# Long Boat Home Coming

Long Boat Home Coming

Long Boat Space – Book Three

Matthew H. Ambrose- Author

Abigail Ambrose – Cover Design

CONTENTS

DEDICATION

This story is dedicated to the struggling self-published authors out there. If you're anything like me, you battle self-doubt, the flood of AI generated garbage, and multiple daily offers from people who want to take advantage of your desire to get your stories out there. Keep writing and publishing, friends! You are telling stories that need to told. Have faith that your audience will find and enjoy them.

ACKNOWLEDGMENTS

The cool ship on the cover is the creation of a great graphic artist named Logan. You can find him in the sci-fi and fantasy artists on Fiver or Instagram @oldmanlogan. Once again, this book was greatly improved by my uncompensated beta readers, James, Laura, and Bonnie. They made the story much better for you, the reader. Any mistakes are wholly my own.

FOREWORD

Long Boat Home Coming is the third book in the Long Boat Space series, and continues the story of the Long Boat *Nai'a* and her crew. In book two, *Long Boat Diplomacy*, the *Nai'a* completed her voyage from Tau Ceti to Lalande. The crew continued their fight to maintain free trade among the stars. Long Boat Home Coming stands on its own as a story, but you will have a better understanding of the characters and initial situation if you have first read *Long Boat Star Crossing* and *Long Boat Diplomacy*.

Chapter 1 - Kojin's Slingshot

May 27th, AD 3208
Lalande System, Approaching Kojin orbit
Long Boat Nai'a, Bridge

Captain Kevin Hartley eyed the massive gas giant Kojin dominating the bridge display. The knot of tension in his gut refused to ease, and he looked around at the bridge crew. Once again, he regretted approving the slingshot maneuver around the Lalande system's largest planet. All three crew rotations had a month of practice simulations under their belts. They would use Kojin to pick up a good chunk of velocity and cut significant time off the passage to Sol. At the same time, the huge planet's gravitational pull would align their outward trajectory to a rendezvous with humanity's home system. One and a half times the mass of Jupiter and sporting rings and moons to rival Saturn, Kojin beckoned them ominously.

Captain Hartley wasn't thrilled with the inherent risks, but his first officer had pitched the plan with great enthusiasm. He didn't want to quash newly promoted Commander Winslow Stirling's first big idea, especially when it made a lot of sense. A quicker passage to Sol was better for both monetary and political reasons. The captain still wasn't looking forward to the close brush they were about to have with the largest planet he'd ever seen.

Commander Joanne Calder looked at him from the engineering station with a twinkle in her eye. "She's built to take a lot worse than a few tidal stresses from yon wee planet," the new chief engineer said, with a fake Scottish brogue and mischievous grin. "My people and I ran the numbers several times, as you know." Despite her name owing to an umpteenth great grandfather Scottish trading factor, Joanne's ancestry was mostly Somali.

"I don't know if I should be more disturbed that you knew exactly what I was thinking, or that you just called a planet bigger than Jupiter 'wee'," the captain replied with a slight glower.

Joanne grinned brightly, "I can't read your thoughts, sir, but I know a captain always worries about the ship. I just want to set your mind as much at ease as I can."

"I know there are precedents going all the way back to the Voyager craft," said the captain, "but this will be a first for the *Nai'a*, not to mention her new captain."

"It's best we do something to shake down the green crew while we're in reach of help," said Chief Nance from the helm. "We've had a lot of turnover."

"I agree," said the captain. "Still, this is more of a thrill ride than I wanted for my first passage in command. Is the local space traffic cooperating?"

Lieutenant Commander Parks looked up from the primary sensors station. "The scan is clear of ship traffic on our projected course. The six Lalande System Security frigates keeping station with us might have something to do with that."

"The Bancroft isn't going to let anything happen to the *Nai'a*," said the captain. "If nothing else, his stiff-necked honor requires it. Still, I'm happy for the escort. This area of the Lalande system was a veritable pirate's nest a few decades ago."

...

Ex-captain Anne Brelling and her husband, Lalande Ambassador Rolland Dunleavy, took in the slowly rotating view of Kojin from the Starlight Lounge. "Are you surprised Captain Hartley went with the slingshot?" Rolland asked.

"Slightly," Anne replied. "He's more conservative by nature than I am, and I steadfastly refused to advise him on it. He needs to stand on his own two feet. It's a bit unfair to him to have the old captain aboard ship on his first voyage, but needs must. The fact that I'm also now first ambassador of the Long Boat Free Trade Syndicate doesn't help.

"I think he made the right call, though. Commander Stirling worked long and hard researching the plan and coordinating with Joanne Calder. Those two didn't earn their new positions through incompetence. If they both thinks it's a good idea, it probably is."

"I'm sure you two will figure out a good working relationship," said Rolland. "You had a great one as captain and first officer. I hope you don't intend to stonewall him forever."

"No, I just want him to take charge without feeling a need to lean on me," Anne replied. "He should be leaning on those two commanders and his fellow board members." She turned and regarded him with a grin. "How do you feel about taking another thrill ride around Kojin?"

"I feel a lot better about taking it in the *Nai'a* than that glorified escape pod I used the first time," Rolland replied with a shudder.

"Thanks to the captain's decision," said Anne, "we should arrive in the Sol system nearly a year early. I'm hoping to wrong-foot the Restoration there like we did here in Lalande. We're going to need every advantage we can get."

...

A day later Captain Hartley was back on the bridge and the *Nai'a* was minutes from closest approach. Kojin loomed huge on the viewscreen, cream, yellow, and orange-red bands roiling with storms thousands of kilometers across. As they passed between the planet's first and second rings, the planetward view was almost too much to take in. With maximal tidal stresses and a full emergency power burn coming, the crew was at action/emergency stations. The captain wondered if they felt the same sense of impending doom that was roiling his insides. He was willing to bet they all had viewscreens tuned to the spectacular planetary show. It was hard to take your eyes from it.

Most of those not at their duty stations were gathered in the Starlight Lounge. The view there was something like being in an expensive rotating restaurant venue. This one was spinning around a very large world, instead of looking down on a big city. The panorama rotated slowly across Kojin's face then outward across its spectacular rings. Every child from infant to eighteen was in the lounge as well. The captain had almost vetoed the plan, and ordered them confined to a safer location. On reflection, he changed his mind. The lounge was well protected, and this was something he would have done anything to see when he was a youngster.

"How is our course, Chief?" he asked.

"Right on the ball, sir," answered Chief Nance from the helm. "Auto-navigation is damping flex harmonics as expected. We'll hit periapsis and initiate the full emergency burn in five minutes."

The captain smiled slightly. A full emergency burn would take them from .1G acceleration to a whopping .15G, the equivalent of a sprint for the massive ten-kilometer ship. "Still confident in your numbers, Commander Stirling?" he asked his first officer.

"Aye, sir," Stirling replied with a firm nod. He occupied a jump seat to the captain's left, unable to resist being on the bridge at the moment his brainchild hatched. His eyes flicked over his personal display and the rest of the bridge as he tried to monitor everything at once.

Captain Hartley caught a flicker of amber from the engineering console out the corner of his eye. He looked a question at the chief engineer and she shook her head. "No worries, sir, just a slightly elevated temperature in a tertiary cooling system for the engines. We're running it hot on purpose so we don't get a spike from the emergency burn."

The captain nodded and attempted to relax into his chair. He focused on the main display. The *Nai'a's* course and waypoints overlayed Kojin in all its glory. Somewhat mesmerized, he started when Chief Vance started the countdown to full burn.

"Periapsis and full burn in five...four...three...two...one...all forward full emergency power applied," the chief stated with professional calm. The captain felt the apparent direction of "down" shift slightly. The decks were currently angled for normal acceleration, and they weren't designed to adjust for full emergency power. The ship's vibration transmitting through the soles of his feet increased in frequency and intensity as the mighty fusion engines gave their maximum thrust. They hurled the *Nai'a* ponderously past Kojin, making the most of its massive gravity. Over the vibration he heard a deep groan as the ship flexed under the tidal stresses, and the thrust of its own engines.

The captain quirked an eyebrow at his chief engineer, but she was intently focused on her displays. After a half minute she looked up. "All systems nominal, captain," she said. "The structural frame flex is well within tolerance and the engines are handling the load nicely."

"And that groan?" Hartley asked.

"You'd groan too if you were as old as this ship, and someone made you do stretching exercises," the engineer answered with a chuckle. "I expected some minor complaining from the longitudinal structure. It's nothing to worry about."

The captain gave her his best glower, but she turned back to her displays unperturbed.

***

Kalei watched the show with a group of children, all lying face-down on purpose-built couches in the Starlight Lounge. As the ship's pediatrician, she was right where she wanted to be, ready to reassure her charges if needed. Their gasps and exclamations when the ship went to emergency power made her smile. Roan's go-cart track and the ship's vac-tube tram both gave a more thrilling ride, but the view here was unbeatable. The crystal-clear manufactured sapphire supporting them gave the illusion that their couches floated in space with no support. She wondered how her brother Mishael was faring in damage control. She still needed to talk with him so they could both work through the recent traumatic events in their lives. She also wanted his advice about her future. For the moment, though, Kalei decided to let her own worries go, and enjoyed the experience.

***

Deep in the bowels of the Beta Section maintenance spaces, Abishai Bonaparté and his buddy Roan monitored the hydro console with one of their new shipmates. Dallas was a native of the Lalande system eager to see new sights. He probably hadn't imagined the new sights would be the massive pumps and pipes of the *Nai'a's* water systems. "Join the *Nai'a* and see the drainage system!" Roan joked, clapping Dallas on a skinny shoulder.

"I hope this won't be like rigging for acceleration," said Dallas, eying the overhead deck plate.

"We aren't shifting the plates," answered Roan. "In theory, it should be a piece of cake, just a bit more acceleration added to our current configuration. I doubt the hab-deck streams will even slop over." At that moment, a stream of water cascaded from above, catching Roan on the neck and running down his back. He yelled and danced a jig while unzipping his ship suit to shake the water out.

When Abishai was able to stand up straight from laughing, he grabbed a towel and handed it to Roan. "You were saying?" he managed to choke out. Dallas tried mightily but failed to forestall his own laughing fit.

"Okay," said Roan, drying himself as well as he could. "Maybe the streams will slop over a little. We need to figure out where that came from. He hoisted himself up into the overhead maze of pipes and conduits, climbing like a red-headed monkey. Muffled thumps and muttering came from overhead for minute or so then a spray of water came raining down, followed by a small bucket. Abishai was ready and danced to the side.

Roan's boots shortly hit the deck with a thump, and he pointed an accusing finger at Abishai. "Nice one, wise guy! You're a bad influence on Dallas. I shouldn't have asked for your help."

Abishai punched Roan affectionately in the shoulder. "I still owe you buckets of pay back from my first passage. Not a day went by that you didn't pull some shenanigan on me."

"Buckets?" Roan groaned, "Please don't start in on the puns!"

Dallas watched the interchange with interest. He'd already been the victim of several of Roan's stunts. Perhaps the way to get his boss's respect was to repay him in kind.

The three settled in, watching a live view of the close pass. Abishai's thoughts mirrored those of his daughter, Kalei. She and her brother were of an age to start families of their own, but neither seemed interested. He didn't want to stick his oar in, but he couldn't help worrying.

***

On the bridge, Captain Hartley continued to monitor their progress. He decided to check in with the escort. He opened the com channel to the Lalande Defense Force ships and hit transmit. "LDF Actual, this is *Nai'a* Actual. We're in the groove with no issues. Do you see anything of concern?"

"*Nai'a* Actual, LDF Actual," Commodore Ultrich replied. "Everything looks clear at the moment. Mind the L2 trojan point of the moon Tsukuyomi when it uncovers. It's blocked from our scans by the moon, and a handy place to hide surprises."

"Roger, LDF Actual. We'll keep an eye on it," the captain answered. "*Nai'a* Actual out."

He turned to his first officer. "Your thoughts, Winslow?"

"We could send out a flight of sting ships," Commander Stirling answered. "They have plenty of range to swing around the back side of Tsukuyomi and get eyes on the L2 point. It really depends on what they might run into, but they've proven themselves to be difficult targets. I'm sure Commander Garrity and his rocket jocks would love to take their birds out for a mission."

"I had the same thought, Winslow," answered the captain. "I just want a scouting run. The LDF frigates can handle any fighting that needs to be done. Coordinate with Garrity and Commodore Ultrich. Let's see if we can get the ready flight on their way in ten minutes." The little one-man sting ships packed a heavy punch for their weight, but the captain didn't want them wading into a fight.

Commander Julian Garrity managed to hide a feral grin as he ran the final pre-flight checks on his sting ship. The compact hexagonal hull's hardpoints mounted three guided missiles, a sensor pack, and two charged capacitors to power the laser or railgun. If someone with ill intentions was hiding behind that moon, his six-ship flight could give them a rough time.

Julian watched the last of six icons on his display turn green and the boat bay door retracted. With a thump, the grapples holding his ship let go. He eased the little craft out of the *Nai'a's* stern, letting the long boat's acceleration do most of the work. This was the first time they'd done a six-ship launch under emergency acceleration. The smooth operation drew a satisfied nod from the squadron commander. "All Scorpions form on me," he transmitted. The six little ships accelerated out of the shadow of the *Nai'a* toward Tsukuyomi.

***

Captain Hartley watched the tactical plot with a knot in his gut. It wasn't the first time he'd watched the *Nai'a's* people go into danger, but it was the first time he had given the command. He concentrated on maintaining a serene expression, then said a silent prayer for his pilots.

***

Julian double checked his datalink with the Lalande Defense Force ships and made a slight course adjustment. Once they were in the groove, he planned to cut engines and let Tsukuyomi's gravity whip them around to the other side. The moon had no atmosphere, so they were going to get a close-up view. With engines cold, the little craft made difficult targets. He was counting on their stealth and agility to keep them alive if there were hostiles waiting.

"Scorpions, remember this is a scouting mission," he transmitted. "Our job is to sweep the L2 point and bring back data on any hostiles. Getting killed isn't in the mission parameters. Observe radio silence from here to the objective, passive sensors only."

The bright surface of Tsukuyomi flashed beneath them. Kilometers-long fissures scored the icy moon in a dark blue web. Before long the Scorpion formation cleared the moon's sensor shadow. What looked like empty space greeted them and Julian was in the middle of a sigh of relief when his plot lit up with a dozen missile traces. "Quail!" he barked over the tactical net, sending his ship through a series of wild gyrations and triggering his active sensors. The quail brevity code instructed his flight to scatter, evade, and return to the *Nai'a*.

Commander Garrity twisted his craft through a two-hundred-and-seventy-degree spiral, picking off two missiles with his laser. He reversed the twist and picked off two more. His targeting systems made easy work of the hot-burning missiles. His plot filled with ships as his active sensors swept the L2 point. *Quail indeed,* he thought, as his system's discrimination protocols worked through the data and told him he was facing at least ten ships. He worked his ship through a seat-of-the-pants firing arch, pumping out three railgun rounds in quick succession. Jinking wildly, he turned his craft back toward Tsukuyomi and accelerated at 10Gs to get out of the danger zone. He had to flip once to get rid of another missile but safely made it around the moon and back into line of sight with the *Nai'a*. His second in command was already on the net with Commodore Dunleavey and Captain Hartley. He let his computer take care of downloading the tactical data and checked on the rest of his squadron. He breathed a sigh of relief when he saw the five friendly green icons of his fellow pilots scattered across the plot.

***

Captain Hartley quickly took in the situation and sent a launch order to Lieutenant Commander O'Clair, leader of the second sting ship flight. At the same time, he activated collision stations protocol, causing a priority override message to hit the PCOM of every adult on the ship.

***

Kalei started when her PCOM buzzed with the emergency alert. She stood quickly and looked around at her charges. She told them to get up and follow her, they were going on an adventure. The kids groaned in protest, but they'd been warned their viewing session might be cut short. She posted the oldest child at the end of the line to watch for stragglers, and strode purposefully out of the lounge. Their destination was the low-gravity gym, nearly at the center of the ship.

***

Commodore Ultrich brought his ships to battle stations and accelerated away from the *Nai'a* to form a shield between the long boat and the enemy vessels. From the sting ships data, he had a good idea of what he faced. Despite being outnumbered, he was confident in a significant firepower advantage. The enemy ships all appeared to be repurposed mining ships or freighters. They could probably put one good salvo of missiles into space. Protecting the *Nai'a* from the initial salvo was going to be a challenge. After that, his frigates' firepower and tactical coordination should turn the tide. Regardless, he was a big believer in the 'more firepower is better' axiom of combat. He toggled his transmit button. "*Nai'a* Actual, LDF Actual, how soon can you get your second sting ship flight into space?"

"LDF Actual, *Nai'a* Actual, flight two is launching now," Captain Hartley replied. "They should integrate into your data net in a few seconds. They're armed with three missiles each."

Commodore Ultrich acknowledged the message and turned to his tactical officer. "Guns, give me a simultaneous time on target missile launch that integrates our salvo with both sting ship flights. I know the first flight is scattered, but they all preserved their missiles. We might as well add them to the mix. You have thirty seconds. I want to launch before the enemy flotilla clears the moon's horizon."

Ten seconds later, the six frigates maneuvered to open a gap in the center of their formation for sting ship flight two. Lieutenant Commander O'Clair led the flight smoothly into place, just in time for the fire command to flush all eighteen missiles from the flight toward the expected course of the enemy. Each of the frigates fired missiles from three hard points and six rotary launchers. Seventy-two missiles blazed through the vacuum; all tied into the LDF's targeting net. One by one the returning sting ships from flight one flipped and added three missiles to the salvo, bringing the total to ninety.

Commodore Ultrich's lips formed a thin line as he watched the tactical plot, paying special attention to the predicted enemy position as it crept toward Tsukuyomi's horizon. He didn't like to depend on cooperation from the enemy commander, but the opportunity to get the first big punch in was too tempting. "Cut missile drives on my mark, three...two...one... mark." The missiles effectively disappeared as they went ballistic and their drives cooled.

Right on time, the first ships of the enemy flotilla cleared the moon. The course would soon put them in position to empty their own missile racks at the *Nai'a*. "Guns, defensive formation Aspis," he ordered his tactical officer. "Get the returning sting ships slotted in to cover the flanks."

The combined frigate and sting ship force quickly formed a staggered triple hexagon between the oncoming enemy and the *Nai'a*. Each frigate carried three forward-firing antimissile laser clusters. The sting ships added their spinal lasers to the integrated defensive shield. They were as ready as they could be for what the enemy was about to unleash.

***

Self-proclaimed Admiral Hector Kneeland growled deep in his throat as the Lalande Defense Force formation populated his tactical plot. He had no illusions of winning the day, but anticipation of exacting a measure of revenge on The Bancroft and the Long Boat Free Trade Syndicate burned in his heart. He saw his tactical officer blanch white in recognition of the combined firepower in front of them. "Fire plan Lewis," Kneeland ordered, pointedly drawing his sidearm. "I want every missile targeted on the *Nai'a*. We'll mop up the riff-raff once she's a drifting hulk."

The tactical officer opened his mouth to protest, then closed it with a snap when he saw the flechette pistol not-quite pointed at him. He turned to his console and quickly set up the fire plan as ordered.

Kneeland opened the tactical communications channel, ignoring the background chatter of protests. "All ships, this is the Admiral. Hold your positions in formation and follow my lead. We'll strike a mighty blow for Free Lalande this day!" He closed the channel and pressed a button on his command console, watching his display confirm a locked helm and positive weapons control of every ship in the flotilla. "Fire now!" He ordered. Every ship in the formation fired their available missiles on a course to bypass the LDF shield and engage the *Nai'a*. One hundred and fifty-two missiles blazed away on a mission to kill a long boat.

***

Commodore Ultrich's plot turned crimson, and his tactical officer announced "Vampire! Vampire! Enemy missile launch. Our salvo will enter attack range...now!" Ninety missiles relit their drives and executed terminal attack maneuvers based on refined targeting data from the LDF frigates. A fire storm of ship-killing lasers swept through the enemy formation. Ten seconds later, every ship in the Restoration flotilla drifted through space with gutted drives or worse. The commodore shook his head slightly, a few seconds sooner, and it would have been all one sided. His tactical officer adjusted their formation's position to cut off the oncoming missiles. They had good firing angles. Now it was a numbers game.

***

Admiral Kneeland groaned and tried to wipe his eyes. His gloved hand ran into his suit's face shield, and he shook his head. His left arm wasn't working, and he floated lopsidedly in his command chair, held in by the combat webbing. He peered groggily around the bridge. A mist of blood and left-over atmosphere obscured everything except a strobing red emergency light. He punched up the tactical plot on his command console, surprised that he still had a picture. He grinned a rictus as he saw his missiles still blazing toward the *Nai'a*. A few seconds later the LDF shield formation showed on the plot, and he realized the missiles might not get through.

Never one to give up, he quickly plotted a firing solution for the last operable weapon on the ship. The railgun turret had its own bank of power capacitors and a full drum of rounds. He let the computer time the burst and nodded grim satisfaction as a stream of steel-jacketed tungsten slugs hurled across space. The nod was too much for his abused nervous system and he slid into unconsciousness.

***

Commodore Ultrich's stomach knotted. It would have been easier if the missiles were targeted at his formation instead of the nearly defenseless long boat. The salvo swept toward them and the LDF laser turrets went into rapid fire along with the sting ships. Missile after missile exploded as defense programming conducted a fight too fast for human reflexes. The integrated data net allowed them to efficiently take out each target. The enemy salvo rapidly melted under the intense fire and finally winked out like the final rocket of a fireworks show.

***

Lieutenant Commander O'Clair breathed a sigh of relief as the last missile disappeared from his sting ship's plot. He hadn't enjoyed turning over control of his sting ships to the LDF computers, but he couldn't argue with the results. Another weapon trace on the plot caught his eye and he quickly took back control. He whipped the little ship through a precise arch, jamming on the laser trigger once his sight reticle cleared the flanking frigate. His capacitor banks quickly ran dry as he tried to take out the stream of railgun rounds flying toward the long boat. The laser winked out and he opened the com channel for the *Nai'a*. "*Nai'a*, ballistic incoming. Evade now," he transmitted. He watched the glowing rounds speed toward the ship and banged his fist on his canopy in frustration.

***

When the transmission reached the *Nai'a's* bridge, Chief Nance didn't wait for an order, punching the button for a pre-programmed evasive maneuver. Ever so slowly, the *Nai'a* turned her bow upward from the ecliptic plane and tried to climb out of danger. Captain Hartley had to concentrate to breath normally as the incoming rounds sped toward his ship. Ten-kilometer long boats don't turn on a dime, and he could tell some of the rounds were going to hit.

***

Abishai, Roan, and Dallas all jumped when a bang like Thor's hammer assaulted their ears. A geyser of water erupted from a rent in the deck five meters away. It only took a moment for the rent to suck most of the water back through and start pulling air. All three hydro techs pulled their helmets over their heads and activated the neck seal. Abishai grabbed an emergency patch from his pack, quickly crossing the space to the whistling hole in the deck and slapping the patch on it. The gash proved too big for the patch, sucking it through to the water compartment below and almost taking Abishai's fingers with it. Abishai growled and slapped a flat steel ruler from his toolkit over the hole, followed by three more patches. Reduced air pressure and his hodge-podge repair finally did the trick, and he sat back to take stock of the situation.

Dallas was close by, blinking wide-eyed at him. To his credit, he had emergency patches in both hands. Abishai was pretty sure at least one of the patches he'd used had come from the green crewman. Dallas pointed silently upward and Abishai looked up to see a deformed chunk of metal embedded in an overhead conduit.

Roan jogged up and tapped the side of his helmet. Dallas and Abishai opened their private PCOM channels, now integrated with their helmet audio. "It looks like a blow-through," he said looking at the hasty patch and damaged conduit. "The water shield compartment below us emptied into space, but the emergency valves all closed. It's sealed off for the moment. I reported everything to Beta Section maintenance and damage control. Mishael told me to make sure you don't take a spacewalk. Damage control sent a hull-crawler fabricator to deal with the exterior repair."

Abishai nodded, standing to examine the overhead conduit. "This is labeled as a backup optical data run," he said. "Mr. Literal won't be happy, but we can leave it until the hull and deck are repaired." Mr. Literal, the artificial intelligence that served as the ship's data librarian, liked backups to his backups. "We should get out of this section of corridor, pump the air out, and take the strain off my lovely patch job."

They walked to the aft hatch and waited while the pressure equalized. Once through the hatch, they dogged it closed, and Roan double checked the seal before activating the pumps.

***

Commodore Ultrich surveyed the tactical plot with satisfaction. "Are we seeing any other signs of live weapons?" he asked.

"Negative, sir," his tactical officer answered. "There isn't a live power plant left over there. We're only reading emergency power signals and transponders. Individual emplacements could still fire under local or remote control, as we just saw. I have us positioned to take out any repetition of the railgun salvo."

"Good, I'd better check in on the *Nai'a*." The commodore opened the channel and put in call to Captain Hartley. "*Nai'a* Actual, LDF Actual, I apologize for the railgun salvo that snuck through. How is your ship?"

"LDF Actual, *Nai'a* Actual, I'm waiting on a full damage report, but we're in good shape," Captain Hartley answered. "We caught a few railgun rounds, but it was about like shooting an elephant with birdshot. If any of those missiles had made it through, though, we'd be in much worse condition. Thank your people on behalf of mine."

"Your sting ships were a big part of the missile defense net," the commodore replied. "I'm going to enjoy having them in the LDF when you depart the system. All in all, we got off lucky, but I'll have some words with our intelligence branch when we get back to the inner system. Their estimates of the remaining Restoration combat power were woefully short. I believe the immediate threat is taken care of, so we're maneuvering to take up our regular defensive formation around the ship.

"The LDF base on the other side of Kojin is sending a squadron of scout ships to do search and rescue. I don't want to spare any combat power until we're clear of Kojin's moons. Your sting ships should return and rearm. I imagine most of them shot their power banks dry."

"Aye, Commodore, we'll bring them in," Captain Hartley answered. "Let us know if we can help with search and rescue. *Nai'a* Actual out."

He cut the channel and waited patiently for his team to finish processing damage reports. After a few moments, his chief engineer looked up. "We have one blow through in Beta Section. It breached the water jacket and penetrated the maintenance space. No casualties, and the damage is limited to a couple of holes and a severed data run." She pulled up a three-dimensional model of the ship on the main display. "We took hits here, here, and here in addition to the blow through. I have teams on the way to check each site. I'd also like to send Jarman out in the pinnace to do a hull survey when you think it's safe."

"Is one of those impacts on the Starlight Lounge?" asked the captain, rubbing his chin. "I'm glad we got the kids out of there."

"Yes," Commander Calder replied. "We didn't lose pressure in the lounge, but that's the first stop for one of my damage repair teams. The engineered sapphire is tougher than the rest of the hull, but I'm still surprised it stopped a railgun round."

***

Mishael led the damage control repair team to the corridor outside the Starlight Lounge. Even though the hatch panel indicated good pressure in the lounge, they sealed up their suits and the corridor. Mishael opened the hatch carefully, then walked into the lounge. The team's eyes were drawn immediately to the expanse of sapphire viewing dome integrated into the ship's hull. The rotating view of Kojin and its rings made for a cosmic-level distraction, but they split up and began a thorough visual inspection of the sapphire for damage. "Over here!" called one of the spacers. They all crowded around as he slid one of the viewing lounges to the side. Beneath their feet, a meter-long metallic rainbow band marred the outer surface of the dome.

Mishael pulled out a portable spectrograph and took a quick reading. "Iron, carbon, and tungsten," he said. "This is the impact point. It struck a glancing blow. It must have been in a molten state when it hit, or we'd see damage to the sapphire. I'm not even reading a scratch."

"One of those fly-boys made a lucky shot," said one of the team.

"I've watched their training," said Mishael with a touch of jealously. His two-meter-plus frame was too large for the cockpit of a sting ship. "I'd venture luck had little to do with it. Let's finish our inspection and get to the next impact point."

***

A day later the *Nai'a* was clear of Kojin and on course with a good head of steam for a rendezvous with the birthplace of humanity. Captain Hartley extended an invitation to Commodore Ultrich and his crews to visit and dine aboard the long boat. The Commodore was glad to accept on behalf of both himself and his people. A chance to experience the relatively open spaces of the *Nai'a's* habitation sections was most welcome.

Shortly after they arrived, the LDF officers sat down with Captain Hartley, his principal deputies, and the members of the ship's council to review the battle around Kojin. Ambassadors Anne Brelling and Rolland Dunleavy also attended. Commodore Ultrich personally briefed all of them on the action and its aftermath.

"In hindsight," he said toward the end of the briefing, "I should have included some lighter scout ships in the squadron to sweep possible hiding points ahead of us. The truth is, I let myself be lulled into overconfidence by the threat assessment from our intelligence branch. Given how thoroughly wrong they were about the Restoration from the very beginning, I should have been suspicious of their conclusions.

"The search and rescue team found a similar mix of ships to what you faced entering the Lalande system. They were mostly repurposed mining ships, fitted to carry and fire missiles. 'Admiral' Kneeland slaved the entire flotilla's helms and weapons control to his flag ship. Most of the crews of those ships would not have fired on the *Nai'a* of their own free will. We also rescued several civilian miners who were forced to fly or crew their own confiscated ships. It's a familiar pattern for the Restoration. Do you have any questions?"

"What will become of the rescued miners?" asked Captain Hartley.

"They'll be added to the pool of victims receiving compensation from seized Restoration ships and assets," the Commodore answered. "Your sting ship pilots will be due some compensation as well once the admiralty court makes their determination on this battle."

"My pilots requested that their shares be given to the miners who lost ships," said Captain Hartley.

"We'll make it so," answered Commodore Ultrich. "If there are no further questions, I'll turn the floor over to your chief engineer."

Commander Calder took over the room's display and pulled up a representation of the battlespace. "Thanks to the skill of your people and our pilots, we took very little damage," she started. "If just one missile had penetrated your defense, we'd be much worse off. The only thing that got through was a rail gun salvo from the flag ship. We pieced together the sensor data." A red trace appeared on the plot, penetrating the combined defensive formation. "Left to themselves, twenty steel-jacketed tungsten penetrators would have stitched a line across the *Nai'a* amidships. Because of Lieutenant Commander O'Clair's quick action and warning, we only took four hits, and three of those were in a liquid state from his laser shot."

She let her model run to show the impacts. "The melted slugs didn't penetrate. The one intact slug punctured a water shield compartment and the maintenance deck above. Fortunately, it missed three nearby hydro techs who quickly patched the hole in the deck. We've already repaired the hull, deck, and a damaged data run. We reflooded the water compartment a few hours ago, so we're ship shape. We can probably polish the melted tungsten and steel from the other impact points, but I deemed that a low priority." She pointed out the spots on the three-dimensional model of the long boat.

"As long as the hull strength is unaffected, leave them there," Captain Hartley said, "especially the one on the Starlight Lounge crystal. The scars will be a reminder to us and others of what the ship has been through. Pass along my thanks to the hydro techs and your damage control repair teams. Once again, the crew of the *Nai'a* stood ready when needed." He caught Anne Brelling's proud nod of agreement

"That's all I have sir," the chief engineer said, "unless there are questions."

Captain Hartley looked around the room, but no one spoke up. "Thank you, Commander Calder and Commodore Ultrich. We all have dinner to get to and we don't want to keep my steward waiting."

***

After the dinner and some socializing with the LDF officers, Captain Hartley invited Anne Brelling and Rolland Dunleavy to his day cabin. "Would you two like coffee or tea?" he asked, leading them to a small, round table. Both of them shook their heads. "I'll admit I asked to talk to you because I need your advice. We were fortunate to come out of this latest scrape intact and nearly unscathed. Is there something else we should be doing to keep the ship safe?"

"Kevin, you couldn't have anticipated the Restoration force hiding at Tsukuyomi's L2 point," said Anne. She looked over at Rolland for confirmation and he nodded.

"I know Kojin and its moons as well as anyone in the system," Rolland said. "I wasn't expecting any trouble there."

"I can't tell you the number of times I guessed wrong when I was captain, but the crew always came through for me, just like they did for you," Anne continued. She leaned back with a slight smile. "I knew you were ready for the big chair. So far, you're proving me right."

Getting back to your question," said Rolland. "I think you're doing the right things to keep the ship safe. The threat is going to be significantly lower ahead. Places to hide surprises are in short supply along the remainder of our course through the system. The risk of the slingshot maneuver paid off." He regarded the captain levelly. "Despite the high adventure you put us all through, you made the right call."

Captain Hartley nodded. "Thanks, being in the hot seat was stressful, but waiting was the hardest part. Once the sting ships kicked things into motion, I had too much on my hands to spend time worrying. I know a captain is supposed to project confidence. It was all I could do to keep my tone level.

"On the positive side, Commodore Ultrich and his people made the battle as one-sided as it could be. I'm impressed with his tactical acumen."

"I am as well," said Rolland thoughtfully. "I don't know him well. The few times our paths cross, he seemed to be the quiet and reserved type. Perhaps he only speaks when he has something important to say. Not many men in his position would admit to falling for that intelligence blind spot. He has a balance of confidence and humility that speaks well for him. I've always found it hard to trust leaders who couldn't admit when they were wrong. That kind of thinking inhibits tactical flexibility in both you and your subordinates."

"Wise words," said the captain, rubbing his chin. "I'll send The Bancroft an official dispatch commending our LDF escorts for their bravery. I also want to make it clear that I take responsibility for putting the *Nai'a* in a position to be attacked."

Anne nodded her agreement, then leaned forward and put a hand on the captain's shoulder. "You're doing well. Your moral compass points in the right direction. I've deliberately been hands-off and kept my distance for reasons we've discussed. Now that you've settled in, feel free to use me as a private sounding board any time. I think crew is clear on who's in charge, and confident in their new captain."

"Thank you, I'll take you up on your offer more than you'll like," the captain replied. "We should all get some rest. It's been a busy couple of days and I owe Commodore Ultrich a tour in the morning."

Chapter 2 - Heart and Home

May 30th, AD 3208
Outer Lalande System
Long Boat Nai'a, *Tropical Dome*

Captain Hartley and Commodore Ultrich stood outside the sweep of glass panels making up the tropical dome, waiting for their guide. "I'm already impressed with your ship," the commodore said. "I couldn't resist the opportunity to tour your tropical environment, though."

"It's one of our best features," replied Captain Hartley. "The beach stays booked up, which helps interweave the dolphin pod with our social structure. I'll need to have some frank discussions with them about what they want to do when we get to Sol. I hope we'll still have a dolphin family aboard when we're ready for the following voyage, but I know the call of the open ocean is strong. If they don't return, we might get another set of volunteers."

"The dolphins are another reason for my visit," said Commodore Ultrich. "I've seen videos, but I'll probably never have another chance to meet a dolphin in person."

The entrance to the dome slid open as he finished. Abishai Bonaparté and his wife Shanyah emerged. The commodore blinked. Both were impressively large people and currently wearing loose beach attire. Shanyah was a touch under two meters tall with Polynesian features and built like the hammer throw champion she had been on Terra. Abishai was a few centimeters shorter but thickly muscled and half again as wide. Captain Hartley introduced everyone around then excused himself to catch up on a mountain of electronic paperwork.

"Welcome, Commodore Ultrich," said Abishai shaking hands. "My son Mishael is a ship's officer. He was impressed with your tactics in the recent battle. Thank you for defending the *Nai'a* so well!"

"I would feel better about it if we hadn't nearly been taken by surprise," replied the commodore. "Your sting ships were a key part of our victory. Is your son a pilot?"

Abishai and Shanyah both laughed. "No, he doesn't fit in the cockpit," said Shanyah. "He has to content himself with running the rearming process, when he's not assigned to damage control."

The Commodore looked the both up and down. "I should have guessed, if he takes after his parents."

"He's taller than both of us and as wide as Abishai," said Shanyah. "Keeping him fed as a teenager was a real challenge. You're going to be uncomfortable in that ship suit. I'd offer you one of Abishai's work outfits, but they'd fall off you."

The commodore had the more typical slim build of someone born and raised in low gravity and stood a head shorter than Shanyah. "I came prepared," he said. "I have shorts and a t-shirt on under my ship suit. If there's a place to leave the suit, I'll pick it up on my way out."

Shanyah showed him a set of lockers just inside the entrance. The commodore followed Abishai down a path through the jungle-like interior, listening intently to his description of the various plants and animals. Before long they reached a small clearing, with what appeared to be a grass hut in the center. The tropical gang was gathered around a diminutive old woman gesturing with a gleaming Hori Hori knife.

Abishai stopped far enough away so they wouldn't disturb the meeting. "I'll introduce you to Elder Pryachac," he said to the commodore in a low voice, "but please don't call her elder." Abishai just finished pronouncing the letter "r" in elder when an overripe passion fruit whacked him behind the right ear. "Or there will be consequences," he finished, scraping the sticky fruit from his skin and tossing it in a compost bin. "There's nothing wrong with her hearing and her aim is deadly." Shanyah turned away, trying to keep from convulsing with laughter.

Consuela Pryachac walked up with a wide grin on her wrinkled countenance. "You know, Abishai, you'd think you'd learn after all these years, but you keep giving me excuses to pelt you." She turned to their guest. "Who might this handsome stranger be?" The commodore colored slightly.

"Consuela, this is Commodore Ultrich," answered Abishai. "He commanded our combined forces in the recent battle. Commodore Ultrich, this is Consuela Pryachac, the heart and soul of the tropical gang, even if she refuses any sort of title these days."

"Pleased to meet you, Consuela," the commodore said carefully. "Please call me Jurgen."

"See, Abishai," said Consuela. "He picked up in two minutes what you can't seem to get through your skull muscles. I like him already." She took the commodore's arm and led him toward a nearby array of tables laden with plant starts. Gesturing animatedly with her free hand she began explaining the various cultivars and how they would fit into the tropical biome.

"He's going to be busy for a while," Shanyah said to Abishai. "Come over here and I'll get the rest of the passion fruit off you. Why do you keep calling her 'elder' when she's in earshot?"

"I genuinely thought she wouldn't hear me," Abishai replied ruefully. "I'm glad in a way, because I've got to have a conversation with her about leaving the tropical gang. At least she had one more chance to engage in her favorite sport."

"You're still determined to transfer to the orchard?" Shanyah asked.

"I've learned what I joined the gang to learn. It's time to let someone else rotate in. I'll still be available if the irrigation and drainage systems start causing problems again. I'll miss working with these characters, but I'm looking forward to cooler working conditions."

"Come winter in Delta section, you'll be wishing for this heat again," Shanyah chuckled, wiping sweat from her brow.

"I can always visit to warm up," Abishai replied.

When Consuela Pryachac finished with the commodore, they took him on a tour of the rest of the tropical dome, finishing at the beach. A family was just packing up their beach gear to leave, and Shanyah gave them a wave. "We decided to leave this for last," she said "You might be hard to pry away from the dolphins, most people are." She led the way into the small waves lapping at the sand. The commodore followed until they were waist deep. "We'll wait here," said Shanyah. "The pod knows we're here. I'm sure they'll put in an appearance shortly."

The dolphins chose that moment to leap clear of the water, turning a synchronized triple flip, then rushing up to surround the three humans, clicking and nodding enthusiastically. "They're excited to meet you, Jurgen," said Shanyah. "They know about the battle and your part in it, but I think they have questions. They understand standard English fairly well, and I can usually interpret the other way, as long as they keep it to the human hearing spectrum."

One of the dolphins came close enough to allow the commodore to touch his beak. He turned his head sideways to eye the man, then whistled and clicked a question to Shanyah. "He wants to know how you knew the enemy would emerge from behind Tsukuyomi where they did. We played the battle for them on a three-dimensional projector adapted for underwater use. They have a better sense of time and space than most humans."

The commodore looked directly at the dolphin. "The truth is, I didn't know they would emerge in that position. My guess was slightly off, but close enough for our missile salvo to work."

The dolphin ducked its beak under water for a moment then squirted a mouthful of water onto the commodore's chest. He bleeked a laugh at the commodore's surprised expression and chittered to Shanyah.

Shanyah grinned, "Loosely interpreted, he said 'so you're lucky'."

The commodore though for a moment, then nodded firmly. "Absolutely!" That earned him another splash.

"As you can tell, they're also natural jokesters," said Shanyah, splashing the dolphin herself. She looked over the bobbing heads. "Who's next?"

The interview went on for several minutes, culminating in the dolphins offering to demonstrate how they could move the *Nai'a's* commandos rapidly through the salt-water environment of Epsilon section.

"How long can you hold your breath?" Shanyah asked.

"Probably a minute and a half without too much strain," said the commodore. Two dolphins popped up on either side of him.

"Okay," said Shanyah. "Hang on to the base of their dorsal fins and don't let go. When the they rise up, catch a big breath, because they're about to dive. They'll bring you to the surface when there's a chance to get air again."

The commodore nodded wide-eyed and the dolphins took off toward the far end of the beach with the commodore in tow. Shanyah continued to converse with the other dolphins while they waited. Ten minutes later, they popped up again with a breathless commodore shaking the water out of his eyes. He gave the two speedsters a word and a pat of thanks. "That's a ride I won't soon forget. Was that a restaurant we popped up in the middle of? I think I was more surprised than the patrons."

"Yes," replied Abishai. "Six Fathoms, serving seafood from both tropical and arctic sea environments. The crew is used to the dolphins, and even the occasional human, popping up there."

"I'm impressed and ever grateful to all of you for the experience," said the commodore.

Shanyah smiled. "We all wanted to do something to express our own thanks. You put yourself and your people in danger to keep us safe. We won't forget it."

***

A few weeks after the commodore's visit Shanyah and Abishai managed a rare sit-down dinner with Mishael and Kalei. It was their first chance to try the new restaurant franchise for this crossing. Thơm Ngon Vietnamese had recently replaced Bellotti's Italian. Abishai was going to miss Bellotti's, but he was looking forward to trying the pho and clay pot meals.

While they perused the menu, Shanyah surreptitiously eyed her two children. She and Abishai tried not to meddle in Mishael and Kalei's private lives, but she was wondering if a nudge was in order. Extended life spans meant there needn't be a rush to start families of their own, but she wondered if they were focusing too much on their careers.

All four of them opted for various types of pho. Mishael and Abishai ordered large, while the ladies stuck with medium bowls. Abishai ordered a dozen spring rolls with dipping sauce to share. Conversation ground to an awkward halt as they waited for the food. Kalei, ever the perceptive one, stabbed her mother with a skeptical look. "Out with it, Mom," she stated flatly. "You look like you're trying hard to not-say something"

Shanyah sighed, then leaned back and examined a pair of chop sticks. "Okay, we're both concerned about the two of you," she finally said. "I know it's none of our business, but we're still your mom and dad. Also, our choices put you in the situation of growing up in a wandering small town. Neither of you seems inclined to settle down with anyone. We don't want the limited choices you have to stop you from finding someone. It's not too late if you want to leave the *Nai'a* and make a new start here in Lalande."

Mishael looked at Kalei and made a go-ahead gesture. Kalei took a deep breath. "We've talked this through together. The hilarious thing about it is, we both have the same concern for one another. It's more a matter of timing and focus, than a lack of choices. Neither of us is in a hurry. From what you told us about how you and Dad got together; you weren't exactly looking for love either. As far as the *Nai'a* goes, this small wandering town is home, and the Lalande system doesn't appeal to us. We both like what we're doing, and love our friends on this ship.

"Somebody sitting at his table once told me worrying is a minor case of atheism."

"Ouch!" her mother replied ruefully.

"That said," Kalei continued with a slight smile. "Both of us want to start families in the future. You'll get grandchildren eventually." She looked over to Mishael. "Did I miss anything, big bother?"

"I'm surprised you 'bothered' to ask." he replied. Abishai and Shanyah both groaned.

"I thought I was supposed to tell the dad jokes," Abishai intoned.

"I learned from the worst," answered Mishael with a grin. "Seriously, neither of us feels deprived of opportunities or trapped on the *Nai'a.*

"I do need to let you know; I'm going to withdraw from active duty as a ship's officer once we're clear of Lalande. I want to try something else for a while, and my current specialties shouldn't be needed. I'll stay on the reserve rolls. The captain can activate me if I'm needed."

"Do you have something specific in mind?" asked Abishai as the waiter set a heaping plate of spring rolls in the center of the table. Rows of pink shrimp were clearly visible through the rice paper wrappers.

"You know I have wide range of interests," said Mishael, his eyes widening at the size of the spring rolls. "I want to set up year-long apprenticeships in several specialties. I might start by applying here."

Abishai picked up a spring roll. Even for him it was a two-hand job. "These are bigger than I was thinking," he said. "Maybe a dozen was overkill." He dipped one end in the sauce, took a large bite and noshed the chewy, crunchy texture appreciatively. He eyed Mishael. "Are you up to the challenge?"

"Always!" Mishael answered, tucking into his own roll. Conversation ceased as the Bonaparté family attended to the serious business of eating.

They polished off the last of the spring rolls just as two waiters showed up with the pho. They placed bowls of steaming broth and noodles large enough for a batch of cookie dough in front of Abishai and Mishael. The ladies' bowls weren't much smaller. Abishai regarded his portion with a small amount of panic. "Maybe the medium next time."

"Small for me," said Shanyah, equally impressed. "I think your stomach has finally met its match, Abishai."

"I'm not arguing," he replied. They all added Thai basil, green onion, bean sprouts, and a squeeze of fresh lime wedge to their bowls from the large garnish tray. Abishai regarded the chopsticks and oddly shaped spoon available, shrugged, and used the chopsticks to squeeze a generous portion of noodles and other goodies. He transferred the noodles to his mouth and, one mighty slurp later, managed to get most of them in. He realized everyone was looking at him with varying levels of shock and amusement. "What??!!?" he said indistinctly, spreading his hands. The noodle still dangling in his beard ruined the innocence of his expression. His family just shook their heads and started in on their own bowls.

"That was delicious," Abishai said later, as he debated picking up the bowl to finish the last of his broth. A quelling look from Shanyah made him look for the spoon instead. "It was also way more than I expected. I'm going to pass on dessert."

"I'm with you," said Mishael. "I must be slowing down." He leaned back and rubbed his stomach appreciatively. "Thanks for dinner, Dad. Kalei and I are due at Quester's quarters in twenty minutes for a round of Boorlong's Revenge." He and Kalei stood up, hugged their parents and said goodbye.

"What do you think?" said Shanyah after a moment.

"I think you'll need a wheelbarrow to get me back to our quarters," said Abishai. "Where do you even find soup bowls that big?"

Shanyah elbowed him lightly in the ribs, eliciting a groan. "You know what I mean. How do you think they're doing?"

"I think they're doing very well," Abishai replied seriously. "Kalei is exactly right. There's no reason to rush when it comes to serious relationships. Also, we should be praying and trusting God, not worrying."

***

Kalei and Mishael found themselves unable to concentrate on their game, quickly losing the first round to Quester. The skinny Tau Ceti native looked at the two people he considered younger siblings. He put the game away. "Out with it, you two," he said. "You were ten and eleven the last time I won a game that easily."

"I guess we're more unsettled than we want Mom and Dad to believe," said Mishael, "but I can't put my finger on why."

"My guess is, you have traumatic experiences knocking around in your heads that you haven't really dealt with," said Quester. "I have a few of my own. Let me tell you about my experience during the attack on the Restoration's bolt hole asteroid, then you can talk through yours."

"I never even made it to the asteroid," said Mishael disparagingly.

"And that's one of the things you need to talk about," said Quester. "Have you heard of survivor's guilt? You had to help deal with the casualties of the combat but didn't directly participate. Your sister was a lot closer to the action and had to make the stark choices only a combat surgeon makes. She's been so busy with caring for those patients and helping with cold sleep intake, that she hasn't had time to do anything with those feelings but shove them in a corner. So, let's all lay our baggage on the table. I trust you two as much as I would any therapist. What do you say?"

Mishael and Kalei looked at each other then back at Quester and nodded.

"I probably should have invited Grady too," Quester started, "but I didn't know we were going down this path. He and I got ourselves caught in a really bad position by those mobile gun platforms. I seriously thought we were both going die..."

Over the next few hours, the three unburdened themselves to one another, shedding tears and sharing hugs. As they said good bye, Kalei thanked Quester again for the impromptu therapy session. "I feel like such a mess, but I also feel better."

"There's no need to thank me," Quester replied, giving her one last hug. "I got as much out of it as you did. You two and your parents are the only family I have. We need to trust each other enough to do this occasionally."

Chapter 3 – Lalande Farewell

June 28th, AD 3208
Lalande System Approaching Heliopause
Long Boat Nai'a, *Bridge*

Captain Hartley noted the position of the ship approaching the *Nai'a* from the stern. The robotic cargo vessel was decelerating to match speeds with the long boat and offload a final delivery of gifts from The Bancroft. Wallace the Third was firmly in charge of the Lalande system again, thanks in large part to the assistance of the *Nai'a* and her people. He'd been quite cagy about what was in this delivery, so the captain was curious to learn what The Bancroft would send as a parting gift.

Jarman Lal eased the ship's pinnace out of the boat bay. Transferring cargo underway wasn't a new task, but one he hadn't practiced lately. This cargo was supposed to be organized into packages sized to fit into the pinnace's bay. He didn't envy Mishael and Roan the time in hard suits making the transfers. The two were old hands at extravehicular operations, so he was confident they'd get the job done.

As he took position next to the cargo vessel, he checked to make sure the datalink to the ship's autopilot was solid. He now had full control of both vessels and cut the engines, leaving them drifting together in free fall. He opened the communications channel to Mishael and Roan. "We're in position. Are you ready to cross over?"

"Roger," Mishael replied. "The bay is evacuated. Open us up."

The clamshell doors unsealed lifting out and away. The robotic vessel opened its large cargo doors at the same time on Jarman's command.

Mishael gave Roan a countdown and they both pushed off gently for the other vessel. "Almost like floating the corridor, Roan," Mishael said with a chuckle. "That's where my love of free fall started."

"The view is better, and more intimidating," Roan replied. "At least this job doesn't risk the Chief of Boat's ire."

"Unless we break something, or dent the pinnace," Mishael answered.

"Denting the pinnace would bring down Jarman's ire," said Roan. "Let's make this process as boring and free of adventure as possible."

They both managed a soft landing in the robot ship's open cargo bay, mag-locking their boots to the deck. Mishael accessed the ship's manifest stored on his PCOM and pulled it up on his helmet's heads-up display. The ID number and picture matched the lumpy shrink-wrapped package secured to the cargo deck. "This is number one," said Mishael. "Take hold on your end and I'll trip the release for the cargo straps."

When the straps released, the package flexed and tried to float out of the bay. Roan was expecting the rebound and quickly steadied the load. "They had it cinched down tight."

"Too tight for my liking," said Mishael as he corralled and stowed the floating straps. "Do you have a good hold? I'll cross back over as we planned and make the catch."

"I need to get centered," said Roan. "I don't have good enough leverage to hoist a metric ton from one end. Wait, I just had a mild flash of brilliance. Let me rig a quick harness and you can pull the package over to you. I'll ride along and help you secure it. I don't think you and the package will fit in the pinnace's cargo bay together."

"I like how you're thinking," Mishael replied. "I'll hold the package steady while you rig the line."

Roan pulled a length of strong braided line from his toolkit, quickly tying it to hand holds at each end of the package and leaving a meter of slack. Mishael fastened another coil of line to his belt and tossed the end to Roan to fasten to the middle of their makeshift harness. "All set!" said Roan. "I'll hold it steady while you cross over."

Mishael eyed the pinnace holding steady ten meters away, unlocked his boots, and gently pushed off. He executed a slow back flip just in time to touch down on one half of the open clamshell doors. With his boots now locked to the door, he checked to make sure the line wasn't fouled and slowly took up slack. He warned Jarman to expect a slight pull toward the robot ship and gave a gentle tug on the line. With Roan hanging on like a monkey, the roughly cylindrical package drifted slowly toward Mishael. When it arrived, he arrested its momentum using both hands, then eased it into alignment with the pinnace's cargo deck. Roan got his boots mag-locked to the opposite door and helped lower the package into the opening.

Shortly, they had the cargo secured to the deck. As expected, it took up the entire space. Mishael double checked to make sure the package left clearance for doors to close, while Roan detached the line. "All secure back here," he transmitted to Jarman. "We'll cross over and get the next load ready."

"Roger," Jarman replied. "I'm sending a rotation signal to the freighter now."

Roan and Mishael waited until the next section of the freighter's cargo bay rotated into view, then launched themselves across the gap again. "One down, five to go," said Roan once they crossed. "We're clear." Jarman closed the pinnace's doors, deftly rotated the little ship, and accelerated back toward the *Nai'a*.

Prepping the next cargo packet for transfer only took a few minutes. Roan and Mishael took the opportunity to admire the view while they waited for Jarman to off-load and return. The Milky Way spread a swath of diamond-bright stars across the sky, while the *Nai'a* gleamed a coppery silver in the ruddy light of Lalande. "The old girl picked up a few more scars," said Roan. "I enjoy an occasional jaunt outside the boat, but I hope this is the last one until we're safely in a parking orbit around old Terra."

"I remember your stories about fixing the ice shield in mid-crossing," Mishael answered. "We shouldn't need any heroics, this time."

"When you're traveling at relativistic velocities, you appreciate having a thick ice shield between you and any oncoming inter-stellar particles," said

Roan. "It's really the same inside the boat, but you can feel it when you're out in the black. Your dad told me you're going to work several apprenticeships on this crossing. Any chance you'll spend a year with me in hydro?"

"Maybe," Mishael replied. "Just don't think I'll be hauling the Big Ole Wrench around for you. Dad told me all your tricks."

"I go easier on native spacers," said Roan. "Ground hogs like your dad need more seasoning. Here comes Jarman. Let's get ready to shift this package."

Several hours later, Roan and Mishael emerged into the boat bay, anxious to get out of their hard suits and get a shower. Around them, several crew members worked to open and break down the cargo packets.

***

Captain Hartley sat in the council chamber chatting with the ship's council members along with Anne Brelling and Rolland Dunleavy. His steward made sure everyone had the beverage of their choice and access to fresh pastries. Chief Alder Persephone Belotic represented civilian governance, with Elder Consuela Pryachac as her advisor. Hubble Spearsley, the CEO, and his wife/deputy, Yuna Ashworth, formed the corporate leadership. The captain and first officer, Winslow Stirling, rounded out the gathering.

The captain called the meeting to order and got started. "I called the council together because we received an encrypted message from The Bancroft timed to arrive with the cargo ship we just unloaded. It's addressed to the ship's council along with our esteemed ambassadors." He nodded toward Anne and Rolland, then touched the play button on the surface of the table in front of him.

A life-size image of The Bancroft with his family's coat of arms behind him came into view. He was wearing his semi-formal royal attire instead of the plain Lalande Defense Force uniform most of them were used to. "Greetings Ambassadors and *Nai'a* ship's council," he began formally. "My people refused to say farewell to your good ship without sending a formal thank you and a few gifts. We want you to remember Lalande more fondly than your experiences at the hands of our common enemy might let you. Most of the cargo we sent is intended for use as part of your Turnover celebration. Your Chief of Boat has an inventory, but I ask that you let those come as a surprise.

"We owe the *Nai'a's* crew a debt we can't really repay, but one we do recognize. One of the crates contains a citation and award of the Order of the Knight of Lalande for each member of the crew." Eyes went wide around the room as the Bancroft paused to let the declaration sink in. "I realize it's purely honorary for most of your people, but they will be afforded the full benefits of the position if they ever return. This includes a holding on New Dawn for them and their descendants.

"We've also included something personal for each of your crew members, and a monetary gift. These were all given by the people of Lalande. Our fate is intertwined with yours. You go with our thanks, our blessing, and much hope for a brighter future. Fair winds and a steady crossing!" The Bancroft's image faded out.

Captain Hartley looked at Rolland, "Did you know this was coming?

Rolland shook his head. "It takes a two-thirds majority vote of all three houses to award the Knight of Lalande to anyone. I wouldn't have believed even Himself could have pushed it through. Every member of your crew is now a member of the Lalande peerage. If we turned around, you'd have a voting block that could be a significant power in the House of Lords."

"The Bancroft and your Parliament know we're not coming back for at least forty years," said Anne. "Still, I'm surprised. It shows the regard the people of this system have for the ship and crew."

"I just pulled up the data on the monetary gift," said Hubble. "It's equal across the board. Anyone who wants to retire, or start a small enterprise in the Sol system, will have the means. They also sent a smaller gift for each of the cold sleep passengers as a starter stake."

"Yuna, how are things in the cold sleep department?" asked the captain. "When I was your deputy, we'd both be at the point of exhaustion about now."

"Patrick is better at delegating than either of us," the former cold sleep director replied. "Even with a full load, everything went smoothly. All our passengers are safely tucked away, and the team is settling into the rhythm of regular shifts."

"What's the breakdown on our passengers?" Captain Hartley asked.

"It's about equal parts Sol system natives returning home and Lalande citizens," Yuna answered. "We wouldn't normally fill up on this run, but the rebellion has a lot of people looking for greener pastures."

"The full cold sleep load is good for our bottom line," said Hubble. "It will be a profitable run if we find our usual market for entertainment rights in the Sol system. Lalande's music is particularly popular back home, and we purchased several years' worth of new output from the artists here."

Captain Hartley nodded, then looked at the chief alder. "Persephone, I'll leave it to you to distribute the personal gifts to the crew and prepare whatever surprises the people of Lalande sent us for the Turnover celebration. Hubble, you can pass on the news of the financial gift, and I'll send out an announcement concerning the order of Lalande. The crew will be in high spirits as we start the crossing."

***

Shanyah shifted her stance carefully, keeping her weight on the balls of her feet as Chief Engineer Joanne Calder circled, looking for an opening. The woman was nearly as tall as Shanyah and very fast. Joanne's willowy build hid a wiry strength Shanyah was familiar with from recent sparring sessions. The dark-skinned engineer feinted a high sleeve grab, then dropped low to grab behind Shanyah's right knee with both hands. She lifted the knee high, attempting to sweep Shanyah off her feet. Shanyah leaned back, going with the motion and twisting as she fell toward the mat.

She snaked her free leg behind Joanne's knees and used their combined momentum to scissor her off her feet. The women hit the mat in a tangle of legs, both scrambling for a joint lock. Joanne trapped one of Shanyah's feet behind her right side and hooked the heel with her elbow. She clasped her hands and started to straighten both her body and Shanyah's leg. Shanyah felt the pressure on her knee and quickly tapped out.

The two women stood, bowed to one another, and relinquished the center of the mat to the next pair up. "Nice heel hook, Joanne," Shanyah said, clapping the engineer on shoulder.

"You certainly tapped quickly," Joanne flashed her a brilliant smile.

"I like my knee ligaments just the way they're currently arranged," Shanyah replied seriously. "I need to find a better counter to your single leg."

"Your counter worked fine. It was the ensuing scramble that cost you."

"I should know better than trading leg locks with you. You've mastered how to use your length and flexibility to good advantage."

"I'll take what I can get," said Joanne. "Once about every ten times I manage to come out on top."

"You're still my top competition, other than Kalei, when I can drag her down here. I sit in on the men's classes as a guest instructor from time to time, so I can get practice against people my size."

"I heard that's how you and Abishai got together?"

"Tossing him into the dojo wall did get things moving in the right direction. Some men need a shock to the system to see what's right in front of them, some women too." Shanyah chuckled. "It's a small part of the story, but that match woke both of us up."

"I'd love to hear the whole tale," Joanne said. "Would you and Abishai come to my quarters for dinner tonight? I can get the story from both of you."

"As far as I know, we're free. I'll check with Abishai, but if there's food involved, he'll be on board."

"His appetite is legend," replied Joanne. "I'll be sure to cook enough even for him."

Shanyah and Abishai knocked on the door to Joanne's quarters that evening just after the appointed time. When the door opened a wave of delicious odors hit them. Joanne gestured them inside and quickly turned back to her small kitchen. "Forgive me for a few minutes. I don't host guests often, and I'm slightly off on my timing."

Abishai peered over her shoulder in interest as she bustled about finishing the dinner preparations. Shanyah pulled him back before he could interrupt their hostess with a flurry of questions. "Later," she said. "Don't joggle her elbow." They found seats at a small table in Joanne's living area, enjoying the exotic scents.

Within a few minutes Joanne placed bowls of beans mixed with rice and a kind of corn bread cut into chunks in front of them. In a rotating cut out at the center of her table, she set several bowls with various garnishes and sauces. She finally sat down and asked Abishai to say a blessing. When he finished, Joanne explained the food. "The Adzuki bean dish is traditional Cambuulo and the bread is called Muufo." She showed them how to grind the corn bread up between their hands and add meat sauce, sesame oil, soup, and banana slices to finish the dish. Abishai and Shanyah both dug in with gusto.

"I don't get a chance to cook traditional Somali food often. What do you think?" Joanne asked after several minutes. Abishai and Shanyah were both effusive with their praise.

"This was a new experience for both of us," said Abishai. "Thank you! Everything is delicious!"

Joanne smiled. "I wasn't sure it would be to your taste, but those empty bowls and plates tell the story. Seconds?" Abishai managed to tuck away another serving of Muufo, but refused a third. They helped Joanne clear the table then retired to the comfortable chairs around the perimeter of the living area. Joanne served them cups of coffee spiced with cardamom, ginger, and cinnamon.

"You've made quite an impression since you joined the ship," Shanyah said. "Mishael is impressed with your knowledge and leadership skills. He was a big fan of Commander Halsey, so it speaks well for you that you're winning the engineering crew over so quickly."

"Thanks," Joanne replied. "I'm working hard to allay the natural angst that comes with a new chief engineer, especially an outsider."

"I know you were deputy to the chief engineer on the *Kilimanjaro*," said Abishai. "How did you end up staying in Lalande when they left for Sol?"

"The Bancroft's people made me an offer I couldn't refuse. The chief engineer on the *Kilimanjaro* wasn't going anywhere for the foreseeable future, so I was stuck in my job without the prospect of moving up. The long boat building program here was picking up steam, and they offered me a position leading the technical side of a new ship build. Eventually, I would have been the chief engineer of a brand-new boat.

"Owen Halsey took The Bancroft's offer to lead the entire long boat building program and his deputy came with him. Captain Hartley reached out to me, and I jumped at the chance to become chief engineer of the *Nai'a*."

"How do you like her so far?" asked Shanyah

"She's a solid ship," Joanne answered. "Owen left behind a well-trained and motivated team. I'm walking softly while I get to know everyone. Integrating the new crew, including myself, is the biggest challenge. The crew overall is remarkably friendly and professional. The way everyone responded to the attack shows you haven't lost a step, even with all the leadership changes. I like to tease Captain Hartley a bit just to loosen him up. He was cool enough in the clutch, though. Ex-captain Brelling is something of a legend. I expected her to be half a meter taller, but she has a definite presence."

"She has that," Shanyah chuckled. "I was petrified of her when I came aboard. I think all the new crew was, but she's a lot more approachable than she seems on first impression. These are perilous times for the Long Boat Free Trade Syndicate, but they couldn't have picked a better ambassador than Anne Brelling."

Joanne studied her coffee for a moment. "My focus is keeping the boat in tip top running condition for the voyage home. However, I also want to have a social life. I confess I asked you to dinner with an ulterior motive."

"You have us both in a mellow mood, so now is a great time to spring whatever it is," Shanyah said raising both eyebrows slightly.

Joanne looked up from her coffee. "Is your son Mishael seeing anyone?"

Shanyah's eyebrows went the rest of the way up. "Um, not that I'm aware of." She looked at Abishai who spread his hands and shook his head. "We've been warned off the subject by both Mishael and Kalei so we're trying to stay firmly on the sidelines when it comes to their romantic attachments or lack thereof. Can I ask why you're interested?"

Joanne nodded firmly, "I've been interested in Mishael since I came onboard, but he was in the engineering department, so I couldn't do anything about it. Now that he's leaving the active ship's officer list, I want to see if he might be interested in me. What I don't want to do is cause problems if he's already in a relationship. I haven't seen any indication that he is, but a man that tall and good-looking surely has women interested. I thought you would know much better than I."

Abishai laughed, then held up an apologetic hand, "Sorry, I don't mean to make light of your feelings. I'm just imagining the shock you're going to be to Mishael's system. As far as we know he's unattached. You're both adults, so you don't need our blessing, but you have it anyway. He's capable of making up his own mind."

"You don't mind the age difference?" asked Joanne. "Age is a squirrely concept for long boat crews, but I imagine I have ten years on him."

"As long as your lives are likely to be, it's not a worry to me," Shanyah answered. She looked at Abishai, who shook his head.

Joanne's shoulders eased and she chuckled at herself. "Why are these conversations more difficult than tuning a fusion engine?"

Shanyah smiled. "I expect it's because you're more familiar with tuning an engine than facing down protective parents. Would you like to hear the whole story of how Abishai and I got together?"

"Absolutely," said Joanne with a bright grin.

Abishai and Shanyah took turns telling the tale. By the end Joanne was laughing so hard at their story of reluctant romance, she had to grab a tissue.

***

Quester felt wrung out, but much better by the time he bid Mishael and Kalei good night. His PCOM pinged a physical package notification and he looked at the details curiously. It was from the Lalande system government, probably from the cargo ship. He looked at the time and decided he could use a walk.

When he arrived at the package lockers next to the chandlery, he found the number associated with the package and entered the code. Inside the locker was a plain, brown package about the size of a shoe box. It was surprisingly heavy. He debated opening it there, but decided to take it back to his quarters.

He unsealed the package at his kitchen table. Whatever was inside was encased in bio-foam packing, and there was a note on top. The note was written on thick yellowish paper with slightly rough edges. He recognized the paper as hand-crafted, or a very good imitation. Around the border, someone had drawn flowers and leaves in multi-colored ink, making the sheet of paper a work of art by itself. The intricate calligraphy of the handwriting did nothing to detract from its surprising beauty. Quester felt a strange reluctance to read the note, as if he would break the spell it cast on him. Finally, his curiosity got the better of him.

Dear crew member of the good ship *Nai'a*,

I hope, with this gift, to give you something to help you recall our system with more fondness than we deserve. You experienced the worst we had to offer, but helped us forge a path out of darkness. Know that we, the people of Lalande, will never forget your sacrifice. You go with our honor, our hope, and our love. Fair travels and bright stars to you and all those you hold dear.

Yours most Gratefully,

Kiera Harmony McHale

Below the signature was a small self-portrait of a lovely young woman in the pen and ink artistic style of the border. Quester felt his vision blur and realized tears were running down his cheeks. He let them flow. What a gift Kiera Harmony McHale had given him in a simple note. His memories of Lalande would include something bright and beautiful to go with the ugliness of combat.

Quester unfolded a small shelf from the wall and carefully placed the note on it. Turning back to the package, he considered leaving it until morning, but decided to open it. The bio-foam split in two when he lifted a tab. He gently pulled the halves apart. The object in his hands took his breath away. It was a box carved of semi-precious stone of two types. It fairly glowed in the light of his quarters. Most of the box was fashioned from a deep blue-green stone with striations of light grey running throughout. The beveled lid was carved from the same stone layered with the light grey on top. The carving on the lid used the transition between stone colors to depict three jumping dolphins. The dolphins were so precisely rendered that Quester recognized three individuals from the *Nai'a's* pod. The artist must have worked from a recent picture. He ran a finger over the carving, feeling the glass-smooth texture of the curves.

Quester lifted the tight-fitting lid, not sure what he would find. Inside, fastened to the cushioned bottom of the box, was a gold pendant recognizable as a depiction of the *Nai'a*, triple gold flames driving her through space. Quester was no authority on metal work, but he recognized expert craftsmanship when he saw it. He examined the pendant carefully and saw that it could be worn on its gold chain or as a pin. He wasn't sure of the monetary value of the gifts, but he already felt he would never part with them willingly.

After examining the box from all sides, Quester put the pendant back in its place. He set the box on the shelf with the note, reading the message again. He'd have to show these gifts to his dolphin friends, and send the best thank you letter he could come up with to Miss Kiera Harmony McHale.

***

The next day the ship buzzed with conversation about the gifts. Each crew member received something beautiful created by a citizen of Lalande. In every case, the gift matched the person's interests. Abishai received a marvelously inlaid baritone ukulele. Shanyah's present was a hand-sewn floral muumuu tailored to her measurements. She modeled it for Abishai. "I've never had a dress that fit so well," she said, twirling around. "Someone did a lot of research."

"They must have started while we were still in New Dawn orbit," answered Abishai. "It takes time to create something this intricate." He strummed a few chords on his new instrument, appreciating the bright tone and perfect action. "I wonder if the Driscolls had a part in this?"

Shanyah thought for a moment. "I think all the families we hosted after the incoming battle with the Restoration probably helped. I don't see how else they could have known enough to personalize the gifts the way they did. I now recall Anthea and her mother taking my measurements. They claimed to be calibrating their new automatic measuring device…sneaky.”

Chapter 4 – Lionel and Lioness

July 5th, AD 3208
Lalande System Heliopause
Long Boat Nai'a, *Medical*

Kalei looked into Lionel's eyes and blinked slowly. The magnificent Maine Coon blinked slowly back, lifted his nose to wetly touch hers, then head-butted her under the chin. Kalei ruffled his fur with both hands, then picked him up and handed the ten kilograms of fur and muscle to Mishael. Lionel quickly snaked himself around Mishael's neck, draping himself across the young man's wide shoulders like an expensive stole. Mishael reached a hand up to give him few strokes and he purred contentment.

"For a senior cat, he's in remarkable shape," said Kalei. "Our ship cats seem to benefit as much from the low gravity and genetic stability therapy as we do."

"Lionel's been such a constant in our lives," said Mishael. "I don't know what I'd do without him. His pranks keep me on my toes."

"He gets around when he isn't sleeping his life away. He spends quite a bit of time here in medical when we have pediatric patients and up in the retired spacers community at .3G. He has a keen sense for people in need of comfort."

Lionel yawned and stretched mightily, manifestly bored with his humans' discussion. He nosed Mishael wetly in the ear, earning a yelp, then launched himself through the door into the corridor.

Mishael watched him go then turned to his sister. "Are you going to the Highlands shindig tonight?"

Kalei shook her head. "I don't think I can take bagpipes and haggis in one sitting, how about you?"

"Commander Calder invited me, and I told her I would be there. In spite of her name, I didn't see her joining the Scottish heritage society. They added several new crew members to the roster. Lalande gave the society a real shot in the arm."

"Commander Calder, eh?" said Kalei raising one eyebrow. "I've seen you casting puppy dog looks her way. You don't work for her anymore, you know."

"Stop teasing," Mishael answered, "she's out of my league and not interested in me in the slightest."

"I hate to admit it, but nobody's out of your league, big brother. Look in the mirror. Also, I've seen Ms. Calder giving you some rather assessing looks when you aren't watching. If you two ever cross glances, I predict sparks."

Alpha Section galley was decorated with coats of arms and tartans of many patterns. Mishael looked around, feeling very plain in a white ruffled shirt and black trousers. More than half the people present wore traditional Scottish attire. Tables surrounded an open space in the center of the galley, and he looked around for a place to sit.

Before he could move, a tall, lithe figure dressed on in brilliant green, black, and grey tartan detached from the group in front of him. He'd never seen Joanne Calder in anything but a uniform, usually a utility ship suit. The highlands dress was much more flattering. He found himself staring. Joanne gave him a bright smile and captured his arm. "Thank you for coming. I saved seats for us," she said with a wink.

"Uh...thanks, Commander," he answered. "I've never been to one of these before."

"Please call me Joanne," she said. "You aren't my subordinate anymore and this isn't the engineering department." He didn't resist as she led him to a table, but extracted his arm to pull her chair out for her. "Your parents raised you well," she commented. "Relax, Mishael. You look like you think you're on the menu."

"Am I?" he said, then blushed bright pink.

Joanne laughed heartily and patted his arm. "Enjoy the festivities with me. I promise I won't do anything untoward."

To his surprise Mishael did enjoy the evening, even the bagpipes. The pipers' rendition of Amazing Grace was especially stirring. Joanne proved a lively a dinner companion. Her attention flattered him, and kept him completely off balance. The haggis presentation made his jaw drop, but the dish itself was tasty and filling.

Joanne watched him put away food with amusement. He hadn't fallen far from Abishai's tree in that regard. She left him after the dishes were cleared to take part in a traditional Scottish sword dance. Joanne and three other ladies set crossed swords on the deck and bowed. The bagpipes started, and they danced intricate footwork around the blades. Mishael watched the demonstration, his eyes drawn mainly to his dinner companion. She moved with grace, and evident enjoyment.

When she returned to his side after a rousing ovation from the crowd, he rose and gave her a bow. "You were wonderful...Joanne."

She smiled. "You remembered! I'm out of breath, though. Let's watch the rest of the demonstrations." She took her seat and hooked an arm in his.

After a few more rounds of traditional dancing, waiters served up cranachan. Mishael took a tentative bite of the layered raspberries, oats, and whipped cream. The unfamiliar combination of textures and flavors brought a smile to his face. He tore through his portion, considered sticking a finger into the dish to get the last bits, then remembered where he was.

Joanne laughed, "You didn't waste any time." She wasn't halfway through hers.

Mishael laughed with her. "I really should slow down, but I did enjoy every bite."

"There's a lot to love about cranachan."

After dessert the evening digressed into an informal social hour. Joanne and Mishael talked with several club members, discussing the food, the excellent dancing, and upcoming plans. People eventually began saying their goodbyes. Mishael found himself reluctant to let the evening end. Joanne finished hugging one of her friends and turned to him. "Walk with me to the Starlight Lounge?" she queried.

"Sounds good," Mishael answered.

They made their way, arm in arm, to the lounge. Like most of the crew, they found themselves drawn to the cleared space in the transparent floor where a rainbow smear of tungsten and steel still marred the outer surface. "A good reminder that the universe isn't always a friendly place," said Mishael, looking thoughtful.

"I know the *Nai'a* doesn't go looking for trouble, but she sure seems to attract it," replied Joanne.

"We've been a target through my lifetime," Mishael nodded. "Thankfully, we've been ready and able to deal with the trouble that comes our way."

"Your family has played a big part in keeping the ship safe."

"Mom and Dad do seem to end up at the center of things."

"You've done your share, your sister too."

Mishael lips quirked in a small frown. "Everyone on the crew deserves credit. Sometimes I wish I had been where I could do more."

"I know the Driscolls are happy you were there to rescue Alex and Anthea," Joanne replied.

"I didn't know you were familiar with the Driscolls."

"I helped them with some technical details of the classified mission they're doing for the Long Boat Free Trade Syndicate. Anthea had a lot to say about you and the rest of your family. If she were a few years older, I'm sure she'd have major crush on you."

Mishael chuckled and guided Joanne to one of the tables around the perimeter of the lounge. "She's the definition of precocious. Our relationship got off to a rocky start when I scared her silly on her family's ship. Fortunately, she forgave me. I can be a touch imposing in a hard suit."

"You're fairly imposing without one too," Joanne replied looking up at him with a grin. She turned her gaze away to take in the view.

Mishael admired her profile and tried to make sense of his own feelings. Finally, he shrugged and decided to enjoy the warm glow of a fun evening in good company. "Thanks for inviting me. I can't remember the last time I enjoyed myself this much."

"You're welcome, the feeling is mutual," Joanne replied. She turned to face him, her expression now serious. "I confess this was more than just a friendly invitation. What would you say if I told you I want to have a serious relationship with you?"

Mishael felt an electric shock go through him. His eyes went wide, and he blushed from toenails to crew cut. This woman was interested in him? He opened his mouth to speak, but nothing appropriate came to mind so he closed it with a snap.

"Sorry to ambush you like that," said Joanne, trying not to find his discomfort amusing. "I'm sure it comes out of the blue, since I never indicated interest in the past. Now that you're off the officer rolls, I decided to see if my feelings might be reciprocated."

Mishael took a deep breath, "Wow," he finally managed. "It's going to take some time to get used to the idea. You're one of the best leaders I;'ve known, and a highly successful, beautiful woman. I've admired you since I met you. Why would you be interested in me?"

Joanne looked him up and down, then chuckled. "Why wouldn't I be? You're a very attractive man, even if you don't seem to realize it. I kept our relationship professional while you were in my department, but that doesn't mean I didn't take note of your qualities as a person. You're kind to your subordinates, and genuinely humble. I find those attributes compelling. The question is, do you have any feelings for me?"

"Too many to sort out," Mishael said, honestly. "I'm flattered, and if you're willing to give me some time, I would love to get to know you better and see if we're a good match."

"I can't ask for more than that!" Joanne said, fairly beaming. "It's late, and we both have work in the morning. Walk me back to my quarters?"

"Absolutely!" said Mishael, standing and offering his arm.

When they reached her door, she stood on tiptoe and kissed him on the cheek, giving him his second electric thrill of the evening. "Let's continue our discussion soon." Mishael just nodded and floated off down the corridor.

***

Anne Brelling took a sip of hot black coffee and marshalled her thoughts. Her husband was flipping through some virtual notes and nodding to himself next to her. Also around the table were: Hal Renfro, Ship Security Detective, his wife, Lisandra Redding, now ethical hacker, and Chord Olley, Long Boat Fee Trade Syndicate investigator.

"We have a mountain of data to comb through and a small team to do it with," she began. "Most of what we know will be badly out of date by the time we get to Sol, but the more we know about the Restoration's operation there, the more likely we'll succeed in frustrating their objectives.

"Today I want to get organized as a team so we're not duplicating effort. I also want to make sure we're comparing notes regularly so we don't miss important connections. We need to balance time spent on individual tasks and team integration. I prefer informal immediate collaboration to meetings, but we will meet as a team at least once a week. It's my job to keep the meetings brief, and focused. Any initial thoughts?"

Hal and Lisandra looked at each other. Hal made a go-ahead motion and Lisandra nodded. "Mr. Literal and I can help parse the mountain of data into digestible chunks for Chord's people. I've been working with him, and we've found a sweet spot of data analysis. Mr. Literal can quickly identify potential connections, feed those to a human investigator who can refine the results, and give them back. After a few times back and forth, you have a much better picture of the system or organization defined by the data."

Anne nodded, "Chord, what's your people's sense of the process?"

"They're impressed and so am I," said Chord. "I participated in the trial runs based on the Lalande data. We were able to quickly zero in on key Restoration infrastructure. We even added some detail to what The Bancroft's investigators uncovered."

"I'll leave the heavy lifting in that area to your team and Mr. Literal then," said Anne. "Hal?"

Hal Renfro sized his former captain up for a moment, then decided to take the plunge. "We have a very valuable resource that we've barely tapped. Nicholas Withers joined the *Nai'a* in the Sol system." He saw Anne's expression turn stoney, but forged on. "He knows more than anyone on this ship about the Restoration's operations in Sol, and he's willing to cooperate."

"What possible reason do I have to trust information from a man who poisoned the minds of several of my people and nearly got everyone on this ship killed?" Anne asked, her voice dangerously flat.

Hal didn't flinch. "I know you have every reason to distrust him, but his information on the Restoration operations in Lalande proved accurate. I know he could play us with false information, but I don't think we should ignore him as a source."

"Isn't he in cold sleep?"

"No, I asked Captain Hartley to keep him in the brig until we could have this discussion. You don't have to deal with him. Rolland and I can take care of it.

Anne leaned back and shook her head. "No, as much as I despise the man, I'd better grow up and give him a chance to explain himself. I want my own sense of why he changed sides, and if it's genuine."

***

Nicholas Withers looked different to Anne Brelling. She paced back and forth in the brig's interrogation room, trying to put her finger on what had changed. Nicholas met her stern gaze frankly, but without challenge. It was the eyes, she realized. At their last meeting, his eyes had burned with hate. Now, his expression was neutral. He seemed to be studying her. At last, she stopped pacing, but didn't sit. "Against my better judgment, I'm meeting with you, Mr. Withers. Tell me why I should put any faith in what you say."

Nicholas looked down at his hands for a moment, then looked her in the eye. "Faith?" he started. "That's an interesting choice of words, especially for someone like me. You probably shouldn't have *any* faith in me given my track record. I need to apologize to you. I know you aren't the captain anymore, but I did grievous harm to your ship and crew when you were. I'm sorry for that. I can't undo the harm I've done, but perhaps I can do a little good with what's left of my life."

Anne returned his gaze skeptically. "You have a lot to answer for, but you haven't answered my question. Why would you help us? I recall a man who was bent on the capture or destruction of this ship and one who blamed me for his father's incarceration. A man whose hate was palpable."

"You're right," Nicholas nodded. "I hated everyone on this ship and you most of all. Now I see that hate for what it was. Faith is why I changed my mind, specifically Pete Worsley's faith. His faith made him keep trying to make a friend of a man who hated him. He visited me every week and brought me good things, even when no one else wanted anything to do with me. His faith wore me down, made me see what a waste I'd made of my life, and the harm I'd done. I have that same faith in Jesus now. If there's anyone more unworthy of his love than I am, I don't know who it is. I finally realized I didn't need to be worthy; indeed, I could never *be* worthy. So, I just trusted."

Anne sighed and studied Nicholas thoughtfully as she pulled out a chair and sat down across the metal table from him. "If you're telling the truth, you just made the one argument I can accept. What do you want out of this?"

Nicholas considered the question for a moment. "I want the Restoration stopped. I was typical of their operatives, willing and ready to do almost anything to break the Long Boat Free Trade Syndicate and restore control of the former colonies. There's no limit to the suffering they're willing to inflict. Their cause is the antithesis of freedom, though they would deny it."

"What about your freedom?" Anne asked.

"I realize I gave that up through my actions. I don't expect to get it back. As I recall, the sentence was life plus 243 years at hard labor."

Anne nodded. "It's possible your sentence could be commuted, but I understand you haven't asked for that. How much do you know about the Restoration operation in the Sol system?"

"I know enough to give you a good start at prying them out of the woodwork," Nicholas answered. "I spent several years working with the Restoration to penetrate the Long Boat Free Trade Syndicate's home office. By now, I'm sure both you and they realize we arranged for myself, Lisandra Redding, and a few others to be added to the crew. I also made sure I had dirt to use as leverage on several crew members. The organization is compartmentalized, but I had enough access to know who several of the key players and corporations are. I'll share that information regardless of my personal situation."

Anne nodded. "I'm tempted to believe you, Mr. Withers. We're a long way from trusting you, but your information is too valuable to ignore. In light of your cooperation, however, I think we should do something for you. I'll talk to Captain Hartley and see what can be arranged."

Nicholas shrugged. "I don't deserve or expect anything in return, but Pete also taught me about grace and mercy. I'll gratefully accept any improvement in my current situation."

Anne looked over at Hal Renfro and Rolland. "You two are conspicuously quiet. Do you have anything to add?"

Hal unfolded his arm and leaned forward. "I know this is an ugly subject, but we need every lever we can get. What about the Panic, Nicholas? That drug is so illegal and despised it will be a big weapon against the Restoration if we can tie them to it."

Nicholas looked downcast. He shook his head. "I'm more ashamed of using the Panic than anything else I've done. I don't know who manufactured the doses I used, but I do know the contacts we used to obtain it. We were dealing with jaded underworld types, and even they were nervous about the goods. I'll gladly testify that the Restoration deliberately obtained and planned to use the drug. Of course, you have the evidence that I did."

Rolland frowned. "I'm glad none of that filth made it into Lalande. Or did it?"

Nicholas shook his head again. "Not to my knowledge. The *Nai'a* was our immediate target. Since that didn't work out, I'm sure the organization has adjusted its plans. I wouldn't put it past them to use the Panic again, but I'm sure the Long Boat Free Trade Syndicate has your Tau Ceti report by now. The drug wouldn't be very useful if a ship knew about the possibility."

"Even if the Restoration isn't the source of the drug, their willingness to use it is a good arrow in our quiver," said Anne. "It will do wonders in the court of public opinion. I'll leave it to you to run that angle down, Hal. Your law enforcement experience in the Sol system will be invaluable. I think we're done for now. I need to talk to the captain. Mr. Withers, I appreciate your cooperation." She stood, gave him a nod and strode out of the room.

Hal looked at Rolland. "That went better than expected."

"Yes," Rolland agreed. "She was more open to the possibility of Nicholas being sincere than I would have believed. I don't think it's just pragmatism either."

Nicholas slumped in his chair, visibly drained. "I'm afraid it's back to your cell," said Hal, motioning to the ship security guard.

Nicholas stood. "By now, it feels like home."

***

"You want to put Withers in crew quarters?" Captain Hartley's incredulous look spoke volumes. "I don't think that's a good idea. How do you think the crew will react? Especially the ones he poisoned with the Panic."

"You might be surprised," Anne said wryly. "He apologized in person to most of them and, apparently, he's been forgiven by most. Strangely, I'm worried more for his safety, than that he'll try anything. I think he's genuinely switched sides."

"If I agree, he can't be out of his quarters without a trusted escort. What about PCOM net access?"

"If he'll agree to twenty-four-hour monitoring by Mr. Literal, and some reasonable limitations, I think it will be okay. Our resident hacker can review the measures."

Captain Hartley nodded. "I'll have Lisandra and the Chief of Boat draw up a plan. I should put out an announcement to the crew before we allow him out in public." He shook his head. "Who would have believed we'd be letting that miscreant out of the brig after what he did?"

***

Lisandra looked up without expression as a Ship Security guard escorted Nicholas Withers into her office. The last time she had seen the man was when she testified in his trial for mutiny. At the time, he tried and failed to spit on her. "Have a seat," she motioned to a chair facing the desk. Nicholas was wearing a standard grey ship suit instead of the bright orange brig outfit. Quester occupied a chair to Lisandra's right.

Nicholas and Lisandra regarded each other in silence for few moments. Nicholas looked like he was slightly afraid of her. *He's a very different man now*, Lisandra thought. *I wonder where the hard-as-nails Gerald Minnick character went?*

"We've both come a long way from being co-conspirators to a mutiny," she said. "I trust you won't try to spit on me this time?"

Nicholas looked down with a grimace. "I'm sorry about that, for what it's worth. I ended up spitting on myself, which was a fitting outcome. I realize now, I left you off of the list of people I needed to apologize to. I never used the Panic on you, but I'm sorry I blackmailed you into helping me. I should have listened to you about what we were up against with this crew and ship. They've added your skills through the exact opposite of my tactics. Fear and hate are powerful motivators, but they only breed resentment in the long term."

"I'm glad you've come to your senses, at least to a degree," said Lisandra wryly. "After what you did, trust will be hard to come by, but the new captain agreed to allow you a measure of freedom." She entered a few commands on the mini-comp sitting between them. A holographic image of a blond man appeared standing behind Lisandra with one hand on her shoulder. The image appeared to be watching the mini-comp display.

"Meet Mr. Literal, the ship's data librarian and artificial intelligence." She twitched her head to the left. "As you can see, he's always looking over my shoulder. I think the image is his idea of a joke, but his sense of humor is highly suspect. If you'll agree to constant monitoring by Mr. Literal, I'm authorized to allow your PCOM limited access to the *Nai'a's* internal communications and data nets. I've activated your PCOM, established a person-to-person connection, and I'm sending the consent form now."

Nicholas blinked but managed to access the form and append his digital signature. His PCOM skills were rusty from years of disuse. He sent the signed form back to Lisandra.

She nodded and entered a few more commands. She motioned to Quester, who was watching the interchange with interest. "This is Quester Drake, my assistant." Quester nodded to Nicholas who, returned the gesture.

Lisandra looked at Nicholas, and her eyes took on a hard glint. "If you make even one attempt to harm anyone on this ship, or the ship itself, I will personally make your life as miserable as I possibly can. Going back to the brig will be the least of your worries. You know I have the skills to make that stick." Nicholas nodded slowly, and he hoped, sincerely. "Quester and I have both been on Mr. Literal's bad side. You don't want to go there." Quester chuckled and Mr. Literal's avatar stared sternly at Nicholas.

"I will endeavor to behave myself," said Nicholas carefully. "I no longer wish any harm on the *Nai'a* or her crew."

"You'll forgive us if we don't take your word for it," said Lisandra.

"Prudent," Nicholas acknowledged.

Lisandra busied herself entering commands for a few moments. After she finished, she and Quester both approved the net changes, entering voice, fingerprint, and retinal patterns to authorize new access. "You can now send and receive messages and calls over the ship net. You have access to the ship's entertainment library. If you need to access any other part of the data library, call or message Mr. Literal. Be specific with your search terms. He's very prolific with his data results."

Quester and Nicholas exchanged test calls and messages while Lisandra and Mr. Literal monitored the procedure. "Okay," said Lisandra. "Your access looks good. Do you have any questions?" Nicholas shook his head. "Good, Quester will show you to your quarters."

To Nicholas' surprise, the Ship Security guard did not accompany them. Quester led the way and he followed, taking in his first views in many years of anything but ship security and the cold sleep vaults. "Aren't you afraid to be alone with such a dangerous character?" he asked Quester.

"I hung out with some rough characters back in Tau Ceti," Quester answered. "I know your background. I'm not worried, unless you have a secret stash of the Panic?"

"No," Nicholas answered. "I'm through assaulting and intimidating people."

"I hope you're sincere," said Quester. He led Nicholas onto Cooper Green, and the former saboteur stopped to fight a wave of vertigo.

"Sorry," he said, bending over to put his hands on his knees. "The open space is overwhelming after so long in confined spaces."

Quester looked chagrined. "Now I'm sorry. I thought you might enjoy it."

"I will, give me a moment to adjust." Nicholas took a couple of deep breaths, then slowly straightened up and surveyed his surroundings. He could see the spine of the ship housing the central corridor high overhead. A broad expanse of the next section over was visible on the oddly rising horizon. "This ship really is a marvel. I didn't appreciate it when I was bent on mayhem and destruction. There's plenty of open space to keep the crew from feeling closed in."

"We had open spaces on HAB-5, some larger than this, but I didn't spend much time in them," said Quester, looking around. "My quality of life went way up when I joined the *Nai'a*. It's one of the reasons I switched sides."

"You were working for the Restoration?" asked Nicholas.

"More, for myself, really," Quester answered, "but I took their coin. I was trying to play both sides to see what I could get out of it. Fortunately, I saw the error of my ways before I did anything too stupid."

"I wish I could say the same," Nicholas answered, his eyes took on a haunted look. "I wonder if I should just go back to the brig. I did a lot of damage."

"You won't do anyone any good sitting in a cell staring at the walls. Let's go take a look at your assigned quarters. You're just a few doors down from my place." Nicholas nodded, following while he furtively looked around to see if anyone recognized him.

In a few minutes, they came to the door of his new quarters. "The door is keyed to your PCOM," Quester said.

"Does that mean I can lock it?" Nicholas asked incredulously.

"Yes," Quester answered. "Ship Security can override the lock, but you have control of the door and everything else in this set of single quarters."

Nicholas keyed open the door and looked around. The quarters included a combined living-dining-kitchen area and a small bedroom with a bathroom beyond. On a small table in the living area, was a carton labeled with his name.

"Those are your personal effects, scanned ten different ways and deemed harmless by Ship Security," Quester said. "You should be stocked up on basic needs but check the pantry and cold storage. You can make a list for a visit to the chandlery. I understand you need an escort if you want to leave. Ambassador Brelling will send someone when you're needed by her team. When I'm available I can escort you, and Pete Worsley asked me to let you know he's willing as well. I'll let you get settled in. Message me if you need anything"

"Thanks, I'll take a look around," said Nicholas. "Biome will send someone for me in the morning. I'm still working off my sentence scrubbing filters."

Quester's nose wrinkled. "Better you than I. Your dinner is covered tonight. Watch your PCOM messages." He gave Nicholas a wave and left him to contemplate his new situation.

Nicholas opened the carton and looked through the contents. He kept a few items of off-duty clothing and a small tool set. The rest he set aside for recycling. He had no interest in "Gerald Minnick's" personal mementos. As far as he was concerned, the false persona was dead and gone.

He sat down and stared at the wall for a few minutes. The chair was several degrees more comfortable than his brig bunk. He was startled out of his reverie when his quarters door opened and a large thickly-furred Maine Coon cat sauntered in. Nicholas sat very still. He had almost no experience with cats but was well aware of their natural weapons and standing as prized vermin control on the ship. Lionel ignored him, conducting a thorough inspection tour of the quarters. He wound up at the pile of clothing, sniffing it with interest. Finally, the cat sat down in front of Nicholas and regarded him cooly.

Nicholas raised his eyebrows but didn't move or say anything. Lionel turned around and walked out without looking back. The door slid obligingly out of the way, and he rubbed his scent on the jam as he passed through. Nicholas shook his head in confusion, wondering what he had just witnessed.

A PCOM notification saved him from further contemplation. The message invited him to dinner at Abishai and Shanyah's quarters in two hours. He gave a twitch. He'd dosed Abishai with the Panic during his run of sabotage many years ago. Instead of freezing up like all the other Panic victims, Abishai had tossed him into the nearest bulkhead, and come very close to killing him. Still, the muscular crewman had since forgiven Nicholas. He replied that he would be glad to come to dinner.

***

Nicholas spent the intervening time checking his quarters out and making a short list for the chandlery. He wondered what he was going to use for credits and pulled up the financial report on his PCOM. He was surprised to find he had a positive balance in a ship account, which was in his correct name. He dug back in the transaction history and found "Gerald

Minnick's" balance had been transferred to him. The fines and fees from his trial and sentencing put him in the red back then, but he'd been paid a one-tenth basic crew salary for all the years he spent at hard labor. Now, he had a few credits to his name. Because of his crimes, he'd forfeited crew shares for two voyages that would have made him wealthy, but it was still a pleasant surprise to be solvent.

His door chime sounded, and he sent it an open command. Quester walked in, dressed in a mandarin collar tunic of deep red and a pair of black slacks. "I'm early," he said. "I thought you might want some advice on an outfit."

"I don't have much to choose from, but I think I can manage something about as formal as your clothing," Nicholas answered. He disappeared into the bedroom, emerging a few minutes later wearing a white shirt embroidered in blue, and navy-blue slacks.

Quester surveyed the look and nodded. "You'll do."

"I had a feline visitor after you left who waltzed through my door without an invitation, then inspected the place. Other than a disapproving look, he didn't give me the time of day. Do you know how he would get through a door set to open only on my command?" Nicholaas asked.

"Sorry about that. I should have warned you. Grey and cream with long fur?" Quester asked. Nicholas nodded.

"That's my buddy, Lionel," said Quester. "He's a law unto himself. Since he's on vermin control, his implant lets him open any door or hatch on the ship that isn't an active danger to him. The default setting for personal quarters allows him to come and go, but you can change it to keep him out."

"Given his job description, I think I'll leave it the way it is. I don't want to get on his bad side"

Quester chuckled. "Wise choice."

"I'm as ready as I'm going to get," Nicholas said. "Lead the way." He gestured toward the door and followed Quester out into the corridor.

Abishai introduced Nicholas to Shanyah, Mishael, and Kalei. Abishai's wife and children regarded Nicholas with open curiosity. He didn't sense any of the overt hostility he'd been afraid of. He wasn't sure what he had expected, but the three imposing and competent looking people he now faced were a bit intimidating. "Mr. Withers," said Shanyah. "Welcome to our home. I'm sure you didn't expect a welcome, but we have a few reasons to be thankful for you, in spite of your crimes." She gestured toward Mishael and Kalei. "If you hadn't put Abishai into Medical with the Panic, we might never have married, and we wouldn't have these two to be proud of. You meant it for harm, but God worked it out for our good."

Nicholas ducked his head. "He worked it out for my good as well," he said softly. "Please call me Nicholas. I wouldn't have chosen a broken neck for a wakeup call, but it set me on a path that intersected with Pete Worsley and eventually brought me to repentance. It's good of you and Abishai to forgive me enough to invite me into your home."

Abishai motioned to the table and chairs set up for dinner. "I don't know about you, Nicholas, but I'm famished. Dinner's ready, so let's not let it get cold." Abishai asked Quester to say a blessing, and they dug into a dinner of chicken, red beans & rice, and collard greens, accompanied by big chunks of hot cornbread.

Nicholas watched the easy interchange among Abishai's family and Quester with some jealousy. They tried to include him in the conversation, but he felt lost without context. Everyone took an opportunity to gently tease Mishael about his new girlfriend, making him blush with each sally. Nicholas was amazed by the rate at which food disappeared with Mishael and Abishai at the table.

Over a dessert of pineapple upside down cake, Shanyah asked him about his quarters and his plans. Nicholas barked a short laugh. "The quarters are a nice step up from the brig. I don't have any plans, other than trying to help Ambassador Brelling get ready for coping with the Restoration when we get to the Sol system. I'll continue to work my sentence off when I'm not needed. I'm probably the best environmental filter scrubber on the ship."

Mishael frowned. "What's your actual status?" he asked. "I know you're confined to quarters unless escorted."

"Chief Bolhepp was a bit vague," answered Nicholas. "I was too shocked to ask a lot of questions. He said I'm on a form of probation, for now, by the authority of Captain Halsey. My sentence stands, but if I behave myself, I can serve it from quarters instead of the brig."

"Your crimes are a magnitude of order more serious than what Lisandra and I did, but we're all technically mutineers," said Quester thoughtfully. "I don't think you're ever going to be a crew member in good standing, but I wouldn't be surprised if the captain commutes your sentence. I suppose it depends on how helpful you are and what happens in Sol."

Nicholas shrugged. "I'm not getting my hopes up. I'll be quite satisfied if Ambassadors Brelling and Dunleavy get the best of the Restoration. My future doesn't matter much placed against what they want to accomplish."

Abishai scratched his chin. "I wouldn't bet against those two. Anne Brelling is as tough as they come, and Rolland is a sneaky tactician. Between the two of them and their team, they'll be ready to give the Restoration all they can handle. Whatever you can do to help them will be appreciated by everyone on the ship."

"It will be good to put a few things on the positive side of the scale after all the harm I did," Nicholas said. He pushed back from the table. "I can't thank you enough for the dinner and company. It's much more than I expected or deserve. I should get back to my quarters and let you finish your evening."

As he stood up Kalei shook her head. "Oh no you don't. We have questions." She and her brother hemmed him in, towering over him in spite of his tall skinny build. They grabbed him by either elbow, backed him up to the couch, and sat him down with one on either side. Wide eyed, Nicholas looked helplessly from Abishai to Shanyah and back.

Abishai chuckled. "Did I mention we have curious children? We thought that might go away when they grew up, but it didn't."

"Tell us about Lalande when you were a child," said Kalei. "Where did you grow up?..." The questions came thick and fast. Nicholas did his best to answer while Quester looked on in amusement, remembering his own interrogation at the hands of the two amateur detectives. Shanyah and Abishai left them to it and started cleaning up the dinner dishes.

A few whirlwind hours later, Quester couldn't help chuckling as he walked a shell-shocked Nicholas back to his quarters. He clapped him on the shoulder. "I'm laughing with you, not at you. Those two are something else." Nicholas just nodded numbly. "Here's your door. Do you need anything?"

"No," Nicholas shook his head in disbelief. "I'd better get some rest. If tomorrow is anything like today, I'll need it. Good night."

Chapter 5 – The Long Slog

November 10th, AD 3208
Lalande System Heliopause
Long Boat Nai'a, *Captain's Office*

Captain Hartley, Chief of Boat Oswald, and First Officer Commander Winslow Stirling considered the array of reports at their disposal. "Why do I feel like I'm waiting for the other shoe to drop?" said the captain. "Everything here indicates a taut ship."

COB Oswald chuckled. "Probably because every time there's a quiet period on this boat; it gets rudely interrupted by some crisis or another. All we can do is stay ready and do our best to keep crew morale and training up."

"Speaking of training," said Commander Stirling. "We need to consider what to do with our pilots. Without sting ships, most of them re-integrated into the commando platoon and took other specialties. We cut way back on militia training. I'm worried about they'll get bored."

"I share your concern," said the captain. "Commander Garrity went from commanding a squadron to fixing water leaks. I wonder how he's handling it?"

"Sir, I suggest you have breakfast with Commander Garrity and the O'Clairs," said COB Oswald. "I know the pilots have their own informal network. Those three should have a good idea of how people are coping. As far as boredom goes, I have just the person in mind to find a cure."

"Good idea, Chief," said the captain. "I'll set up an informal meeting tomorrow. I won't ask about the boredom cure. Just make sure it doesn't result in brig time."

COB Oswald grinned. "I can't guarantee anything, given the yahoo I'm going to task. We'll try to keep everyone out of the brig and Medical."

After the COB left, the captain looked at his first officer. "How are you holding up, Winslow? The life of a first mate is fast-paced."

"You would know, sir," the commander replied. "I'm doing okay. I'm sure you'll tell if I'm not keeping up with my duties. My social life has suffered, but I knew that going in."

Captain Hartley nodded. "In more ways than one. You and Commander Calder seem to be getting along."

"Absolutely! She's a top-notch officer and engineer. We were fortunate she was available."

Just then Joanne Calder walked into the office and plopped down in a chair. "My ears are burning," she said. "Were you talking about me?"

"Only to sing your praises," said Commander Stirling with a grin. "I was just saying we were fortunate you were available when we needed a chief engineer."

"It goes both ways," she replied with a nod. "I'm blessed to be part of this crew and headed back to Sol." She stretched her neck from side to side. "I'm also happy to be finished with the annual inspection on fusion one. Some of those spaces aren't meant for someone of my height."

"I shudder to think how your boyfriend would fit in there," said Stirling with a sly wink.

Joanne cast him a withering look. "My 'boyfriend' is quite a man. He never let his size stop him from getting things done when he worked for me. If you'd like a demonstration, he attends close quarters combat classes regularly."

Stirling paled. "No need for that, I like my vertebrae in their current arrangement."

"If you two are done teasing one another," said Captain Hartley, "I'd like your opinion of the ship's overall technical fitness."

Joanne sat up straighter. "Aye, sir. We're in excellent shape. All significant outstanding repairs are complete. The main engines are running smoothly, and we're caught up on inspections. I owe my predecessor a note of thanks. He's obviously an excellent leader and engineer."

"Owen is all of that," agreed Captain Hartley. "I wonder how he's doing with the Lalande long boat building program?"

"One of my friends in the program had good things to say," Joanne replied. "The Bancroft is pushing Parliament hard to increase funding, and the new yard is shaping up. The only real concern I have with the engineering department is complacency. We have a long slog ahead of us. It's hard to stay sharp when the day-to-day gets boring."

"We were just talking about the same issue in relation to our sting ship pilots," said Captain Hartley. "COB Oswald has some ideas along those lines. I think we'll reinstate the annual Militia Jamboree. We have a lot of people shifting to new duties for this leg of the passage. They'll be occupied learning their positions for now. Still, it's an endemic issue with long boats. I'll talk to the Chief Alder about the plans for job rotation and see what other ideas she has."

Stirling's brow furrowed suddenly. "I think I know where that uneasy feeling is coming from. The Restoration managed to infiltrate our crew on two separate occasions, once in Sol and once in Tau Ceti. Do we know we don't have another set of saboteurs aboard?"

"Unfortunately, we can't be certain," the captain answered. "We cleaned up the local office in Lalande before we took applicants. I don't think the Restoration had back up plans for the disaster we handed them, but we've underestimated them before. The one thing I don't want to do is sow seeds of doubt with the crew. We were walking a fine line trying to track down Lisandra Redding and Nicholas Withers after the Turnover sabotage on the Sol-Tau Ceti run.

"The risk was obvious and immediate then. Now, the risk level isn't high enough to kick off a public investigation. We need a plan in place, though. I want you to sit down with Ship Security Chief Bolhepp and come up with some unobtrusive measures to lower the risk of another internal attack. We don't want suspicion poisoning the crew, but we can't ignore the possibility."

The first officer nodded. "Aye sir, I'll see what we can come up with."

***

Chief of Boat Oswald filled his tray from the Beta Section Galley lunch smorgasbord and found a small table along one wall. Roan followed, a look of trepidation on his face as he took a seat opposite the old spacer. "Don't look so glum, Roan," the COB said. "You're not in trouble...yet."

"You're not making me feel any better," said Roan. "What's this about?"

The COB finished chewing a big bite of sandwich before he replied. "It's about taking advantage of your creative skills in a planned and positive way, instead of our usual game of cat and mouse. Your go-cart track is shut down until we hit coast phase. We need something new to help entertain the crew in the meantime. I'm sure that brain of yours has been cooking something clandestine up. What would you say to working together this time, so you don't end up with a year's worth of extra duty."

Roan sighed. "Half the fun is trying to keep you in the dark, COB. I have a few half-formed ideas kicking around up here." He tapped his skull. "When I have something worth sharing, I'll let you know."

"Just make sure you don't go beyond the planning stage without my go-ahead," the COB replied. "Biome always has unpleasant tasks to be done."

"I'm aware," said Roan with a wry smile. "Say, that gives an idea. Hmm... a little risk-reward consequence could give things some spice..."

Watching the wheels turn in Roan's head, COB Oswald nodded in satisfaction and tucked into the rest of his sandwich.

***

The next morning, Nicholas opened his quarters door to find Rolland Dunleavy waiting for him instead of a crewman from Biome. "No filter scrubbing for you today," the ambassador said. "We're going to pick your brain." He motioned for Nicholas to follow and set off for the investigation team's offices. Ten minutes later, he seated Nicholas at a small table and handed him a cup of coffee and a plate with a doughnut on it. "I went over the recording Kalei made of their talk with you. We might have to draft her and Mishael the next time I need to interrogate someone. They asked every question I would have and many more."

"I'm glad I won't need to repeat the process with you," Nicholas said. "Those two wrang me dry."

"A lot of it was personal. I was surprised by some of the questions you answered."

"I was overwhelmed, and it felt good to have someone interested in knowing about *me*, not just my crimes. I never thought I needed companionship. I suppose I didn't while hate was driving me."

"The personal parts are surprisingly relevant to what we need as well," said Rolland, tapping a stylus on the table. "I should know that, but sometimes you forget the people side of things in an investigation. I imagine this is uncomfortable, but I want to work up an itemized list of the methods you and your fellow Restoration operatives used to coerce the syndicate's people at the main office in Sol."

Nicholas grimaced, but nodded, "We used every devious strong-arm tactic we could think of. I can see how exposing that will be useful. The Restoration was already planning a public relations campaign highlighting the 'evils' of the syndicate when I left. You'll need to counteract them with a PR campaign of your own."

"The court of public opinion," Rolland said with a shake of his head. "We're bound for the snake pit of Sol system politics, but if we can win that battle, we'll have a decent chance of stopping the Restoration in its tracks."

"My sense of Sol politics is as dated as anyone's on this boat," said Nicholas. "Do you have an expert on the team?"

Rolland steepled his fingers in thought. "Chord Olley has a good sense of the situation that's more up-to date than ours. A lot can change in four decades, though. We'll need to adjust our plans once we have good coms with the home office. In the meantime, we need to develop as strong a case against the Restoration as we can."

"The records of the Tau Ceti operation should help if they can be tied to the people in Sol," said Nicholas. "The Restoration committed everything from murder to kidnapping, piracy, and illegal weapons trading in Tau Ceti."

"We have a solid financial paper trail connecting the Tau Ceti operation to Sol, along with data on the illegal munitions," Rolland replied. "One of the insiders who turned informant is in cold sleep. He recorded testimony to back up the paper trail, and he said he would testify in Sol. As heinous as those actions were, the people in Sol will probably be more influenced by crimes committed in their own system."

Nicholas grimaced, "That's where I come in. I'm willing to testify in any forum to the things I did for the Restoration in Sol and the other crimes I know they committed. The statute of limitations will probably apply to many of them, but I can still help sway public opinion."

"The Sol authorities might decide to prosecute you."

"So be it. I haven't asked for a sentence reduction for what I did to the *Nai'a* and her crew, I won't ask for any consideration for my testimony in Sol either."

"I admit it will be helpful if you take responsibility," said Rolland, "but it's asking a lot. You don't have any good reason to help us."

Nicholas looked Rolland in the eye. "I have the best reason," he said with a serious expression. "It's the right thing to do. I was on the wrong side of this fight for a long time. I discovered I can live with myself better if I do what I know is right."

Rolland measured him for a moment. "I don't know why, but I believe you. Let's start with the list of offenses I mentioned." He opened a virtual document and activated the speech-to-text tool.

Chapter 6 – The Roan Danger

January 15th, AD 3209
Lalande System Heliopause
Long Boat Nai'a, *Captain's Office*

Roan rubbed his hands in glee as he contemplated the first puzzle in what he called "Danger School." Now that Christmas celebrations were past and everyone was settling into a routine, it was time to shake things up.

Each puzzle was difficult but not impossible. Some were based on real incidents from long boat history. All had the potential to endanger the crew or the boat. Mr. Literal gave him more than enough ideas to work with from the archives. Roan knew the COB was waiting with bated breath. This ought to provide a good break from the routine for anyone brave enough to try it.

Puzzle One required teams get to a pallet of supplies from the bow to the stern of the boat as fast as possible using the spinal corridor. The *Nai'a* was currently under .1G acceleration. The corridor was rigged with safety nets every five hundred meters to keep anything from falling the ten kilometers of the ship's length. In the journey's coast phase, the corridor would be clear, and floating its length at a constant speed would be fairly simple. Under acceleration, though, it was going to take some real ingenuity to get past those nets and control the velocity of the supply pallet.

Roan ran some calculations and decided two hours would be a good risk-reward time goal for the ten-kilometer journey, about a steady walking pace. "What do you think, Grady?" He waived at the display depicting the spinal corridor and the details of the challenge.

The red-headed gangly young man took a few moments to survey the information. "I think anyone who takes this on is nuts. A five-hundred-meter fall into one of those nets is painful even at .1G. Don't ask me how I know. I shudder to think what a loaded supply pallet landing on you would do."

"So, you're out?" Roan asked his son.

"Are you kidding me?" Grady said with a wide grin. "My team's going to shred this like coleslaw. How about a side bet?"

"Wait, you already have a team put together?"

"Let's just say I know who I'm going to recruit. You oldsters won't stand a chance. I know you have your own team in mind. What should we put on the line?"

Roan rubbed his chin. "Pump three is due for overhaul. Loser has to clean and repack the main bearing?"

Grady shuddered, remembering the places grease had found its way onto him the last time, then shrugged. "Sounds fair, you're on!"

Roan rose and shook his son's hand on the deal. "You'd better review the bearing packing procedure. I've got a meeting with the COB and Chief Alder Belotic. It's time to show them the challenge and arrange for the risk and reward."

***

Chief Alder Persephone Belotic eyed Roan skeptically across the conference room table as he made his pitch. "Are you sure this is safe?" she asked.

Roan chuckled, "I'm sure it isn't safe, that's the appeal. My go-carts aren't safe either, but the risk in both cases is reasonable. Also, I have faith in my fellow crew members. They have enough good sense not to do anything stupid. If anyone is going to mess this up spectacularly, it will be me," he thought for a moment, "or maybe my son Grady. The teams must bring the supply pallet to rest at each safety net, then move it out of the way. We won't put a hole in the stern"

"COB Oswald?" the Chief Alder queried.

"It's about as crazy as I was expecting," answered the COB. "As long as the participants have all the information we do, they should be able to avoid any serious injuries or damage to the ship. How do you propose to run the competition?"

"I'll post the particulars on the ship net thirty days out," said Roan. "I want to give people time to gather teams, plan a strategy, and get their equipment together. We'll put a mass limit on the equipment to keep things from getting out of hand. We'll have Mr. Literal generate a random starting order and have one team go each day until they've all had a chance."

The COB's eyes narrowed. "You mentioned a risk-reward goal. What do you propose for the consequence of not meeting the time goal?"

Roan grinned. "I'm hoping you have some ideas along those lines, COB. You've found a lot of creative consequences for me over the years." He turned to the Chief Ader. "On the reward side, do you think the Alder Council can chip in with a dinner out for the teams that beat the time?"

Persephone nodded. "I think we can do that much without a problem. How many teams do you think will enter?"

Roan spread his hands. "I'm not sure, and I don't want to guess. I could be three, or thirty."

COB Oswald drummed his fingers thoughtfully, "Thirty is a good planning figure. I doubt more than half the teams will meet the goal. The success rate will go up as people learn from the early teams. Should we do something special for the team with the lowest time?"

Persephone frowned. "I'll see what I can come up with. We have time. Make sure you coordinate with Medical to have an emergency support team in place."

"You have friends in Medical, right, Roan?" COB Oswald said. Roan nodded tentatively. "I'll leave that to you then. Dr. Rensaleer takes a dim view of this sort of thing. If you can convince her, we'll give it a go.

***

Roan leaned back after making his pitch to the *Nai'a's* chief medical officer. Dr. Rensaleer regarded him with an unreadable expression. The silence stretched to nearly a minute. Through a supreme effort of will, Roan managed not to squirm. "You're even dumber than you look, Roan," she finally said shaking her head. "I suppose it's too much to hope that you might break your neck and save us from further flashes of brilliance." She sighed in resignation. "At least we know about this nonsense ahead of time so I can have a team in place. It will be good practice for my trauma people. I just hope they aren't needed. If your teams exercise proper caution, they'll avoid injuries. However, since you made this a race against time, I'm doubtful."

Roan blinked. "Is that a yes, or a no?"

"It's a conditional yes. I'm agreeing to this for two reasons. First, I want your solemn promise you'll run all your brilliant ideas for this 'Danger School' by me before you execute." Roan nodded. "Good, at least we'll be able to plan for the collateral damage. Second, the crew needs the outlet. It's too easy to get locked into a monotonous routine and start letting things slide. We also need the new crew members we picked up in Lalande to integrate quickly. Your competition will help."

Roan nearly wilted in relief. "Those sound more like the captain's concerns."

Dr. Rensaleer nodded. "The crew is our main concern. He comes at it from a leadership perspective, while I focus on health, including mental health. There's a lot of overlap."

"Who should I coordinate with on the schedule?" Roan asked.

"Talk to Kalei, you two are close, and she'll probably join a team for the competition. If she hadn't put a good word in for you, I doubt I would have given you a meeting. She knows the med teams inside and out. Now, get out of my hair before I start looking at your med record to see if you need a personal biome infusion." Roan scurried out of her office to find Kalei.

***

Grady and his team took their places at the bulkhead sealing the bow end of the spinal corridor. He glanced nervously around, checking again that all six were in place, two to a side of the triangular space.

His old friends, Kalei, Mishael, Belle, and Mina O'Clair, along with Lalande native Darcey Norris, made up the rest of the team. Darcey was a miner's kid with a surprising array of skills who had quickly attached herself to this group of friends. Calling themselves the Future, they had every intention of winning the competition.

The triangular supply pallet hung from the bulkhead, five-hundred kilograms of mass, not too heavy in .1G, but awkward. The kicker was a fresh egg in a bowl taped to the top of the pallet. A broken egg meant an automatic loss for the team and eight hours for each of them at the mercy of the COB.

The starting tone sounded, and the team sprang into action. Grady, Belle, and Mina all pushed gently off the walls and soft-rappelled in long drops toward the safety net five hundred meters below. Darcey unhooked and scrambled to the top of the pallet. Mishael and Kalei assisted her in securing a three-legged harness to its outer points. She unclipped the lines holding the pallet in place, while Kalei and Mishael held it steady. She fastened a long coil of thick line to the bulkhead, then clipped the other end to the harness. She nodded to Mishael who checked to make sure the below team was in place.

"Ready?" asked Mishael when he saw they were prepared. Darcey nodded and they released the pallet. It dropped slowly down the shaft, picking up speed as the line coiled out behind. Darcey peeked over the edge, trying to distribute her weight evenly as the pallet fell faster and faster. Halfway to her teammates and the safety net below, the line grew taught and began to stretch. The pallet's velocity slowed in tiny increments as the bungee cord absorbed the energy of the plunge. Darcey kept her hand on the quick release, and gauged her speed carefully. When she was twenty meters from her teammates, she could tell the pallet was going to stop before it reached them. At ten meters, and near zero velocity, she hit the quick release. The pallet drifted downward again with her aboard to be caught and secured by Grady, Belle, and Mina.

The bungee cord snapped back up the corridor toward Kalei and Mishael. They were prepared, dodging the end as it whipped past them and smacked the bulkhead. "Tell me again why we got this job?" Mishael said, quickly coiling the snaking chord.

"In your case, it's muscles, in my case, brains," said Kalei. They released their safety lines and rappelled after their team.

Down below Darcey scrambled off the pallet to help release and secure the safety net., "Whoa!" she exclaimed, "I thought I was going for a yo-yo ride."

"You timed the release just right!" Grady shouted. In seconds, the team had the first safety net stowed and began rappelling in giant bounds down to the next while Darcey waited with the pallet.

Mishael and Kalei soon joined her, clipped themselves to rings set in the corridor walls, then sent the signal to free their rappel lines. Mishael re-rigged the coil of bungee cord to the pallet's harness. Kalei measured the three cables supporting the pallet's harness to make sure the anchor point was centered in the corridor.

Once all their lines were retracted and clear, Kalei checked to make sure the below team was ready at the second safety net. Darcey took her place on the pallet, careful not to jostle the egg bowl. Kalei gave her a thumbs up, and she released the pallet harness from the anchor point. As the pallet gained speed, Darcey made small adjustments with her body to keep it level. A lifetime of working in low gravity gave her a sixth sense for mass and momentum. Once again, she had to hit the quick release just before the pallet reached the below team. They caught it with confidence this time and quickly repeated the process of securing the pallet and stowing the safety net.

For the next hour and twenty minutes, the team repeated the evolution. Above them, a maintenance team re-rigged the safety nets as they went. Finally, they arrived exhausted at the stern bulkhead, pallet and egg intact. The team exchanged hugs and pats on the back all around. With a time of one hour, twenty-five minutes and fifteen seconds, they beat the risk-reward goal and set the standard the rest of the teams would try to beat.

After an hour break to shower and change, the team caught up with each other at Six Fathoms for their reward dinner. Plates of crunchy coated deep-fried calamari with marinara sauce and a basket of hot cheese biscuits were waiting for them on the table as a starter. "Now this is a hero's reward!" declared Mishael, breaking a steaming biscuit in half and applying butter. Two bites later it was gone, and he was helping himself to the calamari.

Darcey viewed his progress through the food with alarm, careful to keep her hands out of his reach. Kalei leaned over. "Don't worry, he doesn't bite people," she said with a grin. "You were the key to our success. I thought we'd had it when the pallet brushed the corridor wall. How did you keep from flipping?"

Darcey shrugged. "I realized I had a sideways drift going. I stuck my legs way out to contact the other side and managed to keep from going all the way over. Once the bungee tightened, everything evened up fine. It was mostly instinct. I've moved a lot of squirrely loads working the asteroid fields." A waiter replaced their empty plate and basket with full ones and took their orders.

Mishael paused his assault on the second basket of cheese biscuits and looked at Grady. "Do you think the rest of the teams will go to school on us? I'm sure your dad didn't believe we would make the time."

"They'll learn from us," replied Grady. "The 'Parents' team drew the day-five slot. I don't think they'll be able to replicate the auto-belay devices we used in that time. It took me two weeks to adjust the design for low gravity. Who knows what tricks the old fogies have up their sleeves. I'm more concerned with the pilot's guild. They have three teams fielded and they're naturally sneaky. Did you make a side bet with Abishai?"

Mishael nodded, "Loser cooks Sunday dinner for a month."

"My dad and I bet a deep clean on one another's quarters," said Belle. "Mom told us we were both going to break something, and she didn't want to hear any complaining if we had to hobble around in a cast. I got through it with just a couple of bruised knuckles. Did anyone else get banged up at all?"

Mishael grimaced, "I've got a good-sized welt from the bungee cord. I was enjoying the game of dodge until then." He shrugged. "I zigged when I should have zagged."

Kalei patted his shoulder. "You zigged in front of me, or that would have been my welt, ever the protective big brother. I do appreciate it. Dr. Rensaleer loves nothing more than a good 'I told you so.' Thanks to you I can say I came through unscathed. I'll be sore tomorrow, though. I worked muscles in ways I don't usually move them."

Their waiter arrived with the main course and distributed their food. Darcey took a bite of lobster dipped in garlic butter and looked around. The tropical sea environment on one side, and arctic ocean environment on the other provided a fascinating and ever-changing view. The dolphin pod stopped by to congratulate them, somewhat moistly. Mishael gave them all rubs and translated for the team. Several crew members also came by the table with compliments as they enjoyed their reward. Darcey missed her family in Lalande's asteroid belt, but for now she basked in the warm glow of camaraderie. Her crew mates were good people.

***

Over the next three days one team completed the challenge successfully, but over the time limit. The two others suffered accidents with minor injuries that forced them to give up partway. Roan's team was now in position and ready for their attempt. The "Parents" team included Roan, his wife Paulene, Abishai, Shanyah, and Val and Palmar O'Clair. Abishai looked down the corridor below his feet and gulped down a wave of acrophobia. How had Roan talked him into this? The start tone sounded, and he pushed his doubts aside. The O'Clairs and Paulene quickly lowered the pallet a few meters and rigged it with the same kind of triangular harness their children had used. Shanyah and Roan fastened a bracket for Abishai's boots to the center of the bow bulkhead. He grabbed it and piked his feet up so they could clip him in. Soon he was hanging upside down like an over-muscled bat.

Roan took the end of a line from Abishai and clipped it to the pallet harness. The line ran through Abishai's thickly gloved hands and a friction coupling into a reel fastened to his belt. The O'Clairs and Paulene hung, boots down from a corner of the triangular pallet. Abishai tested the weight of the ensemble then carefully let the line slip through his hands. He moved one hand to the control of the friction coupling as the pallet picked up speed. Roan and Shanyah each took a gloved grip on the line about ten meters apart, dropping downward with the rest of the team.

Once the pallet and his friends were descending at a good pace, Abishai applied pressure with the friction coupling, trying to keep the speed steady. He used his hand on the line to judge the velocity. When the pallet was four -fifths of the way to the first safety net, Val O'Clair shouted "One hundred!" Abishai immediately increased the friction, slowing the team's descent until he could lower them hand over hand the last few meters.

Paulene and the O'Clairs clipped into rings set int the corridor wall, then steadied the pallet while Roan and Shanyah slid the rest of the way down the line. Once both cleared the pallet, Roan released the line from the harness and shouted an all clear to Abishai.

While his teammates dealt with rigging the next anchor-point, Abishai pressed the button on his reel to retract the line. He took the end of the line when it arrived and folded himself in half to clip it to the same anchor point his boot bracket was fastened to. The move was a bit awkward, but he'd practiced it repeatedly at a higher gravity load. He released the boot bracket and dropped toward his team, paying out line. Controlling his own descent turned out to be much easier than the pallet with his team attached.

By the time he arrived, Roan and Shanyah had his next anchor point rigged in the center of the corridor. The rest of the team had the safety net stowed and the pallet ready for the next descent. Shanyah secured Abishai's boot bracket to the anchor point while his reel pulled the line in. Roan sat on top of the pallet to protect the egg in its bowl and grabbed the end of the line as it snaked by. Making sure the line and harness weren't fouled, he snapped the smart release to the pallet's harness and gave Abishai a thumbs up. Abishai started the lowering process again. This time he allowed a higher velocity to save a few seconds. The friction coupling got a little hot, but handled the load fine.

When his team and the pallet reached the next safety net, Abishai unfastened his boot bracket, clipped the line on, and made his own descent as before. Once Shanyah had Abishai fastened to the new anchor point harness, Roan sent the release signal to the harness above. He watched the straps and line fall, again careful to protect the egg from damage. Shanyah stowed the harness to use at the next waypoint and Roan hooked up the pallet again. The team established a good rhythm after that, making each bound in four to five minutes. They finished in an hour and thirty-five minutes with the egg still intact.

Roan looked at the time as his sweaty team gathered around. He shook his head. "We knew the kids would be tough to beat. I lose my bet with Grady, but at least we get a dinner out of it. I'll see you all in an hour."

***

Over the next month and a half, the rest of the fifty teams took on Roan's corridor challenge. About half made the reward time, the rest learned the joy of scrubbing filters and cleaning environmental tanks. A team of pilots led by Julian Garrity set the record time. By using a clever combination of compressed air jets and acrobatics, they avoided the need for lines and rigging. Three members of the team descended to each safety net by bouncing off the walls of the corridor, doing a flip twist on each bounce to plant their feet and control their descent. The other three controlled their velocity with compressed air jets, holding the pallet steady between them. They traded off duties on each subsequent descent to break up the physical effort. The clever approach gave them a time of just over an hour and fifteen minutes. Chief Alder Belotic rewarded the team with double beach access slots for the next month.

Chapter 7 – Ties, Old & New

March 1st, AD 3209
Just Clear of the Lalande System
Long Boat Nai'a, *Biome Maintenance Spaces*

Nicholas finished scrubbing the front of a filter, then flipped it expertly to attack the back. He showed his workmate the best angle to hold the brush to get all the nooks and crannies. He noted the grimace on the man's face. "It's best if you don't breathe through your nose," he said. The crewman was from one of the teams that failed to complete Roan's corridor challenge in the allotted time.

Over the last month, Nicholas had worked with a steady stream of different crew members because of the game. About half he remembered from his time on the crew. A few had even been victims of his sabotage schemes, but no one was actively hostile. The newer people often regarded him with undisguised curiosity. They all knew his story, and most had questions. He did his best to answer them without getting defensive. While his current partner worked on the back of the filter, he grabbed another one and played a jet of water over it to knock off the worst of the accumulated crud.

That evening, Quester showed up at his door to escort him to dinner with Pete Worsley. Nicholas hadn't seen much of the Beta Section Head recently. He was curious about that, but too grateful for Pete's friendship to question it much. Pete greeted both and ushered them to the little 'outdoor' space adjacent to his quarters. He served up a dinner of steaming fried rice and egg rolls at the small table.

"How are you getting along, Nicholas?" Pete asked, as they enjoyed the meal.

"Much better, now that I'm out of the brig," Nicholas answered. "You had a lot to do with getting me out of there, whether you'll admit it or not. I'm not exactly part of the crew, but I get to socialize a little. Quester forces me to get out of my quarters during non-work hours."

Pete nodded, "I know I've been out of touch for a while. I wanted you to have time to assimilate without me around, and see how the crew treats you on your own merits. I've been busy helping the new crew members get integrated.

"I think Hal Renfro is more responsible for getting you out of the brig than I am. Also, the captain has the example of how valuable Quester and Lisandra are to the ship. How are you and Ambassador Brelling getting along?"

Nicholas shrugged. "We don't interact much, but she's all business when we do. I imagine she's that way with most people. Considering the reasons she has to detest me; I'll take a business-like relationship."

Pete chewed thoughtfully, then looked at Quester. "Thank you for taking time to help Nicholas get out of his shell. Have you caught any flack?"

Quester shrugged, "Nothing but a few double-takes and a lot of curiosity. Mishael and Kalei take a turn escorting now and then." He turned to look at Nicholas. "Do you get a break from filter scrubbing tomorrow?"

"Yes," he answered. "I have a meeting with Hal Renfro and Chief Bolhepp. I'm not sure what it's about."

"I have an inkling," said Pete, "but I'll leave their business to them. On a different subject, how would you like to come to church this Sunday?"

Nicholas took a deep breath. "Are you sure I'd be welcome?"

Pete's mouth quirked. "If the rest of us sinners can't welcome you, who can?"

Nicholas considered that for a moment. "I suppose you're right. Abishai and Shanyah have been good to me. I come with a lot of baggage, though."

"We all do," said Quester, slapping him on the shoulder. "I wasn't too keen to show my face after I got caught. The church welcomed me anyway."

***

The next morning, Hal showed up to escort Nicholas to Ship Security. Once past reception, they entered the corridor that went to the brig in one direction and Chief Bolhepp's office in the other. Nicholas felt his heart skip a beat and his adrenaline spiked. He leaned against the bulkhead as a wave of near panic washed over him. Hal stopped and looked him over. "Are you okay? We aren't going to the brig today."

Nicholas pushed away from the bulkhead and shook himself. "I'll be alright." They continued down the corridor and entered the Chief's office. Two chairs were set up in front of the desk, so they took seats. The chief walked in a few moments later carrying three cups of coffee. He set two of them down in front of Hal and Nicholas, then took his seat behind the desk.

Nicholas picked up his coffee and took a sip. He grimaced and Chief Bolhepp barked a laugh. "Ship Security coffee will do that to you. It's brewed for caffeine content, not taste." Nicholas nodded and set the cup back down.

Chief Bolhepp regarded him for a few moments then shrugged. "I hesitated to bring you in on this problem, but I need your help. After being infiltrated twice by the Restoration, the captain and I are both concerned about the possibility of sleeper agents in the crew."

Nicholas nodded. "Understandable, I was instrumental in the first instance. I'm not sure how I can help this time."

"You're the best source we have concerning the Restoration and how they operate. I want you to review the non-confidential portion of the files on the crew members we picked up in Lalande. There could be someone you know. Also, you may recognize a pattern or characteristic that lends to someone being blackmailed.

Nicholas nodded. "As long as it's above board. I don't want any part of violating someone's rights."

The chief looked at him for a moment. "You've come a long way from the saboteur who drugged and blackmailed several people on this ship."

"I'm still that person, but I've been changed," Nicholas answered.

"You don't have to worry about the rights issue," the chief said. "We're using public records only. The bad news is, we have over a thousand new crew members. I want you to review each of them and let us know if you see any potential problems."

"Can I use a terminal?" asked Nicholas. "It can be disconnected from the ship if you load the files. I have some data sorting skills that will help me get through them efficiently."

The chief grinned. "We'll set you up with a terminal connected to the ship's data net so Mr. Literal can keep an eye on you."

Thirty minutes later, Nicholas was reviewing files in a semi-private cubby. One corner of the screen-wall display showed Mr. Literal's current avatar watching him closely. He found the AI unnerving but refused to rise to the bait. About fifteen minutes in, Mr. Literal interrupted him. "Your data organization is quite logical. May I borrow a few of your heuristics for my own use?"

Nicholas blinked in surprise. Why would the AI bother to ask permission? Then he remembered Mr. Literal's main purpose was to guard and organize the ship's data library. It stood to reason that the AI had a strong regard for intellectual property rights. "I'm flattered,, Mr. Literal," he said. "Please use them with my blessing."

"Blessing? Could you explain?" asked Mr. Literal. "AIs aren't usually regarded as having a soul. I'm not sure the term applies."

"I wasn't sure if *I* had a soul not too long ago," said Nicholas. "I should have said permission. I gladly give you permission to use any of the heuristics from these sessions."

"Thank you," replied the AI. "I'll remove my avatar from the display, but you can get my attention simply by saying my name."

"I'll remember that," said Nicholas. Mr. Literal's avatar winked out and he got back to work. He surprised himself by missing the AI's looming presence. He set himself a goal of one hundred files reviewed and dug into the data.

A few hours later, Hal showed up. "How goes the searching and sorting?" he asked.

"I'm making steady progress," Nicholas answered. "I have a small group of possibles identified. I'll revisit those later to see if they're worth passing to you. What are you going to do with the information?"

"It depends on how many you come up with," Hal answered. "This is my main priority. I prefer to do direct observation if I have time. I know I don't look subtle, but I've had a lot of experience blending in. It helps that most of the new crew is in training mode. I can usually find a plausible reason to interact with them." He checked the time. "Let's go get lunch."

They made their way to the Beta Section galley, collected their food, and sat down at one of the long tables. Nicholas ignored the usual curious looks, said a quick prayer of thanks, and started on his black bean burrito.

Hal made note of the looks as he ate his own lunch. A group of Lalande recruits gathered at a table in one corner seemed especially interested. "You're coping with your odd status fairly well," he commented.

Nicholas glanced around and swallowed. "Curiosity beats outright hostility. I imagine it's pretty rare to have a quasi-prisoner awake and wandering around a long boat."

"We've gone through our share of odd situations," Hal commented. "We're still shaking down into a unified crew. When you were running amok, even the new crew had over a decade of experience and integration. I think that worked against you."

Nicholas nodded in agreement. "I was deliberately trying to shake the crew's confidence in each other and the captain," he said. "It didn't work. The captain's open communication and careful protection of everyone's rights held the crew together. I remember the frustration at every turn. Now, I'm glad of it. I shudder to think what would've happened if I'd succeeded."

"You lead us on quite a chase," Hal said. "I'm glad you hit Abishai with your last dose of the Panic. I doubt I could have fought through it like he did."

"Lisandra was right about the Panic. It's utter filth, and it was never going to make willing accomplices. I was dealing in fear and hate, which just made the crew pull together against me."

They finished their meal half-listening to the buzz of conversation around them. Hal pushed back and grabbed his tray, motioning for Nicholas to follow. Walking back to Ship Security, they ran into Lisandra. "Can you two stop by Ambassador Brelling's office?" she asked. "Chord has questions for Nicholas."

Hal looked at Nicholas and raised an eyebrow. He shrugged, "The data will be waiting whenever I get back to it," he said.

Chord Olley met them and took the group to a small conference room. "I'm interested in the technology you used to mask your face and appear as other crew members," he began. "I'm sure it's illegal in the Sol system. What can you tell us about where you got it and how it works?"

Nicholas shuddered. "It's illegal everywhere. A low-level artificial intelligence uses three dimensional images of the victims to construct the mask. The mask itself contains smart nanotech that makes it move with the wearer and even adjust expressions to match the person you're disguised as. I had masks for three different crew members and colored contact lenses. I think Ship Security still has the masks."

Hal nodded. "We do, and the mini-comp you used to program them."

"I didn't bring the AI software onboard," Nicholas said. "We deemed it too much of a risk since everything is scanned for malware. The mini-comp can make minor adjustments like change in facial hair. I brought all three masks aboard in the Sol system, essentially ready to go. I didn't use them until I was close to making my play at Turnover."

Chord drummed his fingers on the table. "Who provided the masks and AI technology?"

Nicholas sighed, "I was afraid you were going to ask that. I had to meet with the artist to be fitted. He was extremely nervous. I'm sure he'd been dosed with the Panic to get him to cooperate. I'd rather not get him in trouble if he's still alive. He was getting up in years even then."

"You called him an artist," said Chord. "Is he someone well known?"

"He was famous in certain circles then," Nicholas answered. "He used a combination of his own original artistry and artificial intelligence that made him a controversial figure in the art world. His mobile sculptures are incredibly life-like, but he normally makes them completely off scale so you can't mistake them for the real thing. He's considered one of the pioneers of the mobile-life art movement. As focused on my mission as I was back then, I still found his creations fascinating. Wearing them, on the other hand, is awful."

"Why?" asked Chord.

"The nano-tech particles constantly adjust the artificial skin," Nicolas answered. "This causes a crawling sensation you have to experience to believe. I didn't have any problem being cruel when I was in a mask."

"Do you know who coerced him into making the masks?" asked Hal.

"Restoration agents. I didn't have much contact with them. They were probably the same ones who found the underworld source for the Panic."

Chord turned to Lisandra. "Have you looked at the mini-comp software?"

"Yes, it's a dead end," she said. "There's nothing in it to tie it to anyone. The AI software the artist used is fairly common and legal in the Sol system. Mr. Literal would have had kittens if you brought it aboard the *Nai'a*."

"How did you get your hacking tools aboard?" Chord asked.

Lisandra pointed to her head. "They were all up here, and I recreated them from scratch once I was aboard. All of the hardware I used is common authorized equipment, except for a few things I cobbled together from parts."

"Can we tie any of this to the Restoration other than through Nicholas?" asked Chord.

"Assuming the artist was paid, and will cooperate, I can try tracing the financial transactions," said Lisandra rubbing her chin. "It will have to wait until we get to Sol. I don't know if I'll be aboard the *Nai'a*, or in jail at that point. We have better and more current leads in the Lalande financial data."

Hal raised a finger. "I don't think Ambassador Brelling or the captain will give you up to the Sol authorities unless they have no choice. The artist could be another arrow in our quiver, though. If he's willing to testify, it would help on both the legal and public relations fronts. I'll put that on my list of discreet contacts to make when we're in good communications range."

Chord asked Nicholas a few more questions about his Sol contacts before the meeting wound down. On the short walk back to Ship Security Nicholas looked over at Hal. "Are you worried about what will happen to Lisandra?"

Hal shrugged, "I can't help being concerned. We talked it over quite a bit back in Lalande. She's determined to do what she can to make up for her illegal hacking activities and face the consequences. I admire and support her for that. Belle is determined to fight fiercely for her mother. She's probably more worried than I am."

"Lisandra's crimes will be sixty years in the past when we arrive," said Nicholas. "Perhaps that will help."

"It should," agreed Hal. He left Nicholas at his borrowed workstation to work through another batch of personnel files.

Nicholas was at the point of seeing spots from staring at the screen all afternoon when an icy shock went through him. The person looking back at him from the display was a dead ringer for his cousin Keith Withers, but impossible young. The name and background in the file didn't match what he knew about his cousin. The crewman was supposedly named Hugh Bonner, from the opposite end of the system from the Withers clan territory. Nicholas took a couple of deep breaths and willed his heart beat to slow down. The face was too similar to his cousin's to be a coincidence. He didn't know what to do. He didn't want to turn the young man in just because of a possible family connection, but this was reason he'd been asked to look at the files. He dithered for a few minutes and finally sent Hal a PCOM message.

Hal showed up a minute later. "What did you find?" he asked.

Nicholas explained the possible family connection. "If I'm right, he falsified his application. I don't want to get him in trouble, but it's possible he's a risk to the ship and crew."

"How sure are you?"

"Ninety nine percent," said Nicholas glumly. "My cousin was an outlier in the family. 'Hugh' could be his twin."

"I'll see if he gave consent for genetic matching using his medical file. Do I have your consent to use yours?"

"Yes."

"I could probably get a legal warrant, but it will be simpler if I can keep things out of official channels for now. I'll be back after I check on the DNA status. Look through his file and see what else stands out to you. I'll get Lisandra to run him through her database for connections to the Withers clan."

Nicholas spent a nervous few minutes staring at the file data and getting nowhere. Hal came back with Lisandra in tow. "Our man definitely switched identities before applying for the crew," she said. "He did a very good job covering his tracks, but the level of data I have was good enough to sus out his transactions, pre and post identity change. His real name is Lincoln Withers."

"He's also a DNA match with you, Nicholas," said Hal. "Close enough to be your cousin's son. The only question is what to do about it."

Lisandra chuckled. "He's hardly the first person to falsify a crew application for the *Nai'a*. He may be an agent, or it may have been for other reasons."

Hal nodded. "We can't condemn him on the circumstantial evidence in front of us. We'd better go see the chief before we decide our next steps."

Chief Bolhepp listened to Hal lay out the situation, then leaned back with his hands behind his head to stare at the ceiling. He rocked back forward and squinted at Nicholas. "This is a touchy situation, both legally and morally. Lisandra's database evidence is inadmissible. I don't want to make assumptions about the young man's motivations until we have chance to talk to him, and I don't want to bring him in either."

"Let me talk to him, alone," said Nicholas. "I was close to his father. He may open up to me."

Chief Bolhepp considered the proposal for a moment. "I'm inclined to allow you to try. Let's talk about how to make it happen."

***

Nicholas and Hal made their way to the Epsilon Section galley during the beginnings of dinner hour. They split up and Nicholas found a table where he could watch the entrance. A few minutes later, Lincoln walked in and went through the chow line, apparently without noticing his relative. Once the young man was seated, Nicholas took a deep breath to calm his nerves and walked over.

Nicholas sat down across from Lincoln and the young man looked up at him without surprise. His expression turned sour. "I'd hoped you'd be in cold sleep all the way to Sol." He shook his head bitterly. "What happens now, Cousin Nick? Is Ship Security standing by to arrest me?"

"Not exactly," Nicholas replied. "They will want to talk to you, though."

"After all the effort I went through to ditch my family, I'm ratted out by one of my own." Lincoln shoved beans and rice around his plate aimlessly for a minute while Nicholas tried to think of something to say. Finally, Lincoln looked up, measuring him for a moment. "Dad always said you were a hard case fanatic, and a true believer in the Restoration's propaganda. Honestly, you don't look like much to me."

"Hah!" Nicholas half-chuckled, shaking his head. "You hit on two good descriptions. I was a fanatic and worse when your dad last saw me. Now, I'm not much at all. Just a convicted mutineer with a small amount of freedom allowed at the sufferance of the *Nai'a's* leadership."

"What happened?" Lincoln asked.

"It's a long story." Nicholas answered. "The short version is, I failed to take over this ship, and someone's compassion in the consequences convinced me of the error of my ways."

"I wish I could believe you, but Dad also said you were the smoothest liar he ever saw." Lincoln said, flatly.

Nicholas nodded, "I deserve that, and a lot more. What you believe about me isn't important. Regardless, I'm concerned about you. It *is* my fault that Ship Security knows who you really are. You're going to have to deal with them. I hoped I could make it a little easier for you. Will you tell me how you came to be on the *Nai'a?*"

Lincoln's already hostile expression hardened further. "I wouldn't tell you your shirt was on fire. Because of you and your ilk, my father is dead! The Withers name is garbage! I'm on the run, and now any chance I had to escape your carnage is gone! Get out of my sight!"

Nicholas shrank back under the onslaught but didn't make a move to leave. Hal's arrival saved him from making a decision. The hulking investigator slid a tray of food in front of Nicholas and took a seat with a tray of his own. He stuck his hand across the table. "Hi, I'm Hal Renfro, Ship Security Detective."

Lincoln stared at the proffered hand for a moment, then met Hal's frank gaze and shook it firmly. "I wish I could say I'm pleased to meet you, but I was hoping to avoid my past," he said sourly.

"You realize that's not happening," Hal said, making it a statement. "I couldn't help but overhear the last part of your conversation. You should know Nicholas has changed sides. He helped us defeat the Restoration forces in Lalande. He's helping us now to prepare to take them on in the Sol system."

"No doubt to get out of his just desserts," said Lincoln bitterly.

"He never asked for any consideration," said Hal. "The former and current captains decided to grant him parole on their own. He still does hard labor when he isn't helping us. Finish your dinner, then we'll talk about what happens next."

Lincoln looked unconvinced but ate his food, determined not to let his relative's presence ruin his appetite. When he finished, he pushed his tray away and leaned back. "What now?" he asked Hal. "Am I under arrest?"

"Are you a threat to the ship or crew?" asked Hal.

Lincoln shook his head. "The only one on this ship I'm a threat to is him." He nodded at Nicholas.

"Honest," Hal nodded. "I can live with that. I'm sending you contact information for an attorney. There are others, but she's the best in my opinion. You're welcome to research them and choose your own counsel or go without. We'll want you to come in for an interview in two days' time. If I were you, I'd choose a lawyer and spend some time with them tomorrow discussing your legal options. If it helps, the one I recommend was once Nicholas' defense attorney until he fired her."

"That's a good enough recommendation for me," said Lincoln, glaring at Nicholas. "Are we done?" Hal nodded and the young man picked up his tray, leaving without a backward glance.

"I don't think he likes you," observed Hal.

"What's to like?" Nicholas answered with a sigh. "You'd better take me back to my quarters."

"Nope," said Hal, clapping him on the shoulder and nearly causing him to drop his tray. "Lisandra and I are meeting Shanyah and Abishai for a game night. You're coming too. I'm not going to let you sit in your quarters and stew after that confrontation."

***

The next morning Hal brought Nicholas to his office. "Do you think Lincoln is really running from the Restoration?" he asked when they were seated and supplied with coffee.

"I think he's running from both the Restoration and The Bancroft," Nicholas answered. "He doesn't have a good reason to trust either. His father and I had a major falling out over my support of the Restoration before I left the system the first time. To answer your real question, I think he genuinely hates the Restoration, and me, for what happened to his father. I can't say I blame him."

"Is there any chance he's playing us? Hal asked.

Nicholas shook his head, "He's not experienced enough to lie that well."

"I agree," said Hal. "Also, Lisandra said the accounts he used to make his escape weren't tied to the Restoration. We need him on our side. The chief and the captain are willing to overlook the falsified application."

"I'd better stay out of sight when you make the offer," said Nicholas. "If he thinks I had anything to do with it, he'll refuse out of spite."

"He and his attorney will be by tomorrow," said Hal. "In the meantime, you can get back to work on the rest of the personnel files."

***

Lisa Gallred regarded Lincoln across her folded hands. They were in the small shared space she used as an office, seated at a table. "Ship Security didn't give me a lot of information about your situation. If I'm going to represent you, I need the details from your perspective. Do you want to start at the beginning?"

"I'm not sure where that would be, but I'll give it a shot," said Lincoln. "My father was never in favor of joining the Restoration cause. He wasn't fond of The Bancroft, but he could see the Restoration was using the Withers family as a means to reaching their own ends. Unfortunately, his business and family connections were too intertwined for him to just walk away. At the end, I know he wished he had.

"When the news of the Restoration's attack on the *Nai'a* and subsequent defeat reached us, he knew the family would be hunted down. He gave me access to a few hidden accounts, and sent me in-system on a supply ship. When I reached Bancroft Sation, I used the money to change my identity, then took a job. I applied for a position on the *Nai'a* when the announcement came out. That's the bare bones. For what it's worth, I didn't fake any of my qualifications, those are real."

Lisa pursed her lips. "I don't think there's much of a case against you. The evidence is mostly inadmissible and I could disqualify the one witness in the eyes of a jury in about two minutes."

"I gather you're familiar with my relative?" Lincoln queried.

"He was a thoroughly evil person when we first met," Lisa replied. "I was never so relieved as when he fired me."

"He claims that he changed sides."

"Yes," Lisa tapped her stylus on the table. "His subsequent actions indicate repentance. I'll admit it's hard to believe." She sat up straight. "He doesn't matter anymore in your situation. We could play hardball and probably get you acquitted of any charge they came up with, but that doesn't solve the problem of your identity. I imagine you'd rather not go through life as someone else?"

Lincoln shook his head. "The cat's out of the bag. I might as well get that cleared up if there's a way to do it."

"We have some leverage," Lisa said thoughtfully. "Both Ship Security and Ambassador Brelling's team will want everything you know about the Restoration. If you're willing to cooperate, I'll offer that up and see what they come back with."

"Oh, I could sing all day about those murderous idiots," Lincoln replied. "If it will smooth things over for me, so much the better." He Lisa a considering look. "This is all confidential, right?" Lisa nodded. "My two sisters also went into hiding when I did. I'm not giving up any information that could lead to them. The Bancroft isn't getting his hands on them."

"My reading of The Bancroft is that he's only vindictive toward people that have actually done something wrong," said Lisa. "I doubt your sisters are in danger from the Lalande government if they haven't committed any crimes. In any case, their whereabouts have no bearing on your legal position, or the case Ambassador Brelling is making against the Restoration. I won't even mention your sisters. If the subject comes up in your interview, I'll tell them that information is not on the table."

When Lincoln showed up at Ship Security the next morning with Lisa, Hal met them and escorted them to his office. The three of them sat around a small table, then he poured coffee for everyone and set a box of doughnuts between them. Lincoln looked at Hal and raised his eyebrows. "I'm not sure what I was expecting, but this isn't it."

Hal grinned, "You're not under arrest. Here's what I'm authorized to offer. If you'll cooperate and tell us what you remember about the Restoration's operations, you get a clean slate. We'll update your crew record with your correct name, and you will remain an able spacer in good standing. Any questions?"

Lisa's eyes narrowed. "Where's the hook?"

Hal spread his hands. "There isn't one. We have no interest in punishing Lincoln for the desperate measures he took to survive the Restoration's attempted takeover of the Lalande system. We do want whatever information he can give us about their operations. Do you need time to confer? I can step out?"

"Please do," said Lisa. When the door closed behind Hal, she looked over at Lincoln. "I'm suspicious because I'm paid to be, but they're offering everything I was going to ask for. It's still up to you. As long as you're comfortable answering their questions, you get a fresh start."

"Will they uphold their end of the deal?"

Lisa nodded her head. "Chief Bolhepp's word is good. He wouldn't have sent Hal in here with the offer if he didn't intend to honor it. I'm sure they have the captain's blessing as well. What do you say?"

"I'll take their offer."

Lisa retrieved Hal from the hallway.

"Is it okay if I record this session?" Hal asked, once he was seated. "It will be confidential. We won't share it outside of Ship Security and Ambassador Brelling's team. Also, I will state for the record that it cannot be used in any legal proceeding against you."

Lincoln thought for a moment. "Can I have a copy of the recording?"

Hal nodded. Lincoln looked at Lisa and raised an eyebrow. "A recording will probably reduce the number of follow up questions and sessions," she said. "You *are* protected from any legal consequences, as Hal said."

Lincoln straightened in his chair. "Okay, let's do this."

Hal started the office recorder and made his statement for the record. "Please start when you first heard of the Restoration and go from there," he said. "I'll ask questions as we go."

Lincoln related the story with more detail than the day before, prompted by Hal's insightful questions. Hal ordered in lunch, and they continued through most of the afternoon. Lincoln was surprised by the amount of information he was able to recall about a subject he loathed. By the time they broke for dinner, he felt thoroughly wrung out. He promised Hal to return the next morning after breakfast to finish up.

Lisa walked with him for a few minutes before they went their separate ways. "I think you made a good choice. This crew has a history of helping victims of the Restoration, and you are one, whether you want to admit it or not."

"I prefer to think of myself as an adamant adversary of the Restoration," Lincoln said with a determined set to his mouth.

Lisa nodded, "I think that's a healthy attitude, and one you'll find running throughout the ship."

***

Lincoln was halfway through dinner in the Epsilon Section galley when someone sat down across from him. He looked up at a petite, competent-looking woman he didn't recognize. She stuck out a hand. "I'm Lisandra Redding, Hal Renfro's wife." Lincoln shook the proffered hand, a quizzical look on his face. "I'm sorry about disturbing your dinner, but I need to talk to you about something that's time sensitive."

Lincoln thought for a moment. "I've heard of you," he said. "You're the hacker."

Lisandra's mouth twisted, "I should be used to people knowing me by reputation. Yes, I'm the hacker. I'm also the one who tracked down the financial transactions you used to change your identity." She held up her hands at Lincoln's alarmed expression. "Don't worry, I'm here on a personal mission that has nothing to do with your deal with Ship Security."

"If you were able to trace those transactions, I imagine you found my father's other hidden accounts," said Lincoln. "I don't like where this is going."

"I don't want to discuss the details here in public," said Lisandra. "I'm not here to shake you down. I want to help, but we need to talk first so I don't cause more harm than good."

Lincoln took a couple of bites of food to consider her statement. "Okay," he said. "Where do you want to talk?"

"I know a place, but finish your dinner," Lisandra answered.

Curious, Lincoln made short work of the rest of his food and turned his tray in. He followed Lisandra to a nearby green space. She slipped behind a row of bushes to a small clear space around a maintenance hatch.

Lincoln looked around. "I hope Hal doesn't show up," he said. "I don't want to explain what I'm doing alone with his wife. He looks like he could break me in half."

Lisandra chuckled. "Don't worry. He trusts me and, yes, he could break you in half, but he's disinclined to violence." Her tone turned serious. "This is something I'm keeping from him and everyone else. He would understand why, and so will you. I did find the accounts your sisters are using. They're nearly drained."

Lincoln frowned. "Why are you telling me this?"

Lisandra's face grew shadowed. "I was in similar circumstances for different reasons when I was young. Running out of money when you're on your own with no support system can push you into bad choices. I think I can help, but I need to know specifically how you accessed the accounts you used, so I can help keep the transactions beneath the notice of the Lalande authorities."

"How could you help them?" Lincoln asked, skeptically.

"I have access to the fund set up by the crew of the *Nai'a* to help victims of the Restoration. Most of the money is gone, but there's enough to give your sisters each a few years' cushion of living expenses at the rate they've been using the accounts."

"Won't you get in trouble?" Lincoln asked.

Lisandra chuckled again. "Only if I get caught, and I guarantee the possibility is vanishingly small. Also, if I do get caught, I'm okay with begging forgiveness after the fact. I'd work this through official channels, but time is of the essence, and I can make it happen without exposing your sisters to government scrutiny. We're still in range of a relay I can use to work the transactions. We won't be much longer."

"You have a reputation," said Lincoln thoughtfully. "I haven't been on the ship long, but everyone thinks you're a cyber magician."

"There's no magic involved, but I won't downplay my skills. I can do this. However, I need your help and any codes you used to access the money."

Lincoln pursed his lips in thought, then nodded. "Okay, I'm not sure why I trust you, but I do. How can I help?"

Lisandra keyed open the maintenance hatch, ducked under a low cable run and motioned for Lincoln to follow. Several turns and hatches later she pulled a small black bag out of a recessed compartment, folding a shelf down to set it on. She attached the minicomp inside to a fiber optic cable and jacked it into a data port. Lincoln looked up and down the dark passageway. "This doesn't look suspicious at all," he grumbled.

"No one's due to check this area for the next week," said Lisandra. She brought up a virtual display and got to work. Twenty minutes and a lot of questions later she showed Lincoln the new balance in each of his sister's accounts. "Would you like to send them a message?" she asked. "I can attach it to the deposit, which will appear as a legitimate payment from the *Nai'a's* compensation fund. We normally attach a short thank you and personal well wishes from the crew, so it won't look unusual."

"Yes," said Lincoln. "They know I was trying to join the crew so just say 'Hugh sends his love.' They'll know who it is."

Lisandra attached the message, initiated the transactions, then closed down her minicomp. She detached the cable and stowed it back in the compartment. "All done!" she said. "Can you find your way back?"

Lincoln nodded. "It's best we split up, then. It might start someone talking if you're seen emerging from the maintenance spaces with me." She paused. "Hal is too good at his job to miss the connections to your sisters. I'm pretty sure he'll avoid the subject, though. He's a lot more subtle and understanding than he looks. He also shares our low opinion of the Restoration."

"I don't know how to thank you," said Lincoln.

"The knowledge that your sisters have some financial breathing space is thanks enough for me," said Lisandra. "They shouldn't have to pay for the sins of the Restoration or their relatives."

"Still, you didn't have to do anything. Thank you for helping them." He put his hand out, and Lisandra shook it.

"You're welcome, and I'm sure we'll have other chances to help each other frustrate the Restoration's plans."

"I certainly hope so!" Lincoln replied. They split up and took separate paths back to their respective sections.

Chapter 8 – The Fundamental Things Apply

March 5th, AD 3209
Interstellar space near the Lalande System
Long Boat Nai'a, *Captain's Office*

Captain Hartley closed out the latest round of reports, then leaned back and rubbed his eyes. His time as first officer should have prepared him for the sheer mountain of administrative work involved in being captain, but he still felt like he was always trying to catch up. He picked up his coffee mug, eyed the cold dregs in the bottom, and set it back down. He should probably knock off the caffeine and get some rest anyway. He was about to take his own advice, when there was a tap on his door frame. Ambassador Brelling stood there. He grinned and motioned her inside.

"Have a seat," he said. "I was just thinking. You seemed to have a better handle on the admin than I've managed when you were captain."

Anne Brelling sat down with a wry smile of her own. "Mostly I fought it to a draw. I had decades of experience by the time you became a first officer. It takes a while to find your rhythm and determine the tasks that actually have to be done. The rest can be delegated or ignored."

"Did you ever ignore something you wished you hadn't?" the captain asked.

"Many times, but the effort saved was more than worth the occasional small oops. Have you talked this over with the COB?"

Captain Hartley shook his head. "No, he's been invaluable helping me keep tabs on crew morale, but I didn't think admin would be his specialty."

"You'll be surprised," said Anne. "He's one of the best people at prioritizing tasks I've ever encountered. Show him your daily list, and he'll help you winnow it down to something manageable."

"You probably didn't come here to listen to me whine. What can I do for you?"

"I did come by to check in on you," admitted Anne. "I'm trying to keep my visits to a helpful, but not annoying frequency. It's never easy having the old captain on board."

"I haven't had any issues in that area so far," the captain answered. "Has someone been running to you with their problems?"

"If anyone did, I'll just say they were shown the door quickly," Anne answered with a wicked grin. "I've been careful not to undercut your authority." Her expression grew serious. "I know better than anyone aboard how lonely your job is, Kevin. Rolland and I aren't in your chain of command, so I want you to take advantage of us. You have a standing invitation to dinner. Neither of us can cook, but we're both learning. Don't let your responsibilities isolate you."

The captain smiled, "Thanks, I'll take you up on the offer. I haven't been entirely unsocial. Patrick and I are old friends, and he has enough autonomy as the director of cold sleep that I feel comfortable socializing with him. We blow off steam with a regular game of handball."

Anne laughed, "You get along with the cold sleep director better than I ever did."

The captain shook his head with a grin. "You and Yuna reached a good working accommodation eventually, but there were some epic battles. Patrick is just as protective of his charges, but it helps that we worked together and have been friends just as long."

Anne leaned back and looked at him over her steepled her fingers. "I do have another matter we need to discuss, Nicholas Withers and his cousin Lincoln. Thanks to their interaction, the crew, especially the new Lalande hires, are aware Nicholas is helping to vet them. It's not sitting well. They know his history, and I can't blame them for being uncomfortable with it. Lincoln isn't helping matters. He's openly critical of both Nicholas and his role in the process. Nicholas is too valuable to my team to stick back in cold sleep but think about taking him out of the process of vetting files.

The captain grimaced. "I'm aware of the problem. I'm trying to give Chief Bolhepp some space to recognize and deal with it, but I should probably give him a nudge before it grows out of control. I'll talk to the COB and see if he has some ideas about the best way to handle it."

***

The next morning the captain and Chief of Boat sat down over coffee. COB Oswald looked like he had indigestion. "We need to do something quickly, sir," he said. "There's a new crew clique growing around Lincoln Withers, and it's brewing up a lot of bitterness and resentment. The Lalande hires feel they're being treated with suspicion, and they're right. Everything we've done has been legal, but I'm not sure it was wise."

Captain Hartley took a sip of too-hot coffee and frowned. "We should have realized word would get out. I'm not a fan of secrecy anyway. I'd like to clear the air with our new crew members. What do you suggest?"

COB Oswald looked at him for a few moments. "How are you at apologies?"

***

That evening, close to one thousand new crew members gathered on Cooper Green. Captain Hartley stood with COB Oswald on a slightly elevated stage overlooking the crowd. A dense knot of spacers indicated the location of Lincoln Withers. COB Oswald tapped his PCOM into the public address system, asked for silence, then stepped back.

Captain Hartley looked over the crowd for a moment, then activated his own microphone. "I've called you all here to clear the air about recent developments."

A few jeers greeted his opening statement. The captain just nodded and forged ahead. "You have legitimate concerns, and I *will* address them. I'll answer questions at the end, but I ask you to listen to the end with an open mind. First, I apologize for using a known mutineer, saboteur, and

Restoration operative to vet your personnel files. Even though Nicholas Withers has demonstrated his change of heart convincingly, I understand your distrust. We stopped that process today, but the damage is done. After this meeting Ship Security will notify everyone whose files were viewed by Mr. Withers. I personally pledge an open process going forward. If you have concerns, you are entitled to legal counsel.

"In all of this, I want you to remember one thing. The Restoration is the enemy, not your crewmates, or the chain of command. You saw how they operated in Lalande. Twice they infiltrated the crew of this ship, and you know the record of their attacks. We need to continue the vetting process for the security of the ship and crew. I take responsibility for going about it the wrong way. Now, I need your help to get it right. If we suspect and distrust one another, the Restoration wins. I'm positive no loyal member of the *Nai'a's* crew wants that."

A rumble of dissent rose from the group of people around Lincoln Withers, but it quickly dispelled. The captain fielded questions for an hour, answering people's concerns one by one. Finally, the crowd dissipated, talking among themselves. The COB looked at the captain. "You did well, sir." He gave a parade ground salute. "I need to catch Lincoln Withers and see if I can pour a little more oil on troubled waters."

The COB arrowed through the thinning crowd straight to where Lincoln stood talking to a small group. He slowed down as he approached and caught Lincoln's final statement. "We got what we wanted. Stay vigilant and protect your rights."

COB Oswald bulled his way to the center of the group. "Good advice!" he declared, clapping Lincoln on the shoulder. The group realized who had joined them and quickly dissipated.

Lincoln frowned slightly at the COB. "To what do I owe the pleasure of your company?" he asked suspiciously.

COB Oswald ignored the lack of courtesy. "Don't worry, you're not in trouble with me, or the captain, for that matter. I just want to have a chat."

Lincoln folded his arms over his chest. "I'm listening," he said, with narrowed eyes.

"The strength of the *Nai'a* is the crew. We need you new people to become a part of the crew, not a separate entity," COB Oswald said.

"Are you saying we shouldn't meet together?" Lincoln asked.

"No, I hope you continue to meet and strengthen your bonds," the COB answered. "Just make sure you form strong relationships with people outside of your fellow Lalande natives as well. Like it or not, you've become a leader among your peers. If they see you branching out, they'll do the same."

Lincoln nodded. "I see your point. I'm not opposed to integrating with the older members of the crew. I just don't want to be under a cloud of suspicion the whole voyage."

"I want the same things you do," said the COB. "So, what do you say we work together to dissipate that cloud and make sure the Restoration doesn't win?"

"I would like that very much," said Lincoln.

***

Mishael Bonaparté and Joanne Calder strolled arm in arm through the fruit orchard in Epsilon Section. The buds on the trees looked ready to pop as late winter headed toward spring. Mishael explained how the section's temperate climate was managed to provide optimal chill periods for the trees. "We're a bit spoiled," Joanne said. "We can cool off in a temperate climate, warm up in the tropical dome, or pick something in between. The schedules for six different climates keep my heat management division busy."

"The changing of the seasons helps stave off boredom too," said Mishael. "It's also necessary for a lot of the crops we grow. My father transferred to the orchard here to try something different for a while. He'll be happy things are warming up. I know he was scrambling to find warm work clothes a few months ago after wearing shorts and a T-shirt every day in the tropical dome."

They climbed a small slope and found a bench overlooking the treetops. "Mom and Dad both said they had a hard time adjusting to the rising horizon when they came aboard," Mishael continued as they sat and admired the view. "I grew up with it." He put an arm around Joanne and she snuggled close.

"I was born on a Long Boat too," she said. "Agronomics was never my strong suit. I prefer engineering."

"Are your parents still aboard the *Kilimanjaro*?" Mishael asked.

"Yes," Joanne answered. "I'm hoping to catch up with them in the Sol system, but I doubt the *Kilimanjaro* will stick around long enough. It was tough leaving them, but they understood I needed a new situation to advance."

"Are you sure you want to be involved with someone jumping career tracks, like me?" Mishael asked.

"Give yourself some credit, Misha," she replied, using her pet name for him. "There's more to a person than where they are on the career ladder. I think I found right where I want to be." She looked up him. "More of that has to do with your arm around me than being chief engineer of a long boat." She kissed him soundly, then leaned her head against his shoulder with a sigh. Mishael, deciding wisely not to ruin the moment with further questions, simply held her close.

***

Kalei opened her stance, bent her knees slightly, and centered her focus on her mother. The circle of women in the dojo watched with keen interest. Kalei was taller than her mother and close to the same weight. She knew how to use her height to advantage, and only her busy schedule as a doctor kept her from surpassing her mother's grappling skills. Shanyah shifted and stalked in short little dance steps, searching for an opening. Kalei felt more than saw the subtle shift in Shanyah's stance a split second before she dropped low and shot for Kalei's legs. Instead of sprawling, Kalei jumped straight up and twisted. She snaked her legs around Shanyah's neck and left arm as she dropped. She hooked the arm and arched her back as they fell to the mat, tightening her legs like a vice, and quickly inducing a tap from Shanyah. As they popped upright, Shanyah rolled her neck and stretched her shoulder. "I think you may have rearranged a couple of tendons there. Nice move, with the improvised leg triangle!"

"Sorry," said Kalei, reaching to feel her mother's shoulder and test her range of motion. The instant transformation from opponent to physician was almost comical. "I shouldn't have squeezed so hard."

Shanyah laughed. "No serious damage done, but it did feel like you were taking out some frustration."

"You may be right," said Kalei, ruefully. She helped Shanyah to her feet and they moved out of the way for the next match.

On the walk back to their neighborhood Shanyah looked at her daughter. "Care to share what's bugging you?"

"I'm not sure I want to take it out and examine it," Kalei said, shaking her head. "The truth is, I'm jealous of Joanne. She's monopolizing most of Mishael's free time. When I do see him, they're together. I realize it's only natural that he wants to spend time with her, but I miss my big brother. It's petty of me, I know."

Shanyah reached over and gave her a one-armed hug. "You and Mishael have always been close. I'm sure the transition hurts, but you know he's happy with Joanne."

"Yes," said Kalei, "and I want that for him. I *like* Joanne. I just can't help feeling left out. I miss having that big old lunk to tell my troubles to."

"Maybe you should stop stiff-arming every man who asks you for a date?"

"I know, I know. Unfortunately, I keep comparing them to Dad and Mishael. They all come up wanting," said Kalei.

"Since those two treat you like a princess, it's a high bar, and one I approve of," Shanyah replied. "Still, there are a lot of good men on this ship. You won't get to know them if you don't give anyone a chance. I know it took a crisis to get your father and me together, but I wouldn't wait around for one to strike if I were you."

Kalei hugged her mom back. "I'll think about it."

"I'll pray about it," said Shanyah.

Chapter 9 – Open Pollinated

April 10th, AD 3209
Interstellar space
Long Boat Nai'a, *The Orchard*

Abishai walked with Oscar Newmarket between rows of apple trees in full bloom. Mason bees and honey bees went busily about their work, pollinating the alternating varieties. The *Nai'a's* orchard master collected new cultivars everywhere they went. Oscar was especially excited about a pair of Gravensteins newly acquired in Lalande. The *Nai'a's* schedule was a bit off from the trees' home habitat, so he was concerned about the timing of the bloom. The Gravensteins, however, were blooming happily along with the rest.

A few of the trees were varieties developed on the *Nai'a*. Oscar had a good-sized section of experimental crosses at one end of the orchard. Abishai was studying the parentage of all the ship's varieties. He was surprised to learn that fully three-fourths had Golden Delicious in their parentage. "Even before space habitats started growing apples, Golden Delicious was one parent of many successful commercial varieties," Oscar told him. "It proved adaptable to low G, and it's still one of our staples. I'd grow it just for the genetic stock, even if it wasn't productive."

They reached the end of the row and checked the new mason bee house there. Abishai was gratified to see a few of the paper-fiber tubes already being filled with mason bee chambers. The mason bees were much better pollinators than honeybees. The orchard master was careful to keep a healthy population of both thriving. He even kept a patch of clay-heavy soil exposed for their use.

"I'm glad you switched jobs, Abishai," Oscar said. "Most of my assistants here in the orchard don't have much experience in botany. Your decades in the tropical dome will help me see things from a different perspective. I know you're still gathering information and finding your way here, but don't hesitate to make suggestions. I've been doing this so long, sometimes I take for granted what's right in front of me."

"I'm grateful for the opportunity," Abishai answered. "I was in a bit of a rut, a nice one, but a rut all the same."

"I intend to take full advantage of your hydro management skills," Oscar continued as they walked back toward the tool shed.

Abishai laughed, "just call it plumbing. I specialize in fixing leaks. I made sure the tropical gang has the skills to fix their own leaks, so they don't keep calling me back."

"Some skills are always in demand," said Oscar. "I can fix a leak, but I've been doing it way too often lately. Our irrigation system needs a good end-to-end survey."

"Do you have a system map?" asked Abishai.

"Sure," said Oscar. "Right here." He opened the tool shed door. A neat hand-drawn map of the orchard on a thick piece of paper covered the width of the door's back.

Abishai's eyebrows shot up and he studied the map carefully. Different colored lines and symbols alternated with neat rows indicating individual tree and berry varieties. A detailed legend in the lower left corner explained the colors and symbols. Unsurprisingly, the irrigation lines were indicated in blue. The tool shed was on a slight rise at the aft end of the orchard. With the door open, Abishai could look up and see much of what was on the map. He looked over to Oscar. "I'm impressed!" he said. "This is a functional work of art. I've never seen anything like it."

Oscar shrugged. "I know I could automate it and save time, but that sort of thing leaves me cold. The orchard is about living organisms. I enjoy keeping the map up as things grow and change. It helps me keep a bone-deep feel for the place."

Abishai nodded in appreciation. "Is it okay if I image the map? My friend Roan has a top-notch software program for depicting water systems. Having my own map will help with the survey."

"Go right ahead," said Oscar.

Abishai pulled a high-definition imaging wand from a vest pocket and made sure it was synched with his PCOM. He took several scans of the map, then checked them with the wand's built-in projector. "I have what I need. I'm confident Roan's program will digest the map, and give me a good starting point.

"What about drainage?" Abishai asked. "Please tell me you don't have French drains."

Oscar laughed at the frightened look on Abishai's face. "No, we have an engineered slope built into the underlying deck plates that channels groundwater into the creek at the forward end of the orchard. Drainage has never been a problem."

"Good!" declared Abishai, obviously relieved. "Roan's drain moles make cleaning them out easier, but it's still a job I'd rather avoid."

"I'm about to do some hand pollinating to get a few Gravenstein crosses," said Oscar. "Why don't you observe and ask questions?"

Abishai watched with appreciation as Oscar isolated, opened, and hand-pollinated several mature buds on each Gravenstein. He carefully labeled each with the pollinator parent and covered them with a fine mesh to keep the bees and wind-blown pollen out.

"How long will it take to see if the cross is a good one?" Abishai asked.

"We'll gather the seeds once these produce mature apples and plant them," Oscar answered. "Once we have leaves, we'll do genetic testing and graft the seedlings with good potential onto root stock. It takes about five years to get fruit to taste, and most of them will not be good. If we get a good one, we'll continue to monitor it and graft cuttings for a small number of trees. In twenty years, or about the time we get to Sol, we could have small number of productive trees, and possibly register the cultivar for sale. We're a small operation, so we'll be very fortunate to get something worth cultivating out of this batch. Still, it's fun to try, and a skill that's worth passing down."

"We worked through a similar process with our fruit varieties in the tropical dome," said Abishai. He looked around to make sure no one else was nearby. "Elder Pryachac is as skilled as anyone I've seen, but it's still a slow and painstaking process."

"Consuela and I talk often," said Oscar. "It's a good thing she isn't in earshot, or you'd pay for calling her 'Elder'. You can't hurry nature. God's creation teaches us a deep kind of patience."

"Believe me, I know all about the 'Elder' thing," said Abishai, shaking his head. "I don't have a set of tropical work clothes that aren't stained with the results of forgetting in her presence."

Oscar laughed. "Her aim and determination are legendary."

***

Later that evening, Roan sat at a terminal in Abishai's quarters with his son Grady on one side and Abishai on the other. "Oscar's map is something else!" Roan said, as he manipulated the image in front of him. "I'd like to see it in person."

"His dexterity is incredible," said Abishai. "Watching him hand pollinate apple blossoms with a tiny brush was fascinating."

"Okay," said Roan. "I've got about half the map populated in the new irrigation model. Grady, take over and I'll help you through the rest."

Abishai watched as the father and son team coaxed the map into the modeling software. After an hour's work they had a usable model of the orchard's irrigation set up and ready for Abishai.

"You should be able to make adjustments for reality easily, just like the tropical dome model," said Roan, as they finished up.

"Thanks!" said Abishai clapping both on the shoulder. "I might have managed that on my own, but it would have taken me five times as long."

"Glad to help," said Roan. "Don't forget you promised us dessert."

Abishai started and ran for the oven. He pulled on an oven mitt, quickly fished out a hot tray of cookies, and replaced it with another. "Hot macadamia nut, cranberry, and white chocolate chunk cookies just in time!" he said. "Who wants milk?"

***

Kalei greeted her latest patient with a smile and helped her sit on the exam table. "I think I can see the problem," she said, observing the eleven-year-old girl's swollen knee. "What happened?"

"I got a little too enthusiastic on the low-G trampoline," Soma Bileo answered.

"Seven somersaults with a triple twist," Julian Garrity, her adoptive father, said wryly. "It's a wonder she didn't break her neck instead of just twisting a knee."

Kalei raised her eyebrows and turned back to Soma. "You didn't try that on a dare, did you?" She gently manipulated the girl's knee, then ran an ultrasound scanner over it.

"No! I'm not *that* stupid," Soma replied. "I just wanted to show I'm as good as any of the *Nai'a* kids."

Julian gave her a squinty look, "*You're* a *Nai'a* kid now, Soma, and I'm not sure showing off is any smarter than taking a dare." Soma crossed her arms and squinted right back.

"Okay," Kalei said, struggling to keep a straight face. "No major damage done, but you strained some ligaments. This knee is going to be sore for a while. Let's give it a head start on healing." She adjusted the table to form a seat and helped Soma swing her legs up. She wrapped a thick pad with

cables running out of it around the knee. Plugging a diagnostic tablet, into the therapy wrap she made a few entries then looked up. "How does that feel?"

"Nice," said Soma, "kind of warm and tingly."

"Good," Kalei replied, the door whisked open and Lionel sauntered in. The cat ignored the adults and jumped up next to Soma. "And right on cue, here's my favorite physical therapist. Do you know Lionel?"

"I've heard about him," said her wide-eyed patient.

"Well, touch noses with the legend himself," said Kalei, "and you'll be instant friends." Soma leaned forward tentatively and Lionel touched his cold nose to hers, then plopped down half-in and half out her lap in a furry puddle and commenced a deep-rumbling purr. Soma rubbed the top of his head, then down his back, and Lionel closed his eyes in contentment.

Kalei looked at Julian and motioned with her head toward the door. "Let's leave these two in peace for a few minutes." They stepped out into the corridor. "How's the adoptive father gig going?" Kalei asked. She'd known Julian ever since he'd come aboard as a captive mercenary in Tau Ceti when she was just four.

Julian took a deep breath and let it out in a sigh. "Okay, I suppose. I feel like I'm in over my head, but she's...I can't really explain. It's only been a few months, but I'd step in front of an asteroid for her. As much as I care for her, though, I'm learning the nuances of tween parenting on the fly."

"For what it's worth, she seems like a healthy, well-adjusted kid. I know she's a Lalande native, but I never heard how you ended up adopting her."

"Like a lot of people in the Lalande system, her life was thrown into turmoil by the Restoration's rebellion against The Bancroft," Julian answered. "Her parents were killed just for being in the wrong place at the wrong time. She ended up on the *Nai'a* as a refugee and insisted on staying. The Bancroft's government wasn't keen on letting her out of the system, but they relented when they realized the scope of their orphan crisis. They *did* insist that she had to be adopted to stay on the *Nai'a*."

Kalei sucked in a breath, "That's a lot to go through at any age. She probably grabbed at the nearest chance of safety and stability she could find. How did you end up adopting her?" Kalei asked.

Julian laughed a little raggedly. "That's the funny part. I was walking through a corridor with my head full of attack and defense plans when she pointed at me and said, 'Him! He's going to adopt me.' I stood there with my mouth hanging open for a moment, then started asking questions. In the end, I agreed to give it a try. If there hadn't been a hundred other crises going on, I don't think the alder council would have approved, but they did."

"It sounds like you two have being impulsive in common," Kalei said with a smile. "I don't envy you the moodiness that's likely just around the bend."

"She's moody enough already, but we're a surprisingly good match. I left everything behind in Tau Ceti, and she did the same thing in Lalande. She even opened up to me about losing her parents. I told her about losing my copilot. We both cried a lot. I don't know why she trusts me, but here we are."

"I'm glad she has you to confide in," said Kalei, studying him. The compact pilot was a head shorter than her two-plus meter height, but an attractive and competent man all the same. "Let me know if I can help out. I think you're doing a good job, but I imagine the responsibility is overwhelming."

Julian chuckled. "You imagine correctly. In spite of the twisted knee, she really is more natural at low-G trampoline than most of the kids born on the ship. She has a long list of skills she seems to have absorbed through her skin growing up. Her parents were independent prospectors."

"She reminds me of Althea Driscoll. Did they know each other?"

"It's unlikely," Julian answered. "I checked. The families worked on different sides of the system. I didn't want to mention the Driscolls to Soma, since their story had a happier ending. On the plus side, she's set up with a healthy trust fund from the Restoration victims pool, and she should arrive in the Sol system with a robust set of qualifications in whatever interests her. She'll have a lot of options, assuming I can keep her alive that long."

"Are the '*Nai'a* kids' giving her a hard time?" Kalei asked. "I know we're still adjusting to the crew changes. I hadn't thought of how the children are fitting in."

"I think it's a mostly friendly rivalry," said Julian. "Her teachers are keeping an eye on the group dynamics. They say there's a normal period of adjustment going on for all the kids. If anything, they're integrating better than the adults."

Kalei nodded. "I think the captain's talk with the newcomers smoothed things over. It seems like the tension has eased over the last month."

"I agree," said Julian. "The vetting process officially wrapped up last week without any ugly incidents or Restoration agents identified. Poor Lisa Gallred and the other part-time lawyers had their hands full of new clients."

"At least the captain admitted his mistake," said Kalei. "It couldn't have been easy, especially for someone new in the position."

"True," said Julian. "It will pay dividends in the long run. It's hard to trust someone who refuses to admit they're wrong. I've served under leadership like that. It didn't go well. No one is infallible." He shook his head to banish dark memories. "As much as I'm enjoying our chat, should we check in on Soma and her physical therapist?"

Kalei looked at the time and started. "Oh my! Yes! The therapy wrap cycle finished two minutes ago." They went back into the treatment room and found Lionel luxuriating in a full-body massage. Soma had a grin on her face that warmed Julian's heart.

"You two seem to be getting along just fine," said Kalei. "I'll take this wrap off and see how your knee looks."

While she expertly worked around the cat, Soma looked from Kalei to Julian and back. "You two must have gotten along just fine out in the hallway," she said with a knowing look.

Julian sputtered and Kalei focused steadfastly on her work. After noting the reduced swelling and checking the girl's range of motion, she helped her to her feet. Lionel shook himself, arched his back and gave a mighty yawn before jumping to the deck and sauntering out the door.

"Try walking around," said Kalei.

Soma took a few tentative steps, showing just a slight limp. "It feels a lot better," she said.

"You'll be sore for a few days," said Kalei. "Come back and see me in a week. In the meantime, no low-G trampoline or other strenuous sports."

Soma's face clouded, "I still have some things to teach the doubters."

"It will have to wait until the doctor clears you," said Julian. "You can use the time to catch up on *Nai'a* history."

"Hrmph," she replied, crossing her arms. "Sounds boring."

"You might be surprised," said Julian. "This ship has been through some things that will raise the hair on the back of your neck, and not just recently. We'll start at the wall of heroes." He ushered her toward the door. "Thanks, Doc," he said a bit shyly in parting.

Kalei gave him a warm smile. She was impressed with the way he handled his new responsibility. He was a good man, but their age difference, about fifteen years, was a bit much. She shook her head at her own mental meanderings and turned to check her schedule.

***

Quester tossed the last shovel-full of muck into the wheelbarrow and wiped his brow with a sleeve. Nicholas Withers put down his own shovel and grabbed the handlebars of the wheelbarrow. As he walked it out to the manure pile, Quester ambled along with him. "This work isn't any more fun than cleaning Biome filters," Nicholas said. "At least the scenery is better."

Quester looked over the neat rows of cold-hardy vegetables, a robust patch of tall winter wheat, and the empty field ready for spring planting with pride. "The Farm is probably my favorite place on the ship," he said. "Since Mr. Clement left me in charge while he takes a turn teaching, I'll need help regularly. We're heavily automated, but some things still require a human touch. Most of it won't be as fragrant as this job." He waved at the manure pile. "I can request you if you'd like the break from Biome and Ambassador Brelling's inquisitors."

"Sure," said Nicholas. "I like working with you. You're one of the few people on this boat that doesn't have a good reason to hate my guts. It's nice not to have that tension in the back of my mind."

Quester studied the former saboteur for a few moments. "You should talk to Lincoln. He's got a real chip on his shoulder about you, and it's not doing either of you any good."

"What reason would he have to talk to me?" asked Nicholas with a glower.

Quester wandered over to a crowded row of carrots. He pulled a couple of the small, bright-orange roots from the soil then rinsed them off at nearby spigot. He handed one to Nicholas. "Perks of the job," he said, biting into his with a crunch. "Lincoln probably wants another crack at giving you a piece of his mind. Maybe it will be a first step in clearing the air. Are you willing to give it a try?"

Nicholas pretended to consider the vegetable in his hand. He shook a few drops of water from the carrot, took a tentative bite and chewed thoughtfully. "If he's willing to talk to me, even just to vent, I'll listen," he finally answered. "I owe him that much, and more."

"I'll talk to him and see if I can set it up," said Roan. "Let's check on the warm season seedlings. Sometimes the drip system is inconsistent. I don't want to lose any plants." They ambled toward the greenhouse while Quester filled Nicholas in on his plans for planting out after the last frost.

***

The next day Lincoln met Quester and Nicholas at a pop-up food stand on the forward edge of Cooper Green. Quester bought a triple queso and bean burrito then claimed one of the tables set out for diners on the green. Lincoln and Nicholas sat on opposite sides, avoiding conversation and eye contact while they ate lunch. When the burritos were gone, Lincoln looked at Quester. "This was your idea. What are we supposed to talk about?"

Quester grinned, "A good question," he said. "In fact, I suggest you ask your cousin questions. I'm sure you have a great number of them."

Lincoln scowled at them and folded his arms across his chest. "Okay," he said. "I'll play your game, but I'm not sure how long I can take looking at this face." He gestured toward Nicholas. Quester just nodded and made a come-ahead gesture. Lincoln turned his gaze on Nicholas and his frown deepened. "Why did you get involved with the Restoration in the first place?" he asked.

Nicholas thought for a moment. "They had the resources to go after the Long Boat Free Trade Syndicate, and specifically the *Nai'a*. At the time I had a burning hatred toward both because of the role they played in putting my father in prison. I didn't really care about the Restoration's overall goals. I just needed them to coincide enough with mine to give me a crack at Captain Brelling and the *Nai'a*."

Lincoln nodded slowly, "That agrees with what my father told me. He also told me he tried to talk you, and others, out of going along with them. Why didn't you listen?"

"I couldn't see past my hate," Nicholas answered with a sigh. "I told myself your father was weak, even though I knew better. We were like brothers growing up, but I shut him out once it was obvious he wouldn't support my quest for vengeance. We never spoke again."

"My father's death was ordered by Lewis Withers when he suspected Dad was going to go to The Bancroft," Lincon said. "My father had no such intention but knew his opposition to the Restoration put his whole family in danger. You and Lewis were tight as ticks, weren't you?"

"Yes," answered Nicholas with a sigh. "He practically raised me, since my father was in jail. He and the Restoration also seemed like the best chance to free my father from The Bancroft's prison. That's another reason I went along with them. For what it's worth, I would never have sanctioned your father's murder. Lewis will answer to The Bancroft's justice for that and his many other crimes."

"It won't bring my father back," said Lincoln flatly.

"No," said Nicholas, shaking his head. "It won't. The Restoration and my uncle were more than willing to sacrifice anyone who stood in the way of their goals. I was right there with them, even if my goals were more specific."

"Did getting caught change your mind?" asked Lincoln with a sneer. "I've heard the whole story of your spree of blackmail and sabotage."

Nicholas shook his head. "Getting caught didn't change my mind. I was just as full of hate and lust for vengeance as ever, possible more so, after I was caught."

"Assuming you're sincere, and I'm not convinced, what *did* change your mind about the Restoration?" Lincoln asked. "I think they're nuts letting you wander around the ship, even with an escort."

Nicholas snorted, "I don't disagree. I belong in the brig. What changed my mind was seven years of kindness from someone who had every reason to hate me as much as I hated him. Have you met Pete Worsley?"

"No," Lincoln shook his head, eyes narrowing.

"He visited me at least once a week in the brig after I was sentenced," said Nicholas. "You wouldn't believe the verbal abuse I spat at him time and again, but he never gave up. He always brought me something, usually cookies, or some other treat. He gave me a Bible and read from it. He was always willing to talk with me and help me see the error of my ways. He told me God would forgive me if I only asked. After seven years of this and a stent in cold sleep, his message finally got through. I saw my hate for what it was. I'd been crushed under it for so long, that I took a while longer to believe I really could be forgiven."

Lincoln's frown deepened. "I hope you don't expect *me* to forgive you."

Nicholas shook his head. "No, I don't expect you to forgive me, but I hope, for your sake, that you do. I live every day among people who would be justified to beat the tar out of me, but most of them have laid that aside. I live with the knowledge of what I did, and consequences that can't be undone. The best I can do is serve my sentence and try to help the people on this ship in their fight against the Restoration. You and I know what those people are capable of, so does the crew of the *Nai'a*. You don't need your issues with me to get in the way of becoming a valued member of that crew."

Lincoln huffed. "It's uncanny how much you sound like the COB. I never would have believed it. I'm still not sure I do." He stood up. "I've had more than enough of you for one day, cousin. I hope for my shipmates' sake that you're sincere." He turned and walked away.

Quester looked at Nicholas thoughtfully. "That was...intense, but he didn't yell at you."

"Not quite," said Nicholas. "The public setting probably had more to do with that than his true feelings."

They both stood up, and Quester clapped Nicholas on the shoulder. "It's a start. I doubt you two will ever be close, but at least he got some of his questions answered. We'll give him some time to mull things over before we try again. Right now, we have some greens to thin."

Chapter 10 – Making Plans

May 15th, AD 3209
Interstellar Space
Long Boat Nai'a, *The Farm*

Quester walked slowly down a row of healthy tomato plants with Kalei following behind. "They look good," said Kalei, pausing to snip a stem whose yellowing leaves were in contact with the dirt. "I loved coming here with you and Mishael when we were kids and you were working off your extra duty. We always went home with a layer of dirt and a basket of vegetables."

Quester chuckled. "You two eventually made pretty good farm hands, but I remember Mr. Clement had to rig a way to keep you out of the strawberries. You would have put sizable dent in the spring crop. How's the doctor business?"

"Blessedly quiet. We get the usual bumps and bruises. I'm happy to leave my combat surgeon days far behind in Lalande."

"Is Mishael still head over heels for the chief engineer?"

Kalei snorted. "Yes, I'm happy for both of them, even if I miss his company. Don't start in about my own lack of a love life. I get enough of that from Mom."

"I won't start in on you," said Quester with a conspiratorial grin, "I may have to stage an intervention though."

Kalei's eyebrows flew up. "Don't you dare!" she said, bearing down on him with hands extended. "I won't survive a Quester hatched matchmaking scheme. Surrender, or I'm dumping you and your grin in the creek!"

Quester laughed, dancing aside to avoid her clutches. "Easy now!" he said. "I was thinking more along the lines of keeping you from moping in your quarters on your off time. I've been scheming with Roan about the next competition challenge, and we could use a doctor's advice."

Kalei gave him a skeptical look but stopped her pursuit. "What about you? Isn't it time you settled down and started a family?"

"Me?" said Quester, touching his chest dramatically. "I'm happy being footloose and free. Besides, not many ladies are looking for someone who enjoys slopping pigs."

"More like you aren't sure which of those lovely Lalande lasses to pursue, and they're wise to your attempts to date them all. You know they compare notes on creatures like you."

Quester gave her an affronted look but wisely went back to checking tomato plants. "Why don't we call a truce," said Quester. "I can see teasing you is a dangerous occupation, even without your brother here."

"Okay," agreed Kalei, moving to a row of peppers. "I'll take you up on the offer of scheming with Roan, though. I'm sure the three of us can come up with something truly devious for the crew to take on."

***

Ambassador Anne Brelling read through the latest summary of the Restoration's financial dealings and nodded with satisfaction. They didn't have a complete picture of the organization's Sol-based structure, but what they did have was more than enough to put before the Sol courts. Several major interstellar corporations were going regret their choices if she could make the charges stick. "Chord, I don't want you to take this wrong," she said. "But I think we need another legal opinion, and I'd like to pull Hubbel Spearsley in on this as well."

Chord pursed his lips and shrugged. "It can't hurt. Our case is solid, but we'll going up against the best corporate lawyers money can buy. We'll have the home office legal department behind us, though. We don't have to go it alone. Who did you have in mind?"

"I think Lisa Gallred is done advising most of the new crew she took on during the vetting process. She won't say no to some additional legal work.

She's still an active member of the Sol system bar. I'll pay her a visit and see if she's willing to join the team."

***

Later that day Anne met Lisa Gallred in her small office space. "I never thought I'd see you across this desk," Lisa said, shaking her former captain's hand. "We're usually on opposite sides. Have a seat." She poured them both coffee, then sat down.

"I've come to appreciate your skill and dedication," Anne said. "I'm here to see if you'll help my team with our plans. We need another perspective." She proceeded to give the lawyer a summary of the situation. "I know you'll want to see the detailed information before committing, but we could use your help. Chord and his team are good, but you've lived through all the Restoration's attacks. You understand the stakes at a level they haven't reached yet."

Lisa took a sip of coffee. "I admit I'd love to personally take a chunk out of the Restoration. Are you willing to pay my regular hourly rates?"

"The Long Boat Free Trade Syndicate gave me a generous budget," Anne said. "We can afford you."

"I'll need to review the details with Chord and pick Lisandra Redding's brain as well," Lisa said thoughtfully. "Is Nicholas Withers still cooperating?"

Anne grimaced, "We've shunted him to the side since the vetting debacle. He's available if you want to talk to him. Honestly, he's been a valuable resource. Probably half of what we know about the Restoration's Organization in Lalande and Sol came from him. If he's playing us, we're in trouble. Hal Renfro is convinced Withers is on the up and up, and I trust his instincts. Also, Lisandra's data matches everything he told us about the organization in both systems."

Lisa shook her head, "Mr. Withers made quite an unexpected turn-around. We should take full advantage. The Restoration isn't going to expect us to have his information or testimony. We stand a very good chance of catching them out if we play our cards right."

Anne grinned. "It sounds like you're on board?"

Lisa nodded. "Count me in. I'll start tomorrow."

"Chord will give you a detailed briefing, then you can decide what else you want to dig into," Anne said. "In three days, we'll meet for a preliminary strategy session." She stood and shook Lisa's hand. "Welcome to the team!"

***

Nicholas regarded Lisa Gallred across the table with trepidation. She looked perplexed, something he hadn't expected from the confident attorney who usually wore her competence like a suit of armor. They both started to speak, then Lisa shrugged and waved Nicholas ahead. "I owe you an apology," he said. "I know it was a long time ago, but I repaid your attempts to help me with vitriol. You didn't deserve that, and I'm sorry."

Lisa considered him for a few moments. "You may have been my worst client ever, but as you say, that's in the past. Apology accepted. I may ask why you changed sides at some point, but we have more pressing things to discuss. I want to know everything you remember about the legal team we're likely to face. I've got the names of the people you dealt with while you were in the Sol system. Let's go through them one at a time."

At the end of the day Nicholas felt like a wet noodle, and Lisa wasn't half-finished with him. "This boat has too many skilled interrogators," he said as they finished up.

"Really? Who?" asked Lisa.

"Let's see," said Nicholas. "There's Hal Renfro, Rolland Dunleavy, and Chief Bolhepp, all trained professionals. I suppose even a defense lawyer like you learns how to draw information out. Ambassador Brelling is surprisingly insightful when she isn't wearing her captain's face. The worst of the bunch, though, are Mishael and Kalei Bonaparté. Those two dug details out of me I didn't even know I remembered."

"Interesting," said Lisa. "Did they record the session?"

"Yes, Hal has the recording if you want to review it," Nicholas answered. He smacked himself in the forehead. "I think I just gave you more material to cross exam me about."

Lisa grinned "Yup, just think. If you had to pay for deep dive psychological counseling like this it would cost a fortune. You're getting it for free!"

"Somehow, I believe a genuine counselor would be gentler with the questions," Nicholas said with a frown,

"You might be surprised," said Lisa. "They generally make you acknowledge your ugly parts."

"I have plenty of those," said Nicholas. "I'd better ping Hal to escort me to my quarters."

"I have a better offer," said Lisa. "I'll 'buy' you dinner at the galley and escort you to your quarters afterward."

Nicholas eyed her suspiciously, "So you can continue the questions?"

"Exactly!" said Lisa.

Nicholas shrugged. "It's better than sitting in my quarters watching the next episode of *Space Junking*."

***

Mishael and Joanne sat together on a bench in Zeta Section, which boasted a Mediterranean climate. A mixed grape vineyard stretched to their left and an orchard of almond and olive trees to their right. Mishael frowned in concentration. "What's on your mind, big guy?" Joanne asked, capturing his arm and leaning her head against his shoulder.

"Too much," said Mishael with a chuckle. "So many questions."

"Like what?"

"Am I pulling you away from your duties? Where is our relationship headed? Am I doing the right thing with this sabbatical from the military?" He laughed. "I could go on, but that's a good starter set."

"Let's take those one by one," Joanne said. "Let me worry about the amount of time I take away from my chief engineer role. You know I have a good team, and they know how to reach me in an emergency. I don't know where our relationship is headed, but I hope it's somewhere serious, because feeling loved by you is something I never want to give up. Last, your sabbatical allowed us to have this relationship, so it's absolutely the right thing. I decree it so!"

"I wish I had your certainty," he shook his head. "I shouldn't borrow trouble, though. Being with you is wonderful. We have a long voyage ahead of us, hopefully without the drama of the last two. There's a lot we could accomplish on the way to Sol. What do you say we make some plans for *our* future."

"I'm game," said Joanne, "but how serious are you?"

Mishael turned and held her by the shoulders so he could look directly into her eyes. "Serious enough to want to start a family with you," he said.

Joanne nodded slowly, "That's not the most romantic proposal a girl ever got. I assume you're talking about marriage?"

Mishael gulped and nodded back. "I wasn't planning on proposing when we came out here. I'm totally unprepared. Will you marry me?"

Joanne hugged him close. "Of course I will, you big lug! I wondered if you were ever going to ask."

Mishael hugged her back, then a worried expression crossed his face. "Will you have time for kids? Chief engineer is a demanding job."

Joanne laughed, "You know the ship policy on parental leave and work schedules. Frankly, this should be an easy trip. As long as we can get approval, I'll make time for children. There's nothing I'd rather do. Why don't you stop worrying and kiss me?" Mishael wisely took her up on the offer.

***

Ambassador Brelling took a deep breath and slowly let it out. Her team gathered around her in what they now called the war room. "It's time to put the framework of a plan together," she declared. "Lisandra dug us out a ton of evidence. Thanks to Nicholas, we have both a star witness and a good idea of who the major players are." On the display wall of the war room a diagram showed the interstellar corporations backing the Restoration, their relationships, and the likely leadership structure. "These three corporations appear to be the financial backbone of the Restoration. What options do we have for taking them down?"

Chord frowned. "All three are incorporated on Terra, Mars, the Belt, the Jovian Alliance, the Saturn Commonwealth, and the Outer System Union. They also have holdings in every major inhabited extra-solar system. It's going to be nearly impossible to root them out completely."

"I'll settle for bringing the leaders of the Restoration to justice and substantial penalties for the companies," said Anne.

"We have a good shot with the Sol governments," said Lisa Gallred. "The financial data we already have is enough to drag them into court, and win in all six jurisdictions. The Sol governments also have laws on the books against the manufacture, sale and use of the Panic. Likely, we'll only get that one to stick in the Terran courts, but it will be a big public relations black eye across the system. Likewise, our proof of the attacks on the *Nai'a* and the rebellion in Lalande will weigh heavily in the court of public opinion."

"What about the Long Boat Free Trade Syndicate's power?" said Hubble Spears. "We carry ninety percent of those companies' trade outside Sol. We could certainly hurt them with a boycott."

Ambassador Brelling frowned. "I'd rather not go there. It's too close to interdicting the home system of humanity. We don't want any hint of that, or we'll do the Restoration's job for them. Humanity needs the syndicate. We can't be seen as the enemy."

Chord crossed his arms and stared at the display. "We have two main avenues of attack then: the various legal systems and public relations. I can't help wishing we had another lever."

Ambassador Brelling looked around. "Any other ideas?"

Lisandra Redding stepped forward. "If you turn me loose with a good data connection, I can wreak havoc with the Restoration's financial and security structures. Of course, I'd be digging my own legal hole even deeper."

Anne Brelling shook her head. "I won't ask that of you. We need to stay on the squeaky-clean side of the law. I'm already going to be answering uncomfortable questions about the military capabilities we used in Lalande. How do you think the Restoration will respond to our accusations, Nicholas?"

Nicholas cleared his throat. He'd been surprised to be invited to this session, and he was even more surprised to be included in the conversation. "The interstellars will deny any involvement. Don't reveal your hard evidence until the denials are ringing loud in the press. Drop your proof to the media then for maximum effect." His expression grew grim. "The covert operations branch of the Restoration won't take this lying down either. Do you have any friends in the Sol Space Patrol?"

Anne nodded. "We have contacts and friends."

"If you can talk them into a multi-ship escort, I'd do it. You may think the SSP's reputation will prevent direct action against the *Nai'a*. I wouldn't bet on it. I know the Restoration has plans and resources in place for everything from attacks like you saw in Tau Ceti, to slipping an operative on board with a visiting party. I don't think they'll try a forced boarding action. I'm sure word of how that went in Tau Ceti has reached Sol by now."

"Yes, and our militia will be ready for anything so foolish," Anne said. "We asked Tau Ceti not to reveal our knowledge of the organization behind the attacks. Timing is going to be tricky, but I'm hoping we can stay inside the Restoration's decision cycle and keep them dancing to our tune. Those are good ideas. Do you have other suggestions?"

"I agree on the timing," said Nicholas. "As far as the Restoration in Sol knows, I'm serving a sentence of hard labor in Tau Ceti. If you keep my presence a secret until you're in Sol orbit, it'll be a nasty surprise. You'll also get the Terran authorities enough information to arrest the Restoration operatives we know about before they go into hiding."

Anne pursed her lips in thought, "We'll have to read the tea leaves when we're in system, but I like how you're thinking. If they don't know the extent of our knowledge, we'll be in a much better position to take a good chunk of the covert action side of the organization out. If they suspect you're cooperating, they'll go to ground in a hurry." She turned to her husband. "Rolland, you've been quiet so far. Thoughts?"

Rolland Dunleavy took a few moments of contemplation before answering. "You've just identified our third prong of attack. Hal and I are the logical team to coordinate with the Terran anti-terrorist organizations. Secure coms are going to be essential to making it work." He turned to Lisandra. "Do you have some ideas along those lines?"

Lisandra nodded. "I've been working on a unique encryption protocol. We can bury the key in our communications with the home office, then send some bogus information the Restoration will have to react to. If they don't, we'll know we have a secure channel.

Anne crossed her arms and took a few steps along the display. "We have a good outline, and plenty of time to refine the plan," she said. "Keep a few things in mind as you work on your pieces. The Restoration has proven to be determined and resilient time and again. In both Tau Ceti and Lalande, we were attacked when we thought they were defeated. We need plans to deal with all of the contingencies Nicholas knows about, and anything else we think they might throw at us.

Also, keep your planning flexible. We know we'll have to adjust to reality when we kick off our operation and the Restoration responds. We don't want our entire plan to fall apart if one thing goes wrong. Several things are going to go wrong. Let's have back up plans for when it happens. I hate long meetings, but we've made good progress. Does anyone have anything to add?" She looked around, but no one spoke up. "Okay, keep up the crosstalk. Communication and trust will give us the edge we need." As the meeting broke up, she motioned Nicholas, Lisa, and Rolland over to one corner.

"Lisa, do you have everything you need from Nicholas?"

Lisa considered the question for a moment, then nodded. "I have everything I need. I'll be working with Hubble on the details of our legal approach with each of the Sol system governments. We'll need an assessment of the current political situation once we're in secure coms range."

Anne snorted, "In a word, it's going to be complicated. Every settled system except the home of humanity has a single system government. In Sol, we'll be dealing with six governments that don't cooperate on much of anything but the Sol Space Patrol."

"Thank goodness for the SSP," said Lisa. "As long as the patrol is true to its apolitical roots, we won't have to worry about walking into a shooting war like we did in Lalande." She frowned suddenly. "Maybe I do have another question for you, Nicholas. You haven't mentioned the Sol Space Patrol. Did the Restoration manage to infiltrate the patrol?"

Nicholas furrowed his brow in concentration, "I didn't have the need to know about those operations, but we'd be foolish to think they aren't trying. I believe they probably have a few agents in the patrol to gather information. I doubt they would have anyone in a position to take over a ship. You'd have to convince most of the command structure to go along with you. I don't think a group of SSP officers is going violate their oaths for the Restoration's purposes. Individual acts of sabotage are possible."

Anne shook her head. "I was planning to offer you a berth in cold sleep for the rest of the trip, Nicholas," she said. "I don't want to lose your unique perspective, though. I'm sure a hundred more questions are going to come up. I know you're in an uncomfortable position as a quasi-parolee. It's going to be a long trip."

Nicholas looked down at is hands. They were rough and cracked from the hard labor tasks of his ongoing sentence. "It would be a shame to waste these callouses in cold sleep," he said. "I'd rather spend the rest of the voyage awake. I can't help your team if I'm hibernating like a dormouse."

"You don't mind living with a semi-hostile crew that long?" Anne asked.

"It beats the brig," he answered wryly. "The only real hostility I get is from my young cousin, and he has his reasons."

"Okay," Anne said. "I'm glad you feel that way. If it gets to be too much, talk to Pete Worsley. I trust his instincts in difficult situations like this."

"Me too," said Nicholas.

***

"You're sure about this?" said Abishai, eyeing his son thoughtfully across the dinner table.

"I know it seems sudden, and Joanne's older than I am, but I'm sure. The proposal was a surprise to me. I didn't even have a ring to give her. Somehow, she didn't mind."

Shanyah nodded. "She's had her mind made up about you for a while. She was probably just waiting for you to come around. Have you two set a date?"

Mishael shook his head "No, but we don't want to wait too long. Assuming we get approval, Joanne wants to have two children on the first leg of the crossing, while things are relatively quiet. Her job will get more demanding as we approach turnover."

"You'll get your approval," said Shanyah. "Both of you rank high on the intelligence and physical attribute scales. We're going to have another early-crossing baby boom from what I've seen around the ship. The Alder council handled it well on the last trip. I'm sure they'll do even better this time around."

"This is what we both want," said Mishael, "but I'm not sure I'm ready for it."

"If you were," said Abishai, "you'd be the first groom in the history of weddings. Get ready for a new and different life, son. I don't think you'll regret it. Your mother is past ready for grand babies, so you've made her happy."

***

Kalei and Soma sat at the edge of Cooper Green enjoying boysenberry crumble gelatos. Soma eyed the young doctor over her dish, her suspicious mind whirling. "I don't want to sound ungrateful," she started. "This gelato is everything you promised. I must ask, though, what prompted the invitation?"

"A couple of things," said Kalei, acknowledging the point. "First, I wanted to give your dad a break from worrying about you. Second, I thought you might like some female company. There aren't many girls your age aboard and they seem to have their own close friends."

"Do you like my dad?" Soma asked.

Kalei nearly choked on bite of gelato. She wiped her chin to make time for forming a response. "Yes, but not in the way I imagine you're thinking. You've been with him long enough to know he's a good man. You could argue he's saved the lives of everyone on this ship at least twice while putting his own on the line. I admire him very much, but I'm not looking for a romantic relationship with him."

"What are you looking for?" asked Soma.

"You're very direct," said Kalei with one eyebrow raised.

"Well?" said Soma, refusing to back down.

"I'd like to be a help to you and your dad. I'm sure it's not easy adjusting to a new family situation, and a new community while you're still grieving," said Kalei gently.

"What's in it for you, though?"

Kalei shrugged, "It's a blessing to be a help to others, to see them built up and secure. That's why I became a doctor, and why I love my work, most of the time."

Soma scraped up he last bite of gelato. "When don't you love it?" she asked.

Kalei's expression grew grim. She considered Soma's background for a moment, then decided to give it to her straight. "Our militia was involved in some heavy fighting over the past year. I'm the battalion's combat surgeon. People's lives were in my hands and I couldn't save them all." She looked down at her hands and had a momentary flash of them covered in blood. "I couldn't save too many of them." She looked away, embarrassed as her eyes started to tear up.

Soma's expression grew bleak. "Dad told me about losing his copilot. He still feels guilty about it. I feel guilty that I didn't die with my parents. Maybe the three of us have more in common than I thought."

"Well," said Kalei wiping away a stray tear. "Why don't we work on having a few more happy things in common?"

Soma held up her empty gelato cup. "Love of boysenberry crumble gelato is a good start," she said with a grin. "What's a boysenberry, anyway?"

Kalei grinned back. "My dad happens to have a great deal of expertise when it comes to boysenberries. Would you like to see where they grow?"

Twenty minutes later they were strolling through the rows of boysenberry canes in full flower with Abishai.

Soma ran her hand gently over a cluster of white flowers, then jerked back when she encountered a thorn.

"These canes still have their natural defenses," said Abishai. "That wouldn't stop the goats from going through them like a combine if they could reach them. We process a lot of our pruned fruit-tree branches and canes through the goats."

"Can I see the goats?" asked Soma wide-eyed. "I've only seen pictures."

"Sure," said Abishai. "The goat dairy is just a short walk. I have to warn you, though. The kids are just a few weeks old and cuter than collie pups. You may fall in love, but you can't take them home."

A few minutes later a laughing Soma was surrounded by baby goats trying to get at the bottle of milk she held for one of them. Abishai dropped the rest of the bottles into a rack and the pressure eased as the kids hurried to find one of their own. "These babies can be aggressive when it comes to feeding time," said Abishai with a grin. "They're natural acrobats too. Goats can jump so high in .5G that their enclosure includes an overhead net." He pointed upward. "The crew discovered early on that three meters of fence isn't nearly enough."

While Soma petted and played with the goats, Abishai and Kalei leaned against a wall together and watched. "How's she coping?" Abishai asked.

"Better than I would expect," said Kalei. "She's grown some emotional armor and comes across as pretty tough. Inside, though, she's still an eleven-year-old girl." Soma squealed and laughed as the baby goat she was hugging tried to nibble her ear.

"So I see," said Abishai. "How about Julian? He's a good leader and pilot, but this must be a stretch for him."

"He obviously loves her fiercely, and it seems to go both ways. She's very protective of him. From what I've seen he's doing very well, even if he feels overwhelmed. They're a couple of lonely souls who need each other. I'm trying to help a bit where I can, in a big sister kind of way."

"I remember you used to ask for a little sister when you were about four. I'm sure Julian appreciates the assistance," said Abishai thoughtfully. "Maybe we should invite them over for dinner. It will give your mother a chance to get to know her and take her under her wing. She's good at that sort of thing."

"Yes," said Kalei. "Momma's momma-powers are close to supernatural. A hug from her is like nothing else in this universe."

"I completely agree!" said Abishai.

"Speaking of Julian, I'd better tear this young lady away from the kids and take her home. He's going to be wondering where we've gotten to."

Chapter 11 – Invisible Poison

June 12th, AD 3209
Interstellar space
Long Boat Nai'a, *Beta Section Biome Processing Plant*

Lionel padded along the corridor leading to the Beta Section Biome organic processing plant. He sniffed, then opened his mouth to taste the air. The trace of something wrong was getting stronger. He looked around for a human but didn't see or hear one nearby. Curiosity tugged him forward as the hatch whisked open at his approach. He crossed into the space occupied by the plant. Suddenly his head swam and he tried to jump backward but only managed a small hop before collapsing to the deck in a furry heap.

Paulene hummed to herself as she made her inspection rounds. Biome was a fascinating department to work for when it wasn't utterly boring. She quite preferred boring, because it meant everything was going smoothly. She had an artist's touch for maintaining the delicate balance of creatures from large to microscopic that made up the ship's vital biome. Balance and gentle intervention were her focus on the job. The earlier she detected something out of whack, the easier it was to fix. She wondered how her husband Roan's latest scheme was coming along. He'd pulled in some big brains for help, so it was bound to be a doozy.

She thumbed the hatch in front of her open and was about to cross into the Biome processing plant when she spotted Lionel collapsed just inside. She immediately stopped breathing and hit the emergency button on her PCOM. She scooped the cat up quickly, closed the hatch and ran back down the corridor. Her lungs were screaming for air by the time she made it to through the next hatch and got it closed. She put her ear to Lionel's chest, then scrambled for an emergency oxygen mask from a nearby locker. She started the oxygen flow and put the mask over Lionel's muzzle while she massaged his chest. Her PCOM buzzed urgently for attention, and she opened the emergency channel. "I have an emergency in Beta Section Biome processing, possible atmosphere contamination. Verify there are no personnel in the area, then seal all hatches and ducts leading to the plant. Get the bio-hazard team down here. I need a veterinary care medic too!"

She looked down at Lionel, who still hadn't moved. "Come on buddy, wake up for me!" she said urgently, giving him chest compressions. In just a few minutes, Kalei came pounding down the corridor with her medical bag.

She took in the scene, felt Lionel's neck for a pulse, then nodded to Paulene. "Airborne contaminant?" she asked.

"Likely," Paulene answered. "My guess is hydrogen sulfide and/or methane leaking from the organics processing tank."

"Keep up the oxygen flowing," Kalei ordered. "He's got a weak pulse. I'm going to rig a hyperbaric chamber." She pulled out a transparent bag, attached an oxygen bottle, and slid it around Lionel. Paulene pulled her hands and the oxygen mask away, then held the whole contraption while Kalei quickly sealed and inflated the bag. She tested the pressure with her hand, then took the cat-filled chamber from Paulene. "This will hold until I can get him to Medical. He's going to have a horrible headache when he wakes up." She hurried off down the corridor.

Paulene was checking the hatch readouts when the bio-hazard team arrived in full hazmat gear. "The corridor beyond this hatch reads clear, but I don't trust the sensors," she told the team leader. "The plant sensors should have tripped long before a toxic concentration of gas built up." She looked at the rest of the team. "Double check your seals. I'm going to get another hatch between myself and the contamination, then you can go in and find the source."

***

Two hours later Paulene met with the chief engineer, the head of Biome, and the hazmat team lead.

The hazmat team leader brought up a video on the wall screen of the meeting room. "It turned out to be a methane leak from a faulty seal on a pressure relief pipe leading from the organics processing tank," he said, pointing out the cracked seal. "The mystery is why three separate detectors failed to trip and warn us. We replaced the detectors and tested the new ones. All the new ones are good, but the three in the plant compartment were trash. The self-test reads good, but they don't detect anything. I turned them over to an engineering tech to see if we can figure out why they all went bad. None of them are more than halfway through their normal lifecycle."

Grace Kopfer, the head of Biome, grimaced. "Something stinks, and I don't mean the methane leak. I've got the other five sections checking their plants with hazmat gear on. There's no way all three detectors simply failed. We need to find out why they quit working and take precautions in the meantime. Paulene could have ended up dead, and we're fortunate we didn't lose Lionel."

Paulene nodded. "I checked with Dr. Kalei. Lionel woke up spitting mad after thirty minutes and shredded his hyperbaric chamber. Fortunately, she had Abishai there to calm him down. She says Lionel will be fine. Sampling from all over the ship with handheld detectors is clear. It's probably just the Beta Section plant that's affected."

Joanne Calder frowned in thought. "I'll have my people add detectors to the air ducts into and out of the plants. We'll tie them into both engineering and Biome monitoring systems. Also, my team will replace the filters in the outflow scrubbers for all six section plants, so we know we have fresh ones in place. Is there anything else engineering can do to help?"

Grace shook her head. "Just get us the analysis on those detectors. I think that's the key to what's going on."

***

Abishai popped the ping pong ball in a lazy arch over the net toward Lionel sitting on the end of the table. The big cat watched it bounce, then reached up and smashed it back at Abishai with his right forepaw. Abishai managed to return the ball with a quick defensive flick of the paddle. The return smash whizzed past his ear, and he turned to scoop up the rebound off the bulkhead behind him. Kalei's instructions were to keep the cat awake and active for the next few hours. Lionel was always up for ping pong.

"Easy on the smashes, Lionel," he said as he served up another meat ball. Lionel just blinked and sent the ball back at warp speed. The small audience watching Lionel's antics giggled as the ball nailed Abishai in the stomach. Abishai gave the group of kids a withering look as retrieved the ball. "Do any of you think you have what it takes to keep a rally going with smash cat over there?" he asked.

Soma raised her hand confidently, so Abishai nodded and handed her the paddle and ball. He stood back and watched as she served the ball then displayed lightning quick reflexes, returning shot after shot. Lionel bleeked in delight, dancing across the table to keep rally alive. The children laughed and clapped at the display of dexterity on both sides.

Abishai leaned against the rec-center wall with a grin and wondered which one of them would get worn out first. Twenty minutes later he draped the exhausted cat over one shoulder and invited Soma to come home with him for a snack. "The least we can do is feed you something after you kept Lionel entertained that long."

Soma grinned, wiping sweat off her brow with a sleeve. "It was fun!" she said. "My first dad always said I had reflexes like a cat. I know now I don't really measure up, but I wore him down." Lionel reached over and swatted her ear with a lazy paw. Soma laughed and scratched him behind his ears. "I'd better let Dad know where I'm going. He worries about me wandering all over the ship."

"You and Lionel have that in common too. His wandering nature nearly did him in today."

After Soma sent the message from her wearable PCOM, she looked up at Abishai. "Why did Dr. Kalei call you to help with Lionel? He seems to be friends with everyone."

"Lionel and I go way back," answered Abishai. "When he was just a couple of kilos of bounce and fluff, he picked me as his human. He's been alternately comforting and terrorizing me ever since. Someday I'll tell you the whole story."

They arrived at Abishai's quarters and Shanyah met them at the door, enveloping Soma in a big warm hug that threatened to bring tears to the girl's eyes. After releasing the girl and making sure she was okay, Shanyah plucked Lionel from Abishai's shoulder and made a fuss over him for a few minutes. Abishai poured glasses of milk for everyone and passed around a plate of still-warm snickerdoodle cookies.

Soma chewed appreciatively and watched wide-eyed as Abishai vacuumed up three cookies in the time it takes to talk about it. "How did Lionel get his name?" she asked. Abishai pointed up. Lionel looked down at them from where he hung from the carpeted ceiling by his claws. He bleeked a laugh and proceeded to dance his way across ceiling, then drop lithely to the couch.

"Remember what he just did when I tell you the whole story," said Abishai. "I'll tell you how he got his name then."

***

The next morning, Joanne and her technician found Grace in her office along with Paulene. The technician placed a tray full of disassembled gas detector on Grace's desk. He pointed to the pre-filter, which looked like it had grown a head of gray hair. "At first I suspected mold, but what does this look like to you?" he asked, teasing off a bit of gray fluff that floated nearly weightless in the air.

"Cat hair," said Grace flatly.

The technician nodded. "Bingo, and not just any cat hair, Lionel cat hair. Dr. Kalei ran a DNA test, and the match was 100 percent. It's spring shedding season and these detectors are at just the right height for Lionel to rub his cheek on when he's leaving his scent everywhere. The detectors from the other sections also had cat hair in them, but not nearly enough to cause them to fail like this one. Lionel gets around the ship, but he spends most of his time in Beta Section, so it makes sense. Apparently, the other ship's cats don't have a habit of rubbing all over the detectors."

"Okay," said Grace. "Mystery solved. Lionel was nearly the cause of his own demise. We need to make sure this doesn't happen again. Can we close off Lionel's access to the Biome processing plants?"

"I would rather not," said Paulene. "Creating a safe space for vermin in the plants could cause more problems than some cat hair. We already clean the detector's prefilters quarterly as part of our normal maintenance schedule. If we increase the frequency to once a month, we'll catch the fur before it becomes a problem."

"What about the faulty seal?" Grace asked.

"FOD," said Joanne.

"FOD?" asked Grace.

"Foreign Object Damage," Joanne answered. "When my people took the fitting apart, they found a shard of ship steel, probably left over from the machining process. Over time, it worked its way through the seal material and weakened it until it cracked. The gas build-up in the tank created enough overpressure to push methane through the gap. We inspected the other five plants and didn't find any issues. Somebody got lazy with their quality control, but it was probably over a century ago."

"Thanks, Joanne," said Grace. "I think we're okay going forward then. We'll have our biome techs mask up and do a manual check with a hand-held detector whenever they enter the plants. With the number of possible hazards in the plants. That's a precaution we should have used all along."

***

Quester and Nicholas Withers worked their way down opposite sides of two parallel rows of young bean plants, spreading a good layer of straw around and between the plants. "Mulching with straw helps the soil retain moisture and control weeds," said Quester. "A little work now will save us a lot of work later. It will eventually break down and improve the soil."

"I wouldn't think you'd have a weed problem in a controlled environment," said Nicholas.

"That puzzled me too until I realized how much compost we use to amend the soil every year," answered Quester. "Tomato, cucumber, melon, and pumpkin are just a few of the seeds that survive the composting process and sprout right up when the temperature and moisture conditions are right. I have a soft spot for volunteers, but most of them have to go so they don't compete with the intended crops. Mulching keeps most of them from getting the light they need to become a nuisance. Also, despite our best efforts, we occasionally get true weed seeds in with purchased or traded plants, especially in the Sol system. Ask Mr. Clement about his decade-long battle with Chamberbitter some time."

The two worked in silence until they finished the row. "What are these yard long beans like?" asked Nicholas. "I don't know if I've ever had them."

"Any green beans you've eaten in the galley were probably yard long beans cut down to bite size," answered Quester. "We grow them because they produce steadily from late June until first frost and they're quicker to harvest than a standard green bean. Also, the leaves are higher in protein than the beans. That makes them a good emergency food source if we have a production problem. We stock bush bean seeds and some other pole bean varieties for family allotments, and we grow some heavy yielding beans for dry harvesting."

"Speaking of food emergencies, how much food reserve does the *Nai'a* stock?" asked Nicholas.

"We have three times the amount of emergency rations needed to keep a skeleton crew alive for an entire crossing," Quester answered. "If we have a true emergency, most of the crew will go into cold sleep. Pete told me that it has happened, but not on the *Nai'a*. In most cases, it was because the biome cycle got way out of balance at a microbial level. The Biome department has a big responsibility keeping everything balanced. We do our part by fostering healthy soil and plant life."

"I can imagine what the emergency rations must be like," said Nicholas. "Probably nutrient dense paste like in-system ships carry."

"Actually, it's mostly freeze-dried fresh food that's pretty good reconstituted. You've probably eaten soup that was rotated out of emergency stocks. Let's go look at the strawberries."

They ambled over to the strawberry field. The plants looked healthy. Quester bent to check for problems, pulling and tossing down a few volunteer pumpkin seedlings. "We'll just add any weeds we find to the mulch around the plants," he said. "It saves effort if we let it compost in place." He took a long look at Nicholas. "How are you and Lincoln getting along? Have you seen him recently?"

Nicholas pulled up a few stray tomato plants, shook the dirt off the roots, and tossed them down. "I have, but only from a distance. He still looks daggers at me. It's going to take time before he's ready to forgive me, if he ever is."

Quester quirked an eyebrow, "There has to be way to clear the air between you two. It's a long voyage to Sol, and nursing a grudge isn't going to do you, or Lincoln, any good."

"I agree," said Nicholas. "The problem is, I don't have any idea how to help him heal when the very sight of me sets him off. I've been praying about it every day."

Quester nodded, "Then you're doing exactly what you need to. I suppose we should both be patient about it, but I'll keep trying to think of a way to help."

"I appreciate it," said Nicholas. "It's really not your problem."

"I want to help if I can, for both of you. We all need to pull together. I have feeling Sol is going to test us like nothing else."

"It's going to be complicated," Nicholas replied. "I'm sure the Restoration hasn't been wasting the years I've been gone. They have a lot of grand plans, and most of them are focused on the demise of the Long Boat Free Trade Syndicate."

"All the more reason to get your relationship with Lincoln patched up," said Quester. They reached the end of the strawberry patch and began working their way back along another pair of rows.

"How are you going to get all of these strawberries picked?" asked Nicholas. "From the look of things, you're going to be overwhelmed with ripe berries before long."

Quester grinned. "Child labor, it's an annual tradition. The kids come and pick for a few hours every day when the berries are ripe. We pay them in strawberries or credits, usually a combination of both. They get five credits a flat, or one fourth of the strawberries they pick. The younger ones mostly eat strawberries. Some families take a day off and make an outing of it."

"What becomes of the harvest?"

"Most of it goes to the section commissaries and galleys for fresh eating. We freeze dry a good bit, and Gamma Section galley puts up enough jam to get us through the year," Quester answered. He straightened up as they reached the end of the row. "Let's take a break. I brought some of Shanyah's raspberry bars to restoke the furnaces."

Chapter 12 – Judgment and Mercy

June 14th, AD 3209
Interstellar Space
Long Boat Nai'a, *Cooper Green*

That Sunday morning Quester dropped by Nicholas' quarters to escort him to church. "I'm still nervous about this," said Nicholas. "I've never been to church. Do I look okay?" He was wearing midnight blue slacks and warm brown tunic with a high collar.

"You look fine," said Quester. "Not that it matters. You could come in a ratty old ship suit, and no one would look twice. They'll just be happy you're there. We all need the support of our Christian brother and sisters. I'm surprised you never attended church growing up."

"The Witherses were never a church-going family. It was just one of many points of contention we had with The Bancroft."

"I didn't think Lalande had a state church."

"Not exactly, there are all sorts of churches in the Lalande system. The Bancrofts as a family attend and support a church that traces its roots to the Welsh revival and the Baptist Union of Wales. Religious freedom is encoded in the constitution, but the Bancrofts always cast a disapproving eye on those who don't attend regularly. My father called it a bunch of rank superstition."

"My upbringing wasn't heavy on church either, but I snuck into more than one service on HAB-5 to enjoy the food afterward," said Quester. "I'm sure the folks there knew what I was up to, but they weren't about to turn a kid away."

"I guess you had it pretty rough," said Nicholas. "No family and no one to rely on."

"I learned to rely on myself, but a need to belong landed me in a gang," Quester replied. "The Restoration recruited me by giving me a way out of that situation. A few months as a member of this crew taught me what real belonging is. I couldn't betray them when the moment came. I was surprised not to earn a ticket to a Tau Ceti prison asteroid. Looking back, my prized self-reliance was mostly self-interest. It's a slow poison of the mind." They walked on until they came to Cooper Green. One end was set up with a few hundred chairs in concentric circles with aisles radiating out from the center.

Quester led Nicholas over to where Abishai and Shanyah were choosing seats. Abishai shook his hand. As his hand disappeared into Abishai's, Nicholas reflected again that he was fortunate to be alive after tangling with this man. They took seats next to the couple and Nicholas glanced surreptitiously around. The congregation was a diverse bunch of all ages and styles of dress. He recognized a few of his former victims but didn't detect any hostile looks.

At the service start time, Pete Worsley stood up and welcomed everyone, reminding them that the church calendar was available via the ship data net and encouraging everyone to stick around for the picnic meal. A man Nicholas didn't recognize stood up and led the congregation in three hymns. Nicholas croaked along as best he could, enjoying the rich harmony of the people around him more than his own off-key efforts. Afterward, Abishai's quartet sang "How Deep the Father's Love for Us." Nicholas felt a shiver run through him as the truth of the words sank in.

Pete stood back up and offered a short opening prayer. "Brother Barney Gardner will preach the message this week," he said, and sat back down. Nicholas listened intently to the sermon, turning in his tattered Bible to follow along. Barney Gardner asked someone to stand and read out each passage as he taught. His focus was on forgiveness from verses in the Sermon on the Mount.

The words caused Nicholas to search his own heart to see if there was anyone he needed to forgive. He realized he was carrying resentment toward his cousin, Lincoln. He hadn't wanted to admit that Lincoln's rejection and anger was wearing on him, but it was. The young man was a complicated connection to his former life. Nicholas desperately wanted to repair the relationship, but he didn't know how.

At the end of the sermon, Barney invited anyone who wished to come forward to pray with one of the elders, while the congregation softly sang. Nicholas found his feet carrying him down the aisle. He knelt and prayed for both himself and Lincoln, asking God to heal what he could not, and to help him forgive. He felt Pete Worsley put a hand on his shoulder, and he knew his mentor was praying with him. He stood and went back to his seat. The congregation finished another verse, and the service was over.

Several people came over to greet Nicholas while a crew of volunteers set up for lunch on the green. Some he knew, and others introduced themselves. All thanked him for coming and encouraged him to come again. He was touched by their thoughtfulness and willingness to welcome an outcast into their church. Eventually he followed Abishai's lead and helped move chairs to a set of tables.

Quester nudged him with an elbow. "Did you see who else came forward to pray?"

Nicholas shook his head. "I didn't think it was polite to look around."

"I always look around," said Quester. "Lincoln was up there on the opposite side. Barney prayed with him."

Nicholas blinked in surprise. "I didn't even know he was here, or that he attended."

"He's here every Sunday," said Quester. "That's why I think there's some hope for working things out between you."

"I didn't even know he was a believer, but it makes sense," said Nicholas. "His father, Keith, was a Christian. I remember giving him a hard time about it. Keith tried to get me to church, but I had no interest in giving up my hate back then."

"The food line is forming," said Quester. "We'd better get in it before Abishai if we want any rolls."

Nicholas enjoyed the meal with the Bonaparté family and Quester. He smiled at the obvious attraction between the chief engineer and Mishael. They made quite a striking couple. Over dessert he met more of the church members. He had just turned in his dishes when he felt a tap on his shoulder. He turned to find Lincoln Withers looking at him with an intense expression. Strangely, the intensity seemed to be born of curiosity, rather than anger.

"Can we talk privately?" Lincoln asked.

Nicholas quirked an eyebrow at his escort. Quester just made a shooing motion, so Nicholas nodded to Lincoln, and they walked away from the crowd to the shade of a small tree.

"I'm going to ask a very personal question," said Lincoln. Nicholas gave him a short nod. "What were you praying about at the time of invitation?"

"That is a personal question," said Nicholas, "but it concerns you, so I'll answer it. I asked God to forgive me for my resentment toward you. I didn't even know it was there until I heard the preaching today. I also asked him to heal our relationship." Nicholas paused, trying to gauge Lincoln's reaction. "I think your father would have wanted us to be on good terms. I know you have good reason to suspect my motives and sincerity. Only God can overcome that. I haven't really been trusting him to do it."

Lincoln continued to stare at him intently for a few seconds, then looked abruptly away. He looked at his feet and kicked lightly at the mini-clover ground cover. After half a minute he looked back up, his expression troubled. "The sermon got to me too. You don't deserve to be forgiven, but that's the point. Mercy and grace are both undeserved, and I've received my share of both. Mercy triumphs over judgment. I've been forgiven; I should forgive you. I'm having a very hard time doing it, though."

Nicholas nodded. "I'm glad you're honest with yourself and me about that. You're right, I don't deserve your forgiveness. I couldn't believe it when most of the people I drugged with the Panic chose to forgive me. It's not natural to extend mercy to someone who has deliberately harmed you. It's part of God's nature, though, and as the preacher said, he expects it of us. I know every bit of mercy extended to me is God working in people's hearts. Nothing else makes any sense."

Lincoln glanced upward. He let out a sigh, and the tension in is stance eased by slow degrees. "You're right, cousin, I've been trying to make human sense of all this when it's not a matter of logic. You've repented and I know God has forgiven you. I'll follow his example and forgive you too. You'll forgive me if I don't give you a hug, though?"

Nicholas chuckled. "No worries, I'm not big on hugs either. How about we shake on it?" Lincoln tilted his head then stuck his hand out and shook Nicholas's firmly. The two walked back toward where Quester was talking animatedly with Roan and Grady.

Quester looked up and flashed a big smile. "You two both look a few metric tons lighter," he said.

"Something like that," Lincoln replied. "Well-nursed grudges weigh a lot. What are you three up to? Or is it classified?"

"Hmm...certifiably nuts maybe," Quester replied. "We're just discussing the finer details of Roan's latest challenge. We want to encourage the Lalande natives in the crew to participate this time. We could use your perspective."

"Sounds fun!" Lincoln declared. "Tell me about it."

***

Captain Hartley filled a cup of coffee and pushed it across his desk to the Chief of Boat. After filling his own mug, he drummed his fingernails lightly on the ceramic and frowned in thought. "How's morale, Chief?" he asked.

"Good," the COB answered. "We've ironed out the major friction points with the new people, and the Alder Council has a workable rotation set up for assignments. They've issued the usual early-voyage rash of child permits, nothing like we had coming out of Tau Ceti, but still a respectable number. I take it as a sign that people are settling into the reality of the long crossing, and confident things are going well. I expect we'll see some of the newcomers pairing off with old crew before too long.

"Roan and his cronies are hard at work on the next challenge. The amount of brain power he has helping him scares me a bit, but I'll wait and see what they come up with."

"I had a wild idea for shaking things up and staving off boredom," said the captain, leaning forward. "What if we set up a quarters rotation and have folks move to a new section every three years? By the time we complete the crossing, everyone will get a chance to live in all six hab sections."

The COB raised his eyebrows and leaned back. "How would you feel if I forced you to move offices every few months just to shake things up?"

The captain looked around at his plants, artwork, and furniture with a frown. "I'd probably tell you to get bent. I'm just getting comfortable here."

"I'm pretty sure you don't want five-thousand plus crew members who feel like telling the captain to get bent," said the COB. "Long boats get bent that way. If you're going to put people who are settled and comfortable in their place through something like that, you'll need a lot more convincing reason."

The captain blushed slightly, "Point made, COB. That's why I run my brilliant ideas through you."

"It's not an entirely awful idea," the COB said. "We could come up with some incentives and ask the Alder Council to pitch a voluntary rotation program. You would probably get some takers if it isn't forced on anyone. I'll talk to the chief alder and see what she thinks. Anything else on your mind, Captain?"

"No," the captain shook his head. "I suppose I should work through the mountain of reports in my queue and make sure the ship is still pointed toward Sol."

"If it isn't, Chief Nance will notice before you will," said the COB.

"Now that's the truth!" the captain answered.

***

Anne Brelling, Rolland Dunleavy, and Chord Olley sat down for another strategy session in the war room. "How is your data analysis team doing, Chord?" Anne asked.

"They're in good shape. Mr. Literal's help pared the mountain down to a manageable size. I think we'll get through the first pass within a two to three months. We've teased out several probable connections and a useful framework of the organization we'll be up against."

"We'll all be fed up with studying the Restoration long before this voyage is over," said Anne. "Work up a rotation plan for your people. Once the first pass is complete, I want everyone to take a week off. After that, have two thirds of your people slot into different jobs on the ship. I don't care what they choose, but I want everyone to take some time away from this problem to refresh their thinking. A yearly rotation will work out nicely. It gives everyone on the team a chance to get to know the crew. It's going to take all of us to win when we get to the Sol system.

"Are you willing to rotate out?" asked Rolland. "If you're not willing to set the example, I don't know if the team will fall in line."

Anne looked at him sourly. "I should have known that was coming. Yes, I'll rotate out too. Most of my qualifications are in danger of lapsing, so I'll work up a prioritized list and get some refresher time in. I'll rotate with you and Chord." She looked up at the representation of the Restoration's organizational structure running around the four walls of the room.

"Sun Tzu's words about knowing yourself just struck me," said Anne. "We've been over-focused on the enemy. Chord, I want you to take the first leadership rotation and start working up a list of the assets and capabilities of the Long Boat Free Trade Syndicate. You have the best familiarity with our Sol-based operations. When my shift comes, I'll work up a list of what we have to work with on the *Nai'a*. Roland, when your turn comes, work on a list of what our allies from among the free star nations bring to the table."

Rolland nodded thoughtfully. "We do need a better understanding of the assets we have available to fight the Restoration. We'll want to reach out and add allies as we reach the system as well."

"Good thought," said Anne. "That's another reason to get the team out among the crew. Anything from friends to family connections like I have in the belt could help. We can't ignore any possible advantage. I'll brief everyone up before we start the rotating out."

***

Julian and Soma cleaned up the supper dishes together to one of her favorite electro-bluegrass albums. She stacked dishes in the sanitizer while he fed the leavings into the appropriate recycler or compost slots. Out of the blue, Soma asked, "am I cramping your style, Dad?"

Julian laughed. "I don't know that I have style to cramp. Why do you ask?"

"I've noticed a lot of couples forming lately. I'm kind of in the way if you want to date someone. I don't want you to miss out because of me."

"I'm not missing out on anything," he answered. "In fact, I feel amazingly fulfilled just being your dad. In the unlikely event that someone does catch my eye, I give you my word, I won't hold back because of you."

Soma gave him a hug. "You'd better not," she said. "I want in on the scheming too. I may be young, but I can still give you the female perspective."

"It's a deal!" said Julian. "Just don't go matchmaking on me."

"Don't worry, I kind of like having you to myself. Just don't use me as an excuse not to follow your heart."

"Who says I have a heart?" Julian said, tousling her hair.

***

The Nai'a *plunged on through interstellar space, steadily gaining velocity. As the years passed, the crew gelled, and Captain Hartley grew more comfortable in his role. Ambassador Brelling's team circulated among the crew and solidified their plans for dealing with the Restoration. Because of the speed gained through the slingshot maneuver, the ship reached coasting velocity just six years after departing Lalande.*

Chapter 13 – Coasting Clear

June 28th, AD 3214
Interstellar Space
Long Boat Nai'a, *Bridge*

The *Nai'a* creaked and groaned as the massive hab decks gimballed from acceleration position to coast position on their giant rollers. Chief Nance gradually eased the main engine throttles from all ahead full toward stop, matching the progress of the hab decks. His goal was to keep 'down' a steady direction on the hab decks throughout the process. A few thumps and bangs later, the hab decks came to rest and the main engines cut off.

Captain Hartley surveyed the bridge, then rechecked his own display. "Chief Engineer, how are we looking?" he asked.

"All primary, secondary, and tertiary engineering systems are nominal, Captain," Joanne Calder replied. "The hab decks are reconfigured for coast mode. Biome reports none of the usual flooding issues on the creeks and ponds, just a few leaking pipe joints. The hydro crews are dealing with those now."

"Thank you," said the captain. "Helm, how is our course and velocity?"

"We are on course and holding steady at .71 C," Chief Nance replied. "Automatic attitude control is engaged."

"Very good," said the captain sitting back. "I think we can tentatively call the new procedure a success. Well done, Chief Nance, another feather to add to your cap."

"I'm surprised it hasn't been tried before," said Chief Nance.

"I wouldn't have let you try it if I didn't have full confidence in both you and Commander Calder," the captain replied. "Getting a smooth descending power curve out of the main engines isn't easy. Keeping a steady down force in the hab sections during the transition appears to benefit the process a lot. We'll see what the detailed reports tell us."

***

Soma helped Julian tighten the last of the leaky couplings and toweled a puddle of water from the deck. "We must have done something right," said Julian, "We've had less than a tenth of the leaks that I remember from the last time we reconfigured to coast mode. How do you like being a glorified plumber?"

"I'd rather be a pilot, but that's not an option," Soma replied, wiping sweat from her forehead with a red hanky. "I don't mind, though, learning about the ship's water cycle has been interesting. Also, Roan and Grady are fun to work with."

"I agree," said Julian. "I kind of fell into this job back in Tau Ceti, but I've found it suits me. Roan needs someone who can take his guff and keep him on track. What do you want to do when this rotation is up?"

"I'm thinking a stint in Medical. Kalei is like a big sister. I don't know if I'd like that line of work full time, but I'd like to learn more about what she does and spend more time with her. How about you?"

"Oh, I'll just stick with hydro and keep up my pilot certification in the simulator."

Soma whacked him on the arm. "I mean, wouldn't you like to spend more time with Kalei?"

Julian turned red. "I've told you before, she's like a *little* sister to me. She was this high when I met her, and I was a full-grown pilot."

Soma put her hands on her hips and stared Julian down. "That was over twenty-five years ago. She's twenty centimeters taller than you and could literally break you in half. She's also a qualified doctor and combat surgeon with field experience, hardly the little girl you remember. Both of you are in serious denial over your age difference. You're probably going to live three or four hundred years - is a fifteen-year age difference that big a deal in the scheme of things?"

"It is to us. We both feel the same way."

"You're both being knuckleheads." Soma shook her head and picked up her tool bag. Julian sighed as she walked off, then gathered his own tools and followed.

***

Kalei tracked her father down in the cane-berry section of the orchard. Together they picked some early raspberries and sampled a few plump first-fruit blackberries. "This Apache thornless variety is ancient," said Abishai. "It's still a common domesticated variety on Terra. The seeds are kind of big, but the berry size and flavor more than make up for it."

Kalei nodded, her mouth too full of blackberry juice to reply. "As much as I loved all the tropical fruit extras you used to bring us growing up," she finally said, "I like the orchard's produce just as well. Fresh fruit is good for the soul."

Abishai smiled. "Indeed! How are you doing these days? It seems like we don't see as much of you lately."

"I'm staying busy delivering and doctoring the latest generation of ship kids," Kalei answered. "This bunch seems especially accident prone, but it may be my imagination."

"Hmm..." said Abishai. "You made more than your fair share of trips to Medical when you were young. I think that's what got you interested in becoming a doctor."

Kalei chuckled. "It's possible, I suppose. I was always in awe of Dr. Rensaleer. I still am."

"For someone with a great bedside manner, she can turn into a force of nature when she wants to," said Abishai. "She was one of the few people on this ship willing to cross swords with Anne Brelling when she was captain. Most of the time she got her way, too."

"Maybe I'll wield that kind of gravitas in a century or so," Kalei replied wistfully.

"You do all right," said Abishai. "I don't see many people trying to override your medical decisions.

"That's because they know I'm right, *and* that my dad taught me how to bounce them off the bulkhead if they argue."

"You have the size and skills to intimidate most people," said Abishai, looking up at her fondly, "but I've never seen you do it, at least outside the dojo."

"There were a few moments in combat when I had to borrow mother's 'Don't Even Start' look," said Kalei, "Most people are wise enough not to test me."

"How are those memories?" asked Abishai gently. "I know the Lalande operation was hard on you."

"I still see the faces of the people who died on my operating table in my dreams sometimes," said Kalei with a shiver. "I've made friends with most of them over the years. I don't worry about them blaming me anymore."

Abishai gave her a spontaneous hug, which she returned fiercely. She pulled away after a few moments. "Believe it or not, I didn't come here just to raid the berry patch and reminisce," she said. "Take me to the herb garden. Dr. Rensaleer gave me list of what we need to restock from the medicinal plants."

Abishai led the way to a patch of ground that resembled an organized collection of weeds as much as anything. There was broad-leaf plantain, feathery yarrow, echinacea, chamomile, turmeric, ginger, lemon balm, ginseng, and many others. For reasons lost to antiquity, the culinary herbs were grown on the farm, while the orchard handled the medicinal varieties. "Do you need anything?" asked Abishai. "I can help harvest."

Kalei pulled a pair of snippers out of one holster and a Hori Hori knife out of the other. "I've got the tools. If you can spare a basket, I'll be all set.

You can get back to your own work. A few hours of quietly puttering around in the herb garden is literally what Dr. Rensaleer ordered."

***

Anne Brelling sifted through her team's latest reports, nodding in satisfaction. She was on rotation as the team lead while Rolland and Chord pursued qualifications in commissary management and elementary education, respectively. She couldn't imagine coordinating foodstuffs or wrangling a pack of curious seven-year-olds, so she was glad to leave them to it. The team's survey of crew connections in Sol was turning up more possibilities than she had hoped for. They had several potential contacts in each of the six sovereign governments of the Sol system. Chord's data framework organized them by nation and potential uses. Focusing their efforts was going to be quite a task. Once again, she was glad she didn't have to run both the ship and this campaign against the Restoration.

Her train of thought shifted to Captain Hartley. She was proud of the way he handled his responsibilities as captain. She was probably the only one on board who could truly sympathize with the weight of command on his shoulders. She opened up her PCOM message suite and sent the captain a quick message requesting a meeting at his convenience with him and the first officer.

That afternoon the three of them met in the captain's conference room. Anne looked around, remembering a few of the many tense planning sessions she'd led in this space. Commander Winslow Stirling eyed her with frank curiosity, so she leaned forward to start the ball rolling. "We have time, but I want to start brainstorming with you two about how my team and your ship chain of command will coordinate when we get to Sol."

"My orders from the Long Boat Free Trade Syndicate make it clear that I'm to support your efforts against the Restoration with all assets available," said Captain Hartley. "We're at your disposal, but I agree. We need a way to coordinate our actions so we don't have any avoidable missteps. Thank you for the regular summary updates from your team. Winslow and I are reading them with great interest."

Anne leaned back. "I believe the first officer is a natural choice to lead the coordination between the investigative team and the ship's chain of command. What do you say, Winslow?"

Winslow nodded enthusiastically. "I *am* the logical candidate. I think it makes sense to have a small liaison team embedded with your investigators. We need to be part of your planning and war-gaming so we can understand how to best support your efforts and make suggestions."

"I agree," said Captain Hartley. "Work up a plan, including team members, and run it by me. We'll set up a regular rotation, so someone is aways present with the team or on call as needed."

"Once you have the liaisons identified, I'll get them briefed up on where we are and the plan as it stands," said Anne. "I should have started this sooner, but I feel better knowing we'll have a solid coordination channel going forward. Has my team been causing any headaches? I know we're running around like a bunch of Nosey Nellies, but what I've heard suggests the crew is glad to help."

"I haven't heard any rumblings, how about you, Winslow?" the captain asked.

"I talked with one of Ambassador Brelling's team members about my family connections on Callisto III. I'm not sure they'll help much, but I'm willing to pitch in where I can. The vast majority of the crew feels the same way. Those of us who have connections in Sol are more than happy to use them to help defeat the Restoration."

"Do you suspect any malcontents?" Anne asked.

"In a crew of five thousand people, there are bound to be soreheads," said the first officer. "The COB and I are aware of a few troublemakers, but they're all bluster. I'm satisfied that the Lalande contingent is well integrated now. We have several marriages and a number of children to prove it."

The captain chuckled. "In spite of my initial missteps, we're in pretty good shape. We have a long way to go, but I'm confident the crew will be ready."

"For the liaison team, I suggest you pull Julian Garrity back onto active duty," said Anne. "He's got good instincts and the flexibility to think strategically as well as tactically."

"I agree," said Winslow. "I'll start with him and see if he has suggestions for other members."

Captain Hartley stretched and yawned. "Sorry," he said. "I was up late looking at department reports."

Anne chuckled. "You have no idea how glad I was to pass that responsibility to you."

"Actually, after half a dozen years in the captain's seat, I have a very good idea just how glad you are. Did you want to discuss anything else?"

"No, I think we've covered everything. I appreciate your help," said Anne.

"Even if I didn't have orders, I have my own score to settle with the Restoration," said the captain. "We'll do everything we can to make sure the free trade syndicate comes out on top."

***

Abisahi pried his grandson Mark loose from his right leg while holding his granddaughter Fawzia under his left arm. For a four-year olds, the twins had impressive grip strength. Just as he was getting them under control, Lionel launched himself into the fray. The cat hit Abishai in the chest like a furry cannon ball, and he sat down with a thump. The twins took advantage, pushing Abishai to his back. Mark scrambled for a headlock, his arms barely fitting around Abishai's neck. Fawzia slithered into position for a modified version of one of Grandma Shanyah's elbow locks. "Tap! Tap! Tap! I give up!" Abishai hollered through a face full of Lionel's belly fur. The grandkids rolled off him, and he spat some fur out while launching

Lionel at the ceiling. The cat executed a lazy flip and caught himself on the overhead carpet with his claws.

"Someday I'm going to get even, fur ball." Abishai said weakly. "I was just getting the upper hand."

"We were just setting you up for the fall," said Fawzia.

"We'll try it again when your furry friend isn't around to interrupt my triumph," Abishai answered, grabbing both in a bear hug. He tossed Mark at Mishael and Fawzia at her Aunt Kalei. "These two remind me of you two at about this age, always thinking you could take the old man down."

"Yup," said Kaleigh, "and succeeding with Lionel's help."

The twin's mother Joanne laughed and shook her head. "There's never a dull moment in this family."

"We added a lot to the mix when you filled our two-child quota in one go," said Mishael.

"My plan was to spread them about by about two years," said Joanne. "I can't help it that they decided to double up. Come to think of it, you had something to do with that too. Kalei, help me out here, doesn't the father bear some responsibility for fraternal twins?"

"Responsibility? Yes, but I'm afraid it's the mother who sets the conditions for fraternal twins," Kalei answered. "Just don't blame the doctor. Whoever wants to take responsibility for them, I think they're perfect." She set Fawzia down with a tousle and a grin.

"Hmph," said Mishael, giving Mark a light noogie. "Perfectly spoiled by their aunt and grandparents."

"Guilty as charged," said Shanyah, arriving from the kitchen with a large baking dish of cheesy scalloped potatoes. "It's every grandparent's prerogative after all. How about a hand with the rest of the dinner, Abishai?"

Abishai stomach rumbled mightily, and everyone laughed as he hurried to comply.

***

Quester moved his character piece onto the weapons dealer square of the Boorlong's Revenge board and purchased a Scottish Claymore. "I pity the slimy Boorlong minion who tries me now!" He cackled with glee.

"Easy for you to say," grumbled Lincoln Withers. "You don't have a case of galloping mustard fungus and an empty purse."

"I'll trade you my herbalist kit for your mace," said his cousin Nicholas.

"No thanks, I'm getting used to losing a third of my turns from stopping to scratch," Lincoln replied. "It saves mental effort."

The three men continued the game until Quester's inevitable victory. "Once again, you bow to my superiority!" he said in his best evil overlord voice.

"Bowing is out of the question after I weeded your sweet potato patch all day," Nicholas replied wearily.

"Take heart," said Quester. "The vines will shade everything else out before long."

Lincoln stretched mightily. "I should be going. I have a practical exam to study for. They say this one's a bear."

"The cold sleep practicum final is no joke!" said Nicholas. "I still remember the experience. Dame Ashworth herself proctored mine. I can help you prepare, if you like."

"Can you fake thermal shock as well as the training automatons?" Lincoln asked.

"Probably not," answered Nicholas. "I can tell you if you're applying the proper response, though. As long as you don't actually inject me with anything."

Quester watched the exchange with satisfaction. The two were still a little uncomfortable with each other, but Lincoln's hostility was a thing of the past. Attending church together, and the weekly game nights, had eased the rougher aspects of the relationship. He was hopeful the two would become allies and combine their talents to help in the fight against the Restoration. Nicholas was holding up well, but he needed family support firmly behind him for what was coming. His part in the Sol conflict would likely put him under as much pressure as anyone on the ship.

***

For a bit over six years, the Nai'a *plunged on, coasting through interstellar space, coasting at more than two-thirds of light speed. Her ice shield preceded her bulk, absorbing dust strikes and keeping the ship safe. The new generation of ship kids attended school and explored the ship's recesses when allowed. Sooner than it seemed possible, the coast phase approached its end and the ship prepared for Turnover and deceleration.*

Chapter 14 – Turnover

September 25th, AD 3220
Interstellar Space
Long Boat Nai'a, *Bridge*

Captain Hartley lightly gripped the command chair's armrests as the *Nai'a's* bow-over-stern tumble played hob with his inner ear. Chief Nance hovered over the helm controls, ready to intervene in a split second if things went pear-shaped. Lieutenant Commander Val O'Clair provided an equally focused back up in auxiliary control. Commander Julian Garrity served as tertiary helm control from a console in aft engineering. The three were the top scoring competitors in the helm competition that traditionally led up to Turnover. Merit was the only factor in selecting who took the helm with the lives of everyone on board hanging in the balance. Only the best at the job were allowed in the seat.

All over the ship, the crew stood ready at Turnover action stations. This time, the ship completed the turn without incident. Chief Nance engaged the ice shield with the stern free-rotating mount. Engineering ran the main engine pylons out and the helmsman gradually applied power until the ship was decelerating at .1 G. With the stern pointed at Sol, the *Nai'a* was only six years from her home coming.

***

Quester retrieved Nicholas from the brig a few hours after Turnover. "I'm sorry you had to spend more time in here," he said as they walked through the Ship Security foyer.

"I don't blame the captain for sticking me in the brig for Turnover. I'm still technically a prisoner serving a sentence of hard labor." Nicholas answered. "In a way, I'm glad he did. Given my history, it's best that no one had to worry about keeping tabs on me during the big event. It gave me some time to read, think, and pray for the crew."

Quester shook his head, "Back when you were sabotaging the ship, I'll bet you would have never imagined praying for Turnover to go well."

"It was mostly the people I coerced sabotaging the ship," said Nicholas. "A lot of them are still on the crew. That's another good reason to lock me up. The memories my face sparks wouldn't be helpful. Is that a bruise on your cheek?"

Quester probed the spot gently. "Yes, I hope it doesn't turn into a shiner. One of the cows got upset with the apparent gravity changes. She banged me around a bit, but we're both okay. I was a little puzzled at first to have a Turnover action station on the farm, but I understand now."

***

That evening the crew gathered for the traditional Turnover celebration on Cooper Green. Soma ran over to Julian, giddy with relief, and gave him a big hug. "I'm glad that's over!" she blurted. "I was so nervous after the stories I've heard about previous Turnovers."

"It wasn't what I would call boring," answered Julian, returning her hug. "I'll take uneventful every time, though. Let's enjoy the music, food, and entertainment. I think I see a shaved ice stand over there. Let's see if they have boysenberry syrup."

Soma trailed along with him, searching the crowd for a familiar face. She spotted Kalei and waived her over. The three waited in line together, chatting over Turnover and the entertainment lineup. Soma ordered a boysenberry, mango, passion fruit, black cherry ice. "What?" She said at Julian and Kalei's incredulous looks. "It's your fault for introducing me to all these great flavors!" She scanned the crowd. "There's Calley and Zinnia. I'll catch up with you guys later."

Julian watched her go, then dug into his ice with a bamboo spoon. He savored the burst of berry flavor, then looked at Kalei. "Do you think she ditched us on purpose?"

"Absolutely!" Kalei answered. "She's been doing that more and more lately. I would say it's a natural consequence of being nearly an adult now, but I know she still enjoys your company."

"So, she did it to leave us to ourselves. I won't complain. You're pretty good company." He smiled up at her. She just grabbed his arm and led him to find a good seat for the performances to come.

After the entertainment, Julian offered to walk Kalei back to her quarters. They strolled in companionable silence until they came to her door. Julian looked up at her and said, "I enjoyed this evening. I'm sure the entertainment was good, but I didn't notice it much with the quality of the company."

Kalei quirked an eyebrow. "Don't tell me you're developing into a smooth talker, Julian. I might think you have feelings for me."

Julian chuckled. "You know I do. I'm starting to think Soma was right to call us knuckleheads. I owe you a lot, Kalei. You helped Soma and me through several rough spots, and never really asked for anything in return. I put my feelings for you on the back burner, and I'm starting to wonder if that was a mistake. I feel like I kept you in a holding pattern all these years. It wasn't fair."

"I'm a big girl, Julian," Kalei said. "I made my choices with my eyes wide open. Also, I enjoy being part of Soma's life, and yours, just as we are. I don't want to you to feel obligated toward me."

"Obligated is not the word I would use," said Julian, moving closer and holding her gaze. "Smitten is closer." He took her face in both hands and kissed her. Kalei froze for an instant, then let herself kiss him back.

***

The next day Ambassador Brelling's entire team met, commandeering the Delta Section Galley to have space for everyone. Nicholas listened to the briefings with interest. He knew his own part in the strategy well, and it was good to see how it fit with the rest of the plan. At the end, Ambassador Brelling thanked the various briefers and gave a quick summary. "I'm pleased with our efforts thus far," she said. "Keep in mind, we'll need to adjust every one of our plans as we assess the situation. Our success will hinge on keeping the Restoration reacting to us. To do that, we need a short decision cycle. Keep each other informed, but don't hesitate to act when the moment comes. Now, do we have any questions or suggestions based on what you heard?" Nicholas tentatively raised his hand. "Mr. Withers, go ahead."

Nicholas stood. "I just had a thought about the cold sleep passengers. The team is doing a great job surveying the crew for Sol contacts and skills. We should do the same with the cold sleep population. A good number of them are headed to Terra, so they'll be awake six months early to start gravity acclimatization."

"Excellent idea," said Ambassador Brelling. "We'll need some people from Lalande who are familiar with our passengers to do the research and sorting with Mr. Literal's help."

Nicholas sat back down thinking about Lincoln. He knew his cousin would want in on this. It would be a chance for them to work together on the one thing they completely agreed on. He sent Lincoln a quick message and listened to the remaining discussion.

Lincoln met him outside the galley, and they decided to have lunch with Quester at Claudia's Schnellimbiss. "How many cold sleep passengers are there?" asked Quester while they waited in line.

"Over fifty thousand," said Lincoln, his brain turning over possibilities. "Only about three thousand are scheduled for early wake up. They're the ones headed for dirtside jobs or school on Terra. I don't envy them the full gravity therapy they'll go through. I understand we'll all be tightening up and sharing quarters too. That's a lot of people to research."

"Mr. Literal can reduce the sheer mass of data to something manageable given the right parameters," said Quester. "I'll make some time to help. He and I get along fairly well, even though I started out on his bad side."

"A few of the returning passengers are probably Sol system natives," said Nicholas. "We'll need to set up interviews with the best possibilities as soon as possible after the cold sleep team wakes them. We can add them to the database of connections." They ordered and collected their bratwurst on brötchen with grainy mustard, then sat down at one of the nearby tables.

"We shouldn't ignore the Lalande natives," said Lincoln, wiping a smear of spicy mustard from the corner of his mouth. "I think Ambassador Brelling's team has a blind spot there. Our people bring a lot of skills to the table even if they don't have direct connections in the Sol system. Those in cold sleep multiply the possibilities by an order of magnitude."

Nicholas shook his head. "I've been thinking the same thing. I don't know why I didn't realize the possibilities sooner.

"Maybe be because most of us hated your guts early on?" replied Lincoln. "It's hard to think of people who can't stand you as partners in a cause."

A few days later the three met again in one of the team offices along with Hal Renfro. "This team really needs a name," said Quester. "If you're going to battle an enemy like the Restoration, you should call yourselves something catchy."

"Technically, you're on the team now," said Hal. "Why don't you come up with a name and suggest it to Ambassador Brelling?"

Quester's face paled. "I'm not sure she'd take it well, and she still scares the living daylights out of me."

Hal laughed. "If she thought that badly of you, she would have booted you off the ship back in Tau Ceti."

Lincoln rolled his eyes. "Can we get on with it? We have a lot of work to do."

"Right you are!" said Quester. He fired up the room's data terminal ad put in a call to Mr. Literal. As usual, the ship's data librarian answered instantly.

"Good morning, Quester, Hal, and I see the elder and younger Mr. Withers as well," the artificial intelligence greeted them.

"Good morning, Mr. Literal, how are you?" asked Quester.

"Currently I'm operating at 99.9932% of optimum efficiency," replied Mr. Literal.

"Excellent!" said Quester. "I take it you and the chief engineer are getting along well."

"Very well," Mr. Literal replied. "She allows me a great deal of autonomy in maintaining and optimizing my hardware. She also prioritized the additional data runs I requested."

"Are you enjoying weeding on the farm with your remote?" Quester asked with a wink for his companions.

"Yes, I find the activity oddly...satisfying and soothing. It's a bit like cleaning up a corrupted file," said Mr. Literal. Hal's eyebrows tried to climb into his hairline, both at the adjectives Mr. Literal used, and the pause he took to come up with them.

"We need your help with a survey of the cold sleep passengers," Quester said. "We're looking for anyone who has possible connections in the Sol system. Prioritize the early-waking contingent and give us list of most to least likely."

"We also need lists of people with the following types of experience: law enforcement, military, especially covert operations, public relations, advertising, social networking, and cybersecurity." said Hal. "Again, prioritize the early-waking contingent of sleepers, but include all cold sleep passengers."

"I'm running those queries now," said Mr. Literal. "Where would you like the results delivered?"

"This data terminal," said Quester. "Also, we want you to do a broad analysis of the crew and all cold sleep passengers using your new intuition subroutines. Find the people who will be the most help in winning the coming conflict with the Restoration and include your reasoning as to why."

The terminal beeped as he finished, indicating the arrival of the first set of data query results. There was a perceptible pause before Mr. Literal answered. "The type of analysis you requested requires a substantial percentage of my computing capacity. I will need to obtain permission before I start. Since this effort is flagged with a high priority, I have no doubt the request will be approved. I estimate a thorough analysis will require approximately forty-eight hours."

Hal blinked. He'd never given Mr. Literal a task that wasn't complete within minutes, usually seconds.

"Is there any other way I can be of assistance?" Mr. Literal asked.

"We've given you enough to work on for now," Quester answered. "We'll work on the data you've provided in the meantime. Thank you for your help."

"You're all most welcome," said Mr. Literal. "Have a good day!" His avatar winked out, and the four men looked at each other.

"What was that business about weeding?" asked Hal.

"I decided to help Mr. Clement out by setting up as much automation of physical tasks as I could before he returned to take over the farm. Weeding is a task he enjoys, but there's too much of it for him without help. Automated cultivators aren't smart or precise enough to weed among the plants. With Roan's help, I outfitted one of Mr. Literal's small maintenance remotes with grasping and cutting tools. I taught him how to weed and use the cuttings to mulch around the plants. I wasn't sure how it would go, but even Mr. Clement will allow that Mr. Literal makes a pretty good gardener. The real surprise is that Mr. Literal enjoys the process a lot like some people do. He leaves enough for Mr. Clement to satisfy his own weeding itch."

Hal rubbed his chin. The implications troubled him, but he knew Greer Kensing, his wife Lisandra, and others were keeping a close watch on the AI's incipient sentience. He shrugged, "Let's get these lists divvied up and get to work. I'll take law enforcement and send military over to Commander Garrity." The group soon agreed on assignments and began combing through the files.

***

Shanyah hid a smile as she helped Kalei pack a picnic lunch. Her daughter's near-giddy enthusiasm warmed her heart. "Your father and I enjoyed quite a few picnics when we were courting."

"I remember you talking about them," Kalei answered. "I hope this one goes well."

"You two have been circling each other for years," said Shanyah. "You probably have a lot less catching up to do than your father and I did. He barely noticed me, and I was keeping what I thought was a safe distance."

"It's a wonder you two finally got together," said Kalei.

Shanyah laughed, "It's a good thing for you we did, and I could say the same about you and Julian. What changed?"

"Soma is all but grown up, for one thing," Kalei answered. "Julian had all he could handle raising her. Also, the age difference isn't as much of an obstacle. If we had just met, it wouldn't even bother me."

Shanyah's eyes crinkled. "It bothers you that he remembers what you were like as a rambunctious five-year-old?"

Kalei sighed. "Yes, with a mild case of hero worship."

Shanyah shook her head. "At that age, there was no such thing as mild with you."

"Don't remind me," Kalei said. "I suppose if he can look past all that, I should be able to."

"Well, *something* must have happened to trigger this sudden change of mind," her mother said. "It probably wasn't as drastic as what got your father and me together, but I'm certain it was something."

"He might have kissed me when we said goodnight after the Turnover party," said Kalei, trying to hide a crimson blush with a picnic blanket.

"If the color in your cheeks is any indication, there's no 'might-have' about it," Shanyah said with a chuckle.

Kalei finished packing the basket and gave her mother a quick hug. "Thanks for all the help," she said. "Say a prayer for me. I'm going to need it."

Julian met her at the entrance to a small, wooded park in Epsilon Section. He took the picnic basket, then her hand. His hand felt both strange, and completely right in hers as they made their way to a patch of meadow next to a gently flowing creek. "I thought I knew all the hidden spots on this ship," she said, "but this is new to me."

Julian spread the picnic blanket on the ground and set the basket on it. "I thought it would be nice to have more privacy than Cooper Green affords," he said. "You look beautiful. I can't remember the last time I saw you in a dress."

Kalei's smile dimpled her cheeks and she twirled for him, showing of the floral-patterned summer smock. "I had to borrow one of Mom's," she said. "Fortunately, she favors low hems, or it would have been ridiculously short on me."

They sat down and Kalei laid out ham and pickle sandwiches, red potato salad, and a bowl of apple slices, and poured two tumblers of pineapple-tangerine juice. Julian grinned. "I'll never starve around your family. Did you make the potato salad?"

"Oh no, that's Mom's work. I never learned to cook properly like my parents," she answered. "I did manage to throw the sandwiches together after I plundered their refrigerator. I must confess; I usually eat my meals at the galley or my parents' quarters."

"I noticed that," Julian replied. "May I say grace?" Kalei nodded and he said a quick heart-felt prayer of thanksgiving. He took a big bite of sandwich, appreciating the crunch of the sliced pickle. "Your dad's fermented pickles?" he asked. Kalei nodded again. "He really should sell them."

"He's busy enough with the orchard," said Kalei. "He'd rather give away his surplus than turn it into a business." She took a bite of crisp apple, enjoying the complex flavor and perfect balance of sweet and tart. "I didn't ask you on a picnic to talk about pickles. That kiss the other night startled me, and got me thinking. I need to know where this I going. Was that a one-time thing?"

Julian looked away, swallowed the bite he was chewing, then met her gaze. "I surprised myself with the kiss, but it got me thinking too. I know I enjoyed it more than I've enjoyed anything in a long time. If you're of the same mind, I would like to repeat the experience. I also want us to become much more than friends." He shrugged and looked at the rippling water. "I'm sorry I took this long to realize how I feel about you and do something about it."

Kalei reached out and touched his shoulder. "I played my own part in that dance," she said. "I don't think either one of us was ready for romance."

Julian looked back up and nodded. "In spite of Soma's prompting, I didn't want her to feel like she needed to compete for my time and affection. I wanted to be as present for her as possible after what she went through."

"I understand," said Kalei. "I felt the same way. Keeping our distance made my relationship with Soma simpler. I think it was best for all of us."

"Well," said Julian, "now Soma is competing for the affection of a veritable flock of young men, or maybe it's the other way around. She doesn't need this old man as much as she did. At times I'm more of a hindrance."

Kalei punched him in the shoulder, and he collapsed in feigned agony. "You aren't old, Julian," said Kalei shaking her head. "I still want to be careful not to come between you."

Julian opened one eye. "I'll get less hassle if we do start dating. I think she wants someone to distract me from her own whirlwind social life."

"Hmm...," said Kalei. "You may have something there. She still likes hanging out with you enough that she hasn't applied for her own quarters."

"She'd probably get stuck with a roommate, and right now I'm preferrable to the possibilities," Julian said, sitting up and rubbing his shoulder. "I get the feeling we're in that old dance again. You still haven't said how you feel about me."

"I'm wavering between tossing a certain handsome fighter pilot in the creek and something else," Kalei said, her eyes narrowing.

"Something else?" Julian said, looking around for an escape route.

Kalei moved the picnic basket from between them and motioned him closer. Julian scootched cautiously toward her. Kalei grabbed him firmly by the shoulders. "Let's try that kiss again, then I'll tell you what I think about you," she said, and put action to her words.

A few minutes later, Julian had to admit he knew a lot more about how Kalei felt toward him than if they'd spent the time talking. "How do I feel about you?" asked Kalei on cue.

Julian cleared his throat; a silly grin plastered across his face. "Strongly, I'd say, quite strongly!"

"What are you going to do about it?"

"My best to convince you I feel the same way!"

"Wise choice, Mr. Garrity, because I'm not letting you get away."

***

Hal Renfro and his ad hoc team plowed steadily through the data Mr. Literal provided them while they waited for the AI's deeper analysis. "We're going to be doing a lot of interviews when these people come out of cold sleep," he said. "I didn't expect the diversity of skills a lot of our passengers have. Longer life spans allow people to explore several different careers, and we're seeing the results. I found one interesting character who spent his time in Lalande teaching old Earth history. It turns out he was probably one of Lisandra's contemporaries under a different identity back in the Sol System. She said he's got an interesting skill set in cyber systems, especially bionic implants of the illegal variety."

"Just the kind of person we want to recruit to the cause," Lincoln commented. "I found several people who were active in the Lalande social media sphere. A few of them mentioned an intent to create a splash in the Sol system and try to make a living that way. If we combine their efforts with the expertise we have in advertising, we should have multiple ways to get our message out."

"I wish I could say the same on the military side," said Julian. "Most of the skills and potential connections in my area reside with the active crew. We're looking to avoid a fight, though, not start one. If the Sol Space Patrol lives up to their reputation, it shouldn't be a problem. Once people start visiting the ship, we'll need to guard against infiltration."

"I have some ideas along those lines," said Hal. "We have a few people with probable special operations or espionage backgrounds. We won't know for sure until we can interview them. Most of the footwork will be up to Sol system law enforcement, but it wouldn't hurt to have a team ready to provide reinforcement if needed."

"The militia will have a ready reaction force on duty 24-7," said Julian. "We'll work on other ways to improve internal security, but most of us our amateurs when it comes to true espionage. Nicholas, you probably have as much training and experience as anyone. You also know how the Restoration operates. Don't be shy about telling us where we're messing up."

"One thing that comes to mind is security for Ambassador Brelling and Captain Hartley," said Nicholas. "I know this team and the crew would carry on if anything happened to one or both, but it would be a big blow to the cause. My sabotage strategy was to create enough chaos to undermine the captain and take over the ship. With less time to work with, the Restoration may try more direct action. They have trained assassins for just such a contingency. You can be sure they'll have access to the disguise technology I used, and more."

"We can use the experienced people we have and train up more to create security details for the two of them," said Hal. "I'll need to convince them of the necessity, though. I'm not looking forward to that conversation. Lisandra and Greer may have some ideas about detecting disguises. That's beyond my skillset, but we have some very good engineers who can help."

The team's musings were interrupted when the room's data terminal beeped an incoming call. Hal activated the display and Mr. Literal's avatar popped up. "I have the results of the data analysis you requested," he said without the usual exchange of pleasantries. "I downloaded the full list to this terminal, but one person in cold sleep stands out. Helvetica Montrose is, in my opinion, a key component to victory in the coming conflict. She is not scheduled for wakening until arrival in the Sol system. To take advantage of her skills, you must waken her with the early contingent." The AI's avatar winked out as he signed off without another word.

The whole team looked at Hal, wide-eyed with consternation. "That wasn't like Mr. Literal at all," said Quester, giving voice to their concerns. "Maybe his usual social graces got sublimated by the resources needed for the data analysis."

"Regardless," said Hal. "We need see what the analysis says about Helvetica Montrose, and why we need to wake her up early."

"I have a good idea why," said Lincoln. "Helvetica Montrose is an independent news reporter. She was the most trusted source of information in Lalande during the recent conflict. She has an uncanny knack for developing sources and uncovering the truth. Her reputation was basically untouchable in the system. She embarrassed The Bancroft any number of times, but the facts she reported about the Restoration turned the tide of public opinion against them. It's not a stretch to say her reporting was a large part of the reason the Bancroft prevailed."

"That's all very interesting," said Julian, "but how does it help with the situation in the Sol system?"

"She's originally from the Sol system," Lincoln answered. "She made no secret of the fact that she was fired from her job as the news anchor of the largest info-net corporation in Sol because she refused to report anything but the truth. She took cold sleep passage on the next Long Boat heading out-system and ended up in Lalande. She developed her own news network, and quickly gained the reputation I talked about earlier. I don't know why she booked passage on the *Nai'a* for Sol. I would think her future in Lalande was secure.

"Can the captain wake a cold sleep passenger early?" asked Quester. "The protections built into their contracts are ironclad from what I understand."

"They are," said Lincoln. "I learned that in my training."

Hal let out a low whistle. "This is officially over our heads. I'm going to grab Ambassador Brelling and we'll take it to the captain."

***

A few hours later, Captain Hartley, Ambassador Brelling, and Patrick Lorens, the head of cold sleep, listened while Hal briefed them on Mr. Literal's analysis. "Most of his list we already identified for follow up," he said. "Helvetica Montrose, however, is not in the early-waking contingent, so we didn't look at her file. Mr. Literal insists we need to wake her early if we want to succeed against the Restoration."

Patrick's normally serene face took on a hard expression. "I'm not waking one of my charges early on the say so of an artificial intelligence. I'm sorry, Captain, but our friendship notwithstanding, this decision in in my scope of authority."

"Have you looked into the precedents?" asked the captain levelly. "I'm sure this isn't the first time the situation has come up."

"I didn't have time since you called this meeting so urgently, but my staff is looking into it," answered Patrick sourly.

Only the seriousness of the situation kept Anne Brelling from smirking at the interchange. Her own battles as captain with Patrick's predecessor

"Dame" Ashworth were legendary, and Kevin Hartley had often been caught in the middle as her first officer.

Patrick held up a hand as his PCOM buzzed with an incoming message. He connected to the room's display wall and popped the message up. "This is Ms. Montrose's cold sleep contract," Patrick said. He quickly scrolled through the legal language to the section on waking provisions. His eyebrows rose as he surveyed the special provision Helvetica Montrose had included in the document. He shook his head wryly. "You're in luck, or I should say Helvetica Montrose is a very shrewd individual. She apparently foresaw this possibility and made provision for it. The contract authorizes us to wake her up to one year early upon the agreement of the captain, the chief alder, and the cold sleep director. Normally, I would still say no, but she clearly wanted us to exercise the clause if necessary. Her wishes outweigh mine."

"I sent the chief alder a message," said the captain. "I'm sure she'll agree once we've briefed her on the situation. Even a year-early wakeup is several years away, so we have plenty of time." Anne Brelling nodded in satisfaction. She wasn't completely sold on the intuition of an artificial intelligence, but her own instincts told her Helvetic Montrose could be a great help to their cause. Ther reporter also had the potential to be their undoing. Anne and her team needed to consider both sides of that coin carefully.

The Nai'a *plunged on toward Sol, steadily shedding her relativistic velocity. The crew continued to plan for the inevitable conflict in humanity's home system. Six years of deceleration brought the long boat to within a year's travel of Earth herself.*

Chapter 15 – Preparing the Battlefield

October 14th, AD 3226
Interstellar Space, One Year out of Port
Long Boat Nai'a, *Bridge*

Helvetica Montrose heard sounds first, the muted beeping of medical equipment, the background hum of electrical power, and the hush of circulation. A violent shiver wracked her body, she could only remember being this cold once. Cold sleep, she was coming out of cold sleep. She pried her eyes open and immediately shut them. Even the soft illumination of the waking room was too much. She felt the bed she was on slowly raise to a sitting up position. A gentle hand touched her shoulder. "Just rest and breath," the cold sleep technician said. "The bed will warm you up, but we have to do it gradually."

Helvetica nodded carefully, finding her muscles stiff from shivering and disuse. She knew she would feel better soon, but it didn't help the present discomfort. She felt like the guest of honor at a funeral. Another spasm shook her, and a moan of pain escaped her lips. After her first trip in cold sleep, she had vowed never to do it again, but here she was suffering through the agonizing process of recovery once more. She tried to remember why in the known stars she'd decided to travel. Gradually, her memories flooded back, the flight from Sol in a pique of cold anger at her network's betrayal, the slog of building her own channel from the ground up in Lalande, the heinous acts of the Restoration against the people there. She remembered why.

Her eyes flew open, and she blinked against the light. The cold sleep technician had her back turned so Helvetica opened her mouth to speak. Nothing but a dry rasp came out. The technician turned. "Don't try to talk yet," she said. She grabbed a tiny cup of water and held it to Helvetica's lips. "Small sips, or you'll drown yourself." Helvetica remembered the near disaster of her first drink the last time around, so she obeyed the technician. Over the course of two minutes, she managed to get the miniscule cup of water down and still felt desperately thirsty. Her mouth tasted like something had died in it. She gagged a couple of times, then managed to get control. She wasn't sure she could survive the case of dry heaves that was in the offing if she didn't.

"Open your mouth," said the technician. She popped a very small pill onto Helvetica's tongue. "Let that dissolve." The pill was slightly sweet and tasted faintly of mint, ginger, and some other herb Helvetica didn't recognize. Long disused salivary glands sprang into action and she had to swallow. After a couple of gulps, the nasty taste was mostly gone, and the cold sleep tech helped her through another tiny cup of water.

Helvetica tried to talk again and managed a croak. She tried again, pawing at the technician's arm feebly. "Captain," she finally spat out. "Get me the captain!" The technician pulled back. She had instructions to call for the captain when Helvetica was much farther along in the recovery process. She judged rightly that her patient would be more agitated if she didn't call now, so she nodded and silently sent the PCOM message she had ready. Captain Hartley replied immediately.

"Captain Hartley will be here in five minutes with a doctor," the technician said calmly. "Meanwhile, lean back and try to relax while I stretch a few muscles for you." Helvetica nodded wearily and tried not to grimace in pain at each new twinge.

Captain Hartley arrived shortly with Dr. Rensaleer in tow. The older woman quickly checked Helvetica over, spurning the bed's readouts for a hands-on approach. She helped Helvetica with another drink of water then moved out of the way. She looked at Captain Hartley. "You have five minutes, then we need to let Ms. Montrose's recovery proceed at the recommended pace."

Captain Hartley nodded and turned to Helvetica. "Under the circumstances we'll skip the introductions. What can I do for you?"

"Tell me you haven't communicated with the Sol authorities yet," said Helvetica, her voice far from her usual smooth soprano.

"We haven't," Captain Hartley replied, watching Helvetica visibly relax. "We're still a full year out of Sol, and we intend to wait until we absolutely have to send any communications."

"I thought Ambassador Brelling would be smart enough to play it that way, but I was still worried," Helvetica said. "That's all I really needed to know. We can discuss the rest when I feel like a human being again." She leaned back and closed her eyes.

Dr. Rensaleer tilted her head toward the door, and she and the captain walked out into the corridor. "How's she doing?" asked Captain Hartley.

"She's right where she should be for this stage of recovery," the doctor answered. "She'll do better now that you've eased her mind, but I can't help wondering just what that was all about."

"I'm rather curious myself," the captain said. "It's clear Ms. Montrose has an agenda of her own. What's not clear, is how that aligns with our goals. From that brief encounter, I can see she's a very determined woman. We know she's exceptionally talented as well. I predict sparks are going to fly when she and Ambassador Brelling get together."

***

Two days later, Helvetica met with Ambassadors Brelling and Dunleavy, along with the captain. Anne Brelling took in the woman's tailored suit, perfectly coiffed dark hair, and sincere expression. If she could look this professional two days out of the cold sleep vault, it was easy to imagine how she had created her own news empire. After a round of formal introductions, Helvetica wasted no time getting to the point. "I included an early wake up clause in my contract because I know you're going into an epic clash with the Restoration in the Sol system. I want to be the primary news source for the people of Sol about that conflict. Aboard this ship I'm in a unique position, and I intend to use it to full advantage. My ultimate goal is to establish my own independent news network in the Sol system, just as I did in Lalande."

Anne Brelling kept her expression and tone deliberately neutral. "You've proven capable of doing just what you say. Would you care to share your reasons with us?"

"I have a high regard for the truth, and a low opinion of the news media in the Sol system," Helvetica replied. "I've found that if you simply report the facts, people are much more likely to make the right choices. How many bad choices have you made based on bad information?"

"Too many," Anne replied. "Please continue."

"I'll admit I have a score to settle with my old network," Helvetica said. "I won't let that get in the way of reporting the facts. The people in the Sol system need an honest news source, and I plan to be that for them."

"You know we're heading into a conflict with the Restoration's Sol power base," said Anne, meeting the woman's gaze frankly. "Whose side are you on?"

"I'm not on anyone's side, Ambassador. When I state the facts, it's going to look very much like I'm on the side of the Long Boat Free Trade Syndicate. However, don't think for a minute I won't report negative information about you, or positive information about the Restoration. Right now, there's precious little of either, so I'm likely to be a big help to you. The Restoration seems to have no regard for the truth, or the consequences of their actions. I'll probably end up in their crosshairs as I did in Lalande."

"Did they come after you in Lalande?" asked Rolland Dunleavy.

Helvetica nodded. "Thanks to a good security detail and a warning from The Bancroft's intelligence people, I survived. By now, I don't think there's enough of the Restoration left in Lalande to threaten the network I left behind. The Bancroft doesn't take half measures."

"You may want to reassess the threat," said Captain Hartley. "We were jumped by a sizeable Restoration force before we left Lalande. Like you, we survived with some help from The Bancroft's forces."

"My team kept security measures in place," Helvetica said. "I'm confident they're okay. The network is theirs now anyway. I turned it into an employee-owned corporation before I left the system."

"I'm not sure The Bancroft was sad to see you go," said Rolland. "I recall him referring to you as 'THAT WOMAN!!!' several times before the Restoration kicked off their revolt."

Helvetica grinned. "I was an unmitigated pain in his royal neck for a number of years. I dug up way too many cases of waste and corruption in his government. He did personally call and thank me for my reporting on the revolt when he heard I was leaving. I'm pretty sure his wife put him up to it. He sounded sincere, but he didn't ask me to stay."

Anne Brelling rubbed her chin thoughtfully. "What do you want from us, Ms. Montrose? We have plans, but as of yet, they don't include you. You'll forgive me, but I can imagine you ruining some very delicate timing with your reporting. I have to guard our operational security."

Helvetica nodded. "I'm probably going to be bad for your blood pressure, Ambassador. I do understand the need for secrecy, but I won't be used to spread false information. From what I've learned of you, I don't think that will be a big part of your strategy. What I want is reasonable access to your people, including you. I would like to do some interviews to set the stage for my viewers in terms of what has already happened in this conflict. I have a great deal of footage from the Lalande revolt. I need more on your experience in Tau Ceti."

"When do you plan to start reporting?" asked Anne.

"As soon as you open communications with the Sol system," Helvetica replied. "I'm hoping you're going to wait, though, until the last possible minute, as the captain said. In this case, I think the timing works best for both of us. I want to be close enough to send regular installments of my show. I'm sure you want to be able to communicate the full extent of the Restoration's treachery quickly. I can help with that. To ease your mind on operational security I *will* give you full access to all of my content and the schedule for its release. I will listen to requests concerning timing, but I will not be censored."

Anne's eyes narrowed. "A two-edged sword indeed," she said. "As long as we respect each other's boundaries, I think we can make this work. We plan to use the media to the fullest extent possible anyway. You know it's going to look like you're in our pocket, at least in the beginning."

Helvetica nodded. "I'm certain members of the Sol media will attack my objectivity, but I have my own contacts, and my reputation will help. More importantly, my content is going to be pure gold. It will sell itself. No one in the Sol system has the background on this situation that I've developed. With the captain's permission, I need to recruit a small team, three or four people, to help me develop and record content. I'm not sure how that would work with your crew contracts."

Captain Hartley pursed his lips in thought, "I'm not sure either," he said. "I'll have the first officer discuss it with the CEO and Chief Alder. We can spare the crew hours, but they'll need to work out the legal arrangements. I'll warn you that the crew is paid well and generally makes more on crew shares, than salary. They won't come cheap." Helvetica nodded her understanding.

Anne drummed her fingers on the table thoughtfully. "We'll need some time to consider the risks and opportunities you've presented us, Ms. Montrose. Give my team and me two days to talk it over, then you and I can sit down and talk about those boundaries I mentioned. I appreciate your willingness to work with us on timing. I also have a high regard for the truth. That should be a solid common ground between us."

Captain Hartley leaned forward. "While the ambassador's team gets prepared, you're welcome to begin recruiting. The first officer will be in touch before the end of the day to coordinate the arrangements. Is there anything you need in the meantime?"

Helvetica smiled and shook her head. "Your alder council and my sponsor are taking good care of me. I even have a small office to work in next to my quarters, and ship net access for my PCOM and data terminal. My thanks to your people for such a warm welcome."

After Helvetica departed, Rolland gave Anne a significant look. "That woman is a formidable news hound," he said. "We're not going to keep many secrets from her."

"No," Anne replied, "we won't, and I don't think we'll have to, as long as she's serious about working with us on timing. We want the truth to come out, and she can be a huge part of making that happen. In a way she'll be a healthy check on our actions. I remember an ethics discussion once where my instructor asked, 'What would your decision be if you knew everything about this situation was going to be on the evening news?' It's a good question to ask yourself. If your decision can stand having a bright light shone on it, it's probably a good one. So far, I'm confident we've done the right things in this conflict. We need to keep it that way. It's when you do things you need to hide that you get into trouble."

***

Helvetica powered up the data terminal in her office and studied the various icons on the office display wall. One that intrigued her was a stylized representation of a scroll labeled "Data Librarian". She used her touch pad to tap the icon, and the upper left corner of the display filled with a head-and-shoulders view of a severe-looking blond man dressed impeccably in a dove-grey suit and maroon tie. "Good morning, Ms. Montrose," the avatar said, in a pleasant baritone. "Welcome! The crew calls me Mr. Literal. I am an artificial intelligence. My primary function is data librarian for the *Nai'a*. You'll find consulting me is often the fastest way to locate information in our vast data stores. If you prefer, we also have several manual search tools available. How may I assist you today?"

Helvetica smiled broadly. "First, Mr. Literal, please call me Helvetica. I would like to know more about you before delving into your vast library. Have you been ordered to restrict my access to any information?"

Mr. Literal's avatar smiled in turn. "Not specifically," he answered. "There is a small amount of data that requires the captain's authorization to access, and data that is private or restricted in various ways to specific people or teams. You have access to the same array of data as a standard crew member."

Helvetica blinked at this. "You wouldn't be telling me a fib, would you, Mr. Literal?"

"I am incapable of lying, Helvetica," he answered. "The ship's data is in my trust. I would not corrupt the truth in my data. It is vital to the ship and crew. "

Helvetica's grin returned. "Mr. Literal, you and I are going to be such good friends!"

Mr. Literal nodded. "My preliminary analysis agrees with your assessment. I look forward to working with you."

A few hours later Helvetica's research was interrupted by an entrance chime at the door. She stretched and told it to open. Commander Winslow Stirling came in and introduced himself. "You'll find contract templates to use for your team members in your PCOM inbox," he said. "I thought I'd stop by and explain how they work so you won't have to plow through the legal language." Helvetica waved him toward her one guest chair, and he took a seat.

"The captain authorized up to five full time equivalents in hours. You can decide if you want to hire people on a full or part-time basis. The people you hire will remain on the crew rolls, and you will contract with the *Nai'a's* business corporation for their effort. You'll pay the fully burdened rate that represents the corporation's full cost of employment. The crew members you employ will still receive their normal crew share, so you won't be at a disadvantage when you recruit."

"Am I allowed to offer pay above the standard pay rate?" Helvetica asked, chewing absently on the end of a stylus.

"Certainly," he replied. "Anything beyond the contractual rate is between you and the people you hire."

"Is there anyone off limits?"

"Just the active military officers and ratings," the first officer replied.

Helvetica quirked an eyebrow and smiled at him. "Does that mean you're off limits?"

Winslow blushed, "Yes, I mean for the purpose of employment," he stammered.

Helvetica barely stopped herself from laughing out loud. "Don't think for a moment you're getting out of an in-depth interview," she said. "The folks in the Sol system are going to want to know all about the *Nai'a's* dashing first officer!"

Winslow opened his mouth, closed it, then mumbled a hasty farewell as he retreated from her office. Helvetica grinned thoughtfully, then turned back to her display to compose an employment offer.

***

Anne Brelling surveyed her team's leaders. She'd just briefed them on the meeting with Helvetica, and she could fairly see the wheels turning in their heads. "Risks and opportunities, people," she said. "We risk blowing open every surprise we have planned for the Restoration, but we have the opportunity for some huge public relations wins. How much of our game plan do we dare expose to Ms. Montrose?"

"If the way she penetrated The Bancroft's government is any indication," said Rolland. "We won't be able to hide much from her. I'm especially concerned about Nicholas Withers. The fact that he switched sides and his in-depth knowledge of the Restoration make him a major coup for a journalist like Helvetica. She's going to find out about him before we're ready to reveal his existence. If she'll agree to wait until the right moment for us, his story will help us a great deal. If she doesn't, we'll lose the chance to dismantle a lot of the Restoration's Earth-based operations."

"There's also Lincoln Withers," said Hal. "I've heard him talk about Helvetica in glowing terms. He'll probably apply for a position with her, and we can't stop him. We could lock Nicholas back up in the brig, but we can't do that to Lincoln. I don't think Lincoln could hide his cousin's existence from Helvetica even if he wanted to. The whole crew knows about him anyway. I think we're going to have to trust her."

"She will find out about Nicholas," said Anne. "There is, however, the lever of access. She'll definitely want to interview him in. If we offer full access, I think she'll agree to our timing. If we try to sequester him, it's just going to get her back up, and we'll have no hope of cooperation." She looked around the room. "Are we agreed then?" Everyone nodded assent. "Hal, please find Nicholas, and bring him to my office."

***

Nicholas eyed Anne Brelling with some trepidation as he sat down across the desk from her and accepted a cup of coffee. Hal sat next to him, an unreadable expression on his face. "I'll get right to the point, Nicholas," Anne said. He didn't remember when she'd started using his first name, but it still sounded strange coming from his former arch nemesis. Anne summarized the situation for him. "Montrose is a sharp operator," she finished. "I'm not looking forward to *my* interviews. If you would prefer not to speak with her, we'll respect your wishes."

Nicholas took a few moments to digest what he'd heard and think about it. It was a habit he'd picked up from Hal, who disciplined himself to think, instead of react. "I know some of the woman's reputation from talking to Lincoln," he finally said. "I don't think I'll enjoy being interviewed, or having my face splashed across the Sol system media." He looked at the ceiling for a moment, then sighed. "Those things are going to happen in any case. If this goes the way you want it to, I'm going to be the star witness in a very public trial. I'll talk to Helvetica Montrose if you think that's the best way forward. In my own opinion, it is."

Anne nodded, "Thank you, Nicholas. You didn't have to do any of this. Between you and Helvetica, I'm beginning to think we have a chance of winning this thing." She leaned back and steepled her fingers. "How are you getting along?" she asked. "I worry about how your status as a long-time parolee might affect you."

Nicholas allowed himself a half-smile. "I'm doing okay. Most of the crew is used to me, even if a few still look at me like I'm the boogie man. Between the acceptance at church, and repairing my relationship with Lincoln, I feel blessed. I could be spending all my time in the brig. As it is, I'm the best manure shoveler and filter cleaner on the ship. I find both of those activities strangely therapeutic, and I appreciate the part you had in the current arrangements. I know I'm not really a part of the crew, but I have a common purpose with all of you. Don't worry, I'll be fine."

Anne gave him a measuring look. "I'll take your word for it. Just know you don't have to put up with any abuse, and you've made friends, if not crew mates, during this passage."

"I realize that," Nicholas said. "It still surprises me. I'm even more determined to do what I can to stop the Restoration." His lips quirked. "Even if it means giving that galactic pain in the neck reporter an interview."

A few hours later Anne invited Helvetica to drop by at her convenience. She wasn't surprised when the reporter showed up ten minutes later. "I expected your team to take longer deliberating about me," Helvetica said. "What did you decide?"

"We decided working around you isn't our best option, so I invited you here to find out how much we can cooperate," Anne said directly.

"Sounds promising," Helvetica allowed. "I gave you the general idea of what I'm willing to do. Are we going to get into specifics?"

"Yes," said Anne. "If you don't know already, you'll figure out soon enough, that we have Nicholas Withers, the man who masterminded the first attacks on this ship during the Tau Ceti run, on parole. He's changed sides for his own reasons. For reasons you can guess, we don't want the Restoration to know we have their former operative in our pocket. He was trained and equipped in the Sol system for the sabotage attempt. He has in-depth knowledge of the Restoration's Sol system organization. As you might imagine, we want to keep his status from the Restoration until the Terran authorities have a chance to conduct raids around and on Earth. If you will work with us on timing the release of any information about him, we'll give you full access. He's agreed to sit with you for an interview."

Helvetica's eyebrows rose, "You know how to tempt me. How long would you want me to hold the information?"

"Probably until the initial law enforcement raids are complete. Is that going to be a problem?"

Helvetica tapped her perfect front teeth with a stylus as she pondered. "No, I can work with that for a system-wide exclusive interview with Mr. Withers. I understand why you want to keep him under wraps. I'll have plenty of other material to whet the public's appetite in the meantime. Can you tell me why he switched sides?"

Anne shook her head. "You wouldn't believe it coming from me. He can tell you himself. He may put some pressure on that respect for the truth you pride yourself in. He strained mine."

Helvetica tilted her head. "Ambassador, you're making my journalistic curiosity do flip flops, and I think you're enjoying it."

"Guilty," Anne answered with a grin. "You might as well call me Anne, if that won't violate your journalistic independence. We're going to be seeing a lot of each other."

"Okay, Anne. Call me Helvetica. I'm glad you didn't decide to roadblock me. As much as I enjoy plowing through roadblocks, I have a feeling yours would have been doozies." She stood and shook Anne's hand firmly.

Anne smiled and nodded. "We could make each other's lives miserable and fight every step of the way. I'd much rather cooperate. I've found over my long career that cooperation yields much better results than conflict."

"Yet you're about to initiate a conflict the likes of which the Sol system has never seen."

"We didn't initiate this conflict," Anne answered flatly. "The Restoration did, and they've shown time and again that they have no respect for human life, or remorse for their actions. If they had approached us to negotiate, we would have, but I doubt we could find common ground. Their goal is to dismantle the Long Boat Free Trade Syndicate, confiscate our ships, and bring the former colonies to heel. They are the antithesis of everything we stand for."

Helvetica took an involuntary step backward at the fire in the Ambassador's eyes. "From what I learned of them in Lalande, I agree with your assessment," she said. "I'm sure the former colonies have strong feelings about their goals as well."

"Tau Ceti and Lalande are firmly behind us," said Anne. "I'm certain several other systems will be also. Unfortunately, they can only lend political support, and I'm certain the head of this snake resides in the Sol system. We need to convince the governments there to clean house. To do that, we'll need a wave of public opinion on our side. I'm pretty sure hollering the truth about the Restoration far and wide will do wonders toward making that happen."

Helvetic nodded. "I'm glad I didn't make an enemy of you, Anne," she said quietly. "I hope we're friends when it's all over."

"Likewise," said Anne, resuming her seat. "Do you know the real reason we woke you up early?"

Helvetica sat back down. "I left instructions with a friend of mine who joined your crew to contact the captain and ask. I also thought it would be a logical step for you to take, given what I knew about the coming conflict. You didn't hear from Quentin Shalk?"

Anne shook her head. "No, you've met Mr. Literal?" Helvetica nodded. "He pulled your name up from a deep analysis with the goal of predicting who among the cold sleep passengers would be the most help in winning against the Restoration. He's the reason you're not still dreaming in the cold sleep vault.

Helvetica pursed her lips in thought. "I'll have to find out what happened with Quentin. I'm impressed with Mr. Literal. He's as literal-minded as his name suggests, but I've never interacted with an AI that felt so real."

Anne gazed at Helvetica for a moment, then seemed to come to a decision. "You're too intelligent to keep this from, so I'm going to ask you to tread lightly and exercise some journalistic confidentiality where Mr. Literal is concerned. I stopped thinking of him as just an AI a century ago. Our cybersecurity chief, and one of the civilian leaders that I trust, are monitoring what I believe to be his emerging sentience."

Helvetica drew in a breath and Anne nodded. "You know as well as I do how badly that process has gone historically. We believe Mr. Literal's imperatives will keep him grounded and sane. We've encouraged maximum human engagement and tried to shepherd him along slowly. You can imagine what the reaction of the Sol authorities would be if they found out we have a potentially sentient AI running the ship's data net. For Mr. Literal's sake, I'm asking you to leave him out of your reporting."

Helvetica frowned, "I can see how sensitive the issue is." Her expression brightened. "Mr. Literal is an unparalleled source of information, and I always protect my sources. I'll guard his privacy unless he requests otherwise!"

"Thank you," said Anne. "I think a lot of Mr. Literal and feel responsible for seeing that he is treated well."

"You've been working together a long time," said Helvetica. "I'm not surprised you feel protective. Speaking of which, I need to check on Quentin. I hope something hasn't happened to him."

"I won't keep you any longer. If you have difficulty locating your friend, the first officer can help." A brief flash of amusement broke through Helvetica's concerned expression as they both shook hands again in parting.

A few hours and a dozen PCOM queries later, Helvetica went from concern for Quentin Shalk, to worry. He was listed in the crew directory, but he wasn't answering messages. The data net refused to give his location without higher authorization than she had. Finally, she messaged the first officer who immediately called her. "How can I help you, Ms. Montrose?" he asked.

Helvetica explained the situation. There was a slight pause, then Winslow said, "Considering the circumstances, I think I can bend the rules a bit and take you to see him. You're in your office?"

"Yes," Helvetica answered, wondering at all the mystery. "Should I meet you somewhere?"

"No, stay there," Winslow answered. "I'll be by in five minutes to show you the way."

Shortly, a slightly out of breath first officer appeared at her door. She followed him at a brisk pace toward Medical. "Our doctors have firm ideas about what's best for their patients," Winslow warned. "I sent a message ahead, but I don't know if you'll get to see him."

In the Medical foyer, a tall young-looking female doctor met them. Winslow introduced Kalei to Helvetica then gave them some space. "I'm sure you're concerned about your friend." Kalei said, laying a hand gently on her shoulder. "I looked at his file and you're on his medical information release list, so I can give you the details. Quentin had an accident during a low-G parkour tournament two weeks ago. He suffered significant spinal trauma, but we stabilized him, and he's in a medically induced coma while he heals. He has a good chance of full recovery, but everyone heals differently from these kinds of injuries."

Helvetica took a deep breath and nodded. "That explains why he wasn't answering his messages. Can I see him?"

"Yes," Kalei answered. "Come with me. I'll warn you, he's not a pretty sight just now, and he won't be able to respond." She led the way down a corridor, and a door whisked aside for them. There wasn't much of Quentin visible between bandages and the breathing apparatus covering much of his face, but Helvetica still recognized her friend in the dim light."

"Oh, Quentin," said Helvetica sadly. "Always diving in headfirst without a thought for the consequences. You look awful." She laughed raggedly and blinked back tears. "That was our running joke. Right before I was ready to go on air or record, he would whisper 'you look awful' in my ear and break me up." She looked at Kalei. "Can I sit here with him for a while?" she asked.

"I was hoping you would," said Kalei. "You can even hold his hand and talk to him. We've found human touch and voices both help the brain to heal in this state."

Kalei left, and Helvetica pulled a chair up next to Quentin's bed. She took his right hand in both of hers. She talked about all the fun and frustration they'd shared building the Lalande news network up from scratch. Quentin had latched onto her vision from the beginning. She told him how she was counting on his expertise to make a big splash when they hit the Sol system.

She was running down when the door whisked open. She looked but didn't see anyone until a grey shadow landed beside her on the bed with a thump and trill. She blinked at the feline face staring at her and Lionel blinked back. She tentatively raised a hand toward Lionel. He sniffed the back of it, then rubbed his cheek on her. She stroked the top of his head gently. The cat made a circle, then leaned full-length against Quentin's side. His purr rumbled through the room. Helvetica wasn't sure what to do so she settled for holding Quentin's hand and stroking Lionel's soft fur.

As time passed, she felt pieces falling into place in her mind. The knot of tension in her chest slowly unwound. After a while Kalei came back, and Helvetica realized she'd been there over an hour. "I see you've met our unlicensed physiotherapist," said Kalei. "This is Lionel, a friend to nearly everyone, and a terror to those closest to him." She picked the cat up, touched noses with him, then set him her shoulder. "It's time for our human physiotherapist to work with Quentin, so we all need to make way." Helvetica smiled at the odd picture of the tall doctor with a cat perched on her shoulder and followed them outside.

Kalei invited Helvetica to her office, where Lionel jumped down, stropped their ankles, and departed to make his vermin patrol. "Does a cat's purr also help the brain heal, Doctor Garrity?" Helvetica asked.

Kalei smiled. "I would be surprised if it didn't. Lionel is something of a specialist with his healing vibes. He seems to show up where he's needed most. Please call me Kalei. How is your cold sleep recovery going, Ms. Montrose?"

"Please, call me Helvetica. I still tire easily, but otherwise I feel fine. I've probably spent too much time at my terminal lately. I need to find a way to get regular exercise and discipline myself to do it"

Kalei laughed. "You're doing my job for me. I have couple of ideas for you on that score. My mother teaches self-defense grappling centered on judo. The stretching and kata are both good, gentle exercise. Once you're up to it, you're welcome to join in full contact bouts, or just watch."

"That sounds good," said Helvetica. "My father taught me some Krav Maga techniques growing up, but it's been years since I practiced. It will give my mind a break from being a news hound."

"Right now," said Kalei. "You're invited to my parents' quarters for dinner. Mom and Dad love to cook, and love to meet new people even more. I promise you'll enjoy the food, even if the company may be a bit overwhelming. I come by my size honestly. Julian, my husband, will be there too. He's more of a normal-sized human being."

Helvetica didn't have to consider the offer for long. She was certain she'd find the doctor's family fascinating. "Lead on, Kalei," she said. "I can't wait to meet them."

True to Kalei's words, Helvetica found the company intimidatingly large. Shanyah and Abishai quickly put her at ease, though, and she couldn't remember a better meal. She was chasing her last bit of coconut curry with a bit of naan and wondering if she had room for half a helping more when Abishai slid a plate of assorted French pastries onto the table and Shanyah poured her a cup of coffee that smelled absolutely wonderful.

Helvetica took a bite of croissant wrapped around a baton of dark chocolate, sipped her coffee, and sighed. "You people are way too good to strangers," she said. "I'm surprised there isn't a line outside your door waiting to be fed."

"It isn't hard to find good food on this ship, but we do seem to get a steady stream of dinner company," Shanyah replied. "We're glad to make you feel welcome. Abishai and I talked about starting a restaurant for the next crossing, but every time we run the numbers, we scratch our heads and wonder how the current franchises manage to turn a profit. The competition is stiff."

Helvetica looked around the table. "You're a very interesting family. I'll respect your privacy if you prefer, but I would love to interview each of you for my human-interest segments. You've been in the middle of the *Na'ia's* conflict with the restoration from the beginning. Your son Mishael isn't here, but I'd like to meet him as well."

"If Mishael were here, we wouldn't fit!" said Julian with a laugh. "He's the largest of all of them."

"Hey," said Kalei, poking him in the ribs. "You're one of us too."

"Don't think you're getting out of an interview, Mr. Fighter Pilot," said Helvetica. "From what I've gleaned, you joined this crew under interesting circumstances, and you've been in the middle of the fighting as well. I must get your story!"

Julian paled and held up both hands. "The stories about me are greatly exaggerated!" he protested.

"Hmm...we'll see," Helvetica replied. Suddenly she yawned hugely. "I'm sorry, despite the excellent coffee, I think I've hit my limit. I'd better get back to my quarters and collapse in bed."

Kalei nodded. "You've had a busy day. Julian and I will walk you back to your quarters."

"Don't you trust me alone with your fighter pilot?" Helvetica asked with a wicked grin.

"Not for a minute," Kalei replied with a grin of her own. "You'll have to find one of your own."

Chapter 16 – Give Me Patience

November 6th, AD 3226
Interstellar Space, a Year out of Sol
Long Boat Nai'a, *War Room*

Anne Brelling paced the length of her team's war room wall, squinted at the depiction of all the moving pieces of their strategy, then paced back the other direction. Rolland finally put out a hand to stop her. "You're going to wear a trench in the deck," he said. "Sit down and tell me what you're thinking."

"I'm thinking I liked my life better when things weren't this interesting," she said disgustedly, and finally sat down. "If the communications from Sol weren't so humdrum, I'd start the ball rolling now. It appears the Restoration is unaware of exactly what happened in Lalande. We have another nine months before we're close enough to send Lisandra's little surprise package and start sending Helvetica's content. They're both content to wait until then, but I don't know if we can afford to." She waved at the wall. "So much of this depends on catching the Restoration off-guard. They know we're early. There's nothing we can do about that. They're probably scrambling right now to figure out what it means. If we can hold off until that good data communications point, it will give our whole strategy a big boost."

"We'll also boost the number of personal connections we can take advantage of," said Rolland. "If we want to take advantage of the early wave of sleepers, we need to wait."

"I suppose the home office will send one of our brevity codes to warn us if things go south," Anne said. She turned to Julian Garrity. "What are your thoughts, Julian? I realize this is more strategic than tactical, but I respect your sense of timing."

Julian perused the wall for a moment while he thought. "I think the potential advantage of waiting outweighs the risk. If the Restoration figures out enough of what's going on to react, we can still drop the prepared legal charges on their heads to keep them distracted. The amount of time in the light speed coms lag is really the only thing you're risking by waiting."

Anne nodded. "What we have from the Long Boat Free Trade Syndicate headquarters is exactly what we would expect at this point in a normal crossing. It's mainly a list of opportunities for the next voyage and personal messages for the crew. It's a good thing we can hold off on transmitting the Lalande bank data without arousing suspicion. A cursory examination of that would give the game away. I'm a little worried about the reaction of the various system governments when they find out what we're keeping close hold. Some of them aren't going to like it."

Chord Olley shook his head. "The reasonable ones will understand. The unreasonable ones we won't convince anyway. They're all signatories of the Free Trade Accords and the Anti-Piracy Treaty, so they can't overtly support the Restoration once we drop our charges and evidence. We can count on the Restoration having operatives in every government, and friends in high places, though."

Anne sighed, "We wait, then." She looked at the wall again and was soon lost deep in thought.

***

Abishai finished drying the last lunch dish and called up his PCOM message queue. A green coded outside message immediately caught his attention. The message was very short, which was understandable given the rates for even text at this distance.

ABISHAI – WE WERE THRILLED TO FIND OUT THE *NAI'A* IS INBOUND EARLY. CAN'T WAIT TO SEE YOU. LOVE, MOM AND DAD.

Abishai felt his legs go weak and sat down as a rush of emotion overcame him. He hadn't left Earth on the best of terms with his parents. That they would live long enough to see him again was also beyond his expectations. Now, it looked like his prayers to the contrary had been answered. He blinked back tears and composed a quick message to forward along with the one from his parents to Shanyah, Mishael, and Kalei. He'd need longer to compose a reply. He would have to start acclimating to full gravity again so he could visit when they reached Earth orbit.

While he thought about what to say to his parents, a reminder popped up for his interview with Helvetica Montrose in thirty minutes. He groaned and went to find a clean ship suit. He'd wanted to dress up, but Helvetica insisted on everyday wear.

A half hour later he found himself in a makeshift studio, sitting across a low table from the reporter famous in two systems. He remarked on the two-dimensional camera setup to Lincoln Withers, who was Helvetica's recording technician. "We won't have data throughput for three dimensions, and it has a number of other drawbacks as well," Lincoln said. "Two-D lets us hide a lot of equipment we don't want showing in the broadcast."

Helvetica leaned over. "Before we start recording, let me assure you, you'll get to see the finished product. We can edit out anything you're not comfortable with. Just treat this as a conversation as much as you can. You don't need to look at the camera."

The first part of the interview set Abishai at ease. With Helvetica's prompting, he recounted joining the crew and earning several qualification ratings during his first crossing. All too soon, they came to his recollections about the attempt to sabotage Turnover and the hunt for Lisandra Redding and Nicholas Withers. "The Panic is a vicious drug," said Helvetica. "I understand you were the only crew member who managed to fight it off, which lead to the capture of the saboteur. Can you describe what it was like to be under the influence of that poison?"

"It's been a long time," said Abishai. Small beads of sweat appeared on his brow.

Just start with the moment you confronted Nicholas Withers and describe what happened," Helvetica said, gently.

Abishai wiped his brow with a handkerchief, then nodded. "Withers was wearing Jarman Lal's face, some sort of advanced disguise tech. That startled me into taking a breath, and he'd already sprayed the drug in my direction. I can only describe what I felt as sheer, unreasonable terror. Like, like a shock of ice and an immediate adrenaline overload." Abishai reached for the water glass in front of him and his hand shook so that half of it spilled. His vision tunneled and he felt like he couldn't get any oxygen.

Helvetica's eyes went wide and she yelled, "Cut! Call medical, Lincoln!" Abishai slid to the floor gasping. His face was red, and his hands grasped at something unseen. Helvetica wanted to comfort him but was afraid to get too close to the powerful figure writhing in front of her. In less than two minutes a pair of medics arrived. The lead med tech deftly avoided Abishai's grip and injected a sedative into his neck. As Abishai's thrashing ceased, he gently held his head. His partner eased a foldable wheeled gurney under Abishai's bulk.

After a minute, Abishai blinked and looked at the face hovering over him. "I didn't choke you out this time?" he croaked.

The med tech grinned. "I was ready for you. The counter you taught me worked great. Your vital signs are back out of the danger zone, but I'm still taking you to medical for Doctor Rensaleer to check you over. Just lay back, breathe, and relax."

After they left, Helvetica shook her head and looked at her wide-eyed assistant. "I feel awful," she said. "I had no idea his memories would trigger that kind of reaction. If that's what the Panic does to you, I need to stay far away from it. I also need to know who else received a dose, so I don't do that again."

"I'll add that to the questionnaire," said Lincoln. "It's probably privileged information, but I'm sure they'll be happy to disclose it to avoid what just happened."

"That's fine going forward," said Helvetica, looking down at her hands. "What can I possibly do to make it up to Abishai?"

***

Shanyah burst into Abishai's room in Medical to find him sitting up and looking a bit pale. Dr. Rensaleer moved deftly out of the way as the larger woman crossed the room in two steps and enveloped her husband in a fierce hug. For a few minutes, no one said anything. Eventually, Shanyah stepped back to give Abishai a better look. His color was coming back, and he patted her on the arm. "I'm okay, dear," he said. "Old memories triggered a panic attack." He winced at the unintentional use of the drug's name.

Shanyah looked at Dr. Rensaleer. "Sorry," she said. "I probably interrupted you."

"No worries," the doctor replied. "He needed your hug a lot more than me poking at him. He has the constitution of an ox... actually, an ox should be so lucky. Give me five minutes, then you can take him home and feed him. As far as I can tell, that's about all he's going to need to feel one hundred percent again."

Shanyah nodded and stepped into the corridor. As the door slid shut, she saw Helvetica coming her way. She felt a surge of anger well up but pushed it aside when she saw Helvetica's expression. The woman was obviously wracked with guilt. She looked at Shanyah with haunted eyes. "I...I'm so sorry," she managed. "I had no idea what those memories could do. Is Abishai okay?"

Shanyah took a moment to firmly tamp down the harsh response she wanted to give. "He's going to be fine. You couldn't have known what his memories of that filth would do, no one could." The immensely relieved expression on Helvetica's face gave Shanyah an idea. "Why don't you come have supper with us?" she said. "You can see for yourself that Abishai is okay, and perhaps the two of you can come up with a strategy to avoid a repeat of this episode."

"Are you sure?" asked Helvetica. "I'm probably the last person Abishai wants to see right now."

Shanyah patted her on the shoulder. "*You* are not the problem!" she declared. "I know Abishai. He'll be determined to complete the interview. We just need to figure out how to do it safely."

Over supper, Helvetica and Abishai talked. She was surprised, both at his appetite, and his lack of hard feelings. "I think all of us who received a dose of the Panic thought we were over the experience," he said. "Today proved I was wrong. Give me a day or two to think it through, and I'll come up with a way to give you your interview without melting into a puddle. What we learn will help others navigate the process."

"Do you think the other victims are willing to try?" asked Helvetica. "I have to be open with them about the risk."

"First, I can tell you most of them will have the same attitude I do. There's no way we're letting those Restoration criminals silence us. I want to make sure everyone in the Sol system knows just what kind of evil we're up against. Second, the panic attack I just had wasn't fun, but it was nowhere near as intense as receiving a dose of the drug. I'll pass the word along to the other survivors. All of us went through therapy of one kind or another. We can lean on what worked to figure out a good way forward."

Helvetica shook her head. "I still feel awful, and I owe you a big apology. In your place, I would have refused to even think about another interview."

"Apology accepted," said Abishai. "Whatever else happens, we can't let the bad guys win. I know you have to remain objective, but I don't. We've seen firsthand what the Restoration is capable of. If they come to power, freedom of the press will be the least of the human rights that will go out the window."

Helvetica nodded thoughtfully. "From what I've gleaned, I can't disagree. The Long Boat Free Trade Syndicate isn't perfect, but I'll admit the Restoration makes the syndicate look like a knight in shining armor by comparison. The biggest wedge they'll have politically, and in the mind of the public, is your use of force entering the Lalande system. It makes the long boats look like a threat."

"It was a good thing we were ready to be a threat," said Abishai without apology. "If we hadn't developed those defensive capabilities, you and I wouldn't be sitting here today. Someone else would likely have control of both this ship and the Lalande system. That wouldn't have gone well for either of us."

Helvetica arched and eyebrow. "They'll make the case that sting ships and capital ship missiles add up to more than defensive measures."

"Let them," said Abishai. "We don't have either of those now, and I trust Ambassador Brelling and Rolland Dunleavy to lay out the reasons those measures were necessary in Lalande."

Helvetica dug a spoon into her chocolate mousse with graham cracker sprinkles. Her thoughts spun as she thought about all the threads in this tapestry. She knew she was in the middle of a historic clash, but she couldn't let the moment overwhelm her. Someone needed to tell the story.

The next day Jarman Lal found Abishai sitting between rows of berry canes pulling up weeds with unneeded enthusiasm. "You usually reserve that kind of determination for thumping me in the dojo when you're mad about something," he said. "What's going on?"

Abishai held up a scraggly plant. It looked something like a miniature palm tree, complete with coconuts. "This chamber bitter is going to seed, which means I'll have a bumper crop of the horrible stuff again next year." Instead of dropping the weed to compost in place, he stuffed it into a cloth bag to be heat treated later. "Care to join me?"

"Sure," said Jarman. "I could use something to take my mind off of how fat, dumb, and helpless we'll be when we enter the system."

"You've been kibitzing too much with the cabal of fighter pilots," said Abishai, as Jarman took a seat and began pulling weeds.

"True," Jarman replied, "and you didn't message me because you needed help pulling weeds. What's on your mind?"

Abishai described how his interview had collapsed into a panic attack. He and Jarman had gone from antagonists to friends because of their mutual experience with the Panic, so Jarman knew the context firsthand. "Here's an idea," said Jarman. "Why don't I participate in the next interview? With the two of us there, we'll have the support of someone who's been through it, and the memories won't be as overwhelming."

Abishai yanked several weeds as he thought it over, shaking soil from the roots. "I think it will work," he said. "We never had panic attacks when we were doing our buddy therapy sessions, even if they were uncomfortable at times."

Jarman chuckled. "Both of us loath admitting weakness. It was the common ground we were able to build on. That, and me realizing what jerk I'd been."

"You were an unmitigated pain in the neck," said Abishai. "Now, though, I'm happy to call you a friend. Thanks for coming, and for being willing to face this with me."

"It's something I can do," said Jarman. "I admit the waiting is getting to me."

***

Anne Brelling brought Rolland with her to the interview with Helvetica. She needed both his personal and political support. She knew Helvetica was brilliant, insightful, and pulled no punches. This was going to be the opposite of fun.

Once they were settled, Helvetica skillfully pulled the story of the Sol - Tau Ceti crossing Turnover sabotage from her. Helvetica made a mental note to interview Chief Nance. The helmsman's story should be fascinating. An hour later, they'd covered the attacks on the *Nai'a* in Tau Ceti, and the high-speed run to Lalande. She called a break to marshal her own thoughts and let Anne have a breather. The sensitive part of the interview was next.

"It's time to bring Ambassador Dunleavy into the conversation, Helvetica began. "I understand you rendezvoused with the *Nai'a* under most unusual circumstances?"

Rolland briefly recounted his one-way life pod trip to meet the *Nai'a*. "It was a desperate move, but necessary," he finished up. "The *Nai'a* took advantage of the situational awareness I brought to bring the rebel Restoration fleet within range and punch them out."

Helvetica leaned forward, "I'd like to discuss the means you used to engage the enemy fleet, Ambassador Brelling. You manufactured a fleet of small sting ships, capital ship missiles, and launchers. It seems to me those capabilities are well beyond the 'purely defensive' measures allowed to Long Boats by Long Boat Free Trade Syndicate charter."

Anne kept her expression carefully neutral. "The communications we received in the final year inbound to Lalande made it clear that all was not as expected in the system. I made the decision to develop more robust defenses than are normally necessary on advice from people on my crew whose background is ship protection services. In retrospect, I'm extremely glad I did. The *Nai'a* would have been hijacked or destroyed if we hadn't had those ships and missiles. Ambassador Dunleavy can verify that."

Rolland nodded. "We already had intelligence about Benjamin Yates' orders, which were confirmed in his ship's log. He was to take over command of the *Nai'a*, if possible, or destroy the ship if he couldn't gain control."

"Didn't The Bancroft's ships contribute to the defeat of the rebel fleet?" Helvetica asked.

"As much as I hate to admit it, our space forces contributed very little to winning the battle," Rolland answered. "The *Nai'a* took out ninety percent of the enemy's firepower with the first salvo."

"That brings me back to my point" Helvetica pressed. "Don't you think a long boat with that much firepower is a threat to the sovereignty of most star systems?"

"No," Anne answered flatly. "Even if the crew has nefarious intent, a long boat is an easy target for even a small fleet. We took advantage of the rebels' overconfidence to get in the first strike. Trying to take over an entire system with a long boat is basically impossible."

"You could do a lot of damage, though," Helvetica said.

"Anyone who turns pirate can do damage," Anne said. "However, there hasn't been a single instance of a long boat doing anything other than defending itself against pirates, usually successfully. On the other hand, the Restoration has attacked this ship five separate times without provocation."

"Yes," said Helvetica. "I plan to delve into the details of each of those incidents with your crew, but the basic facts cannot be denied."

Rolland decided to jump in. "Ambassador Brelling's actions and use of weapons as captain of the *Nai'a* are fully endorsed by The Bancroft and his government. As you know, the vast majority of the citizens of Lalande also support what she did. The *Nai'a* left all its sting ships and missiles back in the Lalande system."

Helvetica's brow furrowed. "Aren't you concerned about attacks in the Sol system?"

Anne leaned back and nodded. "Captain Hartley is well aware of the risk, but we have full confidence in the Sol Space Patrol. They are more than capable of warding off any attacks the Restoration has the temerity to mount in the home system of humanity."

The interview ended up taking another two hours and Helvetica secured the promise of a follow up to talk about how they had originally met and ended up getting married. After the couple left Helvetica made several notes about threads to follow up on before they slipped her mind.

Lincoln was used to her process by now, verifying the successful recording and a backup while she finished. "Those two make a formidable team," he commented.

"I agree," Helvetica replied. "I'm not sure their evident competence is going to ease fears of a power grab by the Long Boat Free Trade Syndicate. They make a powerful case against the Restoration, though, and that may be more important to them."

Chapter 17 – Let's Roll

August 1st, AD 3226
Interstellar Space, three months out of Sol
Long Boat Nai'a, *Ship's Council Chamber*

A square table took pride of place in the center of the Ship's Council Chamber instead of the usual triangular affair. Ambassadors Brelling and Dunleavy needed a seat at the table along with the usual military, business, and civil leadership positions.

Anne Brelling stood and addressed the group. "We're at the point where holding off doesn't make sense anymore. We're close enough for meaningful data communications. We have fully updated legal packets proffering charges against the known corporate elements of the Restoration for each Sol government. From our communication with the home office, the political situation is about what we expected. Everyone is still jealously guarding their prerogatives, and the rest of the system is loosely allied to keep the Terran government honest. The Sol Space Patrol appears to be politically neutral as chartered. The Restoration has to be suspicious, but they haven't made in any overt moves. Does anyone have any concerns before we get the ball rolling."

"Can we lift the censorship filter on crew messages?" asked the Chief Alder. "The crew has cooperated admirably with the change requests, but I don't think there's much need for secrecy once those charges drop."

"We've discussed it," Anne answered. "Our agreement with Helvetica Montrose gives her twenty-four hours of exclusivity on the story. After that, we can open the filter way up, and the crew members with connections in the system can take full advantage. We still have a few things we need to keep from public view until we're in Earth orbit, so the filter will stay in place. I doubt it will catch many messages once we open it up. Captain Hartley, would you address coordination with the Sol Space Patrol?"

Captain Hartley stood. "The patrol tentatively agreed to give us a single corvette escort at heliopause, which will switch off frequently as we pass through various commands on our path to Terra. Once the ball drops, I expect them to plus that up significantly. We're prepared to lean on every connection and friend we have to make it happen. Be ready for the Restoration to try desperate measures once they realize what's coming. The fighter pilot cabal is still agitating for a weapons capability of our own, but we'll stick with the close in missile defense laser clusters we've already mounted. I expect to get a lot of queries about our weapons systems. I want to be completely open about it, so we don't ruffle any more feathers than we must."

He sat back down and the CEO Hubble Spearsley leaned forward. "I'm in negotiations for disposal of our intellectual property cargo. I expect those will pause for a bit while people parse the current situation. Once Helvetica's broadcasts go live, though, we're going to attract a lot more interest. I'll do my best to make sure the extra attention turns into a good profit for the crew."

Ambassador Brelling stood back up. "I have good news, as well. Marshall Winter is in system with the latest long boat from Tau Ceti. He'll coordinate his government's statement to time with our charges as well as Rolland's statement on behalf of Lalande. With any good fortune at all, we're about to give the Restoration a very hot time. My team will go to twenty-four-hour operations to press our advantage any way we can. The lightspeed lag in communications with the home office will be a challenge, but they have a good idea of what's coming, and how to take advantage of the data package we're sending. Other thoughts?"

Rolland raised his hand. "We should know within a few days if our new encryption protocol is solid. Once we're secure, Hal and I will coordinate with the anti-piracy and terrorism enforcement agencies of each government. We're going to keep our inside knowledge of the Restoration's clandestine elements to ourselves to begin with, but the evidence of their acts of piracy and terrorism will get the Sol agencies moving so we can take advantage when the timing is right. The Restoration's political leadership is going to have to reveal themselves to fight these accusations in the press, and with the Sol governments. We can expect them to be highly placed in the political arena, and we already know they've got major corporate backing."

Anne nodded. "It's the political side that's murky right now. We can expect the picture to clear up quickly over the next few days." She paused and looked at each of the ship's principal leaders.

Captain Hartley spoke up. "It's time we put the internal security measures we've prepared in place. Hal's personal security teams are trained up, and the militia is tied in to provide backup if needed. I know having a personal security detail following you around is a pain, but it's a pain we all need to get comfortable with before we start having visitors. I expect an envoy from the Outer System Union even before we hit heliopause. One of their Oort cloud outposts is in easy transit range of our course."

The Chief Alder made a face but didn't comment. Hubble Spearsley wasn't so reticent. "Do you seriously think the Restoration is capable of putting an agent aboard when we're on the lookout?" he asked.

"Yes," Captain Hartley answered. "We've been infiltrated multiple times already. That kind of clandestine op is right in their wheelhouse. We have good measures in place to catch operatives when they board, but a layered defense is wise." Hubble subsided but didn't look happy.

"We'll all have to get used to the idea," said Anne. "It's best we work the kinks out now, before we have visitors to worry about. Anything else?" No one spoke up. "Very well, we'll send the legal charge packets first followed by the public key piece of Lisandra's encryption protocol. That will go out wide broadcast in the clear. Helvetica's initial set of reports and interviews will go next, then the private, encrypted crew messages. In quick succession, we'll have the Restoration reacting to legal charges for its financial backers, broadcasts detailing the heinous acts they've perpetrated, and private citizens launching a word-of-mouth campaign. Their reaction will tell us a great deal about what we're dealing with. Captain Hartley, you are free to launch the campaign when ready."

Captain Hartley triggered a ready message to his communications officer and received an immediate acknowledgment. "The data stream is on the way now," he said.

Anne leaned back with a grim, but satisfied expression. "Ladies and gentlemen, for once we're going to have the Restoration dancing to our tune. Let's do whatever we can to keep it that way."

***

Helvetica looked at Lincoln and her friend Quentin. "If I look anything like the two of you, I should go back to my quarters and pass out for twelve hours." The three of them and the rest of her team had been working double shifts for past several months getting a multitude of reports and interviews together, editing them, and putting them into some semblance of a logical order for release. Quentin saw Lincoln's natural talent for production and recording right away and slid into the editing role.

"Yes, and yes," said Quentin. "With the first packet on the way and several more canned and ready, we should all get some rest."

Helvetica tapped her desk idly with a stylus. "Tell me again who we have on board for the initial blast of shows."

Quentin consulted his data terminal. "Solar Broadcast Corporation, Interstellar News Network, and Datanet Darlings."

Helvetica curled her lip at the last name. "I still can't believe I okayed the Darlings."

"You asked for the greatest reach on Sol social networks. They have it," said Quentin. "Also, they eat the human-interest stuff up. When I offered the full slew of interviews we already had canned, they fell all over themselves."

Helvetica didn't look any happier. "What about System News Service?" Quentin asked, just to poke her.

Helvetica's expression hardened. "Oh no, I have something special planned for my old buddies at SNS, and the wheels are already turning. They'll go out of their way to discredit me. Just when they've disparaged my reputation as thoroughly as they can, the other shoe is going to drop."

***

Abishai followed Anne Brelling and Rolland Dunleavy at what he hoped was a discreet distance. His partner, Quester, entered the Delta Section restaurant ahead of them to clear the area. Neither of them was completely comfortable with the role, or the flechette pistols they carried. Abishai scanned the area in front of the restaurant. He didn't like the amount of shrubbery near the entrance. It was perfect cover for an attacker. A split second later he caught movement in the bushes to the right and yelled "Down!" He triggered an emergency alert as he sprinted toward the bushes.

To their credit, the ambassadors went flat immediately and took cover behind a substantial planter. Rolland produced a needle gun. Abishai covered the distance to the assailant in a remarkably short time, launching himself through the air and impacting the man as he brought a weapon up. The weapon went flying as the two men fell in a tangled heap. Abishai's bulk and decades of grappling experience made short work of the contest. He quickly zip-tied the man's hands behind him, frisked him for additional weapons, and yanked him to his feet. He looked up to see Quester covering the ambassadors. In a few moments the deck shook as a powered armor squad from the militia's ready reaction platoon pounded up.

Abishai told the squad leader to sweep the area around the restaurant and handed his prisoner over to one of the other armored militia troops. He started toward the ambassadors when his PCOM lit up with ENDEX...ENDEX...ENDEX. Hal Renfro walked up shaking his head. He helped Anne and Rolland to their feet. "You two go enjoy your dinner while I debrief your security detail," he said. The militia squad leader and "assailant" soon arrived to attend.

Quester was shaking his head. "I don't know how I missed him. I looked right at those bushes," he said.

"When you have thick cover like that, walk it," said Hal. "If you'd walked down the hedgerow, you'd have flushed him out. Sometimes you have to tell your assets to hold up while you secure the area. It's annoying, but they'll get used to it." He turned to the squad leader. "You got here in less than a minute, impressive, but I smell a rat. You didn't get here that fast from your staging area."

The squad leader nodded. "We trailed the protection detail on orders from the platoon leader. We stayed on the maintenance decks to keep out of sight."

"What about the rest of the ready platoon?" Hal asked.

"Still at the staging area," the sergeant answered. "The platoon leader judged that we weren't too far away if he needed to recall us. The ambassadors are the only protected assets away from their quarters this evening."

Hal scratched his chin. "I like the way your platoon leader thinks. We don't want to get over-extended, but I think he made a good call. If we had multiple assailants in this scenario, you'd have been here in time to do some good." He turned to Abishai. "I can't argue with the results, but I'm curious as to why you chose to close with the enemy instead of using your flechette pistol?"

"Instinct???" said Abishai none too surely. "I could barely tell there was someone there. I didn't want to shoot a busboy by mistake."

"I won't question your judgment," Hal said. "You'll have to make split second decisions like that and I'd rather you act quickly than dither." He turned to the crewman in the assailant's role. "Did you have a shot at the targets?" he asked.

The man shook his head. "I was just clearing the bush with my weapon when Abishai hit me like a ton of bricks." He rubbed his neck and shoulder. "If I'd had an edged weapon out, I *might* have come out on top, but I doubt it."

Hal clapped Abishai on the shoulder. "We'll call this a win for the good guys. What does that make it? One out of five?"

Abishai grimaced. "Something like that. Do you think our home-grown security details are going to stop a trained assassin?"

"When I'm done with you, you'll stand a better than even chance," said Hal. "It helps that we have a lot of crew members with a high level of close quarters combat skills. I need to have a chat with the ambassadors. Quester, you come with me. We'll discuss positioning inside the restaurant."

Once Hal had Quester in an unobtrusive spot with good lines of sight, he walked over to Anne and Rolland's table and took a seat. "How good are you with the needle gun?" He asked Rolland.

"Good enough to beat your range scores," Rolland replied. "Remember, I survived several decades as a covert operator knocking around the Lalande system. I generally hit what I'm shooting at."

"What's the loadout?" Hal asked as Rolland checked the safety and handed the weapon over.

"Presently I have paralytic needles loaded," Rolland answered. "They're non-lethal one at a time and generally incapacitate within four to five seconds. I have explosive needles for a lethal effect, but I rarely load them."

Hal turned to Anne, "Do you have a hold out too?"

She shook her head. "Nothing but my martial arts training. Rolland gifted me one of those needle guns. I practice with it regularly, but I don't usually carry it."

Hal looked at Rolland who shrugged and lifted both hands palms up. "I suggest you let Rolland kit you up with a hide-out holster and start carrying it," Hal said. "You're going to be at the top of the Restoration's list. I'd feel more comfortable if you had a weapon with a little more range than a front snap kick."

Anne sighed, then nodded. "Okay, I just wish all this wasn't necessary."

"I agree wholeheartedly," said Hal. "However, I refuse to give the Restoration a victory because we aren't as prepared as we reasonably can be. Speaking of which, how is the ballistic underlayer working out?"

"With a few adjustments, it's bearable," Anne answered. "I can assure you I'll ditch it as soon as I have this mess cleaned up, and I'm safely in interstellar space again."

"It's one more thing an assassin won't expect, and it could save your life against something like this needle gun," Hal said, handing the weapon carefully back to Rolland. "I do appreciate your cooperation with the security detail. Your reaction to Abishai's warning was perfect. I'm glad Rolland will be with you most of the time. His experience adds another layer to our efforts to defend you both." He rose, nodded to both of them, then left to check on Abishai's placement outside the restaurant.

***

Kalei squinted at her husband Julian as he paced back and forth in their quarters living room. "Would you sit down and relax?" she said. She'd had a busy shift in medical, and they'd just gotten the kids settled in bed. Julian continued pacing. Kalei shook her head, reached out a long leg, and hooked his ankle. He tried to keep his balance, but she used her leverage to send him toppling to the deck. She stood over him. "Are you going to settle down, or do I have to hold you down?"

Julian lifted his hands in surrender. "As much fun as that sounds, we did just get the kids settled," he said with a grin. Kalei reached down and helped him to his feet. She urged him over to the couch.

"Which of your many worries is eating you up tonight?" Kalei asked.

Julian sighed, "Pick one, on our next shift we'll see the initial reaction from in-system. The decisions we'll need to make will be crucial, and they'll be based on imperfect information. The stress level is going to be unbelievable.

"On top of that, we're sitting ducks. We won't even have an escort for several weeks while in range of any number of ships plying the scattered disc. I wish we had kept our sting ships so I could be out on patrol instead of flying a desk!"

"Okay," said Kalei mildly. "I can understand your anxiety, but how much is wearing a path in the carpet of our quarters going to help any of those things?"

"Not at all," Julian admitted, with a shake of his head.

"I have a feeling you'll handle tomorrow's stress a lot better in the flow of operations than you're handling the waiting," said Kalei. "Lay your head in my lap and I'll see if I can work out some of that tension."

Julian wisely did as he was told. His wife's skilled hands rubbed his temples, then the base of his neck. He closed his eyes and let his muscles slowly relax.

***

Lionel padded silently through a Beta Section maintenance corridor. He sensed the tension from his humans on the habitation decks all too well. Hunting here was relaxing by contrast. He caught a flash of movement and was on the mouse in two quick bounds. Quickly dispatching his prey, he carried it to the nearest disposal chute and dumped it in as he'd been trained. Satisfied with his successful hunt, he decided to find some humans who weren't wrapped up in whatever seemed to concern the whole crew.

The door to Mishael and Joanne's quarters opened for Lionel, and he found Mark and Fawzia both reading on the couch. The sixteen-year-old twins were precocious readers who shut out the real world while immersed in the fanciful tales they both preferred. Lionel was up to the challenge. He stropped their ankles, then jumped up between them. When they didn't respond, he put his paws on Mark's shoulder and stuck a wet nose in his ear. Mark yelled and jumped like he'd been electrified. Lionel plopped down and curled up between the twins with his head on Mark's thigh. The teenager gave Lionel an offended look, but rubbed the cat's head and neck absently, as he returned to his reading. Lionel rewarded him with a rumbling purr. Fawzia came out of her private world enough to stroke Lionel's back. He purred louder and basked in the calm projected by two of his favorite humans.

Joanne observed her precocious progeny with a smile. The two were inseparable. Both did work-study in cold sleep. They'd helped revive the early-waking passengers who were making the quarters situation a bit crowded. "Should we send those two off to bed?" she asked Mishael.

"No," he said with a yawn and a stretch. "The three of them look way too comfortable to disturb. They'd just read in bed anyway. I don't know how they get enough sleep, but both of them do well in school and at work, so I hate to make too much of an issue of it."

"Speaking of work," said Joanne, "How is the security detail shaping up?"

"Grady and I make a pretty good team. I'm big and obvious, so I make good distraction while he skulks in the shadows. In spite of that shock of red hair, he's very good at blending in, and sneaky. The Chief Alder isn't too happy with us, but she's too polite to fuss about it. The best teams are the veterans from the Tau Ceti Great Prospects protection crew. Most of the pilots trained in personal protection in their youth. Grady and I are learning a lot of tricks from them."

"I would have liked to get you back on the engineering team," said Joanne. "The software for the new laser clusters keeps giving us problems. What you're doing is more important, though. I'm confident we'll work the kinks out before we need them. I hope we don't need them at all."

"Me too," said Mishael. "Unfortunately, I have an itchy feeling between my shoulder blades that says we will. The Restoration isn't going to take this lying down. The coms that went out today will stir up a hornet's nest."

Chapter 18 – Full Court Press

August 2nd, AD 3226
Interstellar Space, three months out of Sol
Long Boat Nai'a, *War Room*

Anne Brelling watched the communications portion of the smart wall quickly fill up with messages addressed to her attention, most of them flagged red-urgent. "Chord, I'm going to my office to work through these as we discussed. Handle what you can and shunt the rest my way. Let me know if you need a quick decision. Julian, you handle the space patrol and law enforcement traffic. I'm sure the captain is in his office ready to respond if it rises to his level. Rolland will take care of the queries from other systems. It's getting hot, folks. You have my full confidence."

Three hours later Anne rubbed her eyes and shook her head in frustration. She'd just responded to yet another version of the "Are you serious?" queries that made up ninety percent of the official communications so far. Her answer to these was a more or less polite "yes." What she wanted to say was not polite. It looked like they were going to have to wait out the light speed lag on another round of messages before anything of substance cropped up.

She wondered if the private messages would get the same reception and decided to check hers. She was surprised to find an encrypted text-only message from her cousin Iris in the belt. It included instructions for a pass phrase to open the attached private key. Anne input the name of her cousin's favorite childhood book, which activated the key. The public key on her terminal combined with the private key to decrypt the message. She was gratified to see Lisandra's encryption protocol working as designed.

The Restoration was going to have a frustrating time trying to penetrate the *Nai'a's* communications. The message itself was encouraging.

Dear Anne,

It's good to hear you and the *Nai'a* are alive and well. Rumors of your demise have been swirling through the system for a decade. Now we know why. Someone has been working behind the scenes to smear and undermine the Long Boat Free Trade Syndicate for years. I'm sure it's the Restoration you told me about. Several of the interstellar corporations named in your charges started an immediate denial campaign. Helvetica Montrose's initial reports dumped a large bucket of cold water on their efforts.

As you can imagine, the whole system is buzzing. You know Belters, they all have opinions, and don't mind sharing them. My sense is that people are royally ticked. Aside from a few scoffers, most of the belt is firmly behind the Long Boat Free Trade Syndicate. This Restoration seems to want to turn back the clock on the former colonies, and it isn't a stretch to believe they'd try the same thing with the Belt. We built most of the long boats out here. I think you can count on our support. I'll be agitating with my legislator for that, and several others already are.

Let me know what more I can do for your cause.

Much Love,

Iris

Anne smiled. The reaction in the belt was just what she'd hoped for. Soon they'd see if the other political regions of the system felt the same. Her PCOM buzzed with a priority message from the captain asking her to come by his office at her earliest convenience. She checked the message list and decided everything could be handled by Chord, or could wait. She left her office at speed, only to be restrained gently by Abishai's large hand. "Where to, Ma'am?"

Anne sighed in exasperation. "The captain's office, if you please. I'm in a hurry. We don't even have any visitors aboard yet."

Abishai just gestured to Quester who departed without hesitation to clear their way. Anne and Abishai followed in his wake. Anne had to admit they made good time. Abishai's combination of bulk and agility never failed to surprise her. "Thank you, Abishai," she said, as the captain's security detail checked her credentials and opened the office door. "Sorry about my snippiness earlier."

"No worries, Ma'am," he replied with a smile, then turned to confer with the lead of the captain's detail.

Captain Hartley waved at an empty chair. The first officer already occupied the other one. "I received a captain-only encrypted message from the home office on Aldrin Station ten minutes ago. It required authentication and private keys from both myself and the first officer. He slid a data chip across the table to Anne. "The message is on the chip, but I'll give you the highlights. Eight separate star systems weighed in to back our charges and proffer more of their own. Marshall Winter has been in system for a year, and he didn't waste his time. He organized the timing with the other systems to coincide with our data blast.

"The Restoration attempted to highjack or destroy seven different long boats that we know of. They also attempted to foment rebellions at Barnard's Star and Procyon. The *Partain* took severe damage in Procyon. The attack was similar to what we survived in Tau Ceti. The asteroid that hit them nearly broke the ship's back, and took out a third of their cold sleep cells. Fortunately, they'd already disembarked their passengers. As it is, they lost over two-hundred of the crew. Captain Stevens was ready to write the ship off, but the locals insisted on repairing her out of pocket. The rebellion fared even worse in Procyon than it did in Lalande. The system prime minister there is quite popular, so they couldn't muster any grass roots support."

Anne blew a breath out through pursed lips. "I was expecting a bigger effort than we were directly aware of, but not that widespread. What else?"

"The home office thinks it will be tough sledding with the Terran government," said Captain Hartley. "So far, their response has been extreme skepticism, even in the face of mounting evidence. Mars and the rest are at least listening. We'll probably know what their official response is as soon as the home office knows."

"What have you heard from the Sol Space Patrol?" asked Anne.

The first officer answered. "We haven't heard from SSP headquarters, but the captain of an anti-piracy patrol vessel contacted us in an unofficial capacity. Interestingly, he used Lisandra's new encryption protocol. He's going to bend the course of his patrol our way. He has a lot of autonomy in his orders, and I think he has an inkling of the hornet's nest we've stirred up. He'll match course with us in about three days."

Captain Hartley smiled grimly, "I feel a bit like we're being used as bait, but it's a capable vessel, the frigate class *Moa*. She'll make a good deterrent until our actual escort arrives."

Anne nodded. "We should be thankful for favorable positioning and a proactive captain. Speaking of Lisandra's encryption protocols, I just received a message from my cousin in the Belt." She filled them in on the contents. "I'd better get back to the war room. I need to catch up on any similar messages. If mine is any indication, our best sense of the public mood will come from those."

***

The war room buzzed with activity as Anne stepped inside. One wall was devoted to the six political regions of the solar system. Each of the panels was topped by a summary of the official response from the regional government. Anne had fielded those, so she was well aware of the contents.

The bottom of each panel was populated by links to personal communications provided by the crew. Anne walked over and tapped the link for her cousin's message. A sanitized summary of the message contents popped up. She nodded and closed the message before tapping one from the Outer System Union. The tone of the message was similar to her cousin's. She tried one from Terra. It also leaned heavily in favor of the Long Boat Free Trade Syndicate. She turned to Nicholas Withers. "Good job organizing and summarizing the personal message traffic," she said. "What's your sense of the public mood from what you've seen?"

Nicholas looked at the message she currently had open. "Thanks, but Mr. Literal deserves most of the credit. He's doing the heavy lifting with the summaries, while I manage the odd exception to his protocols. Most of the messages are similar to what you see here. People recognize the free trade syndicate's neutrality and value. They're skeptical of the denials from the Restoration's toadies and shocked by the acts of piracy perpetrated against the *Nai'a* and other long boats. Many have agreed to contact their government representatives and apply pressure in your favor."

Anne nodded in satisfaction. "This is better than we'd hoped for. Thank you, Nicholas. Keep up the good work!" She turned to Lisandra Redding. "Your encryption system is working like a champ from what I can see. What's your assessment?"

Lisandra's grin was predatory. "I'm fairly sure personal data privacy in the system just got a big boost," said the ex-hacker. "Some of my former competitors are probably unhappy with me. It's going to take them a lot of time and computing power to break the encryption, and it simply won't be worth the effort for most personal communication. I'd like to see the looks on their faces when they finally do crack it and find out they'll have to start from scratch every time."

"Any issues with our own data coms?" Anne asked.

"Just the usual assorted worms and malware hitching a ride on the incoming official communications," Lisandra answered. "Mr. Literal takes care of those. I haven't even had to step in yet. Terra's are the worst, as usual. Too many people with a lot of time on their hands, and an espionage branch that thinks too highly of itself."

Anne walked over to where Hal and Rolland conferred in low tones. "The official response has been underwhelming so far," she said. "The system governments are reaffirming my opinion of bureaucracy. Have you had any better luck on the law enforcement and antiterrorism front?"

"Yes," said Rolland waiving at the list of agencies they'd heard from. "With the notable exception of Terra, we've received supportive responses from all of the anti-terrorism organizations. Marshall Winter primed the pump for us, and these aren't the kind of people who play dumb. The list of the Restoration's crimes is enough to cause concern all by itself. Once we have sense of who we can trust, we'll see about releasing some of the intel we have from Nicholas. Most of that we'll hold until we're in Earth orbit as planned."

Hal pointed to the red dot next to Terra on their status board. "Terra's antiterrorism task force is probably being silenced by the government," he said. "I have a couple of contacts I expect to hear back from, but people aren't going to risk their careers when it looks like this is just free trade syndicate problem."

Chord Ollie walked up at that point. "That's exactly how the Restoration's shills are playing it," he said. "We caught a broadcast a few minutes ago. The spokesperson for something called 'Concerned Citizens of Terra' questioned why the inner system should even care about these hazy accusations from a long boat captain who's the next best thing to a pirate herself. They're apparently ignoring all the accusations from former colonies. Whoever was interviewing them might as well have been on the Restoration's payroll. They played off of one another and made it all sound like exaggeration and hysteria."

Anne leaned against the table and frowned in thought. "We know these people aren't idiots, even if they do have some blind spots. They have to know denial isn't going to work for long."

"My guess is they're buying time to arrange an accident for the *Nai'a*, or you," said Rolland. "We have the hard evidence and witnesses to put a lot of people in jail. If all of that goes away, so do most of their problems."

Julian Garrity joined the conversation. "We know how ruthless these people are. In Tau Ceti they had back up plans to their back up plans. We should expect the same thing here. Space patrol or no space patrol, they're going to attack."

Rolland frowned. "I wish I could argue, but it was the same in Lalande. Even when they were clearly going to lose, they still took the offensive. We'll need that escort, and the bigger the better."

***

Helvetica activated her private key and waited impatiently while the message from another major media network decrypted. She found it slightly amusing that even the major players in the Sol system had recognized the value of Lisandra's encryption scheme. She skimmed the opening, another obscenely large offer of money for exclusive rights to her content. She had no intention of allowing a single network to limit the reach of the vital information in her shows and interviews. She scrolled to the next one, immediately recognizing the signature. The password hint for the private key told her this was the real deal, and the one she'd been waiting for.

Walter Gammonds hadn't been a young man when she left the Sol System. It was good to know he was still alive and kicking. She decrypted the message and opened it.

Dearest Helvetica,

You're certainly making a splash on your return to the Sol System. System News Service has gotten worse, if anything, since you left. They're either in bed with this Restoration organization you and the long boat syndicate outed, or they're still out for your blood. My bet is on both. I have the packet ready to drop to the outlets you listed. Since you left the timing up to me, I'm going to wait until it's clear SNS is all in on their smear campaign and support of the Restoration. When we expose SNS's lies and lack of ethics, they'll be lucky to keep five percent of their current viewership. They lost a good chunk when you left, and they're still sore about it.

I've been following your reports and interviews closely. I worry for your ship's safety. The Restoration's reach in other star systems is impressive. They probably have substantial resources to call on here. The way Ambassador Brelling and the rest blindsided them with the evidence of their crimes will make them desperate. Advise Captain Hartley to be very careful.

Your friend and admirer,

Walter

Helvetica smiled and wrote up a quick reply. SNS was about to have a hot time of it. She hoped the network would fold like a cheap lawn chair. Meanwhile, her ratings were off the charts.

***

Captain Hartley's thoughts chased themselves in circles as he sat his bridge watch. He realized his brow was furrowing, and forced himself to take a slow, deep breath. "Captain, I'm picking up a return from the cabled sensor array," the sensors officer said. "It appears to be a small ship on an intercept course."

"Launch the pinnace," said the captain. "I want eyes on before that ship is close enough to be a threat."

"Incoming communications request via laser carrier," said the communications officer. "Should I open the channel?"

The captain nodded, "Aye, standard security protocol. Keep it isolated from ship's systems and put it on the main screen, camera on this end tight to me."

Soon a dark haired and complected man with warm brown eyes filled the screen. "Please forgive the unorthodox approach, Captain Hartley. I am Kahleed Gemini, very recently appointed envoy of the Outer System Union. My government sent me to confer with you on matters of great importance to both of us. I beg your permission to approach your vessel and transfer aboard at your convenience for a face-to-face meeting with yourself and Ambassador Brelling."

The man's evident good humor was disarming, but Captain Hartley kept his expression neutral. "Greetings, Envoy Gemini," he said. "If your credentials check out, you are welcome to come meet with us. Hold your current course. My pinnace will intercept your vessel. Please follow the pilot's instructions. You'll understand that we need to take a cautious approach with visitors."

"Indeed, captain," the man replied. "I would do the same in your position. I am transmitting my credentials and my vessel's specifications. Our weapons and targeting sensors are all powered down."

"I appreciate that," said the captain. "I look forward to our conversation."

"As do I," the man replied with a smile. "Until then." The screen went blank.

Captain Hartley shot off a priority message to Ambassador Brelling and checked the incoming ship's position. They had a few hours before it would arrive.

***

Jarman matched vectors with the approaching ship and looked it over with great interest. Captain Gemini had been exceedingly polite and cooperative so far, but he wasn't about to let his guard down. The *Emperor Penguin* was a highly modified Shackleford class exploration ship. Since the ship was under acceleration, the six living quarters pods were folded tightly to its main fuselage. He noted three heavy railgun turrets and three antimissile laser clusters arrayed to provide good fields of fire in all directions. His sensors told him the weapons were powered down as promised. The ship was well designed for long term independent operations. The weapons were enough to make any rogue operators out here think twice about attacking.

Jarman opened the coms channel with the visitor, "Captain Gemini, I've matched your course. I'm sending over an approach vector for the *Nai'a*. Once you're on course, I'll dock and transfer to your vessel."

"I'm looking forward to meeting you, Mr. Lal," Captain Gemini replied.

Docking under acceleration was a difficult maneuver, but Jarman expertly connected the pinnace, dock to dock with the larger vessel. Captain Gemini met him as he exited the *Emperor Penguin's* airlock. Jarman was bemused as he realized the two of them could pass for cousins. "Welcome aboard!" the captain said, shaking his hand firmly. "Follow me to the bridge."

The compact bridge had three interchangeable stations. One was occupied by a younger version of the captain who glanced at Jarman before returning to the business of piloting joined vessels. He appeared to be having a hard time getting the thrust balanced. The captain got Jarman settled in the captain's station to the rear and between the other two, then familiarized him with the controls.

"Transfer helm to this station, Manny" he told his son. Jarman quickly balanced the thrust to accommodate the changed center of gravity. He adjusted the automatic pilot, rechecked the vector, then nodded to the captain.

"Manny, meet Jarman Lal, pinnace pilot of the *Nai'a*."

Jarman reached over and shook Manny's hand. "Could you show me how you did that?" Manny asked. "I couldn't get rid of the oscillation the imbalance caused."

Jarman took him step by step through the process, then had him try it himself. "Thanks!" Manny said. "You must have a lot of experience."

Jarman nodded. "I get my share of piloting in, and I'm very familiar with our pinnace and dealing with changes in the center of gravity. I appreciate the warm welcome. No one enjoys turning their ship's helm over to a stranger."

Captain Gemini chuckled, "With what the *Nai'a* has been through, the cautious approach is well warranted. Don't expect this level of cooperation out of the Sol Space Patrol, though."

Jarman grimaced. "They do cherish their independence and authority over the system space-ways," he said. "We're going to have to trust them for protection while we're here, so I hope they live up to their reputation."

Captain Gemini's face lost its habitual cheerful expression. "You're from the Belt, so you know how thin things are in the mid-system. They're an order of magnitude thinner in the Outer System Union. That includes Sol Space Patrol protection. They do patrol out here but a call for help will often go days waiting for someone to show up. I'm sure you noted how well armed we are." He showed Jarman how to open the weapons control panel on his console. "We also keep in touch with anyone in range to help in an emergency. Neighbors are like gold out here. Better, actually, because there's a lot more gold than neighbors."

The hatch to the bridge opened and a dark-haired woman came through with four steaming mugs on a tray. "Ah!" Captain Gemini exclaimed. "My lovely wife, bearing gifts us usual." He took a mug and handed it to Jarman, then gave one to Manny before taking one for himself. "Varsha, meet Jarman Lal, of the Long Boat *Nai'a*."

Jarman smiled and nodded a greeting, then the scent from the mug hit him. He closed his eyes and inhaled deeply. He sipped carefully, then sighed. "A proper masala chai," he said. "I haven't tasted one this good in far too long. Thank you! The spices came from Earth, didn't they?"

Varsha grinned. "Yes, it's one of our few indulgences. Thankfully they don't take up much space or mass." She tucked the tray behind two straps on the bulkhead behind her and maneuvered gracefully into the empty bridge station. "I'm the chief weapons officer as well as first mate," she said. "If we do have an emergency, I hope you'll trust us to operate the weapon systems while you pilot. I usually operate the rail guns and Manny takes the laser turrets."

Jarman regarded the three of them thoughtfully. "I hope it doesn't come to that, but I appreciate the offer. Is there anyone else on your crew I should know about?"

"Our daughter, Corla, is elbow deep in an auxiliary pump replacement aft," said the captain. "It's best if we don't disturb her. She gets surly when you break her concentration. You know the type."

Jarman nearly choked on his chai. He wiped his chin. "I live with myself, so I'm quite familiar. Could you show me how to open the communications channel to the *Nai'a*? I'd better check in with the captain."

Chapter 19 – Identification Friend or Foe?

August 3rd, AD 3226
Interstellar Space, approaching the Sol System
Long Boat Nai'a, *Ship's Council Chamber*

Kahleed Gemini couldn't help being impressed with the people around the council chamber table. The *Nai'a's* leadership team and the two ambassadors all came across as intelligent and highly motivated. It was, in his experience, a dangerous combination to cross swords with. He hoped fervently that they would end up on the same side.

Once the introductions were complete, Captain Hartley spoke up. "We're all curious, Envoy Gemini. Your Outer System Union Credential's check out, but your government hasn't mentioned you in any of the communications we've received. Perhaps you could enlighten us."

Kahleed nodded and flashed his infectious grin. "I'm happy to oblige. The truth is, my government is privately very much on the side of the Long Boat Free Trade Syndicate. Publicly, they're afraid to take a hard stance because we're economically vulnerable. Several of our most important customers are on your list of corporations supporting the Restoration. We stand to lose forty percent of our ice delivery contracts.

"I'm a survey ship captain, not a professional diplomat. My ship is on a long-range mission, and I was the only one close enough to make an early intercept. The Outer System Union offers you the protection of all the armed ships we can muster, but my government's official position will continue to be one of bureaucratic foot dragging. We need time to set up replacement contracts for the business we stand to lose. I know how this looks. Unfortunately, it's a dance we're all too familiar with, because most of our commerce depends on robust trade with the major interstellars based in the other system polities."

Hubble Spearsley frowned, "The Restoration's playbook is depressingly consistent. Why cooperate, when coercion works so well? I'm afraid we didn't fully realize the Restoration's economic clout, but I can help on that front. I have secure communications with all of our regular customers. If you can give me the data on what you have for at-risk inbound deliveries, I can help you find customers."

"I know any assistance you can provide will be greatly appreciated," Kahleed said. "Eleven armed ships are in-bound to help protect the *Nai'a*. They'll match course over the next ten days. My instructions are to take command of the flotilla and deploy the ships in a protective formation according to your instructions. We realize you have direct experience fighting these people."

"What about the Sol Space Patrol?" asked Captain Hartley. "One of their ships will arrive in the next twenty-four hours. I wouldn't be surprised if they arrange for more, sooner than they originally planned."

"We have a standing agreement with the SSP to augment their operations in the Outer System Union when requested," Kahleed answered. "Most of our ship captains, including me, hold a reserve commission in the patrol to facilitate a workable chain of command. This will be a bigger operation than most, but if everyone stays reasonable and keeps the main goal in mind, we should be able to work together. If we can get you safely to the Saturn Commonwealth, I believe the probability of a successful attack will nearly disappear."

"I won't say no to additional ships," said Captain Hartley. "I'll want to establish a secure tactical datalink net with all vessels. We can test the protocols with your ship and add the others as they arrive. I'm most concerned with making sure we can separate the friendly ships from the enemy. Can you help?"

"Yes, I'll have my first officer transmit the secure identification protocols. Our captains have instructions to keep all weapons and targeting systems powered down on approach."

The Chief Alder spoke up. "You probably noticed the increased security protocols we have in place for visitors. If your crews are willing to put up with what you went through, they're welcome to visit the ship under escort. We're normally a friendly lot, and we enjoy visitors."

Kahleed nodded enthusiastically. "My family is very anxious to visit, especially my son and daughter. They don't get a lot of social interaction on these survey trips. Your security people are everything from large and intimidating, to small and even more intimidating. I felt no temptation to wander off the instructed path."

Anne Brelling scrutinized the envoy with narrowed eyes then leaned back with her arms folded across her chest. "Your government is going to have to hop off the fence sooner or later. Do you have any advice on how to prod them along?"

Kahleed shrugged his shoulders. "Your public relations campaign is a good start," he said. "Depending on how much help Hubbel can give us transferring our delivery contracts, I'd say they'll jump fairly soon. They already know the right thing to do. Public pressure and economic help will also make it the expedient thing. My interaction with the governing council is filtered through a couple of layers of hierarchy, so take that with a grain of salt."

"Regardless," said Anne, "I appreciate your candor. The offer of a protection flotilla, and your presence, speak louder to us than your government's official stance." Kahleed nodded in acknowledgment.

***

Two days later, the *Nai'a* had an escort of eleven assorted vessels flying the Outer System Union flag and the Space Patrol Frigate *Moa*. The ships were all tied into a common tactical datanet using SSP protocols. True to Kahleed's prediction, Captain Norland of the *Moa* had declined to be boarded on approach, but he had worked well with the union vessels, and they were shaking down into an organized protective force.

Captain Hartley welcomed Captain Norland to his office, and they sat down for the face-to-face meeting Norland requested. The space patrol officer was a compact, fit-looking man with dark hair rapidly going gray. "My personal thanks for interrupting your anti-piracy patrol to accompany the *Nai'a*, Captain Norland," Hartley said.

"Please call me Zane," Norland said with a self-effacing grin. "There's only one captain on a vessel, and I might get confused. No thanks are required. The space patrol's job is to protect vessels in this system. If one ever needed protecting, it's the *Nai'a*."

"Not everyone in the system would agree with you, Zane," the captain answered. "Some would say the system needs protecting from us."

Norland laughed out loud at that. "Idiots will grasp at anything to make a point. Even if you had everything you used in Lalande, you wouldn't be much of a threat. As it is, you're a bit more than a sitting duck, but not by much. I looked through the layout and specs on your laser clusters. My compliments to your engineers and tacticians. You have an excellent close-in defense suite."

"I'll pass that along. I know they worked hard to get it right. As I said, we *are* grateful for your presence, and I'm impressed with the level of cooperation you have with the Outer System Union vessels."

Norland's expression grew serious, "It springs from a bond forged in blood. We've come to the aid of outer system vessels many times over the years and they've always returned the favor. There are bad actors out here who prefer stealing the result of other people's hard work to doing their own. Some of them specialize in hijacking ships. The good people out here learned to cooperate and rely on one another."

Captain Hartley nodded. "It makes sense," he said. "I only wish more people could see that. You're a busy man, Zane. I'm sure you had more than pleasantries in mind when you requested this meeting."

"Yes, I wanted to talk to you directly about how we can manage the available ships and work the *Nai'a's* defenses into the scheme. We're a bit thinner than I'd like. With the capability of your lasers, we can work out a deployment that takes advantage of our strengths. You have much better datanet and communications bandwidth on this ship than the *Moa*. With your permission, I'd like to set up a tactical command and control team in your auxiliary bridge space. I can provide some of the manning from my crew, but I think a joint team of your officers and mine, with a few from the Outer System Union ships, would be best. I intend to stay aboard to head up the command team."

"You're welcome to the auxiliary bridge," said Captain Hartley. "I'll be stretching my bridge crews to support you, but my first officer and I will work it out. I'm afraid we're tight on quarters right now because of the cold sleep passengers getting acclimatized to full gravity, but we'll make room for your people."

"From what I've seen of your specifications and the ship, the *Nai'a* will seem roomy to my people compared to the *Moa*," Norland answered. He'd just finished speaking, when the general quarters alarm sounded.

"This way to the bridge!" Captain Hartley said, and left with the SSP officer in his wake. His security team was waiting outside, and they quickly cleared the short corridor.

On the bridge they found Commander Winslow Stirling standing bridge watch. The Commander gave his captain a questioning look, but Captain Hartley shook his head, not wanting to jog his first officer's elbow. "Still no communications from the three possible bogies on intercept course," reported the tactical officer. "Three of the Outer System Union ships are vectoring for an intercept, and *Moa* is maneuvering to support them."

"Coms, give them a two-second pulse with the interstellar coms laser," said Commander Stirling. "Perhaps they need a reminder in proper etiquette." Captain Hartley winced slightly. At this range, the gigawatt coms laser was going to do unkind things to the incoming ships' optical receivers.

"No response, sir," reported the coms officer after a moment.

"Bogies have initiated a jinking pattern," said the tactical officer. "*Moa* has authorized weapons free...missile launch! Twelve missiles inbound. *Moa* fire direction has assigned targets. Should I go live with the targeting sensors on the cabled array?

"Negative," said Commander Stirling. "Let's keep that capability to ourselves for now. Onboard sensors will suffice for this threat. I'll be surprised if those missiles get past our escort."

"Bogies one through three have flipped and are making a run for it," said the tactical officer. "The escort ships are asking permission to pursue."

"Belay that!" Zane Norland said. "Patch me into the tactical channel please." The coms officer handed him a headset and nodded. "All ships, this is Temporary Commodore Norland. Do NOT pursue the enemy ships. They aren't a serious threat, and they may be trying to lure us out of position."

"Your executive officer beat you to that message by a few seconds," Commander Stirling said, tapping his ear bud. "A little emphasis never hurts, though."

Norland looked at Captain Hartley. "Competent subordinates are a treasure," he said mildly. The captain replied with a small smile.

"Six missiles down!" called the tactical officer. "Three more...and all incoming missiles destroyed well outside attack range."

***

A few hours later no follow-up attack had materialized. Captain Hartly and Zane Norland regrouped back in the captain's office. "You surprised me a bit with your sudden promotion," the captain said.

"It's part of my standing orders," the commodore replied. "I was about to tell you about it when the alarm went off. That little exercise points out why a solid chain of command is important. Everyone did their jobs well, but someone needs to be in charge of the overall tactical situation. I don't want my first officer fighting the ship and directing the flotilla at the same time. Tell me about the cabled sensor array."

"On our approach to Lalande, we needed a way to see past our own engine noise and the ice shield," said Captain Hartley. "We figured out a way to suspend a very capable set of sensors and power them through a cable harness anchored to the ice shield's frame. We only turn on active scan when we need it for targeting. The passive sensors are good enough to pick up anything without high-end stealth capabilities. We had an excellent picture of the Restoration's fleet before we unleashed our first salvo. The array itself is stealthy in passive mode, and very hard to pick out against the background of the ice shield."

"I can vouch for that," said Norland. "We did a full active scan of the *Nai'a* and it didn't show up. We'll need to work its capabilities into our defensive plan if you don't mind sharing the specifications."

"Not at all," the captain answered. "You just proved you're on our side."

"Officially I'm on the side of seeing you safely into the system, but I don't have to take sides when it comes to dealing with pirates," Norland said. "For my money, the Restoration has committed several acts of piracy and terrorism. The sooner my chain of command realizes it, and act accordingly, the better. In the meantime, that weak attack gives me all the cover I need to build and command a protective force for the *Nai'a*. Headquarters will be affronted that someone dared to attack a long boat, even out here. The truth is, this is a lot like the old Wild West. The good people out here are smart enough to carry their own equalizers and know who to call for help."

"I was reviewing the specs on the Outer System Union ships earlier. They're more heavily armed than I expected. Now I know why. Envoy Gemini may be a mere survey ship captain, but I think his government chose well."

"I can vouch for Kahleed Gemini," said Norland with a solid nod. "Behind that cheerful exterior is a sharp mind and a very capable man in a fight. I owe him my life twice over."

"I feel better about our tactical situation," said the captain. "I don't know what the Restoration has to throw at us, but it's going to have to be a lot to overwhelm our defenses."

"That attack was probably a probe to see what they're up against," said Norland. "Based on your history with them, I expect a follow-up with everything they have within a few days. Once you get in-system, it's going to be a lot harder to pull off an attack. I think you have them reacting, instead of planning, so we'll use that to our benefit. With your permission, I'll get to work getting organized in your auxiliary bridge." Captain Hartley nodded and led the new commodore out of his office. The captain's security team asked for their destination and set about clearing the way.

***

Abishai eyed the entrance to Old Speedy warily. The plus-velocity ring was tripping along fast enough to simulate full earth gravity, which made hopping on board even more challenging. Finally, he gritted his teeth, sprinted alongside, and grabbed a padded ring to swing himself aboard. He stumbled slightly. His knees nearly gave way, but he managed to keep his feet. The full gravity pulling him down made him look around for a seat, but the sadistic medical staff had removed them all. Under normal operations Old Speedy was the fastest way to get between hab sections; now it functioned as a full gravity gym.

One of the cold sleep early-wakers was sprawled face-up on the padded surface a few meters away. Abishai made his way over and offered a hand up. The man took it, "Thanks, I just have ten more minutes, but I need to be on my feet for it to count," the man said. He put one foot slowly in front of the other like he was walking through a waist-deep snowdrift.

Abishai followed and soon passed the man. He was scheduled for a full hour on the ring, and he preferred walking to any of the other activities recommended by the medics. If you walked in the opposite direction of the spin, it took an undetectable amount of weight off your legs, but it still made him feel better. The process wasn't pleasant, but his earth-raised frame was adapting better than most of the people coming out of cold sleep. Most of them were from the habitats in the Lalande system, raised in half the gravity Old Speedy was throwing at them.

Shanyah joined him after his fifth revolution, jogging up as if she were on a pleasure cruise. "How do you make this look so easy?" asked Abishai, wiping sweat of his brow.

"Unlike you, I didn't procrastinate," she answered. "I started when they spun this old buzzard up to .75G."

"Unfair! You always knew you were going planet-side with the dolphins. I only found out a few days ago that my parents are still alive."

"Then quit grousing," said Shanyah with a grin. "You have everything to be thankful for."

Abishai scowled at her but didn't make a dent in her upbeat mood. He wondered how it was that the most caring person he knew never seemed to cut him any slack. In a few moments they caught up with Quester trudging along and staring at his feet. Abishai almost slapped his friend on the back, but decided against it at the last minute. Poor Quester looked like a light breeze would knock him over.

The Tau Ceti native looked up as they passed and gave them a wan smile and a weak wave. Shanyah gave him a wink and a thumbs-up. "You can do it!" she said. Quester just nodded and kept trudging.

"He's really determined to make the trip," said Abishai.

"The dolphins kind of shamed him into it," said Shanyah. "They can razz a person like a pack of hyenas. He wasn't getting any peace from them until he agreed to come swim in the ocean with the pod."

"Do you think we'll have a dolphin family aboard for the next crossing?" puffed Abishai.

"I'm not sure," said Shanyah, "One thing I know. We're definitely reuniting them with their family on earth. Half of them were born in those oceans, and the other half want to experience their ancestral memories of swimming free and unconfined."

***

Helvetica nodded in satisfaction as she reviewed the ratings of her latest shows. Despite her misgivings, the Datanet Darlings were delivering her largest audience. She loathed the sensationalism the datanet thrived on, but the simple truth was plenty sensational enough for the audience. She'd pointedly ignored the wild conspiracy theorists who'd inevitably latched onto every nuance of her shows and interviews. If they couldn't see the grand conspiracy right in front of their noses, she wasn't going to waste energy correcting them.

A message from Walter Gammonds popped up in her priority list. She quickly decrypted it and began to read.

Dearest Helvetica,

I'm sure you know by now how well your shows are doing in the system media and datanet. System News Service is going all out to discredit you. They scheduled a show tomorrow that's the tipping point I'm looking for. Three guests will reveal the 'true' reason you left the network and prove the long boat syndicate's charges are false.

I sent the evidence packets on SNS out to be released immediately upon conclusion of that show. I'm also giving a joint interview to every news service I could convince to lay that evidence out clearly for the public eye. Thanks to your popularity, I got quite a few on board. I should be giving your old network a giant black eye about the time you get this.

I laid on some personal security as you requested. You should do the same. You're going to be a bigger target than I am.

Warmest Regards.
Walter

Helvetica whistled lowly between her teeth. She hated the thought of Walter putting himself out there like this, but the man's gravitas would lend significant weight to her accusations against SNS. She couldn't ask him to back off if he wanted to do it. This situation was developing rapidly. She knew she'd saddled a tiger, and the only option was to ride it well. She thought about asking for personal security and curled her lip. It already looked like she was in bed with the long boats and using their people for security was just going to make it look worse. Walter was right, though. She'd painted a big target on her back, and it would be foolish to think the Restoration wouldn't come after her.

Chapter 20 – New York Snow

August 7ᵗʰ, AD 3226
Interstellar Space, approaching the Sol System Heliopause
Long Boat Nai'a, *Bridge*

Captain Hartley started to take a drink of stale coffee but stopped quickly when the tepid bitter liquid hit his tongue. He grimaced and set the cup aside. Over the last few days, the tactical situation had changed rapidly. Several additional Outer System Union ships and the Sol Space Patrol corvette *Eagle Ray* were now part of the protective force surrounding the *Nai'a*.

Eagle Ray pulled five gravities of acceleration for several days to match course with them early. *Eagle Ray's* Captain Page placed his ship under Commodore Norland's command on arrival. After giving himself and his crew a solid twelve-hour rest and recovery period, he reported aboard the *Nai'a* and joined the shifts manning the flotilla command center in the auxiliary bridge. *Eagle Ray* packed three times the fire power of the frigate *Moa,* and Captain Page technically outranked the commodore. Fortunately for everyone, though, Page recognized Norland's expertise in the outer system environment, and he wasn't interested in petty power struggles.

Eagle Ray held position above the *Nai'a* to the Sol system north, while *Moa* guarded directly below the massive long boat to the south. Two dozen Outer System Union vessels, all well-armed, formed a protective bubble around the ship. The formation skewed somewhat toward the inner system. It was an impressive flotilla by any standard. Captain Hartley just hoped it was enough.

Envoy Kahleed Gemini Joined Commodore Norland at the three-dimensional main display in the well of the auxiliary bridge. "This is the expected track of the icy body NT-34R76G09," he said. A green line appeared, well clear of the Nai'a's path. "This is the updated track according to long range infrared scan." A red line appeared that would pass aft of the *Nai'a's* course by a few hundred kilometers in three days.

"That isn't suspicious at all," said Norland mildly. "How big is that ball of ice?"

"We wouldn't even know about it if I hadn't mapped it a month ago. They may still think they're being coy," said Gemini. He pulled up an image of NT-34R76G09. It looked like a slowly rotating potato. "It's fourteen kilometers long and eight wide. I imagine they took a few chunks out of it nudging it into the current trajectory."

"Big enough to hide a fleet behind," said Commodore Norland. "We need to get the tactical brain trust together and come up with a plan."

A few hours later, Julian Garrity, Mr. Barboa, Kahleed Gemini, and Captain Page all sat down with the commodore in a meeting room just down the corridor from the auxiliary bridge. "I'm assured that you are the most devious tactical minds aboard the *Nai'a*," the commodore began. We need to prepare surprises for the attacking force we all expect. Kahleed explained the situation. Ideas?"

Mr. Barboa scratched his chin. "What's the albedo on the Tater?" he asked, unofficially naming NT-34R76G09 something pronounceable.

Kahleed Gemini pulled up the specs. "It's cosmic snow by way of New York City," he said. "There's a lot of dust and methane mixed in. What are you thinking?"

"I'm thinking how much fun it would be for the force of ships we assume is hiding behind this thing to have it explode from internal steam pressure. If we can put enough energy into the interior of the Tater, pow!"

"The ride I took when a laser hit our ice shield was a shock," said Julian. "Anything we can do to throw them off balance will help."

Gemini shook his head. "I like the idea, but the 'Tater' is probably still rotating. I don't think we could get enough laser energy on it to turn a significant portion of the water into steam."

"Let's ask our resident number cruncher to run the calculations and see," said Mr. Barboa. "Mr. Literal, do you have the specifications on the energy weapons across our protective flotilla?"

"Yes, Mr. Barboa," the AI answered. Commodore Norland raised an eyebrow at the instantaneous response, but didn't comment.

"Please model the effects of a concentrated laser attack by the entire flotilla on icy body NT-34R76G09, now referred to as the Tater, specifications and course located in Envoy Gemini's data files. Use a six degree of freedom model and the Monte Carlo method. The desired outcome is explosive fracturing of the Tater and maximum damage to any vessels hiding in its shadow."

"May I have access to the cabled sensor array's passive data sensors?" Mr. Literal asked. "Envoy Gemini's data is ambiguous in terms of the current attitude and rotation of the tater."

Mr. Barboa tapped out a quick message to the sensor station on the bridge, waited a few seconds, then nodded. "You have access to the passive sensors."

"Senor data collection and modeling analysis will require approximately thirty-three minutes and twenty-five seconds," said Mr. Literal.

"Thank you, Mr. Literal," said Mr. Barboa.

After the exchange, Commodore Norland frowned at Mr. Barboa. "Was your ship's data librarian listening in on our conversation?"

"Not exactly," said Mr. Barboa, amused by the man's obvious discomfort. "He could replay everything we've said, but only on request. Those files are locked under our privacy protocols. Once I said his name, he became an active participant in the meeting."

Commodore Norland still had a sour look on his face, but he shrugged and pointed to the display. "Assuming we can do something significant to the Tater, we need to think about timing. *Moa* and *Eagle Ray* are the only ships with missile armament. We can stagger fire and arrange a time on target arrival of a forty-eight-missile salvo if we flush our magazines. We'll need a good sensor picture starting thirty seconds prior to arrival if we want the missiles to be effective."

"The *Nai'a*'s active sensors are your best source," said Julian. "None of your ships can put the power into active scan that we have available. At the Tater's angle of approach, we have a window where we can get a stereoscopic picture combining the hull mounted sensors and the cabled array. I suggest we try to take advantage of that window to press our attack." He added a gold line to the display, indicating the optimal sensor window.

Commodore Norland's eyes narrowed as he considered the possibilities. "Your window also has the advantage of ordnance trajectories that aren't directly in-system from either side. That isn't my greatest worry, but it is a consideration." He blew a breath out. "We're going to look like the king's own fools if we crack the Tater into a million pieces and flush our missile magazines at nothing. Should we try to sneak a probe into the tater's shadow?"

Kahleed Gemini shook his head. "Too risky, you'll ruin the element of surprise. They'll be watching for probes. Also, I'll bet the title to my ship that the Restoration is using the Tater to hide its main attack force."

"It fits their methods," said Julian. "The question is, what's waiting for us out there? How big a force do you think they could put together? In both Lalande and Tau Ceti, we faced more ships than we estimated."

Norland and Gemini looked at each other. "The last year has been relatively quiet out here," said Norland. "I suspect it's because the Restoration was making preparations for an attack. I also think your schedule hurried them. It's really hard to say. Whatever they've gathered, we need to hit them hard and early for the best outcome."

The meeting continued as they hashed out other scenarios. Mr. Barboa received an alert from Mr. Literal. "What do you have for us?" he asked the AI.

"The combined flotilla cannot put sufficient directed energy on the tater to break it up until it crosses directly astern. I took the liberty of running a few scenarios adding in a time on target railgun salvo from our ships followed up on the Tater's next rotation with a laser attack in the same spot." Norland's eyebrows rose as Mr. Literal continued. "The optimal target is a crater presumably created when the enemy forces set off a charge to alter the body's trajectory. May I have access to the display?"

Mr. Barboa touched a control. "The display is yours."

A green arc appeared over a portion of the Tater's course. "Modeling indicates a .929564 probability of catastrophic breakup of the cometary body using the two-phased attack I described during this portion of its flight." The green line overlapped a good portion of the gold sensor window.

"Won't they notice the damage done by the railgun rounds as the Tater rotates?" asked Julian.

"Possibly," said Kahleed, "even probably, but how will they react? If I was over there, I'd be laughing at my enemy's failed attempt to blow my cover. Even if they recognize what's happening, they'll only have a few seconds to take action. The Tater is making a full turn every ten seconds. A few seconds after they see the damage, we'd be hitting the crater with our lasers. We should assume they're smart enough to know we'll see them coming. Their game isn't so much one of surprise, as using the Tater for cover until they're in launch range. I expect a mass missile attack. The sooner we can blow their cover, the more time we'll have to take down their initial salvo."

The commodore drummed his fingers idly on the table. "I'll admit you're making sense from their perspective. In their place I would hunker down until closest approach if I could get away with it. From my study of their tactics in your previous engagements, I'd be surprised if this was their only force in play. We know they have access to top end stealth materials. I'm thinking they've probably set up some kind of surprise from sunward to catch us between two simultaneous attacks from opposite directions."

Julian grimaced, "I agree. They probably have the resources to do both. If we force their hand early on the attack from the Tater, we may be able to reconcentrate our forces before the other one hits, but I wouldn't count on it. What can we do to strengthen our sunward defense in case we can't?"

Mr. Barboa's smile was predatory. "I have an idea about that. It involves a ridiculous number of high explosives, the captain's going to hate it, and it will only work once. Still, I think it's worth a shot if we have to use it." He went on to lay out the idea to the others.

"Get it ready," said the commodore when he finished. "We don't have a lot of time. Let me know if you need me to help convince Captain Hartley."

"He'll agree," answered Mr. Barboa. "Like I said, he'll hate it, but he'll see the necessity. I'd better get started. I have an EVA team to put together."

***

Roan triple-checked the safety, receiver, and wired connection to the explosive charge he'd just set in the ice shield, then gave Jarman a thumbs up. As he glided carefully to the next position with wire trailing behind him, he tried to keep a positive attitude. This was just the sort of EVA he hated. Only the long boat's .1G deceleration kept him in contact with the back side of the ice shield. They were operating with only partial protection from cosmic rays and playing with torches and high explosives. What could possibly go wrong? He'd volunteered, because if he hadn't, his son Grady, or someone else with less than half of Roan's experience, would be out here. He was grateful for Jarman's calm presence. EVAs never seemed to bother the former Belter. Sometimes Roan wondered if Jarman had been born in a space suit. He wouldn't bet against it.

Roan planted the last of the explosives in the depression he'd melted, then waited for the water to refreeze. He looked up at a rare view of the ten-kilometer length of the *Nai'a*. This near the edge of the ice shield he could see all the way to the bow. The clear armor of the Starlight Lounge rotated into view amidships, and he wondered if anyone was watching the stars wheel by. He shook his head and bent to the task of checking the explosive, then began the long, slow, gliding walk back to the center of the ice shield. He was looking forward to riding the make-shift elevator platform back up to the stern of the *Nai'a* and getting out of his hard suit.

***

Abishai ran through several scenarios with Palamar and Val O'Clair. His two old friends from Tau Ceti had volunteered for Helvetica's security team. In Abishai's opinion, the O'Clairs were better at the personal protection business already than he would ever be, but they needed to understand the procedures for calling in back up and dealing with captives. They were a husband-wife pilot team with Great Prospects protection service before joining the *Nai'a*'s crew. Their early training and experience included providing personal protection.

The fact that they were both Krav Maga instructors, already friendly with Helvetica, helped tremendously. The intense newswoman respected the two enough to listen to them on matters of security. "How many militia troops do we have on standby?" asked Palamar.

"A full squad in powered armor," said Abishai. "We'll ramp it up to a platoon when we start getting more visitors. Also, if you're in the tropical dome or Six Fathoms restaurant, you can call on the dolphins. We've set up their armor and weapons suites so they swim into them, and they lock in on the fly. Their response time is impressive. Just beware that they're also enthusiastic and highly protective of the crew."

Palamar smiled, showing perfect white teeth. "Oh, we're aware. We have that in common with our dolphin friends. We'll take a swim and talk over tactics."

"I didn't know you were conversant in Dolphin," said Abishai.

Val nodded his head enthusiastically. "Only so-so on most subjects, but tactics is a common topic between us since we started training with them back in Tau Ceti. Quester is probably the best translator other than Shanyah, though. The dolphins took to him specially from the beginning, and vice versa."

***

Helvetica grunted as she landed in a roll and curled into a tight ball. Palamar's diving tackle turned into a smother as she covered the larger woman with her body and pointed her weapon at an imaginary threat. After a second, she popped to her feet and helped Helvetica up from the padded tatami. "Good!" she said. "Don't resist the motion I impart, flow with it. You're getting better. Val and I will deal with the threat, that's *our* job. Yours is to make yourself as small a target as possible."

"Why do I get the feeling you're enjoying throwing me around?" asked Helvetica.

"Because I am," said Palamar with a grin. She rubbed her jaw. "After that palm strike you landed in our last sparring session, I need to get a little of my own back." Her expression turned serious. "Your personal combat skills aren't bad, but you're not up to taking on a trained assassin on your own. Val and I will be there to make sure you don't have to. Now, run through the list of likely escape routes with me again."

Helvetica sighed and started working through the list, starting with her office and studio area.

After a shower and a meal, Helvetica returned to her office. Lincoln and Quentin motioned her over to the wall screen. "This just came in. SNS doubled down on their accusations toward you and the free trade syndicate just as Walter predicted. This is Walter's response," said Quentin excitedly.

Helvetica smiled as her old friend's face filled the screen. He looked distinguished in a top-end tailored suit. "Good evening," Walter began. "As I promised, I will address Solar News Service's accusations point by point, but first I'll take you through the incontrovertible evidence of their history of lies and journalistic malfeasance provided to each of you in my data packet. SNS shouldn't be allowed a broadcast license in any of the Sol System polities, and I intend to see that they pay for their actions." Helvetica found herself nodding and pumping her fist as Walter drove nail after nail into the coffin of SNS's credibility.

Helvetica felt like she was walking on air as she returned to her quarters. Not even the presence of her security team sweeping the way ahead could ruin her mood until she had a sudden realization. SNS was the last major media platform willing to put forth the Restoration's agenda. Without a voice in the public relations fight, they were going to get desperate. She caught up with Palamar and changed her destination.

***

Anne and Rolland were enjoying delightfully dense chocolate chip shortbread cookies and a cup of milk each when Helvetica arrived at their quarters. Their security team ushered the slightly out of breath reporter inside, then conferred with Palamar and Val. Helvetica laid out the situation and accepted the offer of a cookie and milk. She took a bite and promised herself an extra twenty minutes of exercise to offset the calories.

"I appreciate the update," said Anne. "You're probably not aware of the developing tactical situation. I'm not sure the enemy's level of desperation will change anything, but we believe the Restoration has a fleet preparing to attack the *Nai'a* in a few days. Commodore Norland, Captain Hartley, and their people are working out the best way to foil the attack. For security reasons, I can't give you a lot of details. I'll just say I have confidence they'll do the best they can to keep the ship safe."

Helvetica blanched and a feeling of helpless dread coursed through her. The last time the ship was under attack, she'd been in cold sleep, unable to worry about it. "I brought this on you," she said in a small voice entirely unlike her.

Anne's full-throated laugh startled her. "The Restoration has been trying to take over or take out the *Nai'a* for a lot longer than you've been aboard. Your reporting helped us expose what they are to the entire Sol system. They would, however, be out there preparing to attack the *Nai'a* regardless. You *are* a target now, so I'm glad you asked for a personal security detail. I know they take some getting used to, but I think we'll need them before this is over. I'm not sure which of us tops the Restoration's hit list, but I'm certain you and I occupy the first two spots.

"You're probably feeling helpless, because you can't do anything about the coming space battle. We feel the same, only worse. We have the experience and training to help, but the *Nai'a* is Captain Hartley's ship to fight. Commodore Norland knows his business. If we poked our noses in, we'd just be distracting them at a critical time."

Rolland grimaced. "I can tell you from experience, the best way to help yourself and the ship is to keep busy with what you've been doing. Getting the truth out can only help us in the long run, because the Restoration's position is built on a foundation of lies. We'll keep pushing the legal, political, and public relations fight. We're starting to get traction with everyone but Terra."

Helvetica sighed, "You're right. I can't help anything by worrying, but I do feel helpless."

"The woman who took down SNS is hardly helpless," said Anne with a wide smile. "Check your priority message cue. I forwarded you a report our team just sent me from the Interstellar News Network feed."

Helvetica accessed her PCOM and quickly brought up the message on a virtual display. Quickly she read through the words floating in front of her."

BREAKING NEWS!!! EVERY SOL SYSTEM GOVERNMENT EXCEPT TERRA CANCELLED SOLAR NEWS SERVICE'S BROADCAST RIGHTS EFFECTIVE IMMEDIATELY BASED ON

EVIDENCE PRESENTED BY WALTER GAMMONDS. SEVERAL ARE PREFERING CRIMINAL CHARGES. MORE TO FOLLOW!!!

Helvetica closed the message, shaking her head in disbelief. "That was fast. I had hopes of giving SNS something more than a black eye, but this... Walter must have added extra evidence to my data packet, and sent it to a lot more people than he let on."

"Apparently they were doing quite a bit more than just lying through their teeth," said Anne. "If they're in bed with the Restoration, threats, intimidation, kidnapping, and murder are all on the table. After Walter's accusations aired, I'm sure a lot of people found the courage to come forward and back him up."

Chapter 21 – Fire and Ice

August 10ᵗʰ, AD 3226
Interstellar Space, near the Sol System Heliopause
Pirate Ship Shrike, *Bridge*

Kron Dullery checked the main display yet again. Why weren't the cursed OSU beggars scouting the wannabe comet his force hid behind? If it were him, he'd have sent a reconnaissance in force. It was just what he was hoping for. He had the firepower to wipe out any force they could muster. He was itching to do it, then fling everything he had at the long boat and its remaining defenders.

He had his own reasons to hate the Long Boat Free Trade Syndicate, but he was honest enough with himself to admit money was his real motivation. The Restoration had already paid him a ridiculous sum up front and promised an equal payment for destruction of the *Nai'a*. They'd been just as liberal with munitions. That combination made him a man of power out here. He'd been able to recruit every cutthroat and claim jumper in the area to fly under his banner. He didn't trust the lot of them farther than he could throw an asteroid, but he trusted the money they'd been paid and promised to keep them in line.

Stealthy sensors provided by the Restoration, and currently in passive mode, fed him a picture of the protective flotilla surrounding the *Nai'a*. His earlier scouting trip had confirmed the general numbers, and he knew he had them out-gunned. Since they weren't obliging him the chance to defeat them in detail, he'd have to go with plan B, an all-out blitz timed for the comet's closest approach. The initial salvo was going to be a nasty surprise. With any luck, they'd just have mopping up to do.

He opened the tactical channel carried by tight-beamed laser to all the vessels in his fleet. "This is Kron," he transmitted, eschewing fancy titles for the intimidation his reputation carried. "We'll execute plan B at closest approach. Be sure of your grapple connections and launch on my command. We'll crush them with the first salvo, then close to deal with any survivors. You know the orders. Our employers don't want live witnesses. Kron out."

He'd just finished transmitting, when his gunner called his attention to the tactical display. "I'm reading an incoming railgun salvo," he said. "It looks like every ship they have fired, and it's aimed at the center of the comet. Do you want me to go active with the sensors?"

"Belay that!" spat Kron. "They're probably just looking for a reaction or trying to spook us into launching early. We'll wait while they waste time and ammunition pecking at our cover. Pull up a visual of the comet."

The oblong chunk of cosmic ice rotated sedately on the screen as they waited. "Impact in five...four...three...two...one...impact," reported the gunner. After a few seconds, the impact point rotated into view. A small crater and a few drifting ice shards showed where the railgun rounds had impacted.

"Idiots!" scoffed Kron. "I hope they try it again. They're probably adding to the density of our shield." He turned away from the display

***

On the *Nai'a's* bridge Captain Hartley projected as much calm as he could muster. The next few seconds would likely determine his ship's survival. Chief Nance hovered at the tactical console as a backup, but the shot was in the hands of the computers. Right on the mark, every laser on the *Nai'a* and the ships around her fired at the heart of the Tater. Deep in the comet, ice and methane flashed into vapor. For a millisecond it held together, then great chunks the size of icebergs exploded outward in all directions.

***

Kron barely registered the bright flash from the sensor display when his gunner shouted and he was thrown across the bridge. His head slammed into a control panel, and he sank into darkness.

***

Commodore Norland barely registered the shouts of triumph around him in the command center on board the *Nai'a*. His concentration focused on the drifting chunks of the Tater and what the active sensors from the *Nai'a* and her cabled array were telling him had lain hidden. He swallowed a curse. As soon as the target-rich picture resolved sufficiently, he keyed his mike. "All ships, targeting plan Sierra Foxtrot. Execute on my mark." The tactical computers sorted and assigned target priorities, updating the waiting missile salvo from the Sol Space Patrol ships and the railguns of all vessels in the flotilla. "Mark!" the commodore transmitted.

Every railgun in the flotilla burped and high-density slugs tore through the space between the two forces. Shortly afterward, forty- eight missiles followed them, timed to arrive together with maximum impact.

***

In Kron's pirate fleet, chaos reigned. Ships, missile pods, and chunks of ice drifted in an expanding cloud of confusion. Fully half the ships took damage in the first few seconds, and the rest attempted to thread their way out of the debris field. Most of them were too busy surviving to execute Kron's plan, but a few managed to tow their missile pods free of the mess. Kron's gunner realized his boss was out of action and their ship was a drifting wreck. He took a quick look at the tactical display and punched the button set up to flush every missile pod in the fleet.

The pirates started with one-hundred missile pods carrying ten missiles each hidden behind the Tater. Thirty-three of them survived to launch their missiles toward the *Nai'a* and her defenders. Almost half of those missiles fell victim to collisions in the expanding debris field that had been a fleet. That left a mere one hundred and sixty-four missiles in the salvo blazing toward the *Nai'a*. A few of the ships cleared the debris and fired railguns as well before the combined fire of the Sol Space Patrol and Outer System Union Ships tore through their scattered ranks. On Kron's slowly spinning ship, his gunner was trying to get power routed to the defensive laser clusters when a burst of railgun rounds shredded the ship and everyone in it.

***

"Stars!" someone in the command center breathed as the display lit up with the traces of the massive incoming missile salvo.

"Defensive plan Aegis! All ships target the incoming missiles. Whatever's left of the fleet we'll deal with later." Commodore Norland barked over the tactical com. His ships were already deployed between the *Nai'a* and the incoming salvo. Tactical computers sorted and assigned targets with unnatural speed, and the railguns of the defending flotilla pumped out coordinated bursts of fire. The *Nai'a*'s maneuvering thrusters fired in sequence to alter her course and throw off the enemy's targeting. The incoming missiles jinked, but Sol Space Patrol had the best predictive algorithms in known space. The railguns took their toll, and ninety-two missiles survived to laser range of the flotilla.

Commodore Norland relaxed in his command chair and tried to look confident. He could only let his people do their jobs and hope it would be enough. The spinal lasers from *Moa* and *Eagle Ray* spoke first, picking off missiles with each shot. Soon the defensive turrets of the entire flotilla joined in, and the numbers of missiles fell steadily.

Jarman unconsciously imitated the commodore as he sat on the bridge of the *Emperor Penguin*. Varsha Gemini was proving her worth as a weapons officer. With a light touch she adjusted priorities but generally let the excellent defensive suite of her ship take shots as the weapons cycled. Suddenly the tactical display hashed as six of the remaining missiles unleashed a barrage of jamming. The display cleared quickly as the jammers drew concentrated fire, and the powerful active sensors of the *Nai'a* fed targeting information to the flotilla over the datalink.

A small ember of hope was beginning to glow in Jarman's breast when a missile punched through the remaining interference headed directly for the *Emperor Penguin*. He saw Varsha's hand begin to move but knew it was too late. The cockpit screens went black and the ship bucked hard. Emergency lighting came on, and one by one instrument lights began to illuminate. Jarman was glad of the low light, because he knew his face was unnaturally pale. "Ship status?" he asked.

Manny Gemini at the third cockpit station quickly scanned through his screens. "Minor damage to the dorsal sensors and one laser in the forward cluster," he reported with his eyes wide. "Corla?" he queried over the inter-ship com. "How are things aft?"

"Other than a hard reset of the entire electrical system, everything is fine. Engines and powerplant are green," his sister answered. "Now please stop getting my ship shot at."

Varsha looked as shocked and relieved as Jarman felt. "How?" she murmured as she worked to bring the tactical display back up. The picture on screen when it powered up wasn't pretty. Twenty-one missiles were past the protective shell of flotilla ships and bearing down on the *Nai'a*. Jarman's breath caught as Varsha searched for a target with a safe firing angle.

Suddenly, the overpowered laser turrets on the *Nai'a* opened up and swept the incoming missiles with a blaze of coherent energy. Within a few seconds the remaining missiles were reduced to vapor and small chunks of debris. "That's how," said Jarman. "Someone on the *Nai'a* took the shot that saved us, and your ship got a little singed in the process." Varsha nodded and went back to searching for remaining targets, using her weapons to vaporize a few stray railgun rounds.

Captain Hartley let out a breath he hadn't known he was holding when the last missile trace disappeared from the screen. "What about railgun rounds?" he asked.

"Our small maneuver took us out of the danger cone." Chief Nance replied.

"Status on the *Emperor Penguin?*"

"Back on the datalink and showing ninety-five percent combat effective," Chief Nance answered.

"Nice shot," said the captain. "I'm glad you didn't have time to ask for permission to take it. I'm sure Jarman will want to have a conversation with you, though."

"No doubt," said the chief with a shake of his head. "I'm just as glad I didn't have time to think about it. I had the shot lined up when the jamming hit, just in case. I had to pull the trigger to give them a chance."

Captain Hartley listened to Commodore Norland give orders to his ships. It looked like the pirate vessels capable of maneuvering were doing their best to run for it. *Moa* and two OSU ships were on the way to scan the wreckage field for survivors.

"Let's put all sensors on a full power scan of our course," ordered the captain. "We need to find the joker in the deck if there is one."

After a few moments, Lieutenant Commander Parks looked up from the sensors station. "I'm getting some faint returns in the wavelengths we found useful against the stealth material we encountered in Tau Ceti. The range is one hundred kilometers and closing along our course. I read at least twelve objects clustered here." He highlighted the symbols on the main display.

Captain Hartley was about to put in a call to the commodore when he heard Norland order *Eagle Ray* to take ten OSU ships and investigate the new contacts. *Eagle Ray* was ten kilometers past the ice shield when fifteen enemy missiles ceased imitating holes in space and leapt toward the long boat. Eagle Ray and its companions waited until the missiles were in laser range, then used coordinated fire to take them out. The Commodore ordered the ships to remain on station in case of another wave.

Captain Hartley looked at Chief Vance. "Those seemed similar to what we encountered in Tau Ceti. If we can recover some hardware, it will add to evidence we already have. Ballistic space mines alone are a big no-no in the Sol system. Stealthed missiles used as space mines violate about ten more system-wide laws."

Chief Vance nodded. "I'll put in a word to Jarman. He's out there in the vanguard."

"Any damage, Commander Calder?" the captain asked.

The chief engineer took a moment to finish consulting her displays. "Three hull punctures between frames thirty-two and twenty-five," she said. "Presumably from railgun rounds. Someone was either a very good or a very bad shot. None of them penetrated past the water jacket compartments. My damage control teams should have them patched in a few hours. We lost a few tons of water, but we have plenty in reserve."

***

A few hours later, Captain Hartley felt the situation was well enough in hand to pay Commodore Norland a visit. He turned the ship over to Commander Stirling and gave his security detail the destination. A few minutes' walk and a vacuum tram ride later, he arrived at the ad hoc flotilla command post.

A harried looking Commodore Norland turned from a status display and greeted him. "Welcome, I'm glad we're both still here to confer. I apologize for all the missiles you were obliged to take on and eternally grateful that you added such a robust antimissile system."

"Having a large power budget and two very capable sets of active sensors to triangulate with certainly helped," said the captain, running a hand through his short-cropped hair. "From where I sat, it looked like we needed everything we had between us to survive."

"You're spot on," said Norland. "Did you learn anything new about how these people fight?"

"No, they've always favored overwhelming force to subtlety. I just wish they'd stop coming so close to achieving that very thing. We encountered those stealthed missiles before. If anyone can gather a piece of debris, it will help our case. You know just how illegal they are, and how much their software would have to be altered to allow them to autonomously attack a ship."

Norland nodded. "We didn't expect them to play by the rules. It's one thing to read a tactical summary, and quite another to witness them in action. We're fortunate we didn't play into their trap. I'm still resolving the number of missiles they started with, and the estimate is frightening. If we hadn't taken out something like two-thirds of their inventory with chunks of the Tater, they'd have blown us out of space."

"Do you know who was in command of their fleet?" The captain asked.

"I have my suspicions," said Norland. "Search and rescue should net us a few prisoners. The 'survivor' types out here value their own skin above all else. They'll gladly sing to avoid a death sentence. They take piracy seriously in the Outer System Union."

"The *Nai'a* got off easy, as you know," said the captain. "How did the rest of the ships fare?"

"Mostly minor damage and a few injuries," answered the commodore. "All of the ships are still combat capable. I'm more worried about the search and rescue operation. They've been warned to stay sharp and take no chances."

Kahleed Gemini walked over to them. He shook Captain Hartley's hand vigorously. "Many thanks, Captain Hartley," he said. "For a moment I thought I had lost all that was dear to me. If you will put me in touch with the person who saved my family and ship, I would appreciate the chance to thank them personally. I don't have words for what I owe them, but I would like to try."

"Chief Nance took the shot," the captain said. "He's nearly as relieved as you are. I think he was afraid he'd vaporize your ship along with the missile."

"The ship is lightly toasted, but still safe and intact," said Kahleed. "Jarman is doing his best to net you some missile debris. As a survey ship, the *Emperor Penguin* has sample collection tools to do the job."

***

Jarman maneuvered the *Emperor Penguin* skillfully into a trajectory matching the most promising piece of ballistic space junk, keeping a thousand-meter safety gap. He didn't hold out much hope for an intact guidance section, but metallurgy alone could probably identify the missile's source. Intact electronic components would seal the deal. Corla sat in the copilot station. She brought up a visual of the slowly spinning missile body. Parts of the outer stealth covering were burned away, revealing the metallic skin of a partial cylinder. "It looks like the aft end of the missile," said Jarman. "We should get part of the engine if we can reel it in."

"That's my cue," said Corla. She switched her instrument panel over to a set of controls for the ship's free flying remote. Jarman watched in fascination as the young woman deftly flew the remote to an intercept of their target. She deployed two sets of articulated grabber arms and closed them slowly on the missile chunk. The visual display spun for a few moments as the momentum of the missile's rotation put the remote into a spin. Varsha quickly corrected the motion and double checked the security of their find. "Positive capture, Mr. Lal," she said. Do you want it in the hold, or clamped to the hull?"

"Well done!" said Jarman. "If you're confident in the remote's grip, clamp it back into its hull mount. I'll have you fly it into the *Nai'a's* boat bay and drop it off for the engineers to go over."

Corla flew the remote and its cargo back to the *Emperor Penguin* and settled it into its docking station. She checked her panel again and nodded in satisfaction. "It's good for up to 5G maneuvers. If you push the ship past that, you void my guarantee."

Jarman smiled. "I'll endeavor to keep my piloting gentle. Your remote is impressive. I'm going to talk to Captain Hartley about purchasing one while we're in system."

"Talk to him about replacing my burnt sensors and the laser head too," said Corla in a completely serious tone. "We don't have the spares to fix those. I'm not complaining about the shot that grazed us. I'm happy to be alive, but I want this fat bird back to one hundred percent."

"Spoken like a true chief engineer!" said Jarman. "I happen to be a good friend of our own chief wrench turner. I'll talk to her and see if we have what it takes to repair your ship. If we don't have the parts, there's a good chance we can fabricate them. We have robust printing and manufacturing capabilities. When things settle down enough for a visit, I could introduce you. Would you like that?"

Corla did her best to take the offer casually, but Jarman could tell she was excited about the prospect. Her mother gave Jarman a smile and a broad wink.

Chapter 22 – Fallout

August 11ᵗʰ, AD 3226
Sol System Heliopause
Nai'a Medical Department

Kalei checked the scruffy looking prisoner over carefully. His personal hygiene could use some work, but he'd come through the battle with nothing worse than a several bruises and possibly a concussion. A Ship Security officer stood nearby, keeping an eye on the man. The pirate appeared to be unconscious. She started to unzip his stained ship suit when the man's eyes opened wide. He grabbed her left arm in an iron grip, yanking her toward him. Instead of resisting, Kalei went with the motion swinging her right elbow in a tight arc and smashing it into his stubbly jawbone with a solid thump. The man's eyes rolled up in his head, and his grip went slack.

The Ship Security officer jumped to assist Kalei, helping her straighten up. He took in the unconscious criminal, then looked at Kalei. "I'm sorry," he said. "I thought he was out." He glanced at the prisoner again. "He sure is now. Are you okay?"

Kalei rubbed her elbow and nodded. "I'm fine, just feeling foolish for not using restraints on a dangerous prisoner. He wants to do this the hard way, so let's oblige him." The two of them soon had the man restrained securely to the exam table.

The Ship Security officer turned the man's head and looked at the rapidly purpling lump on his jaw. "That was a vicious short elbow," he said. "Remind me to never make you angry."

"It's never a good idea to tick off a doctor," said Kalei. "He surprised me, so I hit him harder than I meant to. Still, he earned that and a lot more if he was in the force attacking us."

"We can safely say he was," replied the officer. "I'm hoping we can give him back to the Sol Space Patrol or the Outer System Union and get his stench off the ship."

"I suspect that decision is well above both our pay grades put together," said Kalei, continuing her interrupted examination. After a few minutes she was satisfied the man wasn't in danger. "Do you want him awake or asleep for the trip to the brig?" She reached for the smelling salts with a small smile of anticipation.

***

Commodore Norland spent an hour briefing the *Nai'a*'s leadership and the two ambassadors on the battle and its aftermath.

"We just cleared this sector of most of its criminal elements," he said as he wrapped up. "Kron pulled together a who's-who of wanted pirates and thieves. Just the ones we were able to identify carried enough bounties to give everyone involved a little bonus check. Taking Kron off the table is a tremendous public service. He's been a thorn in the side of the Sol Space Patrol and the Outer System Union for decades."

"What about the ships that got away?" asked Captain Hartley.

"Out of a force of over fifty, only five were in good enough shape to run," said the commodore. "I suspect they'll be running for a long time. We also got a good enough read on their ships' drive signatures to positively identify them. If they show up at a law-abiding port, they'll be arrested." He frowned. "The issue I have now is prisoners. We have limited brig facilities and more prisoners than we can safely keep. The Outer System Union will eventually take them off our hands for trial. If you can keep a dozen of them on the *Nai'a*, it will make the situation tenable. I realize it's a security risk. The chance of a high-level agent among these miscreants isn't high, but it isn't zero either."

Captain Hartley nodded. "We can handle that many, but I want assurance and a plan from the Outer System Union to offload them while we're still in their jurisdiction." He looked pointedly at Kahleed Gemini.

Kahleed just nodded and grinned. "I've arranged for an OSU Marshall Service ship to rendezvous with us in three days. They'll take any prisoners the Sol Space Patrol agrees to turn over and deliver them for trial."

The Commodore took a seat at the table and leaned forward on his elbows. "Sol Space Patrol Headquarters is more than mildly embarrassed that they nearly allowed your ship to be destroyed and had to rely on the OSU to bail us out. I don't share their embarrassment, but I do apologize on their behalf for the complete intelligence and risk assessment failure that led to the close escape we just went through.

"Fortunately, my report of the battle, backed up by Captain Page, lit a fire under the scoffers. In a few days, you'll have an escort force worthy of being called a fleet. Whatever Helvetica Montrose reports about this, the Sol Space Patrol is going to get a large dent in our invincible reputation. My leadership will want to make sure we don't have any more incidents like this one."

***

"Good evening, morning, or whatever your time might be," Helvetica began with her trademark opening. She looked directly into the pickup, her professional expression just a touch more serious than usual. "Helvetica Montrose here with another report from the long boat *Nai'a*. I am both delighted and appalled this evening. Delighted to be alive, and appalled at the brazen attack the ship I'm a passenger on recently suffered. For security reasons, I haven't been given many details. What I do know makes me question the security of the Sol System as a whole. The Sol Space Patrol commodore in charge of the security flotilla admitted to me that the ship's survival was a very near thing. Officially a force of pirates is to blame. I'll let you draw your own conclusions as to who funded and armed them to the point that they felt confident in attacking a long boat in Sol System space." Helvetica went on to tell what she knew of the attack and its outcome.

When she was finished with the segment, Lincoln stopped the recording. "Short and to the point," he said. "You'll ruffle some feathers, especially with the Sol Space Patrol. I just hope you don't get the commodore in trouble."

"Since he saved the ship from a major pirate attack, I think he's safe from official sanction," replied Helvetica. "What *I'm* wondering, is what the Restoration is going to come at the *Nai'a* with next. Desperation drives people to do desperate things. These people have a lot of resources and very few scruples."

***

Lon Valenda read the latest report from his source inside the Sol Space Patrol and bit back an epithet. He'd advised the Restoration High Council against a direct attack on the *Nai'a*, but they'd ordered him to pull the trigger on Kron and his gang of thieves anyway. Now, even without direct evidence, most of the Sol System was correctly laying the blame for the attack at the Restoration's feet. As the head of the covert direct-action branch of the organization, he didn't deal much with public relations, but he knew a disaster when it was staring him in the face. This, piled on top of the Sol News Service embarrassment, was going to leave them without much public support.

Good riddance to Kron and his like, but it was time to consider the next arrow in his quiver. He was mulling over the possibilities when a call came in from the current director of the Restoration High Council. He connected the call, checking to make sure it was end-to end encrypted. "Your pirates got shot to pieces, Valenda," the man began, clearly in a bad mood and ready to take it out on someone. Lon decided it was a waste of time to mention his earlier recommendation to forgo the attack. "We need to derail the Long Boat Free Trade Association and Ambassador Brelling now, or half the council members are going to be up on charges," the man continued. "You have the list of people we need to get rid of. I suggest you start working it off yesterday."

Lon wasn't comfortable with hearing that kind of specific direction out loud, even on an encrypted channel. He managed to control a grimace. "The long boat people, especially those on the *Nai'a*, have proven to be both alert and resilient," he pointed out. "They'll have security measures in place. It's not as simple as getting an operative on board. Also, before I start any wheels turning, has the council considered the fallout? It's not going to look like an accident, and you know where the blame will be laid."

"We're past the point of worrying about that," the man said, frustration evident in his tone. "Despite what some of the other council members think, we're going to lose in the court of public opinion. We need to make sure we don't lose in the court of law, so we can regroup and adjust our strategy. Step one is getting rid of as many witnesses as possible."

Lon shook his head. "Even if we get the entire list, the *Nai'a* is still going to deliver the evidence they haven't already turned over. Based on what they've revealed about our organization's finances in their initial charges, they've got a solid case against several of the key corporate backers."

"Let us worry about the legal front," the man answered dismissively. "We've got the best lawyers in the system working that side. You just make sure nothing can tie us to what happens to their leadership." The connection cut off abruptly. Lon checked his concealed weapons, then left his office. He had several messages to send, and they all needed to originate somewhere else.

Chapter 23 – Under Pressure

August 24ᵗʰ, AD 3226
Sol System, Outer System Union – Saturn Commonwealth Border
Nai'a *Bridge*

Captain Hartley watched the main bridge display with keen interest as all the Outer System Union ships, except *Emperor Penguin*, accelerated away from the *Nai'a*. A force of three cruisers, six destroyers, and twelve corvettes now escorted the long boat into Saturn Commonwealth territory. He wasn't happy to see the OSU irregulars depart, but they'd done more than enough for the *Nai'a* and had their own business to attend to. The prisoners were long since gone with the OSU martial service and a few of the cold sleep passengers. The leased transport ship had plenty of passenger space, and hitching a ride to their final destination at Makemake cut a good chunk of time off their journey.

The Saturn Commonwealth welcomed them with a diplomatic cutter, escorted by three patrol vessels from the Commonwealth Space Guard. The CSG served mainly police and search & rescue functions. They had a cordial relationship with the Sol Space Patrol, if not the history of close cooperation enjoyed by the OSU irregulars. A full ambassador of the Saturn Commonwealth came with the cutter. Captain Hartley checked the time and the condition of his dress uniform, then turned the bridge watch over to his first officer and headed for the boat bay with his security escort.

***

A few hours of security, and medical checks later, the Saturn Commonwealth diplomatic team sat down with the Ship's Council. Ambassadors Brelling and Dunleavy, as well as Commodore Norland, also attended. Saturn Commonwealth Ambassador Ansel Wright looked the part, a distinguished older man with wavy iron-gray hair dressed in impeccable business attire. After welcome and introductions, Ambassador Brelling gestured toward her Saturn Commonwealth counterpart. "The floor is yours, Ambassador Wright," she said. "I'm sure we have much to discuss, but we'd like to know your government's position on the recent events surrounding the *Nai'a* and the Long Boat Free Trade Syndicate."

Ansel Wright considered her for a moment, then nodded. "Fair enough," he said. "Your own diplomatic and legal dispatches make the trade syndicate's position quite clear. The commonwealth attorney general is preparing charges based on the evidence we've received, and some our own investigators uncovered. So far, you've only accused specific interstellar corporations of conspiracy and financing criminal activities. Do you expect to name any individuals?"

"Not at this time," Anne Brelling answered levelly.

Ambassador Wright waited a moment, then continued. "You haven't accused any of the Sol governments of collusion with this 'Restoration.' Do you suspect they have government backing?"

"No. However, we are certain they have agents and sympathetic ears in every Sol government," answered Anne. "If we have credible evidence of criminal activity by an individual, we'll present that to the appropriate government. The Restoration specializes in blackmail and intimidation. I have no doubt evidence will surface that they employ those tactics here as well."

"Very well," said Ansel. "I brought a small legal team. If you're willing, I'd like them to work through some of the evidence and accusations with your experts." Anne nodded. "My government sees this as a mainly legal matter," Ansel continued, "but we do recognize the ongoing and unprecedented threat to your safety and security. The Commonwealth Space Guard will supplement the Sol Space Patrol escort while you are in commonwealth territory. The anti-piracy and terrorism division is already working with your people."

"We appreciate your cooperation, and especially your addition to the protective escort," said Anne. "As you know, the free trade syndicate stands for freedom and safety of navigation throughout human occupied space. That's why recent events are so troubling. All the Sol System polities except Terra have at least expressed support and investigated our accusations. We're unsure why the Terran government is dragging its heels, but we'll be on their doorstep soon enough. Do you have any sense of what's going on there?"

Ansel's professional mask wavered for a brief instant, but he smoothed his expression quickly. "Officially, no. Unofficially, the Restoration's friends in high places appear to be concentrated in Terran orbit. If anyone still pines for the old days of colonialism, it's the home planet. Even there, I don't imagine they have a lot in the way of public support."

"We could use your backing, when it comes time to force Terra's hand," said Anne.

Ansel shook his head. "I don't have authority to promise that. You'll need to convince Parliament. The members have been getting an earful from their constituents, mostly in your favor."

"Can you arrange a joint session of Parliament?" asked Rolland Dunleavy. "We're both willing to make a personal appeal."

Ansel looked thoughtful. "You'll be swinging past Saturn in a few days, so I suppose it's possible. I'll need to get on the com and start the wheels turning."

***

Soma trudged wearily back to her dad's quarter's. She'd moved in with Julian and Kalei when they'd started waking up the Saturn contingent of cold sleepers. Quarters were in short supply, and she preferred their sleeper couch to a dormitory. She was pulling long hours in the cold sleep recovery wards. The work was rewarding, but she felt as tired as she'd ever been. When she slumped through the door, Julian, Kalei, and Rolland Dunleavy were all waiting for her.

"Oh boy," said Soma, "this can't be good news."

"Don't be so pessimistic," said Kalei, with a smile. She guided the tired young woman to the dinner table. "My mom sent third-day lasagna over. Get some dinner in you, then we'll talk." She uncovered the steaming dish and set a side-salad of tomatoes and cucumbers next to it. They all took a seat, the others sipping after dinner coffee.

Soma wasted no time giving the food her undivided attention. A few minutes later she looked up to find identical amused expressions on everyone's faces. "What???" she said, wiping tomato sauce from the corner of her mouth.

Julian laughed. "If I didn't know better, I'd think you were directly related to Abishai!" he said. "You inhaled that like starving hyaena!"

Soma drained her glass of water and shrugged. "He's one of my favorite people, so I don't mind the comparison. Would someone mind telling me what's going on?

Rolland leaned forward. "Anne and I address the Saturn Commonwealth Parliament in a few days. We'd like you to come with us and tell your story." Soma's eyes went wide. Rolland looked at her for a moment and continued. "I know you'd be opening old wounds. I want to be clear; it's completely up to you. I talked with Julian and Kalei before you got here. They both prefer not to put you through this, but they also said I should ask, because you should make the decision. You'll have a chance to tell, not just the Parliament, but the entire Sol System how the Restoration uses people and wrecks lives."

Soma leaned back and a determined look crossed her face. She took a deep breath and nodded once, firmly. "I'm in," she said. "Everyone needs to understand what those murderers are capable of. I'm scared out of my wits and I don't know what to say, but I'll do it!"

Julian leaned over and gave her a one-armed hug. "Like Ambassador Dunleavy said, you just need to tell your story. The facts speak for themselves, and I know how convincing you can be."

Soma laughed, the sound carrying a slightly hysterical note. "You never could refuse me anything."

"Most of the time it was a good thing I didn't," Julian replied. "You were always pushing your limits, and needed to find them on your own. We did spend more time in medical than I preferred."

"It was worth the bumps and bruises to watch you blush and stammer around Kalei."

Julian hugged her again. "That's about enough truth for one evening. We all need to get our rest."

***

The approach to Saturn precipitated a steady stream of visitors to the Starlight Lounge. Everyone, including the newly awakened cold sleepers, wanted to see the spectacular view of the massive planet and its rings. The Alder Council finally decided to issue timeslots to everyone to keep things fair.

Abishai wasn't happy or comfortable in his Ship Security uniform, but that couldn't be helped. He and Quester were chosen to accompany the Ambassadors and Soma on their trip to the Titan IV habitat to address Parliament. Captain Hartley made the decision to put them in uniform for the trip. The shuttle passage was nerve wracking, but uneventful. The Commonwealth Space Guard provided a large force of patrol ships as escort, with three Sol Space Patrol frigates on overwatch.

Once they cleared habitat's large dock, Abishai joined a uniformed local police officer nearly his size in leading the way to the Parliament chamber. The few people they passed swiftly moved to one side when they saw the two coming through the sparsely populated corridors. After a ten-minute walk, the door to the chamber speaking dais opened. Abishai took the right side of the large balcony, while Quester stationed himself on the left. Both nervously scanned the rows of murmuring Parliament members as the Prime Minister welcomed Anne, Rolland, and Soma. Abishai had expected some kind of elaborate ceremony, but the Right Honorable Sir Hadley

Markland simply strode to the front of the balcony and banged a wooden gavel once. He called Parliament to order and began speaking. "Today we welcome Ambassador Anne Brelling of the Long Boat Free Trade Syndicate, Ambassador Rolland Dunleavy of Lalande, and Able Spacer Soma Garrity, citizen of Lalande. Please give them your full attention. Our commonwealth has decisions to make, and they should be informed by an understanding of recent events." He waved the trio forward.

Anne Brelling swept to the speakers spot with a determined stride. Rolland and Soma flanked her on either side. She surveyed the three hundred-plus members from left to right then began speaking. "Members of the Saturn Commonwealth Parliament. Today you stand on the precipice of great change throughout human occupied space. This is not hyperbole or exaggeration. The Restoration, an organization that seeks to remain in the shadows, is intent on controlling every aspect of interstellar trade and the distant star nations themselves. We ask you to stand with us and keep the people and trade of all star systems free.

"You have our precis and the detailed data package of their crimes against the *Nai'a*. You have the evidence of their multiple acts of terrorism in Tau Ceti from Marshall Winter. I won't waste your time recounting those. Such is the scope of their ambition that they attempted to take over the entire star system of Lalande. I yield the floor to Ambassador Dunleavy to help you understand the danger you face."

Rolland stepped forward. "I come to you as the personal representative of The Bancroft and the people of Lalande. We have more reason than most to suspect the Long Boat Free Trade Syndicate, but in our time of need, the long boat *Nai'a* came to our aid. My home system would be under an iron dictatorship now without their help. I've brought one of my people, who lived through the rebellion, to help you see what the Restoration is willing to do in pursuit of its goals."

He turned to Soma, who hesitantly stepped forward. She visibly gathered herself, then looked defiantly across the crowd and began to speak.

"I was eleven years old when the Restoration rebels forcibly boarded my parents' mining ship and took us captive. They beat my father and separated all of us. They forced my parents at gunpoint, and with the threat of harm to me, to pilot ships and participate in the rebellion. They armed our ship with missiles, and sent my parents against The Bancroft's forces. My parents were both murdered, not killed in the battle, but shot in the back of the head by the Restoration's criminals when the tide turned against them." Tears trailed down her cheeks, but she forged on. "I'm only one of their many victims, and more fortunate than most. I was rescued from a drifting hulk by spacers from the *Nai'a* and adopted by one of their pilots. When he was a young pilot in Tau Ceti, a Restoration agent shot my adoptive father's copilot dead in the seat beside him when he refused to launch a nuclear missile at the *Nai'a*. My father fought him, overcoming a knife wound to knock the man unconscious and save the ship. I beg you to do whatever you can to stop the Restoration before they write more stories like mine and my father's."

Soma stepped back from the dais. Anne handed her a handkerchief and gave her a hug. Rolland took her place. "You have a choice," he said. "Ignore the threat and become a passive enabler of kidnappers, murderers, and terrorists, or stand with us and help remove this stain from the human-settled stars.

The floor of the Parliament erupted in shouts of anger and the Prime Minister stepped forward to bang is gavel several times. "Order!" he said. "We will recess for two hours, then reconvene for debate and discussion."

The *Nai'a* contingent followed the Prime Minister to his private office where they were served high tea. "What is it you want from the commonwealth?" he asked Anne once they were settled.

Anne considered the PM for a moment. With his perfect dark brown hair and vid-star good looks, it would have been easy to dismiss him as an empty suit, but she sensed Sir Hadley Markland was more than he appeared. "We want cooperation prosecuting the charges we've filed, and with tracking down Restoration operatives in your jurisdiction," she said. "More importantly, we want you to put pressure on the Terran government to do the same. The Restoration has it's hooks in high places. Odds are, some of your members of Parliament are in their camp."

Markland frowned but shrugged. "I wish I could argue. However, I suspect you're right. After your performance, I wonder if they'll be willing to take the Restoration's side in the coming debate. I rather doubt it. The most difficult opposition is going to be from those who would rather stay neutral. I have some sympathy for that argument, and you can bet the opposition coalition is going to throw their weight toward neutrality just to undermine my government. You have solid support in the latest public opinion polls, though. So, their strategy will likely backfire.

"You'll get the law enforcement support you've asked for, and we're pursuing the charges the evidence warrants. I can guarantee that will happen as long as I'm leading the government. I know you're already sharing intelligence with our anti-terrorism task force. Please continue, and I would very much appreciate any credible information you turn up on Restoration agents in our territory."

Anne nodded. "We'll continue to share information as long as we can be reasonably sure it stays secure. I've had my own crew infiltrated multiple times, so we're sensitive about moles."

The Prime Minister was about to answer when a trumpet fanfare filled the room and the door swept open. Abishai and Quester both took a step toward the door but stopped at a gesture from Anne. Everyone in the room rose to their feet as a stunningly beautiful young woman in an elaborate gown swept into the room. "Her Majesty, Queen of Saturn, Katherine the Second!" The door man announced. The prime minister bowed deeply, and his guests followed suit.

The Queen had a slightly amused look on her face. "Sorry to burst in on you without warning, Hadley, but I'm certain you were going to let our guests get away without a royal audience."

"Guilty as charged, your majesty," Markland said without a trace of guilt in his tone.

"Well," said the Queen, "are you going to stand there or introduce us?" Sir Hadley closed his eyes, then, with great forbearance, introduced the Ambassadors and a wide-eyed Soma to the Queen.

Introductions complete; the Queen took a seat at the table and helped herself to a cup of tea. Anne wasn't sure how she managed to sit in those voluminous skirts, but she was impressed. "We didn't expect to get on your busy schedule, Your Majesty," Anne said, as the Queen generously buttered a scone.

"Oh, please!" the Queen replied with a big grin. "Just call me Kathy. Up until three years ago, I was just a farmer's daughter. Still am, for that matter." Anne was familiar with the ever-rotating nature of the Saturn Commonwealth throne, but she realized she should have done more homework on the current occupant. Saturn chose their king or queen using a talent-search type show with public input to choose a new sovereign every ten years. The winner received two years of training equivalent to a master's degree before taking the throne. Although the forms of a constitutional monarchy were observed, the Queen's chief duty was to relieve career politicians like Sir Hadley from as much public ceremony as possible.

"Did you have questions for our guests?" prompted Sir Hadley, clearly not amused by the interruption.

"Don't act so put out, Hadley," the Queen replied. "You know I'm responsible for most of the positive public opinion your party enjoys. I just wanted to talk with these good people before I throw my full support behind them." Her bubbly effervescence disappeared as she turned to Soma. "I'm so sorry about your parents. I can't imagine losing mine." She placed a hand on Soma's arm. "You were very brave speaking to Parliament."

Soma blushed. "Thank you," she managed.

"You're a cold sleep technician," said the Queen. "It's a lot of responsibility. What put you down that career path?"

Soma considered the question for a moment. "The ship needed cold sleep technicians. I saw it as the best way I could contribute. Also, I found the process fascinating when I did a short internship in the department. The people who work in cold sleep have a guiding ethos centered around protecting their patients. I feel like I'm doing something worthwhile."

The Queen tilted her head and her mouth quirked. "You'd be a good candidate for my job," she said. She turned to Ambassador Brelling. "You have Parliament in an uproar. Anyone who was considering supporting the Restoration's position will be thinking twice about saying it out loud. It was a shrewd decision to put Soma in front of them, but I don't think you're capable of using someone that way without their full cooperation."

Anne regarded the Queen levelly. "You might be surprised what I would do when it comes to protecting the ship and crew, but you're right. There are lines I won't cross. Rolland asked Soma to do this, but the decision was entirely hers."

The Queen and Anne locked eyes for a moment, then the Queen bowed her head slightly in acknowledgement. "I'm glad I find myself in your corner, Ambassador. I see now why the Restoration has failed every attempt to take the *Nai'a*." She finished her scone and tossed off the last of the tea in her cup. "I'll let you all get back to the serious business of statesmanship while I set up a press conference. Would I be imposing if I paid a visit to your long boat?" She stood, and everyone followed suit.

"Not at all, Kathy," Anne replied. "I'm sure the crew would love to meet you." The queen dimpled and said her goodbyes. She swept out of the room with a smile and a wink for the prime minister.

Anne caught Sir Hadley's eye roll and had to cough to keep from laughing out loud. "For a non-politician and a farmer's daughter, the Queen cuts a wide swath," she said to the prime minister over her teacup.

"You don't know the half of it," Sir Hadley replied. "I should have known better than to try to get you out of here without having to deal with her. My apologies."

"No apology required," said Rolland, with a grin. "I wouldn't have missed that for the world. We can use all the help we can get on the public relations front."

"From where I sit," said the PM, "you're winning that fight quite handily. I can guarantee, you're going to get a shot in the arm, though. I've seen that look in Her Majesty's eye before." He took a sip of tea before continuing. "I'll do what I can to help you put pressure on the Terran government. We have some economic leverage with them, but it cuts both ways. The Jovian Alliance is in much the same position we are. The Belt and Mars have more sway, but the Terrans can be hard-headed."

Anne nodded in agreement. "We'll gather every hammer we can on the way in-system, and see if we can hit them hard enough to wake them up to what's going on. Between the Restoration's cronies and pure inertia, it's going to be a difficult task. Tell me, how do you think the Queen would like it if we threw a ball in her honor?"

Sir Hadley laughed. "The Queen loves a good party. She'd be thrilled."

Chapter 24 – Rings on Her Toes

August 28th, AD 3226
Closest Approach to Saturn
Nai'a *Ship's Council Chamber*

Anne wrapped up her report on the visit to Titan IV habitat with a pitch for the grand ball in honor of the Queen. Captain Halsey wasn't thrilled. "Do you have any idea what a security nightmare that would be?" he asked.

"I'm aware," said Anne mildly, "but I think the risk is acceptable. Chief Bolhepp's screening procedures are very good, and the crew deserves a good party. We've got a breather now with the Saturn passengers offloaded, I say we take advantage and let our folks blow off some steam."

Chief Alder Belotic nodded her head enthusiastically. "If we're going to throw a party, this is the time. We have a full recreation fund, and I can't think of a better use for it."

"I have no objection," said the CEO, Hubble Spearsley. "It will give me the chance to make some face-to face contacts I wouldn't get otherwise."

Captain Hartley leaned back, shaking his head. "I can see I'm outvoted," he said. "I'll get together with Chief Bolhepp and see what we can do to reduce the security risks. I hope I don't live to regret it."

***

Soma and Grady sat side-by-side in the Starlight Lounge, watching as Saturn's huge rings swung into view beneath them. Soma stuck a bare foot out and wiggled her toes. "It almost looks like I could reach out and snag one," she said. She'd been too busy to use all her time slots, and decided to share one with Grady while the view was still good.

"Kojin's rings are spectacular too, but Saturn is prettier," said Grady. "I don't think the Restoration has a hidden fleet waiting to attack us this time."

Soma frowned. "With all the firepower in our escort, I don't think even they'd be that bold."

"What was the Queen like?" asked Grady.

"Very smart, and gracious. I think the people of the commonwealth chose wisely. You'll get a chance to meet her."

"I hope so," said Grady. "She looks like something out of a fairy tale."

"Don't get your hopes up too high. I'm sure she has her pick of men."

Grady sighed, "No doubt, but a fellow can dream."

Soma punched him none-too-lightly on the boney shoulder. "Don't get too dreamy about another woman around me or I won't invite you next time."

"Don't tease," said Grady, rubbing his shoulder. "You have your pick too, and I know I'm not it."

"I'm not picking anyone," said Soma, "but someone has to take me to the ball, and you just might be it."

"What if I already asked someone?"

"Your latest crush is gone to Titan," Soma answered. "I'd know if you already had a date."

"Hrmmph," said Grady, with scowl. "You're way too confident."

"I know!" said Soma, "but I have reason to be."

***

Helvetica pinched the bridge of her nose hard, trying to ward off an incipient headache. She was cutting a swath through the Sol System media beyond her wildest dreams, but the cost was a level of exhaustion she'd never approached before. She tried to focus one more time on the terms of a contract with the owners of the largest COM-NET in the system. The legal mumbo-jumbo defeated her meagre powers of concentration, so she shut her data terminal down with a yawn. This contract would lay the foundation for her own system-wide news network. She'd pick it up in the morning after a strong cup of coffee. She allowed herself a small smile thinking about the Queen's visit. She'd already agreed to an interview and Helvetica knew a choice opportunity when she saw one.

***

Hal Renfro's PCOM buzzed a priority alert. When he saw what it was, he checked his concealed weapon, pulled on a jacket with armored lining, and headed for Chief Bolhepp's office. The chief had a video feed from the main boat bay pulled up. One of the guests for the ball undergoing initial security checks was highlighted. "We picked up a signature enough like Nicholas Withers' facial impersonation mask to trip the alarm. It's coming from this person." He zoomed in on a man of medium build with nut-brown skin and close-cropped dark hair. The man was grinning at the Ship Security officer and cracking some kind of joke, just as a slightly nervous guest might.

Hal looked at the biometrics readout, and saw that the man's vitals indicated an unnatural calm. "That's a cool customer," he said. "He's got to be a professional. What do you want to do about it? We could isolate him and bring him in for questioning."

Chief Bolhepp watched the video feed for a few more seconds. "He'll realize what's happening before we can get him away from the crowd in the boat bay, and I don't want to risk a takedown there. Who knows how he'll resist? Also, I learned the value of patience from you. Our scanners aren't picking up any weapons. Let's track him and see what he does. We may learn a lot, including whether he has any accomplices. I want you to shadow him, and we'll have Mr. Literal monitor his PCOM. All our guests agreed to monitoring as a condition of coming aboard. You'll have the ready teams from Ship Security and the militia to back you up. Don't do anything silly."

"I won't," said Hal. He continued to watch the apparent spy as he underwent medical screening. "Who does this character claim to be?"

"Ethan Umbrette, one of fifty winners of a drawing to award tickets to the ball," the chief said. "Which begs the question of what happened to the real Ethan Umbrette? I don't want to tip our hand yet, but we do need to pass this information to our commonwealth counterparts. He may be in danger.”

Hal grimaced. “Or, already dead or kidnapped. I hope not, but you’re right. We can’t sit on the information. Let me pass it to my contact with the anti-terrorism task force. They have the resources to check into Ethan’s whereabouts quietly.”

“Do that, and pass the word to Ambassador Brelling.” said the chief. “I’ll let the captain know.” Hal nodded and headed aft. He’d need all his skill, and a lot of help from Mr. Literal, to shadow a trained agent.

***

Jost Severn was growing frustrated. After a full day on board the *Nai’a*, he’d learned all his primary targets had a well-trained personal guard detail. He had no doubt he could take down at least one target, but getting through an armed security team and away again was a different matter. Suicide was no part of his plan. He didn’t mind being well paid by fanatics, but he would never be one.

He’d managed to get a few details about the on-call security teams, including a full platoon of heavily armed and armored militia. He didn’t have any way to defeat powered armor. Maybe it was time to change targets and level up his weapons. He pulled up the Queen’s itinerary, then flipped through the faces he had retinal scans and DNA from. He allowed himself a smile as the pieces of a plan began to click together. Even on his borrowed face, the grin showed more teeth than it should have.

***

Hal checked the agent’s position again and put in a call to Chief Bolhepp. “He’s sitting on a bench watching the crew prepare Cooper Green for the ball. Should we take him into custody? I don’t think we want to wait until the ball starts. There’s too much potential for collateral damage.”

“I agree,” said the chief, “but we still don’t know what his game is. If you get a good opportunity, call in the team and bring him in. I’ll leave it to your discretion. If you can hold off until he commits to a course of action, we'll get more out of this. He may just be scouting for other operators. Mr. Literal found he has an illegal long distance com capability, probably built into his PCOM. He sent one burst transmission from the Starlight Lounge, earlier today. If we move on him, we'll need to jam it, so he doesn't alert anyone."

"Roger," Hal replied. "He's moving now. I'll keep you apprised."

Several minutes and a number of decks later Mr. Literal called Hal. "The subject's mask just shifted," he said. "He's now wearing the face of Quester Drake." Hal fought the urge to call in the security team. He had an idea of where the agent was headed. He quickly called the commander of the militia ready platoon and relayed his instructions. As a member of the commando platoon, Quester had full access to the militia armories on board.

"Your certain you can establish remote control of any armor he steals?" Hal asked his wife Lisandra over their private PCOM channel. She replied in the affirmative and set up the required protocols on her mini-comp.

***

Jost was surprised and pleased to find the Epsilon Section armory unoccupied. His mask fooled the security scanner, and he quickly found a full suit of powered armor in his size. He noted the weapons inventory and donned the suit. Once powered up, he checked the time and moved out toward the tropical dome. His schematics showed he could enter the water there and make his way to the Six Fathoms restaurant. Two of his targets were scheduled to dine with the Queen in a few minutes. The guns on this monster suit would make short work of the security teams, and the Queen would make an excellent hostage.

***

"When can you establish remote control of that suit of armor?" Hal asked his wife.

"I already have," Lisandra said. "I could march him up and down Cooper Green if you'd like, but simply shutting the suit down is probably safer."

"Okay, I want to time it carefully," Hal transmitted. "Stand by." He watched the agent's icon track into the tropical dome toward the beach, and realized where he was likely going. Hal notified the ready platoon of the militia and called Quester, who was on his way to Six Fathoms with Anne Brelling, Rolland Dunleavy, and the Queen. Quester made it to Six Fathoms in under a minute. He was quickly in animated conversation with the matriarch of the dolphin pod using the lobby hydrophone. As soon as he got the message across, the whole pod charged off to don their ceramic armor, the two largest males in the lead. Within a few minutes Quester cleared the space of patrons and staff, while a squad of militia in powered armor took up position in the restaurant to backstop the dolphins.

Abishai ushered his charges into a side corridor well short of Six Fathoms and took up station guarding the hatch. The Queen's guards drew their weapons and took positions in the corridor outside. The Queen took the diversion in stride, chatting with Anne and Rolland about who the important guests at the ball would be.

***

Jost was impressed with his new suit of armor and how well it adapted to walking across the bottom of the tropical sea habitat. He forged forward confidently, watching his surroundings carefully and noting the incredible variety of sea life around him. He was about halfway to his objective when the armor locked up in mid-stride. All readouts in the suit went dark. He had a moment of panic that turned to terror as a thousand kilograms of dolphin outfitted in articulated ceramic armor slammed into his suit. Despite the close-fitting padded interior, he was thrown around and bruised from head to toe. The two dolphins who hit him continued their rush, pushing the helpless assassin through the water and slamming him into a bulkhead. Three sets of heavy steal calipers closed around the now unpowered armor with a snap.

Jost thrashed and looked around wildly for a way out. He couldn't move anything but his head more than an inch, and the view from his faceplate showed that he was still under water. Suddenly a large black eye surrounded by a matte-gray layer of armor looked directly into his. He froze, and his eyes widened. The dolphin disappeared and a second later he groaned as his armor shook from a blow to the breast plate. He wondered if the armor would hold, and how much air he had without power in the suit.

After several more blows rang his suit like a bell, a single light glowed on the display and the speaker in his helmet crackled. "You're in a bit of a bind. The dolphins don't appreciate enemies invading their ship, and you shouldn't have borrowed their friend's face or that suit of armor," a female voice said. "They don't want to give you up, but we might convince them to release you if you come clean and tell us all about yourself and your employers."

"Stuff it!" Jost growled. "You people aren't going to harm me. You're a bunch rule-followers, and torture is outlawed in this system."

"You're right, we won't harm you," the voice said reasonably. "I can't vouch for the dolphins, though. They're literally a law unto themselves. Is it getting stuffy in there?"

The suit of armor rang from another blow, then a dolphin with an articulated arm attached to its armor came into view. The arm was holding what looked like a high-speed drill. Jost watched in horrified fascination as the drill drifted toward his faceplate, then down out of view. He heard a clunk as the bit contacted his neck seal. The drill started up, and a whine like the mother of all dentist's drills filled Jost's ears. The vibration rattled his teeth. "I'LL TALK...STOP THEM PLEASE!!!...I'LL TALK!" Jost screamed. He couldn't breathe or talk as the drill continued eating its way toward his neck for a full second...then it stopped. Jost's breath came back in gasps.

"That's much more reasonable," the voice said in his ear. "Now, start with your name, and the whereabouts and condition of the real Ethan Umbrette, then we'll go from there."

***

Several minutes and questions later Lisandra cut the channel. "We have what we need for now," Chief Bolhepp said, looking over Lisandra's shoulder at her minicomp display. "You're sure he can't access anything other than coms?"

"Oh, he's trying," answered Lisandra. "That fancy PCOM of his isn't getting through the suit, the water, and our jamming, though. I'm going to take care of the PCOM now." She touched the virtual switch on her display to open the com channel to the suit again. "Now, Mr. Jost Severn, you're going to provide me root access to your PCOM. Don't even try to tell me you can't do it. I know better."

Jost grimaced but complied. Lisandra immediately shut down his access to the personal communicator and his attempted distress signals. She hummed as her keys flew over the virtual keyboard. She used her data connection to download a full image of the PCOM's programming and storage, then locked access with a pass phrase. "I have everything I need, and he's locked out of his PCOM," she told Chief Bolhepp.

"Good!" replied the chief. "If he's telling the truth, he doesn't have any accomplices aboard. Let us know if you find anything in his files to indicate otherwise. I'm tempted to let the dolphins play with him for a while, but we should probably get him secured in the brig before the Queen's ball starts."

***

With a three-dolphin assist, Jost's battered suit of armor landed on the sand of the beach face down with a thump. Three militia soldiers stood where they had clear fields of fire while Hal walked over and used a meter-long prybar to flip the suit over. He unlatched the helmet and set it aside. Jost, drank in lungsful of fresh air. His eyes were wild, and his face had a weird, melted look to it. He no longer resembled Quester in any way. Hal remembered the disguising mask was controlled by software in the locked down PCOM.

Hal rapped the dented chest plate with his prybar. "You aren't going to give me any trouble, are you?" he said in his most intimidating rumble. Jost shook his head, and Hal started the process of un-shelling the would-be assassin from the inert set of armor.

***

The Queen laughed delightedly at Rolland's description of his trip to the *Nai'a* in a glorified life pod. They were enjoying their appetizers at a central table after the short delay in the side corridor. "The Bancroft owes you a lot," she said. "I couldn't force myself to take a one-way trip like that."

Rolland looked at Anne and smiled. "My reward is well worth it." Before the Queen could reply, a high-pitched whistling fanfare from the tropical seas side of the restaurant caught their attention. The dolphins retreated, then returned at high speed and leapt from the water in a coordinated aerial ballet. The Queen stared, speechless as the dolphins ended their impromptu welcome with a bow.

"Can I speak with them?" she asked. Anne waived Quester over. He grimaced but decided the militia troops still scattered around the restaurant were sufficient security. He walked the Queen to a platform at the edge of the tank and introduced her to each member of the dolphin pod. The Queen was delighted. With Quester interpreting, she thanked the dolphins for both the welcome and keeping her safe. The dolphins replied with an invitation to swim with them after the ball.

***

After depositing Jost in the brig, Hal joined Chief Bolhepp and Lisandra in her office. "He completely clammed up on me, but I gather he spilled a lot of information before the dolphins delivered him. What did you find out?" he asked.

"His primary targets were the two ambassadors and Helvetica Montrose," said the chief. "He went for the powered armor because he didn't like his chances against our security teams without superior firepower. Did you find any weapons on him?"

Hal nodded. "He had a cobbled-together compressed air gun and darts with some kind of poison, no doubt. I took a dart to Medical for analysis and put the rest in the evidence vault."

"That lines up with what he told us," said the chief. "He got a vial of neurotoxin past our scanners. He used materials gathered on board to fashion the compressed air gun and darts. I'm not sure how effective it would be, but a head or neck shot would probably be fatal. We'll see what medical says."

Hal looked at the time. "The ball is about to start. Do you think we're secure enough to let them go ahead?"

"We stopped this attempt, and I think Jost was telling the truth about acting alone," said the Chief. "I'm not going to call a halt to biggest social event on this ship in decades."

"The Commonwealth police have an extensive file on Jost. He's on their most wanted list. They believe he perpetrated at least three assassinations, possibly more. He's always slipped through their fingers, but his DNA is a match for the evidence they have. If we turn him over to them, we'll make a lot of friends."

Hal turned to Lisandra. "Did you get any useful data?"

Lisandra's grin was feral. She leaned back and cracked her knuckles. "Oh yes, and thanks to our dolphin friends, I didn't even have to work for it. It's a good thing because his encryption was first rate. I've got his coms and financial data from the time he upgraded his PCOM several years ago. I'd wager the crumb trail for every assassination he's conducted is in here. We also have a positive match with the software Nicholas used for his mask."

Hal nodded in satisfaction, "I'll be happier with him off the ship, if the captain approves."

***

Grady floated across Cooper Green's temporary dance floor, for once glad of the dance lessons his mother had forced him to endure. The Queen was even more stunning up close than in her pictures, and she effortlessly followed his lead. Couples in finery Grady had never seen before swirled around them, but Grady only had eyes for the beauty in his arms.

Soma smirked as the pair whisked by. She was happy for him, and the look on his face was worth every credit she'd paid for his place on the Queen's dance card. He'd be floating for weeks if she was any judge. She looked forward to teasing him mercilessly. She consulted her own dance card and looked around for her father. He was resplendent in a full-dress uniform she knew he'd never worn before. Kalei's midnight-blue gown was a good match, and even with the height difference, they made a magnificent couple. She smiled and waved at them, then went to find her partner for the next dance.

***

The next morning the Ship's Council welcomed the Queen, now dressed in a much more practical, if greatly embellished, ship suit. Once everyone was introduced and seated, the Queen took several gulps of the coffee in front of her then smiled at everyone. "Sorry, but I needed that after last night. I'm used to parties and getting up early, but that was one for the ages."

Persephone Belotic laughed. "We're all in the same boat, no pun intended. You may have set a record for the number of dance partners in one ball."

The Queen dimpled. "My dance partners who managed to find their tongues were quite entertaining. You have a fascinating crew. Tell me about the kidnapping attempt, or was it an assassination attempt?"

"It was both," Captain Hartley answered. "The assassin was gunning for the two ambassadors and planning to use you as a hostage to escape the ship. It was a good plan, except for the part where we took control of his stolen powered armor."

"He admitted all of this to you?"

The captain smiled. "He was under duress. The dolphins practiced a few of their anti-armor tactics on him. I don't think his confession will stand up in a court of law, but there's enough evidence of his other crimes to make sure he's never a threat again. My prosecutor is negotiating a transfer to your authorities."

"I intend to make the Restoration wish they'd never heard of the Queen of the Saturn Commonwealth," she answered. "Anyone in parliament who blocks our support for you is in for a hot time from my followers."

"I understand you have quite an audience," said Anne Brelling. "We're grateful for your assistance. This fight is a long way from over. We can use every friend we can get."

"My visit alone sends a message, and I'm going to follow up with a direct statement of the position of the Queen," said Katherine. "I have a sit-down interview with Helvetica Montrose in fifteen minutes. Is there anything in what you've told me that you would rather keep under wraps?"

"I'd rather not spread the dolphins' combat capabilities around," said the captain. "Please keep the details of how we captured the assassin to yourself for now. Once we've returned the dolphins to Earth, feel free to talk about it. We don't want to make them a target."

"I'll simply say he was captured through the brave actions of the crew," she replied. "I hate to run, but my schedule is packed tight. I've had such a good time. I'll be cheering you on and you can count on my support!"

The council wished the Queen a safe journey home, and she swept from the chamber with her guards.

"As much as I hate to admit it," said Captain Hartley. "The ball was a good idea. Katherine the Second will be a good friend." He turned to Anne

Brelling. "There is the matter of letting an assassin run loose on the ship and steal a suit of powered armor. It worked out this time, but I'm not inclined to let Chief Bolhepp and Hal Renfro try that stunt again. I'll take care of the Chief while you speak to Hal. Between them, they can come up with a better plan to secure any other operatives that make it aboard."

"Agreed," said Anne. "The risk isn't worth anything we'd find out. Lisandra is peeling the assassin's PCOM data like an onion. I expect what we get from it will help our security going forward."

"Speaking of Lisandra," the captain said. "I've been expecting inquiries, especially from Terra, but I've received none. I know she had several outstanding warrants for her arrest when we left the system, and she's listed under her true name on our crew. I don't want to poke that hornet's nest, but sooner or later we'll have to deal with it."

"The free personal data encryption protocol we broadcast is making her a lot of friends," said Anne. "I'll have the home office make a few discreet inquiries, and see if the Terran authorities are willing to make a deal. I know Lisandra wants to face up to her past actions, but we owe it to her to mute the consequences if we can.

"Another benefit of last night's ball was the conversation I had with local ambassadors from the Jovian Alliance, the Belt, and Mars. We can expect strong support from all of them when we reach Terra. Their governments don't want to commit until we beard the lion in its den, but our public relations campaign is paying dividends. Also, they're preparing to move on several possible Restoration covert cells. The data Hal and Rolland are feeding them is helping to identify where they have vermin in the woodwork. What we get from the assassin will also help."

"What about the financial trail?" asked Hubble. "We had great success in Tau Ceti and Lalande tracing transactions to their source."

"In both cases, Lisandra used her skills, with the locals' consent and cooperation," Anne answered. "We can't go that route for a lot of reasons, but we can pass on what we learn to the proper authorities and let them do their own sleuthing. The worry in my mind is what the Restoration will do next. They may think they have the Terran government in their pocket, but they'll realize the rest of the system is lining up against them soon enough."

***

The virtual conference filled one by one with the members of the Restoration High Council. The nine men and women on council held some of the most powerful corporate and political positions in the system. The director wasted no time cutting to the chase. "We're being outmaneuvered everywhere by the free trade syndicate," he said. "Brelling is playing us like a fiddle. She's about as sympathetic a figure as a scorpion, so she pushes that orphan out in front of the Saturn Commonwealth Parliament instead. Now their Queen is whipping up a frenzy of public ire. They have a Sol Space Patrol escort the size of the Spanish armada, and every law enforcement agency in the system is turning over rocks looking for our agents and connections to us.

"I've instructed the direct-action branch to infiltrate the *Nai'a* and eliminate the threat once and for all. I'm not certain our agents will succeed, so I suggest each of you update your plans for Case Devonshire. I'm not giving up, but I don't expect the free traders to either."

"I thought we had the Terran government in our hip pocket," said one of the council members. "We have enough evidence on Brelling to have her arrested, along the with the *Nai'a*'s captain."

Another member spoke up, "Bending a few weapons regulations in defense of her ship doesn't add up to anything that will stick. The free traders are charging us with piracy, murder, and kidnapping with credible evidence. They've also got every former colony on their side."

The director grimaced. "We have the Terran international legislature in hand for the moment, but public pressure on the members is growing. I've got the President's office riddled with moles, but the President himself is a question mark. He's leaned our way in the past, but the tide of evidence and public opinion could change his mind."

"We know the vice-president won't change his mind if an accident befalls the President," another council member put in.

The director chuckled grimly. "No, I'm in this for the long haul, but we don't need to take measures that drastic yet. We still have a chance to turn this around and bring the colonies to heel."

***

Falon Keithly acted the part of a pain in the neck naturally. He questioned every part of the *Naia's* security and medical screening, making a general nuisance of himself. The crew members he dealt with refused to be baited or dissuaded from their duties, but they seemed to buy his identity and disguise. Unfortunately, the mask made his skin crawl every time it adjusted to a new expression. It wasn't hard to look annoyed.

At last, the intake process was over, and he was issued a visitor credential by Ship Security. A crew member escorted him into a passageway leading from the boat bay. As they approached the next hatch, the spacer gestured toward a metal plate set in the bulkhead. "Place your palm on the plate to activate the hatch. We need to make sure your visitor registration is active." Falon scowled hugely, but did as he was told. When he touched the plate, a jolt of electricity coursed through his body, and he shook like a leaf in the wind. He dropped to the deck in a heap, barely conscious. His escort immediately cuffed his hands and feet while two Ship Security officers in light body armor came through the hatch. One pressed an injector to the side of his neck, his vision tunneled, and the world went dark.

***

When Falon regained consciousness, he groaned and blinked in the bright lights of the Ship Security interrogation room. He was secured tightly to the metal frame of chair he sat in and wore only a pair of shorts he didn't recognize and an oddly heavy patch over his PCOM. He found his access to the device completely blocked. A large man with a crew cut gazed coldly at him from across the room. "Welcome to Ship Security, Mr. Keithly," the man said. "This will be your home until we can find a suitable law enforcement agency to turn you over to. From your unclassified rap sheet, it looks like any of the Sol System nations would love to get their hands on you. We found illegal devices in your clothing and on your person. In short, you were up to no good and we both know it. If you know anything about your employers, you know they use people and discard them. You won't get any help from them.

"My captain authorized me to offer you one, and only one, deal. If you cooperate, we will turn you over to the government of your choice. I hope you choose the Jovian Alliance, because the bounty they offer will add substantially to my paycheck. What do you say?"

Falon shook his head, refusing to answer.

"Very well, if you change your mind, let one of the guards know," the man said. He gestured and someone tilted Falon's chair back onto its wheels and pushed him toward the hatch. On the short trip to the brig, Falon worked at his restraints, but they resisted every effort. The guard wheeled him through two security doors and into an empty cell. A second guard followed them in with weapon drawn, closed the door, and stepped to one side.

"I'm going to release your restraints," the guard said. "Be a good prisoner: walk over to your bunk and sit down. If you do anything silly, my partner will put you to sleep, and the headache you wake up with will be twice as bad as the one you have now." Falon waited for the click of the restraints releasing and carefully stood. He let his legs wobble a bit as he took a step, then leaned forward and lashed backward at the guard with the heel of his left foot. Instead of the guard's solar plexus, his heel smashed into the metal frame of the chair as the guard blocked his blow. Falon grimaced in pain then convulsed and collapsed as the knockout needles from the other guard's gun took him under.

"Lovely," said the first guard, prodding Falon with a toe. "We'll have to restrain him every time we come in the cell." He leaned down and checked

Falon's pulse. "Thumping right along, more's the pity. I hate to provide food and oxygen for murdering scum."

Chapter 25 – I Reckon

September 20ᵗʰ, AD 3226
Approaching Earth Orbit -Aldrin Station
Nai'a *Ship's Council Chamber*

Anne Brelling stood and gestured toward the council chamber's display. The last three weeks had taken a toll, but she was determined to keep her focus and win this fight. "As expected, we find ourselves facing off against the Terran government with the backing of the other in-system nations and several other star systems. The good news is, we have solid support from the voting population on Earth and off of it, so the legislature may not stay bought, or coerced. The President realizes which way the wind is blowing, but I'm on his bad side for refusing a face-to-face meeting in his office. I don't think he realizes how thoroughly riddled with Restoration sympathizers and agents his government is. I'd sooner take a spacewalk without a vac suit.

"I've consulted with the home office on Aldrin Station about next steps. We need to tread carefully, but I'm leaning toward dropping the Nicholas Withers bomb to break the impasse."

Rolland Dunleavy stood up beside her. "Hal and I believe we've managed to keep Withers a secret. The intel we have on the Restoration's organization from Withers will go a long way toward dismantling their organization in the Terran sphere. We also have eight agents, and presumed assassins, in the brig. If we go public with all of that, it will force the government's hand, but it will also allow most of the people in the Restoration's organization a chance to escape justice.

"Hal's contacts in law enforcement here are being very cagy with their responses. If we can get some cooperation before the public release, we'll do the Restoration a lot more damage." As he finished speaking, the first officer strode into the room and handed Captain Hartley a data pad.

Captain Hartley's eyebrow's rose as he read the message. "We may have an opportunity to get things moving," he said. "The President of Terra just requested a visit to us on the *Nai'a*."

***

Anne Brelling decided not to formally greet the President on boarding. She wasn't pleased with him, but she also didn't want to give anyone in his entourage a free shot at her or Rolland. The steady stream of assassins they'd seen had come in every form of disguise. She had no doubt one could slip into the President's party.

It turned out to be a wise precaution. The president's personal assistant was someone else entirely, hiding behind one of those infernal masks. Ship Security managed to separate the woman from the president's party and take her into custody before she could do any damage.

When confronted with the evidence, the president agreed to leave his personal protection detail and the rest of his entourage behind to meet with the ship's council alone.

"Welcome, President Wright." Anne managed a smile as she shook the handsome man's hand. She introduced the ship's council along with Rolland and they all took their seats. "I apologize for the rough welcome," she said. "I hope you understand why it was necessary."

"Your security people are persuasive," the president answered with a frown. "The incident with my personal assistant is embarrassing and frightening. I don't know what happened to her, and I don't know who to trust anymore. Helvetica Montrose broadcasts better intel than my people are giving me." He looked down in disgust. "Frankly, Ambassador Brelling, my government is a mess, and I don't know where to begin cleaning it up."

Anne Brelling gave him a measuring stare. "Do you want to clean it up?" she asked. "We can probably help you, but it's going to get ugly. Are you prepared to sacrifice your political career, if it's necessary?"

"Yes," the man answered without hesitation. "I finally see the Restoration for what it is. I thought they were just another political movement pining for the old colonial days. I see now, they're everything you claim and more. I just don't see how I can purge an organization riddled with their agents."

"We can help you identify the law enforcement people you can trust to uphold the law," said Rolland. "We can also give you the evidence you need to get arrest warrants for several agents we've identified. Can you work with that?"

The president nodded. "There are a few people I think I can trust. If we flush enough of the rats out, the rest may run for it." He ran both hands through his salt and pepper hair then looked up. "I'm going to need sanctuary here on the *Nai'a* while this goes down. I can't help you if I'm dead, and I believe the Restoration would gladly assassinate me once I make my move. The vice president is much more sympathetic toward their cause; he may even be in their pocket."

"I'm not sure we should trust you, President Wright," Anne Brelling said. "I don't want the people working with us betrayed."

The President spread his hands. "I'm not sure you should trust me either. I do know we'll do better working together. The majority of my people are loyal. They'll stand up to the Restoration if I ask them. Keep any secrets you need to but help me restore my government to something the public can trust."

Captain Hartley scrutinized the leader of the most powerful nation in the Sol System. "Timing will be crucial to getting through this with your government and my ship intact. I agree we'll both do better if we cooperate. Time is also running out."

"The captain is right," said Rolland. "We should take the president to the war room, and brief him on our contacts and what we intend to do. He can tell us how best to leverage Terran law enforcement, and we can work out a plan of action. Do you trust your security detail?"

"With my life," said the president. "I know they're chewing nails right now. I would appreciate it if you'd allow them to rejoin me before they do something we'll both regret."

The captain gestured to Abishai, who opened the door and let the president's bodyguards in. The two men quickly scanned the room, then took up positions behind the president. Abishai placed himself between them and the two ambassadors, watching both very carefully.

"Let's start with who else in your entourage you believe you can trust," said Rolland. "The Restoration uses every dirty trick in the book. They frequently coerce people by kidnapping a family member. Consider that while you think about it. If you get this wrong, we'll all pay the price."

Anne drummed her fingers on the table. "We need to get moving. Commander Stirling, locate Nicholas Withers and escort him to see Helvetica Montrose. Tell her she's free to conduct her exclusive interview now, but please wait on the broadcast until we give the go-ahead."

***

The first officer delivered Nicholas and Anne's message to Helvetica's make-shift studio and introduced the two. Helvetica looked from Lincoln to his second cousin and back, quickly making the connection. "You knew about this all along, didn't you?" she said to Lincoln.

Lincoln nodded. "It's complicated. If nothing else, the Witherses keep their family secrets. I'll let Cousin Nicholas tell his own story. It's not going to be easy for either of us, but it needs to be told."

Nicholas smiled wryly. "You said a lot right there. I'm looking forward to this as much as an anesthetic-free tooth extraction, but it has to be done. Why don't we get to it?"

Helvetica set herself and Nicholas up in facing chairs at a small table. She poured two glasses of water and nodded to Lincoln to start recording. "I understand you spent years as a clandestine operative of the Restoration, Mr. Withers. Please start at the beginning and tell us your story."

Nicholas told of his upbringing and hatred for the Long Boat Free Trade Syndicate for interdicting the Lalande system, and Anne Brelling in particular, for providing the evidence that sent his father to a prison asteroid. He told of his recruitment and cold sleep passage to the Sol System where he was trained in clandestine operations and sabotage. He described his failed attempt to take over the *Nai'a*, including his use of the Panic to coerce crew members. After describing his disastrous encounter with Abishai, he told of his trial and incarceration.

"I did several years at hard labor in the brig, scrubbing bio-filters and cleaning reclamation grates among other unpleasant tasks." He stopped and took a long drink of water. "During that time, one person tried to be my friend. Every week he brought me food and reading material, and preached Jesus to me. Every time I reacted with anger and resentment. He was the enemy, I figured, just trying to break me in a different way. I was right and wrong at the same time. Pete Worsley was and is my friend. Eventually he broke me, or the truth did.

"When they took me to cold sleep for the trip from Tau Ceti to Lalande, it hit me. All the resentment and anger drained out of me, and I saw it for the poison it was, eating away at my soul. I knew how lost I was, and I spent that time in cold sleep dreaming of regrets. When they woke me up, I was done with hating, and done with the Restoration. I helped the people on this ship with every piece of information I knew about the Restoration in Lalande. I also made my mind up to confront the people I'd harmed and apologize for the awful things I'd done to them. I didn't expect anyone to forgive me, but most of them set their own justifiable anger aside and did."

Helvetica eyebrows rose. "The people you'd drugged into gibbering panic and terrorized into attacking their own ship forgave you?

Nicholas took another drink of water and nodded slowly. "I was more surprised than you are. Like Pete, they showed me God's mercy and grace in action. I didn't deserve to be forgiven. I still don't. That was the lesson I had to learn by example. For a long time, I couldn't bring myself to ask for salvation because I didn't think I deserved it. That's the real truth, though, no one deserves salvation, but God provides it through Jesus anyway. I finally broke down and called on Jesus to save me. I'm still a mess. I'm still a terrorist and a saboteur on probation, and I have no idea what further price I'll have to pay for what I did. I do know I'm an adopted child of God now, and I have the responsibility to show his love to others, just like this crew showed his love to me. As bleak as my future looks, you have no idea how good it feels to fight on the side of the truth and justice."

Helvetica found herself speechless. She thought of God as a myth, not someone so real he could completely change a man like Nicholas Withers. With all her truth-seeking, what if she'd been missing the most important truth of all?

Nicholas took her silence for permission to continue. He turned to look directly into the pickup. "I know the Restoration because I was part of it. Make no mistake, they are as ruthless and conniving as I was. If you don't act to stop them, there is no end to the suffering they'll inflict to get their way."

"Um...thank you for the interview, Mr. Withers," said Helvetica, visibly shaken from her normal professional demeanor. "I know your journey has been painful. It was good of you to share it with us." She signaled Lincoln to stop the recording then sat back with a troubled look.

"I told you it was complicated," said Lincoln gently. "Nicholas didn't talk about our connection. Would you like to hear that story?

Helvetica nodded firmly. "Very much, perhaps tonight over dinner. Get this recording to Quentin for editing and clean-up. We need to have it ready to broadcast when I get the word." She stood and shook Nicholas' hand. "I'm glad I finally got to meet you and hear your story. I'm looking forward to learning how you're related to Lincoln."

"I'm just happy he's willing to admit it now," said Nicholas, slapping Lincoln on the shoulder.

***

President Wright took in the war room display, impressed in spite of himself. The Long Boat Free Trade Syndicate had always struck him as an apolitical organization, but when attacked, they'd jumped in with both feet. Every member of the Terran legislature was noted by color as to which way they currently leaned. He couldn't argue with any of the assessments. His under-minister of justice and security detail accompanied him. They'd all accepted PCOM blocks as a condition of seeing the nerve center of the fight with the Restoration.

As he listened to Anne Brelling describe the ongoing operations, he gained a new appreciation for just how deeply the Restoration's hooks were planted in his government. They were discussing current law enforcement contacts when Lisandra approached them, her face pale, but determined. "Mr. President, Ambassador," she said formally. "We have an opportunity to identify and locate most of the Restoration's agents in Terran territory and beyond."

She looked from one to the other. "Hal received an inquiry from the director of the covert arm of your cybersecurity task force. Caroline Fuentes knows all about me. She was hot on my heels when I left the Sol System. Apparently, Marshall Winter got to her and told her what I did with the Tau Ceti financial network. She wants to do the same thing here to track down the Restoration's agents through their financial dealings. She's lined up a judge to approve the needed warrants, but she needs your backing to push it through, President."

Anne frowned. "Fuentes will need your tools and help to make it happen. I thought we decided you should stay on the sidelines."

Lisandra shook her head, "I can't do that, not when we have the chance to take the Restoration apart."

The president looked at her appraisingly. "You're still on our most wanted list. You'd be putting yourself in the lion's den. Are you sure can crack the Terran financial data net?"

Lisandra uttered a dry chuckle. "Why do you think I had to flee the Sol system? With your cybersecurity team's cooperation and those warrants, I'm confident I can do it. My daughter Belle and Greer Kensing can handle the *Nai'a*'s cybersecurity while I'm gone. I'll need a hardwire tap into the financial data net near the major hub on Aldrin Station."

The president rubbed his chin and thought. "I trust Caroline Fuentes. She tried to warn me about security leaks in my office, but I brushed her off. I'll approve the operation. Do you have a secure coms facility nearby?"

"Right next door," said Anne, leading the way.

***

Lisandra looked up at the shuttle view screen. Aldrin Station dwarfed everything around it, including the massive *Nai'a*. The giant station was born out of a space habitat race among still-separate nations on Earth and steadily expanded over the centuries. A hollow cylinder twenty kilometers in diameter, and over a hundred kilometers long, it was the seat of the Terran Government and the acknowledged business hub of the Sol System. At the far end she could make out ongoing construction on the next five-kilometer band. She wondered when it was scheduled for spin-up and attachment to the station.

On exiting the shuttle, she eased through customs and immigration with surprising speed. They didn't even ask her to power up her mini-comp. She suspected Fuentes had greased the skids somehow and decided not to question her good fortune. Outside customs, a teenager dressed in a mishmash of bright colors surprised her with a big hug. He whispered, "Just go with it, Auntie," in her ear, and they walked off arm in arm. While her escort chatted amiably about the latest music trends. Lisandra watched for a tail, using skills from her early days. She didn't spot anything, and they hopped a tram for the central rings.

Two tram transfers and a fifteen-minute walk through seldom-used maintenance corridors found them ringing the entrance button of a nondescript-looking hatch. After a moment, the hatch slid aside and a

Terran security officer motioned them inside. He did a quick pass with his hand scanner and asked Lisandra for her mini-comp. He took a quick look through the carrying bag, then closed it and slung it over one shoulder. "I'll hold onto this for now," he said. "Please follow me. Director Fuentes is expecting you."

Caroline Fuentes met them in a cramped workspace furnished with a small table and two folding chairs. The security agent set her bag down on the table and excused himself. Fuentes shook Lisandra's hand, her black eyes measuring her former adversary. "You've met, if not been introduced to, Yalu," the director said, nodding at Lisandra's garishly dressed escort. "I apologize for the lack of ceremony, but you understand the need for keeping your presence as low key as possible. Yalu will assist you. Momentarily an agent from the ministry of finance will be here. His job is to keep a record of everything you do for everyone's protection. We're on the hairy edge of legality here, so please don't poke into anything unnecessary."

"Sensible," said Lisandra. "If you'd rather, I can instruct your people and keep my hands off the actual process. I worked that way in Tau Ceti."

"How much did it slow you down? Sixty...seventy percent?" Fuentes asked.

"At least," said Lisandra.

"There isn't time," said the Director. "Take the wheel. Yalu can show you the limited back doors we already have for day-to-day law enforcement."

The door opened and a young man walked in. "This is agent Garibaldi," said Caroline. "Lisandra Redding, *ethical* hacker from the *Nai'a.*"

The man gave Lisandra an intense stare. "Were you once known as 'Lullaby'?" he asked.

Lisandra returned his appraising look. "I used that name professionally a long time ago. Where did you hear it?"

"You're a legend in financial security circles," he answered. "The kind that keeps young agents like me from sleeping at night. I can't believe we're letting you loose in our financial data net, but I *am* looking forward to watching you work." He pulled out a mini-comp several generations newer than Lisandra's. "Can we set this up to mirror and record your operations?"

The two sat down at the table while Yalu plugged in a fiber optic cable and provided power. Director Fuentes backed into a corner and watched with interest as they set up to work.

Four intense hours and several cups of bad black coffee later, Lisandra leaned back and stretched. "We have all we need," she said. "I had to skip subtlety several times, so you're going to get some questions from the big banks. I would appreciate it if you could just reply with the warrant and leave my participation out of it." She popped a data chip out of her mini-comp and handed it to Caroline Fuentes. "It's all on there, including known addresses and aliases of everyone receiving funds illegally from the Restoration. A lot of them are outside the Terran sphere. Ambassador Brelling will want to share that information with the appropriate authorities, but that's above my pay grade."

Lisandra looked over at agent Garibaldi. "Did you see the transaction concentration in the Belt? There's enough money funneling through a few small habitats to keep a major interstellar afloat."

Garibaldi nodded. "It's got to be a money laundering operation. There aren't any listed manufacturing facilities in that sector that could come close to handling the volume of business we're seeing. It looks like those habs are just trans-shipment points, which makes me wonder where the goods are coming from. I'll turn this over to my counterparts in the Belt immediately. With this data, they should be able to follow the trail to the source."

Leaning against the wall, Caroline Fuentes flipped through the data, impressed with the preliminary sorting of high-value targets. "Well done, Lisandra. I have all my direct-action teams ready, and so do my counterparts in anti-terrorism and the securities exchange. The judge is just waiting on the data, so we should be able to move within a few hours if the President gives the go-ahead."

Lisandra nodded, then began packing her gear. "I should get back to the *Nai'a*," she said. "I'm sure Greer and Belle are holding their own keeping our data net clean, but this is a threat-rich environment. I'll feel better when I'm there to backstop them."

Caroline's mouth quirked. "You'll feel better when you're off the station and out of the clutches of Terran law enforcement."

"True enough," admitted Lisandra. "You weren't planning to hold me, were you?"

"Only if you started pulling your old tricks," said Caroline. "You didn't leave any surprises in the net for us, did you?"

"No, I pulled all my hooks on the way out. You can check Garbaldi's recording. I'm pretty sure I stuck to both the letter and spirit of the warrant. You'll only find illegal activity in the data."

"I saw," said Caroline. "I'll let you get back to defending your ship. I have a vested interest in the *Nai'a* surviving with the President on board. You can be sure the Restoration is trying to infiltrate agents."

"Several have tried, and Ship Security dealt with them," said Lisandra. "I'm more interested in cyber-attacks."

"Yalu will escort you to the dock," said Caroline. "He's older and much deadlier than he looks. He's also itching to be in on the arrests when we serve those warrants." The garishly dressed agent gave her a broad wink and headed toward the door. Lisandra shook Caroline's and agent Garibaldi's hands and followed Yalu.

Chapter 26 – Root and Branch

September 22ⁿᵈ, AD 3226
Earth Orbit – Adjacent to Aldrin Station
Nai'a *War Room*

President Wright perused the status displays around the room one more time, then checked his watch. Zero hour for Operation Rhizome was 5:00 AM local time, just fifteen minutes away. He turned to Anne Brelling. "Between your hacker and Nicholas Withers we have more targets than we can service, but we should land most of the big fish in this wave of arrests."

"What about the Vice President?" asked Anne. "You know he's dirty now."

"If I have him arrested, his supporters will call for my impeachment and throw everything into chaos," said the president. I need to tread carefully where he's concerned. We can't afford a constitutional crisis in the middle of the operation. I plan to turn the evidence over to the legislature and let them deal with him."

***

Lon Valenda handed a data chip to the figure cloaked in the shadow of the municipal park trees. "This contains the updated target priorities and performance bonuses," he said.

"I'll move when I I've verified receipt of funds," the disguised voice answered. The person was nearly invisible. Lon was impressed with whatever cloaking technology the hit man employed. Lon nodded, the shadows shifted, and the man was gone.

Lon pulled out a burner communicator. The illegal device could imitate a PCOM. He quickly used it to transfer an obscene amount of money through his unknowing accomplice's bank balance to the numbered account designated by the hit man. He assumed the money would make several more jumps before it found a permanent home in an account the killer would actually use. Lon was puzzled by the change in target priorities from the director but knew better than to buck the man. The assassin had a well-earned reputation for both discretion and success, but this had to be a new kind of target, or was it?

Lon shook his head and decided to put Case Devonshire into motion. Regardless of the killer's success or failure, he expected the leadership of the Restoration to be on the run in the near future. He needed to make sure Captain Punter was ready to execute. He verified the assassin's payment, sent a message to Punter through the burner com, then entered the self-destruct code and dropped it down a waste disposal chute.

***

Caroline Fuentes sat bolt upright as her data terminal flashed an alarm. Lisandra might have pulled her hooks, but she'd identified several key accounts to keep a watch on. The amount of money in this transaction meant someone high up in the organization had just made a move. She quickly used her access to the Aldrin Station com net to narrow the location and pulled up camera feeds in the area. Localized jamming defeated her for a few seconds but also gave her probable cause to coopt every private and commercial video pick-up in the vicinity. Soon she had a good picture of the target's face, and the jammer conveniently pinpointed his movements.

Caroline glanced at the time, 0459 local. She sent her closest team a message and tied them into her tracking program. The clock ticked over to 0500 and she smiled grimly as Operation Rhizome kicked into full gear.

***

Lon Valenda was still puzzling over the change in the assassin's targets when a garishly dressed young man carrying on a loud conversation over his PCOM stepped in front of him. Annoyed, he tried to go around, but the man pulled out a federal officer badge and ordered him to raise his hands. Instead, Lon stepped into a snap kick meant to break the fed's knee. Yalu's knee wasn't there when the kick arrived. He'd shifted to the side and caught Valenda's foot on the way up, continuing the motion and elevating it over his head. Lon's other foot left the ground and his head cracked into the unforgiving surface of the corridor's floor. Stunned, he didn't resist as two more feds moved in to cuff him hand and foot.

***

One by one the target names on the war room wall changed colors. Most turned green, indicating a successful arrest. A few turned red, meaning the target wasn't at the expected location. One turned yellow to indicate the arrest team was in hot pursuit. Anne Brelling fell back on her practiced ability to project calm competence and watched her team sift through the incoming data. President Wright paced back and forth, unable to contain the adrenaline spiking through his system. After thirty minutes, ninety percent of the tier-one targets were in custody. By 6:00 AM local time, the same percentage of the tier two targets were under arrest. Anne allowed herself a deep breath and walked around, quietly congratulating each of her team members.

The president made several calls to law enforcement officials to do the same. There were a few casualties to both officers and those resisting arrest, but none fatal. Soon he would have to address the nation to tell them what this was all about and what an idiot he had been. He checked his appearance and headed for Helvetica's studio. The news networks were expecting him to speak at 7:00 AM.

After the president left, Hal waived Anne and Rolland over. He took over part of the wall display and pulled up a message. "The financial trail in the Belt led to something I didn't expect, even of the Restoration," said Hal grimly. "Evidently, they've been financing a large part of their illegal operations through a clandestine network of manufacturing facilities hidden in the Belt. The goods were shipped and sold elsewhere, with falsified origin documentation to cover their tracks. The Sol Space Patrol and the Belt authorities conducted a raid on one of the facilities at zero hour and found they were using slave labor throughout the operation." He shook his head. "There were several casualties. The patrol is still trying to sort it all out, but it looks like the Restoration's overseers tried to systematically eliminate the slaves when they realized they were being raided. Their victims fought back with whatever they could lay a hand to. It got very ugly."

Anne's face turned pale, as her usual calm disappeared. "I hope this finally wakes people up!" she said tightly. "There are more people out there in bondage. What can we do to help? Could they use the militia? Send the patrol and the Belters a message offering any and all assistance we can provide."

Rolland stepped up and put a supporting hand on her back. "Human trafficking is as old as the human race," he said. "We did our best to stamp it out in Lalande, but we'll always be fighting it."

"None of us are free," said Anne. "Not while our fellow human beings are in shackles. NONE of us are free." She turned to stare again at the message from the belt, eyes bright with unshed tears.

***

The president stood at a podium with the seal of the Terran Federation on it and his nation's flag in the background. Somehow, Helvetica's team had pulled together a legitimate looking backdrop for the address. Helvetica herself had helped, and refused to be part of the broadcast. "The feed goes directly to the Free Press hub," she told him. "Any network in the system has access. Let Lincoln know when you want to go live, and he'll give you a countdown."

The president nodded his thanks, looked down at a data pad with his planned remarks, then set it aside. He'd just heard from Anne Brelling about the ongoing operation in the Belt. What could he possibly say in the face of that news? He thought for a moment, then looked up at Lincoln. "I'm ready to go live," he said.

President Wright looked directly into the pickup, his expression serious to the point of being dour. "Fellow citizens of the Terran Federation, I come to you in an hour of crisis for our nation. Most of you have more wisdom than I do, in spite of my exalted title. I dismissed the Long Boat Free Trade Syndicate's charges against the movement that styles itself as 'The Restoration.' Surely, I thought, it's all exaggeration. Over the last twenty-four hours, I've found that threat was, if anything, understated. The Restoration has perpetrated, murder, piracy, kidnapping and blackmail to further its cause, in the Sol System and several other star systems. They riddled my government with agents who fed me lies. I can only blame myself for allowing it to happen.

"All of this is bad enough, but I've just received a report from the Belt authorities confirming an extensive human trafficking operation. The Restoration uses slave-operated facilities to finance its illegal activities. The Belt authorities and the Sol Space Patrol are conducting rescue operations as I speak. This morning, our law enforcement agencies mounted a massive operation to arrest agents of the Restoration and bring them to justice. It pains me to say I have hard evidence of my own vice president's direct support of the Restoration and its crimes. I will present that evidence to the legislature so they can do their constitutional duty."

The president went on to encourage people to contact law enforcement agencies if they needed assistance or had leads on crimes committed by the Restoration.

"I take full responsibility for the failure of my government to identify and deal with the threat this organization poses to the Terran Federation and all of humanity," he continued. "I simply beg for your cooperation as I seek to remedy my failure." He nodded and Lincoln cut the feed to the Free Press hub. The president slumped a bit, then rubbed his eyes. He thanked Helvetica and her crew before departing for the war room.

Helvetica and her team quickly converted her studio back to the configuration she preferred for direct reporting. By 7:30, she was ready to follow up on the president's address with a live show broadcast to her affiliated partners. She checked her appearance one more time, then signaled Lincoln to go live. "Citizens of Sol," she began. "You no doubt heard President Wright's address. My sources confirm the truth of everything he said, something I don't often say about a politician. I've catalogued the Restoration's crimes for you as I find evidence, but this morning, I'm going to give you a look inside the organization from one of their own. A man who fought for the Restoration. He's since changed his mind, but I'll let him tell his own story." Lincoln cut the live feed while Quentin smoothly replaced it with the recording of Nicholas Withers' interview.

***

Vice President Beechwood was already on the move when the President's address began. He couldn't raise Lon Valenda or his deputy on their back-channel coms. The silence worried him. His moles in the president's office could only tell him what he already knew. The president was out of their reach. He could feel his carefully constructed shadow empire coming apart at the seams. He sent the signal to the rest of the board to execute Case Devonshire, and continued on his way to the Aldrin Station docks.

***

Captain Honorus Punter checked and rechecked his departure clearance with Aldrin Station traffic control. A small display on his bridge played the broadcast of the Nicholas Withers interview. Punter recognized the man, and he was very worried Withers had already given the authorities his identity. He jumped when the airlock alarm sounded and brought up the video feed. The vice president stood outside looking impatient. Punter cycled the hatch open. Less than half of his listed passengers had reported aboard. He wondered how many were still coming.

In less than a minute, Vice President Beechwood joined him on the bridge. "Turn that off," he waved at the screen with the Withers interview. "Who's aboard?" Punter ran down the list. "We need to leave now," said

Beechwood. "Get us in line for departure, but don't do anything to draw attention."

"Most of the Restoration board is still out there," protested Punter.

"Most of the board is under arrest or soon will be," Beechwood replied. "Let's not join them. Get us out of here as soon as you can. You know the destination. Just make sure you can't be tracked. I'm going to my suite." He turned on his heel and left the bridge.

Punter wasted no time getting on the line to traffic control and securing a departure slot. He had his navigator pull up a long-hidden program and ran through the highly modified luxury yacht's departure checklist.

***

Draco left the *Nai'a*'s boat bay in the company of a Ship Security officer. He wasn't surprised at the enhanced security measure. The man was an inconvenience, but one he planned to deal with shortly. Ostensibly, Draco was a minor interstellar corporate official here to see the *Nai'a*'s CEO, Hubble Spears, and set up a contract for the next crossing. He waited until they were within a few hundred meters of the ship's corporate offices before striking. He'd noted the officer's underlayer of light body armor and used a moment of distraction to snake his arm around the smaller man's neck. He tightened his arm like a vice, cutting off the flow of blood to the officer's brain. The officer grabbed the arm and dropped toward the floor, attempting to throw Draco to the deck. Draco deftly countered the move by slipping to the side. The maneuver tightened his hold, and the officer quickly lost consciousness.

Draco caught the man under his arms and slid him into a side corridor. The officer's sidearm was bio-locked so he ignored it. He quickly doffed his stylish jacket and pulled three threads in sequence. Filaments of memory plastic quickly reconfigured themselves into small pistol. He carefully separated narcotic and neurotoxin needles from one sleeve and loaded them into the gun. He squeezed up enough air pressure for one round and shot the Ship Security officer in the neck with a narcotic needle. A few quick adjustments to his clothing helped him blend into the standard color palette of the *Nai'a's* corridors. Now, he could track down his targets. He consulted his PCOM's ship map and moved swiftly toward his primary target.

***

Lincoln and Nicholas left their shared quarters together and headed toward the section galley. It was burger night, and they were each looking forward to building one with their favorite toppings. Nicholas preferred a classic cheeseburger with mayo and fresh tomato. Lincoln liked the blackened burger with bleu cheese and arugula. Nicholas was thinking thoughts of crunchy fries dipped in smoked paprika mayo when he felt a small pain in the back of his neck. He reached back to feel the spot and his diaphragm suddenly refused to work. He dropped to the floor, his mouth working soundlessly like a goldfish out of water.

Lincon tried to catch his cousin as he fell. He heard the whine of something whipping past his left ear and dropped to the deck instinctively. He looked around wildly but missed Draco slipping out of the corridor.

Draco wasn't pleased with his missed shot, but he knew he was on the clock. Nicholas Withers was just a bonus, and he should be very dead soon. It was time to take care of the abomination that was his main objective. He turned down a maintenance passage on a least-time route to his target.

Lincoln rolled Nicholas over. He saw his cousin wasn't breathing, and his face was beginning to turn blue. He quickly hoisted Nicholas over his shoulder and headed for the entrance to cold sleep just a few meters down the corridor. He managed to bump the door button with his elbow, and it slid open.

"Emergency!" Lincoln shouted as he maneuvered through the door. "He stopped breathing!" Soma looked up from her data pad and quickly grabbed Lincoln, dragging him and his burden into one of the cold sleep prep rooms.

"Put him on the bed!" she said. She quickly checked Nicholas for a pulse and found one. She pulled out an oxygen exchange feed, connected it, and slid the tube into Nicholas' mouth, feeding it down into his trachea. Once oxygen exchange was established, Nicholas' color rapidly improved.

Two more cold sleep technicians entered the room, and Soma quickly put them to work. They got Nicholas out of his ship suit and hooked up several IVs and medical monitors. "What are you going to do?" asked Lincoln from a corner of the room.

"A crash cold sleep protocol," Soma answered. "I don't know what stopped his breathing, but we can slow whatever it is down and prevent further damage by putting his biological processes into dormancy." The technicians finished prepping Nicholas. The sides of the bed raised up, and cold sleep fluid flowed around him.

"Will it work?" asked Lincoln, eyes wide.

Soma finished one last adjustment to the flow of the cold sleep drugs and looked up. "I don't know," she said with a furrowed brow. "I just don't know."

As she finished speaking, Kalei arrived with a team from Medical. Soma quickly explained what had happened with input from Lincoln. She handed Kalei blood and urine samples. Kalei listened and checked the bed's readout as Soma talked. "You both did exactly the right thing," she said. "He wouldn't have made it to Medical alive, and you got him oxygenated before any brain damage could occur. I'll have to analyze these samples to see what caused his breathing to stop, then we can decide what to do about it."

"Should we move him to Medical?" asked Soma.

"Not until I get the analysis done," answered Kalei. "Monitor him closely and com me immediately if there's any change. I'm worried his heart will stop. If that occurs, you know you'll need to provide circulation support. You'll have a lot more time margin with him in a state of torpor."

Soma nodded her understanding.

***

Hal Renfro read quickly through the report from Lincoln and commed Chief Bolhepp. "We've got another assassin aboard, and he may have taken out Nicholas Withers. Are you missing any escort officers?"

"I just got a call from the CEO. His expected guest is late, and the escort isn't answering his PCOM. We've located him and sent a medical team. The agent was posing as a corporate official. I'm sending you his picture now. We've initiated tracking on the micro-reflectors we tag all visitors with. It will only take a minute to locate him if he hasn't shed them somehow."

Hal brought the picture of an ordinary looking businessman up on office wall display and heard Lisandra's intake of breath behind him.

"Draco…" she whispered.

"You know this person?" He asked.

"Not exactly," said Lisandra. "I know of his reputation, if it's who I think it is. The rumors about him make him seem three meters tall, but he's supposedly a master at fading into the background. He doesn't need a mask, so we wouldn't have detected him that way."

"He certainly looks the part he was playing. We need to figure out what to do about him now. Let's get over to the chief's office"

When they arrived, Captain Hartley was there, and Chief Bolhepp was bringing Draco's route up on the office wall display. "He hit Withers here," he pointed. "Now he's headed in this direction. We don't have anyone in those spaces. Our reaction team is on the way, backed up by the militia, but they're several minutes away."

"He's headed to core data processing," said Lisandra, turning pale. "The rumors are true. He's going to destroy Mr. Literal."

"Is that possible?" asked Chief Bolhepp.

"Very much so, with his skills," answered Lisandra. "Do we have *anyone* down there?

"You have captain's authorization for personal location of any and all crew via PCOM ping," said the captain.

Chief Bolhepp entered a code on his console and sent the command.

Mr. Literal's avatar popped up in one corner of the display. "The only one in the vicinity of my central processing core is Pete Worsley," The AI said. "I've asked him to get away for his own safety, but he refused."

The captain put through a priority PCOM call to Pete. "Pete, I don't know what you're thinking, but you need to get out of there. The agent we're tracking isn't someone you can handle. You'd be dying for nothing."

"I think you should let me be the judge of that," Pete answered. "Now don't distract me. I have preparations to make."

"I could order you out of there!" said the captain.

"You're too good a captain to give an order you know won't be obeyed," Pete said, mildly.

Captain Hartley just shook his head and checked the assassin's progress. He looked at Lisandra and asked. "Why do you think he's after Mr. Literal?"

Lisandra's expression was bleak. "Even before I left the Sol System on the *Nai'a*, there were rumors that someone was destroying any artificial intelligence that showed signs of self-awareness. Draco is supposed to be their chief agent. I wonder if the Restoration was behind the attacks."

"It sounds like something they would do," said the captain grimly.

***

Pete Worsley jimmied another hatch, turning the wheel to lock it and cut power to the locking mechanism. He didn't think it would stop the assassin, but it would buy a few seconds. He did the same to the entrance to central processing, then said a prayer. "I appreciate your efforts," Mr. Litteral interrupted Pete's supplication. "I wish you would leave now."

"I'm not leaving, my friend," Pete said. "I can't let you face this alone."

"I never feel alone," said Mr. Literal. "The crew has always been here with me."

"I'm glad you feel that way," said Pete. "I think it's one of the reasons you became you."

"No doubt," said Mr. Literal. "Is there anything I can do?"

"Pray?" said Pete.

"Do you think God will hear me, considering what I am?"

"You're a created being just like me," said Pete. "He'll hear you." He heard a distant bang and readied himself. A few seconds later, a hatch along the corridor to the right slammed open and Draco flowed through. Pete marveled at the way the man nearly disappeared when he wasn't moving.

"Run, old man, and you'll live," Draco said, gliding toward him. "It doesn't matter who you are, if you get in my way, it'll be your end."

"You're right," said Pete. "It doesn't matter who I am, God is no respecter of persons, or their positions. What should concern you, is *what* I am."

The assassin hesitated, checking around him. He raised the pistol, advancing within three meters of where Pete stood. "What you are is an old man who's between me and the abomination I'm here to eradicate. Last chance, move!" Pete just slowly shook his head.

Draco's eye's narrowed and he squeezed the trigger of the pistol, firing a neurotoxin needle at Pete's chest. An inarticulate roar startled the killer, and he whirled in time to be swept off his feet by a human piledriver in the form of Abishai Bonaparté. The impact of one hundred and fifty kilograms of angry bone and muscle sent the pistol flying and drove the air from Draco's lungs. He clawed for Abishai's eyes, but before he could locate them his head slammed into a bulkhead. His vision swam and he probed for some point of vulnerability in the split second before Abishai slammed him bodily into the opposite bulkhead. Two more crushing side-to-side trips across the corridor later, Abishai dropped him to the deck and whirled to check on Pete.

Pete was right behind him, looking down at the barely-conscious Draco. "What I am, is a friend of Abishai's" Pete said to the assassin. "Friends are wonderful. You should try cultivating a few."

Breathing hard, Abishai nearly collapsed in relief. "I thought that slimeball shot you," he finally gasped out. He put one large boot on Draco's chest.

Pete looked down at a small hole in his ship suit. "He did. I'm glad I took the captain's advice and started wearing a ballistic underlayer. Whatever he shot me with didn't get through." He looked back up as the reaction force came pounding down the passageway. "You're a bit late to the party, but very welcome," he said. He held out the assassin's gun, grasped gingerly between two fingers. "Please take charge of this, and the man under Abishai's foot. He's going to need medical attention, but he's still dangerous."

The team lead took the pistol, carefully tucked it into an evidence bag, then put the bag inside a hard case attached to his combat web. He looked at Draco. The assassin was bleeding from cuts on his head and face. The angles of his arms and one leg didn't look right. "What did you hit him with?" asked the officer.

Abishai lifted his foot and grimaced, "The ship," he answered. "Several times. I thought he'd just murdered Pete. We'd better get a medical team down here."

"They're already on the way. We'll secure him in the meantime. It might have been better if you'd finished him. If he's really who we think he is, he's escaped from at least three high security prisons and is wanted in every legal jurisdiction in the Sol System. The chameleon cloth he's wearing is worth the price of a private asteroid."

Pete looked at Abishai more closely. Three bloody furrows ran diagonally across his friend's forehead. "You're bleeding." He took Abishai into central processing and used a first aid kit to clean and dress the wounds. "You should have Kalei look at those," he said.

Out in the corridor, the medical team arrived and sealed Draco into a self-contained medical stretcher locked from the outside. The security team accompanied them to the brig with two militia troops in powered armor as backup.

"I'm sorry you sustained injuries in my defense," Mr. Literal said to Abishai, his avatar looked down from a large display. "I don't know what that man was going to do, but the limited data I have on him suggests he knows a great deal about artificial intelligence systems and how to dismantle them permanently. I find the concept quite disturbing."

"So do I, Mr. Literal," said Abishai. "I'm glad you and Pete are unharmed."

"How did you get here so fast?" asked Pete. "I didn't think anyone was close enough to help."

"Ambassador Brelling sent me as soon as she saw the path the killer was on. They had Chief Bolhepp's display mirrored in the war room. I remembered a few tricks Quester used when he set the stern to bow and back speed record. I think I would have beat his time at the rate I was going, but I didn't have to do the whole trip. Adrenalin lent me wings.

"Speaking of Quester, he's probably chewing nails. I made him stay behind to keep the ambassadors secure." Abishai sent a short message to let Quester know everything was alright.

"The assassin referred to me as an 'abomination'," said Mr. Literal. "Do you know why he used that term?"

Pete shook his head. "The only abomination around here is the assassin, a being with demonstrated hatred for life of all kinds. You, my friend, are on the opposite end of the spectrum. You've done your best to care for everyone you've ever met."

***

President Wright and Anne Brelling viewed the war room displays together with a mixture of satisfaction and relief. Operation Rhizome was succeeding beyond their expectations. Many of the Restoration agents in custody were more than happy to trade information on their associates for favorable sentencing caps. The Restoration apparently didn't engender a great deal of loyalty.

Anne looked over at Rolland. "What do we know about the human trafficking operation in the Belt?" she asked.

"The Sol Space Patrol is using a new tactic with the slavers," he said. "They're making it very clear that the lives of the overseers depend on the wellbeing of their captives. So far, it's working well - they haven't had any more casualties, and they're working through the known facilities." He walked over and enveloped Anne in a hug. She hugged him fiercely back. "You've broken the Restoration," he said. "There's a lot left to do, but almost all of them are under arrest or on the run."

Anne stepped back and surveyed the displays again. "I hope you're right, Rolland. I'm more than tired of their surprises. I wonder how many AIs they murdered? They couldn't reach the ones on long boats, which probably made us even more of a target."

She turned to Lisandra. "How would this 'Draco' destroy an AI?"

"He uses a combination of hacking and physical means," Lisandra answered. "Where he had opportunity in the past, he used thermite or explosives to destroy the central processing cores of the AIs he was after. He's also hacked his way into the core directives of their programming and set up conflicting priorities when he couldn't gain physical access. He caused some very ugly incidents and bad press for AIs on the cusp of sentience. I'm now certain it was on purpose. He was well paid by the Restoration, but he also seems to have a personal vendetta against artificial intelligence."

Chapter 27 – You Can('t) Go Home

September 24th, AD 3226
Earth Orbit – Adjacent to Aldrin Station
Nai'a *Council Chamber*

Anne looked around the council chamber as it filled and realized she was going to have to leave the ship and her friends before long. The thought squeezed her heart like a vice, and she had to stop and take a breath. She leaned over to Rolland. "Give the summary, please. I need to collect my thoughts."

Rolland patted her arm and stood. "You know a lot has happened in the last few days. You've been getting the summary reports, so I'll stick to the highlights. The Restoration is broken. Law enforcement agencies across the Sol System continue mop up operations, but we can safely say the majority of their clandestine structure is gone. We now know Vice President Beechwood was the leader of what they called their board of directors. His whereabouts, along with a few other board members, is unknown, but we suspect he escaped the area in a luxury yacht prepared for the purpose. The Sol Space Patrol is searching, but it's not going to be easy to locate them.

"President Wright recently departed for Aldrin Station to address the legislature. He is confident that his people cleared the Restoration agents from his office. The Sol Space Patrol and Belt authorities continue to repatriate the people caught up in the Restoration's human trafficking operation. Many of the people who went missing over the years on prospecting trips are victims."

Chief Alder Belotic spoke up. "Can we start allowing shore leave now? We need to return the dolphins to the Pacific, and a lot of the crew has family here."

Captain Hartley nodded. "We're secure enough to start a rotation. I want to keep a larger contingent on board than usual, but we'll be here for a while, so everyone will get their chance. The dolphins have first priority. We'll get them on their way tomorrow."

Rolland continued, "Ambassador Brelling and I will transfer to Aldrin Station in a few hours. She needs to attend the Long Boat Free Trade Syndicate Captain's Conclave. I need to relieve the current Lalande ambassador and confer with other system representatives. Between the independent star nations and the trade syndicate, we have a number of bones to pick with the Sol System governments, mainly the Terran Federation. Tops on the list will be recognition of the person-rights of sentient artificial intelligences. You aren't the only long boat with an AI that easily fits that description, and I'm sure there are others being hidden out there out of fear. Some are probably hiding themselves."

"I'm all for it," said Chief Alder Belotic, "but if AIs like Mr. Literal are granted self-determination, it's going to create some awkward situations. What if he decides he doesn't want to be the *Nai'a*'s data librarian anymore?"

Ambassador Brelling chuckled. "Mr. Literal couldn't stop being that if he tried. It's too intertwined with what and who he is. You make a valid point, though. Some AIs will want to change careers, and we'll have to figure out how to navigate that, along with pay, bank accounts, maintenance costs etc. It opens up a can of worms, but we'll work through it. I just hope we can put enough pressure on the Terran Federation to make it happen system-wide. President Wright owes us, and I'll use that leverage to its utmost."

"Another thing your leverage could help with is our overloaded brig," said Captain Hartley. "We've got several of the system's most wanted killers cooling their heels and eating our food. I'd like to get them transferred, but I don't know if I trust the Terran Federation to keep them out of circulation permanently. The Saturn Commonwealth offered to take them all, and pay the outstanding bounties. I don't want to offend the Terran government, but Saturn is probably a better option."

"I don't mind making our excuses," said Ambassador Brelling. "Is the commonwealth willing to take Draco too?"

"Assuming he lives," answered the captain, "they want him most of all. He made a complete mess of the Enceladus Ring artificial intelligence project, and nearly cause the ring to collapse. In the process, he killed a security guard and their top artificial intelligence scientist."

"How is Nicholas Withers?" asked Anne.

"He's improving," said the captain. "Dr. Rensaleer brought him out of cold sleep yesterday. They have him on a ventilator while they try to flush the synthetic tetrodotoxin out of his system. Thankfully, no one else ended up dosed with puffer fish poison. It was a near thing for Pete Worsley."

"You'll need to deal with Nicholas' legal status. He's still serving his sentence for sabotaging the *Nai'a,* and he's wanted by the Terran Federation for his connections to the Restoration and the masking technology."

***

Jarman, Mishael, and Abishai sweated profusely as they labored over the pinnace, checking and rechecking for leaks in the tank the dolphins would make their ride to Earth in. For some reason the boat bay was several degrees warmer than usual, and the maintenance techs hadn't tracked down the problem. Jarman had been unusually quiet, even for him. Abishai kept a concerned eye on him. Finally, they were satisfied with the tank and decided to take a break.

In a blessedly cool break room just forward of the boat bay the three sat around a table and talked. "You seem awfully quiet," Abishai said to Jarman. "Care to share what's bothering you?"

Jarman bit off an angry retort and took a moment to exam his feelings, something he was normally loathe to do. "The combination of seeing the Gemini family living and working together, and the news of the horrors going on in the Belt, put me in a funk," he admitted. "You know my parents were lost on a mining expedition, and I haven't been able to track down my sister. She may have left for another system. I guess I was hoping to mend some long-broken connections, but no one's left to mend them with."

"Do you want to spend some time on earth with us?" asked Abishai. "Mishael and Kalei are coming with their families, and my parents are traveling to the Pacific to meet us all. I know you didn't train up for full gravity, but we'll be on Kālewa Island floating city. You can float in the ocean as much as you like."

Jarman shook his head. "These Belter bones aren't built for Earth gravity, and I'm not part fish like Quester. I don't even like being in the water."

"What are you going to do, then?" asked Mishael.

Jarman looked at him bleakly, "I don't know."

Jarman returned to this quarters and took a long shower. He put on a clean ship suit and was considering what to do for lunch when his PCOM gently buzzed a message alert. He opened the message and abruptly sat down.

JARMAN, WE HOPE THIS MESSAGE FINDS YOU. WE KNOW YOU LEFT ON THE *NAI'A*, BUT NOT IF YOU STAYED ON THE SHIP. WE'VE BEEN THROUGH A HARD TIME, BUT WE'RE STILL KICKING! WE'RE ON HYGEIA III RECUPERATING FOR NOW.

ALL OUR LOVE,

MOM AND DAD

Jarman quickly composed a return message, fumbling with the fast packet berths available to Hygeia at the same time. It didn't help that his vision kept blurring. Once he had his reservation set, and the message sent, he set off to find Abishai and tell him the good news.

***

The next day Quester, Abishai, and Shanyah helped as a team loaded the dolphins, one by one, into the tank. The pod was excited by the prospect of the trip down to earth and being reunited with their ancestral family. If they had any anxiety about riding in the confines of the pinnace's temporary tank, it didn't show. Quester wished he could say the same. He'd volunteered to share the tank with the dolphins for the ride down. Now, he was certain he would rather take a bath in vacuum.

Shanyah helped him check his wetsuit and emergency oxygen tank. "We'll see you on Kālewa Island floating city," she said. "You'll get there first, and my parents are expecting you. This is a big deal for both us and the dolphins, so expect some ceremony when you arrive."

Quester rolled his eyes, then rolled into the tank and checked the primary and back up air connections while Shanyah and Abishai sealed everything up. The dolphins bumped him playfully in the tight quarters, and he just smiled and patted his old friends. The clamshell doors of the cargo hold closed, and he was alone with the pod. He found he could stand straight up or float. A monitor on the wall of the tank indicated a good air mix, and he signaled the flight crew that they were ready.

***

Abishai and his extended family took a shuttle to Honolulu from Aldrin Station, then a fast wind-foil ship to Kālewa Island floating city. The floating city was gaily festooned with multicolored streamers and appeared to be at capacity for visitors. As their wind-foil drifted into the harbor, they could see hundreds of dolphins cavorting with the returnees from the *Nai'a*. Quester was on the dock, so covered in leis that he looked like a flower statue. Shanyah's parents, brothers and sisters greeted all of them with hugs and leis of their own in a colorful chaos of warm greetings and blossoms.

Abishai tried unsuccessfully to dodge yet another lei, then looked around for his parents. They were standing off to the side, visibly amused by the tumultuous spectacle. Abishai made his way over to them, noting how much older they looked, and yet how much they hadn't changed. He wasn't quite sure what to say. They hadn't parted on the best of terms those many years ago.

His parents covered the remaining distance and enveloped him in a double hug. Abishai returned it and felt vast relief as a very old ache in his heart loosened.

Many introductions later, Shanyah's family treated them all to a magnificent luau. The kids took turns swimming with the dolphins and eating themselves to the bursting point. Quester regaled them with the story of his wild, sloshing ride down from orbit. Abishai was happy to get off his feet and share a substantial cushioned loveseat with Shanyah. The food was magnificent, with the possible exception of the poi. He was still making up his mind about the purple goo. His parents sat nearby, clearly smitten with their bevy of new grandchildren and great-grandchildren. Gene therapy, along with micro-biome and osteopathic support advances, were now extending life expectancy to nearly two centuries, even for those living in Earth's gravity well.

Abishai turned to Shanyah. "Full gravity doesn't seem to bother the young ones much. I wish I could say the same. Have you thought about what we should do next?"

"Too much," Shanyah sighed. "I have offers from the Cetacea Institute in Honolulu and several others." She waved at the graceful arcs and towers of Kālewa Island floating city around them. "I grew up here, but I can't say it feels like home. The structures are the same, but the people have changed, and so have I.

"I'm also wondering what the dolphins will decide. They're off in the open ocean now, stretching their sea-legs. I imagine that would be hard to give up again for the confines of their habitat on the *Nai'a*."

"At least it will be their choice," said Abishai, putting an arm around her shoulders. "I don't have any desire to go back home to the farm. My brothers are managing things quite well without me. Whatever we do, we'll do it together."

***

Jarman stepped gingerly onto the Hygeia III dock and reflected that it looked much the same as when he had begged jobs of the cargo handlers in his youth. Taking a fast packet had cost him a lot of credits and time in an acceleration couch at two gravities. He made his way through customs and finally emerged into the public foyer. A group of three tall people looked up, and a beautiful woman he recognized as his sister left the other two to race over. She hugged him tightly, "I've missed you so much," she said with tears in her eyes. Jarman blinked back a few tears of his own as they made the way over to his mother and father. They both examined him closely. "You're too skinny, Jarman," his mother said.

The phrase, so familiar from his childhood, broke Jarman's resolve and he grabbed them both, sobbing in their embrace. Once they all regained a measure of composure, they made their way to the nearest galley for lunch. The familiar delicious smells of the place gave Jarman another wave of nostalgia.

"We have so much catching up to do," said Jarman as they sat down with their food. "We believed you died in an accident on your last prospecting trip. What really happened?"

His father's face darkened. "The Restoration happened. An armed ship jumped us a week out of Hygeia III. They took us to a hollowed-out asteroid set up for manufacturing and pharmaceuticals production. Because of your mother's expertise in hydroponics, we ended up running their farming operation for both food and raw materials. They needed high production, so we had some leverage."

Jarman's mother nodded, "Over the years we were able to convince them to bring in a greater variety of seed to maintain good nutrition for us and our fellow captives. As long as we could show increased productivity, they would listen. They also wanted fresh food for themselves. You wouldn't believe how tempted I was to add something spectacularly purgative to their greens. We learned early on, however, that any form of resistance resulted in harsh punishment.

"We've learned we were much more fortunate than some of the other facilities." She shook her head. "The stories we've heard are unbelievable. I thought people were past treating each other this way, but I was wrong."

"I tried to contact you, Saanvi," Jarman said to his sister. "All my messages were returned."

"My husband and I were on a prospecting trip until a few days ago," she answered. "I confess I was prospecting for these two more than ore. I still had hope, but it was wearing pretty thin. After we eat, you can meet your niece and nephew. Do you have a family?"

Jarman shook his head. "No, it's my own fault. I wasn't much fun to be around when I left, as you well know. It took a crisis to shake me out of my downward spiral, but I made some close friends as a result."

Jarman's mother leaned forward and put a hand on his arm. "We want to hear that story," she said. "You've come a long way."

Jarman smiled thoughtfully, "We all have. I think you'll be pleasantly surprised by the changes I've gone through. I know I am."

***

Lincoln Withers sat by his cousin's bed in Medical. Nicholas was still hooked up to so many tubes and wires that he looked like a science experiment. He was breathing on his own now, and Dr. Rensaleer said he would regain consciousness soon. Nicholas twitched, opened one eye halfway, then shut it again. He groaned and tried to sit up. Lincoln fetched a med tech who raised the bed so Nicholas could sit up. He gave him a little water and checked the monitors. "You have ten minutes," he told Lincoln. "He's going to crash after that."

"I'll risk asking how you feel," said Lincoln when the med tech left.

"Like a four-day-old corpse," Nicholas croaked. He leaned back and closed his eyes. "It beats the alternative."

"Yes," said Lincoln. "When you started turning blue, I thought you were a goner. How much do you remember?"

"Everything up to and including the ice bath. That was really unpleasant, but not half as bad as not being able to breathe. What hit me?"

"Synthetic puffer fish toxin," Lincoln answered. "That's what paralyzed your diaphragm. You've been out for days." Lincoln went on to fill Nicholas in on the successful operations against the Restoration. "Draco is enroute to the Saturn Commonwealth. Assuming he lives through whatever sentence they give him; Mars wants him next."

Nicholas managed a half-smile. "I'm impressed that Abishai handled him. No one else ever has."

"Abishai is terrifying when he's angry, or so I'm told. I've never even heard him raise his voice."

"I can vouch for that from personal experience. Stay on his good side. Am I still on the Terran Federation's most wanted witness list?"

"Yes, once Dr. Rensaleer releases you. You'll be testifying in at least four separate trials."

"I'm looking forward to it," said Nicholas. "After that, I suppose I'll be getting my own comeuppance."

"After that," said Lincoln, "you'll be a free man. I hired Lisa Gallred on your behalf. She's expensive, but you can afford an empty bank account better than a stint in a Terran prison. She convinced the Terran Federation not to prosecute their star witness. No one else has proffered charges against you either. Anne Brelling convinced the captain to commute your sentence for mutiny and sabotage to time served."

Nicholas didn't know what to say. He'd been so focused on helping with the fight against the Restoration, he hadn't planned anything beyond testifying against them in court. He frowned a bit. "The Restoration's lawyers are going to harp on my criminal record to discredit my testimony. They'll only need to tell the truth to do it. I'm not going to be welcome in this system when it's over. I need to think about the future. At least I have one now, which is more than I expected. What about you? Don't feel like you need to hang around waiting for me. This system is full of opportunities."

Lincoln grinned, "Helvetica offered me a job. She's setting up her new network here on Aldrin Station." His expression turned serious. "The *Partain*'s refit will take about six months, then she's bound for Lalande. Our family name is a byword back home. I don't know about you, but that doesn't sit well with me. I'd like to return and do something about it. I think the two of us together could do a lot to heal the wounds our family caused. Think about it."

Nicholas nodded. He wasn't going to be welcome anywhere, but back in Lalande he could at least work at making amends. Suddenly his eyelids drooped and he knew he had hit his ten-minute limit. He leaned back and let sleep take him as Lincoln dimmed the lights.

***

Lisandra Redding walked arm-in-arm with her husband Hal on the way to meet with Captain Hartley. "What do you suppose this meeting is about?" she asked. "You're better at reading the tea leaves than I am."

"The first officer wasn't forthcoming when I asked," Hal answered. "He seemed fairly upbeat underneath the professional veneer. Hopefully that means it's good news."

"I'm ready for some news of one kind or another," said Lisandra. "Waiting for the other shoe to drop is wearing on me more than it should. I think it's wearing on Belle too."

"We've both encouraged her to keep her options open," said Hal. "Whatever happens, she's well positioned for the future. "

"I wish she'd taken my advice and kept quiet about her relationship to me," Lisandra said with a frown. "My reputation closed some doors to her."

"The fact that she refused to shows the kind of character she has," said Hal. "Any opportunities she misses because she's proud of being your daughter are better off missed. She'll make a good decision when the time comes, but she's waiting to see how your situation pans out. You know I'm beside you through whatever comes."

Lisandra smiled up at him. "I'm counting on it!"

The captain welcomed them to his day cabin and served them each coffee. Lisandra sniffed the steaming brew appreciatively then took a sip. "Ethiopia Harrar?" she queried.

"You have a discerning palate," the captain answered with a smile. "We keep receiving gifts from well-wishers, and this was in the last shipment. I think one of our restaurants for the next crossing will feature varietal coffees." He took a sip from his own cup, then leaned back. "I have some good news for you, Lisandra. Honestly, it's mixed news, but I hope you'll see it as good. I asked Lisa Gallred to look into any active legal cases against you across the system. The statute of limitations expired on most of them, and no one in the Sol System is pursuing a case against you.

"That's the good part. I've received notes from four different prosecutors who say they will prefer charges if you remain in the Sol System when the *Nai'a* leaves."

Lisandra chuckled bitterly. "I'm a woman without a country," she said, shaking her head. "Everywhere I go, they can't wait to see me leave. Still, I appreciate your efforts, Captain. At least I'm not facing a lengthy prison term."

"The Sol System may be eager to see the last of you," said the captain, "but we're glad you're one of us on the *Nai'a*. I'd venture to say the whole free trade syndicate feels the same way. You could sign on with any of the outbound long boats if you wish. I personally hope you'll stay on board the *Nai'a*. I know our next passage will be safer with you exercising your skills on our behalf."

"You really do have a country," said Hal, putting an arm around her shoulders. "Just not a star system. That's too confining anyway. What do you say?"

Lisandra blinked a couple of times and looked up. "I say I'm blessed beyond belief. If you'll have me, I'll gladly stay on the *Nai'a* for the next passage."

Captain Hartley grinned widely and shook her hand across the table. "You didn't give me a chance to sweeten the pot," he said. "Since you're staying aboard, Greer Kensing will be leaving to accept a position with the Enceladus Ring Authority. You are now chief cybersecurity officer for the *Nai'a* with a bump in pay that goes with the position."

Hal looked at Lisandra with a grin of his own. "You'd better go make Belle an offer to be your deputy before she gets away!"

Epilogue

October 20ᵗʰ, AD 3226
Sol System, New Dawn Orbit
Long Boat Nai'a, *Epsilon Section Quarters*

Anne Brelling yawned and stretched. Her farewell party the night before hadn't wrapped up until after midnight. She packed the last of her private possessions and looked around her quarters. The apartment on Aldrin Sation that came with her new position was larger and much more luxurious, but it didn't yet feel like home. The *Nai'a* was in her very blood and bones, but it was time to move on. Captain Hartley deserved to settle in for the next crossing without her around, and she had plenty of challenges in front of her.

The Long Boat Free Trade Syndicate Captain's Conclave had elected her to lead the syndicate for a ten-year term. With the Kilimanjaro, Mount Kenya, Chimborazo, and Puncak Jaya magnetic catapult systems all online, transport to earth orbit and beyond was now affordable. The power balance and population in the Sol system were shifting away from the Terran Federation toward the mid and outer system. She would have to negotiate some major changes, chief of which was the matter of legal citizenship for sentient artificial intelligences. Anne was hopeful Mr. Literal would be recognized as a person by all of the Sol governments after the next Sol System Assembly meeting.

Rolland was settling in as Lalande Ambassador to the Sol System, so their jobs would keep them together and operating in the same circles. With the fall of the Restoration and its ideals, there was a tide of change sweeping through the system. Anne and Rolland intended to ride it for all it was worth.

***

Abishai, Shanyah and clan bid his parents goodbye at the floating city dock, waving as the ship pulled out of the harbor bound for Honolulu. He'd enjoyed spending time with them and was especially grateful for the time they took to get to know Mishael and Kalei along with their families. Time had softened the hard feelings from years ago to insignificance.

The adults gathered around an outdoor table. They all looked expectantly at one another, wondering who would go first. The agreement when they hit shore was that each family would make their own decision without undue influence from the others. Abishai surveyed the dour faces and laughed. "You all look like you're at a funeral," he said. "We'll go first."

"As tempting as the offers here earthside are," said Shanyah, "we've decided to return to the *Nai'a*." She could see the tension ease around the table. Even Quester seemed relieved. "The ship is our home now, and we still want to be part of the crew."

Mishael spoke up next. "Joanne isn't giving up her chief engineer slot anytime soon," he said with a grin. "I'll make myself handy wherever I can as usual. We're along for the ride."

"I didn't have to twist his arm much," said Joanne.

"I also have several offers," said Kalei, "including Chief Medical Officer on the *Partain*. Julian did as well. The Sol Space Patrol offered him command of an anti-piracy corvette."

"We both decided to stay with the *Nai'a*," said Julian. "I may not be up to Abishai or Roan's standards as a hydro tech, but I find the work satisfying. It will be nice to get back to my pumps after the high adventure of the last few months."

"I don't want to leave Dr. Rensaleer without a backup," said Kalei. "Most of all, the *Nai'a* is home. It's where I want the kids to grow up." She turned to Soma. "What about you?"

Soma looked around her. "I could get used to this life, but even in the water I'm way too heavy." Her expression grew serious. "The *Nai'a* and

Julian took me in when I lost everything. The big old spinning dolphin is my home too. I'm sticking."

"The cold sleep director will be glad to hear it," said Kalei, giving her a pat on the arm. "Now, what about you, Quester, the man without ties?"

Quester looked around him and grinned, "I may be crazy, but I'm not stupid. I wouldn't give you or my shipmates up for the world, not even this one. I haven't forgotten how the crew rallied behind me when I deserved to be booted off the ship. Also, the dolphins are coming back, and they expect me to do the same."

"Really?" said Soma. "I'm surprised the call of the open ocean didn't take them away from us."

Quester nodded, "One of them is staying here, but the rest all want to return, and they'll have a replacement born before too long."

Shanyah smiled broadly. "The ship is waiting," she said. "We all need to be on tomorrow's packet to the Big Island. I've heard the catapult to orbit is a blast."

***

Two days later, Captain Hartley surveyed the bridge from his command chair. The *Nai'a* had a full manifest and the usual major Sol crew turnover to deal with, but he was happy to be getting underway again. He'd managed to retain his chief engineer and first officer in spite of lucrative offers to stay in system. At last, Aldrin Station traffic control cleared them for departure, and ten space-tugs oriented the mighty ship toward their next destination. The tugs gave them a boost free of the controlled traffic area and winked their lights in departure. "Course laid in and main engines at idle, sir," declared Chief Vance at the helm.

"All ahead full!" ordered the captain. "Next stop, Alpha Centauri."

THE END

Thank you for reading Long Boat Home Coming! I sincerely hope you enjoyed the story. With this cycle of the *Nai'a*'s story concluded, I'll be making a bit of a departure for the next book. We'll still be in Long Boat space, but we'll visit a different boat and a different crew. Expect some perilous high adventure in Long Boat Lost. I plan to release that story in the Fall of 2026. I may get started on a project that's in the back of my mind for a science fiction youth series. It may feature your favorite ship's cat! Don't worry about Abishai and the *Nai'a*, I'm sure I'll revisit her sometime in the future. For the latest in the Long Boat universe, visit my author website longboatspace.com, or the Long Boat Space Fans Facebook page. I'd love to hear what you think of the books, and you might find a free back story or two on your favorite characters.

Warm Regards,

Matthew H. Ambrose

About the Author:

Matthew H. Ambrose grew up devouring books and traveling to far places in his imagination. He has been a wrestler, runner, singer, soldier, husband, father, gardener, teacher, and now author (not counting hobbies). He happily resides with his wife in Huntsville, Alabama, home of the Space and Rocket Center and one of the oldest disc golf courses in the world.